Marsha Orr
(A.K.A. L. M. Nisgow)

ELPIE IMPERATIVE

Book Three Of The Elpie Trilogy

By

L. M. Nisgow

Book Cover Design by Todd Hebertson
BookCoverArt.webs.com

ACKNOWLEDGEMENTS

I would like to thank all the firefighters and paramedics at Fire Station 41 in San Antonio, Texas, for their willingness to share their experiences and thoughts, and to give their time and expertise in acquainting me with their routines, machines and firefighting equipment. Their group picture with their names are as follows: From left to right, bottom row:

Roger Garza, Fernando Villa, Lieutenant Ruben Sanchez, Sean Kirkeby, Nathan Colvin, and Captain Ruben Cruz

Top row from left to right:

Javier Gutierrez, Jamin Scott, Paramedic Alfred Noriega, and Paramedic Miguel Acosta

Not shown are Paramedics Joel Fox, Firefighters Chris Navarejo, Domingo Carlin, and Lieutenant Kraig McCullough.

My appreciation for the Jiu Jitsu info and demonstrations from Josh Lauber, owner of Relsin Gracie Jiu Jitsu San Antonio, and his friends, who graciously allowed themselves to be choked for my edification. (Yes, they did survive.)

Thanks to my sister-in-law, Cathy Nairn, DVM, for sharing her knowledge, and to my sister, Carol Riley, for editing, always encouraging, and for being an all around great sister.

Thanks to my email friend, author Marie Dellavalle, for her encouragement and her Italian.

And finally, thanks to the real Elsie, for her unconditional love and devotion for sixteen and a half years. She only got sweeter with time.

Elsie girl, you were truly a great dog, and you'll never leave my heart. I can only hope that when I leave this world, you'll be there to greet me on the other side with a squeaky toy in your mouth.

Elsie
December 1999-June 2016

This book is dedicated to

Firefighters

The brave men and women who
rise and go to work each morning
to risk their lives for those
they have never met.

Thank you

ELPIE IMPERATIVE

BOOK THREE OF THE ELPIE TRILOGY

BY

L. M. NISGOW

CHAPTER ONE

Today he would face his greatest fear. As a firefighter, he had more than his share: getting disoriented in a smoke filled house, unable to find his way out until it was too late and his tank ran out of air; falling through a roof of rotted timber and crashing down into a room full of flames; being trapped by collapsing ceilings and becoming food for the enemy.

Today Enzo Uccello, after taking his turn at mowing the fire station lawn, would take a shower and wash his hair *while on duty*. Some of these men, his brother firefighters, would boldly step into the shower as if it were nothing, invariably coming clean without anxiety or incident. But he, Enzo Uccello, knew without a shadow of a doubt, that if *he* dared to strip down, wet down, and lather up, the alarm would ring while he was at his most vulnerable.

He stood straight, and laughing in the face of fear, grabbed a towel, tore off his clothes, and stepped into the shower, disdaining to even test the water temperature first. *They call me The Fearless One, Signorina.*

He soaped himself all over, lathered shampoo into his hair, and just as he was about to rinse off, thinking he had escaped the danger and proven to himself that his angst was groundless—WAA,-waa, WAA-waa, WAA-waa--the alarm sounded.

Maledizione! He frantically swiped at his hair, trying to flush out the shampoo with one hand, while attempting to rub and rinse the soap off of every place else with the other. He heard shouts from three different directions, of "Hey Enzo, snap it up!" and "Uccello, we got to go!" and "Move it, Uchie!" He grabbed the handle and slammed off the hot water, fully aware that he'd done a half-ass job of rinsing—literally.

But you, Signorina, may call me Sticky Buns.

He made one big blot with the towel and threw his clothes more or less on before running to the truck. "Well, if it isn't Mr. Clean!" greeted him as he grabbed for his gear.

He stepped into his boots, always left inside the crumpled protective trousers, and in almost one continuous motion, yanked the boots on by their straps, pulled up the pants, and heaved their suspenders onto his shoulders, finishing in half the time most people would take. He'd just tugged his suspenders up, when two pairs of hands reached down and hauled him into the truck with shouts of "Come on, come on!" as it began rolling out onto the street, sirens wailing.

Once in the truck, the process of gearing up continued. He pulled on the knit hood that covered his head and neck, leaving only face exposed, then grabbed his coat and slipped into that. Next came the mask, minus the regulator attached to the canister of compressed air. The crew breathed through the openings in their masks while on the truck, only attaching the regulators when they were about to engage the fire.

After donning the mask, he leaned back into his seat, put his arms through the straps of his pack, and cinched it tight. The packs were attached to the seats, so that once a crewman put his arms through the straps, all he had to do was pull a cord to release the pack, and he was loaded up. This was always a time saver, but today, Enzo was especially thankful that he didn't have to think about anything past sitting and pulling the cord, since he was bound to have screwed up something.

He put on his gloves and lastly, the helmet—symbol of the firefighter, recognized and honored as a badge of courage throughout the civilized world. It always gave Enzo a little added sense of purpose when he finally put on that helmet each time, as if with the donning of it, he took on the mantle and truly became a fireman.

Firefighters are taught to pay attention to their ears when they're working on a fire. If the ears are starting to burn, it's getting too hot for safety. Enzo sat in his wet pants and shirt, and from beneath his hood, his hair dripped a few die hard drops that began itching crazily as they meandered down his spine. But what was killing him was the soap. He was still sticky all over with it, and his whole head felt slimy under his hood. How the hell was he supposed to know if his ears were burning when they were already burning from the shampoo?

"Why, just look at Mr. Uccello, all nice and fresh from the shower! And *what is* that lovely fragrance? You *must* tell me where you shop." Enzo punched Ernesto on the arm, laughing as his friend began sniffing the air around him with a blissful smile on his face.

Normally, he would be loving this ride. The camaraderie, the air blowing through the truck, the siren blasting, that weird sensation when they turned a corner, that the truck just might tip over in the process, and that sense of energy/excitement/fear that was almost palpable in the atmosphere on the way to a fire. Loving the rush, but praying that nobody got hurt, and that he and the others would do everything right.

They always passed people on the street when responding to a call, and occasionally someone would salute them as they drove by. Others, especially the elderly, sometimes made the sign of the cross. It always touched Enzo when he saw that show of respect, and even more to think that someone he didn't know was praying for his safety.

Yeah, normally he would feel all of that, but today he was too distracted by the prickling and itching sensation from the soap. And now with the hood pressing the unrinsed shampoo against his scalp, along with the slight increase in temperature caused by the helmet, his head was beginning to feel really irritated. In some places it was starting to burn, especially on and around the all-important ears. He couldn't even scratch anywhere, with gloves and protective gear all over. This was going to be one miserable fire.

It had already been a miserable day. He'd turned his alarm off in the morning without actually waking up, and when he did wake up, it was so late that he'd had to skip breakfast and his morning workout. He cut himself in a rush to shave, and then knocked over a lamp and shattered it when he lunged for his keys on the end table in his dash out the door. He'd left the broken ceramic all over the floor, jumped in his car, and—nothing. It wouldn't start. Engine wouldn't even turn over.

He had no friends in the area yet that might give him a ride, and he knew that none of the guys on his shift could pick him up without making themselves late, so he'd called a taxi. Of course, he'd never hear the end of his arrival at the station in a cab, just as several of the guys were going out to their cars to bring in supplies. He'd been "Prince Enzo" for the rest of the morning, and who knew, maybe for the rest of his life, the way things were going.

After being late, suffering the expense of a taxi and the replacement of his broken lamp, worrying about what was going on with his car and how much that was going to cost him—after all that, putting up with the good natured but still obnoxious kidding from the other guys was almost more than he could deal with.

Then when he'd taken his turn at mowing the lawn, the ancient machine he'd had to use for the job wouldn't start at first, and for icing, the grass catcher fell off about a hundred times while he was working, so it took him at least twice as long to finish the job as it should have. On a hot, humid, San Antonio day, that meant that he was grunged out, completely soaked with sweat, and fragrant as a dung heap by the time he was done. It was only to be expected on this kind of day, that the alarm would go off while he was in the shower.

When they rolled up to the house, a neighbor had already gotten an elderly woman, her dog and a couple of puppies out of the house, and had her sitting on the lawn in a chair, since she refused to leave the scene. There was smoke coming out of several windows and the door, but no flames were visible from the outside.

The engine carrying the hoses and water tank pulled up, and the engineer moved to the control panel behind the cab while the Captain and Lieutenant sized up the situation. The rest of the crew jumped off the truck and as soon as their feet hit the ground, the Lieutenant sent them to shut off the utilities.

Regulators went on, and the Captain sent Enzo and Raul through the open door of the house. Enzo was the nozzle man, going in first, and Raul held the thermal imaging camera, (TIC), sweeping it back and forth to try and find the source of the fire through the smoke.

At any structure fire, Enzo's heart always skipped a beat when he walked through that door for the first time. What was he walking into? He still took that step, though—all of them did, trusting that their officers understood the situation.

Once inside, even though they were only a few feet from the doorway on a bright, sunny day, it was another world. Darkness—they could see nothing through the smoke, but the TIC gave them a view of where the hottest spot was, so they aimed the hose in that direction. A couple of the other guys tried to shift what little furniture and other belongings they could see to the middle of the room to try and protect them by covering everything with a tarp. Even with smoke damage, these things might be irreplaceable to the owner, particularly if she had no insurance.

It looked like they were making progress, when suddenly flames leapt up in a different section, and boards started falling from the ceiling. The heat intensified, more flames appeared, and the lieutenant called the crew out.

Enzo was burning all over now with the heat from the fire raising the temperature of the already irritating soap and shampoo residue. He felt like he was frying, so he was guiltily overjoyed when they were called out of the house. Just as they emerged, the old woman started screaming and pointing at the house, saying something in Spanish, over and over, and crying hysterically. The neighbor, whose Spanish was minimal, couldn't understand the words through the crying, but Abel, the engineer, caught it and yelled down to them.

"It's her puppy! She's missing one of the puppies! She says it was in the front room, near the back right corner."

Enzo grabbed the TIC from his belt, put his regulator on again, and ran back into the house before the officers had a chance to tell him not to. A couple of weeks before, they'd gone on a call to a house fire where a dog and cat had been trapped inside, and they were too late to help them. It had made them all sick at heart, and he wasn't going to see that kind of thing again if he could help it.

The heat was worse, but luckily, the flames weren't to the front of the house yet, because the thermal imaging wouldn't work around flames, where *everything* was hot. In the smoke, the screen showed body heat and even footprints where the men had just walked, and hopefully it would pick up on the puppy.

Come on, come on, little guy, where are you? He headed towards the back corner, and there it was, right where the woman had said, the screen leading Enzo through the total darkness of the smoke, directly to the helpless creature. He grabbed the tiny thing in one hand and used the TIC to trace his tracks back through the disorienting smoke and out the door.

The Battalion Chief had seen what was happening and already had the oxygen and mask ready for the pup. Only the Chiefs, who responded to all the calls in their battalions, carried the special equipment made for animals. Enzo rushed over and handed him the limp little body, and the woman cried out at the sight, overjoyed that Enzo had retrieved the pup, but terrified that it might be too late. The puppy was brown with white patches across his face and one side, though now his color was largely obscured with soot. It didn't look like he was breathing, and Enzo caught himself holding his own breath, hovering over the chief as he put the mask on the pup's face and rubbed his chest and belly gently.

A whole minute went by without seeing any movement, and everyone figured it was no use, but the Chief kept the mask on another minute anyway. Suddenly, the little body jerked convulsively, and the chest started moving. Enzo felt a surge of happiness and fulfillment as he looked at the old woman and nodded with a smile. This kind of thing gave firefighters a reason to keep going despite the dangers---a life saved. Even one as tiny as this.

She hobbled over to them with the help of her neighbor, and leaned over to kiss the coat sleeve, first of Enzo, and then of the Chief. Both men, gratified but embarrassed by the emotional gesture, automatically patted her arm in return, not knowing how else to respond. *Maybe this wasn't such a lousy day after all.*

"Senora, you need to take this puppy to the vet right away. You could still lose it," the Chief told her in Spanish. But when he tried to hand it to her, she shook her head and pushed it back at him, replying that she had no money for a vet, and that she couldn't keep the puppies now anyway, because she had no house to keep them in. She would probably stay with her son, and his apartment didn't allow pets.

Realizing that arguing would be futile and cause even more anxiety for the woman, Enzo volunteered, "Hey Chief, if we can drop it off at the vet's office down the street, I'll cover the bill and see if maybe they can find it a home after they treat it."

Chief Gonzalez, who had several dogs himself, looked at him for a moment and then nodded. Enzo breathed a sigh of relief, thanked God that the puppy had made it, and thanked Him again for the rest of his crew, who'd kept going on the job at hand while he'd been busy with the pup.

Times like this made all of the men appreciate being part of a team. When they pulled up to a fire and their Lieutenant and Captain began directing the crew, the men put their lives in the hands of these two, and their judgement had yet to fail them. They put their lives in the hands of each other, too, and every one of them felt that responsibility keenly. On this team, somebody always had your back, and you would literally walk through fire to cover your buddy's, in turn. It was a team, but it was a family, too.

#

Between the increasing itching and burning and his worries about the pup, the rest of the job was sort of a blur in Enzo's mind. When they finally finished up and the truck and engine pulled away, the engine headed back to the firehouse, and the truck with Enzo and the puppy on board went in the opposite direction, towards the local veterinary office. He only hoped they could get there before his own head burst into flames.

CHAPTER TWO

Thunk. Thunk. Thunk. Baseballs hit the bullseye and dropped to the ground. The target was homemade, and only the bullseye had a piece of metal inserted behind it so the sound would be different when it was hit. If she missed and hit the straw stuffed area around the bullseye, only a soft thud would reward her. She hadn't heard a thud in years. This was definitely a twenty ball day, so Genevieve snatched the next one out of the bucket and continued her sublimated hissy fit.

When she was a little girl, she'd become obsessed with watching baseball after seeing the weird, rubber-limbed appearance of major league pitchers shown throwing in slow motion on TV. She'd begged her dad to buy her a bucket of baseballs, and then she'd set out on her own private mission to become the best pitcher in the world. Her dad, Simon, was always quick to encourage any interest that his children showed in sports, art, music, science, or any other endeavor that was legal and made them use their brains and bodies. Not only had he bought her the longed for bucket of balls, but he'd made the special target for her as well.

Aside from watching the contortions of the pitchers, however, she soon found that she had little interest in the rest of the game. She'd never lost her love of throwing a baseball though, and had spent thousands of hours in perfecting her aim. Having her pitch clocked had never appealed to her—she deemed the speed of her throw irrelevant. But as the years went by, she had definitely developed muscle and speed along with accuracy. Now she never left home for any extended period of time without her target and bucket of balls, which made for some very expensive plane rides.

Pitching came in exceptionally handy as an outlet for her anger, which in this job, was of paramount importance. Colder, one of her brothers, called the balls and target her "anger management team." As a recent veterinary school grad, she wanted to do at least a year of practice as an intern under a good general practice vet before she decided if she wanted to specialize, and for the most part, her time at this clinic in San Antonio had been very positive. But days like today, having to bite her tongue almost destroyed her. This was not her practice though, and she had been told very pointedly when she'd been taken on by the partners, that she should keep negative opinions to herself. She'd also been warned by them that there would be days like today.

A woman had come in with her female Fox terrier/Jack Russell mix. The dog was only about three years old, full of energy and affection, and looked to be in perfect health. The woman had put the dog on the table, and when she'd happily wagged her tail and covered Genevieve in kisses, she'd remarked on what a nice dog she was.

"Oh, thanks. Yeah, she's always been a little charmer. And she's sooo good with the kids and our other pets."

"Well, what can we do for you today?" she asked, while the little dog bounced around on the table, alternating between slathering kisses on Genevieve and her owner.

The woman sighed, shook her head sadly. "I'm afraid we're going to have to put her to sleep."

"Oh my, I'm so sorry. Are you here for a second opinion about that? What kind of diagnosis has she been given?" Genevieve automatically assumed that a malignancy had been found by another vet, but the energy and robust appearance of the little dog didn't fit the picture she would have expected.

"Oh, no, she hasn't been diagnosed with anything. But she keeps getting out of our yard and getting pregnant. We just don't want her having any more puppies."

She couldn't keep her jaw from dropping—couldn't believe what she'd just heard. "You want to *kill* her because she gets pregnant?"

Looking appalled at the idea, the woman shook her head and replied, "No, not *kill* her. We just want to have her put to sleep."

Could she really be so stupid, that she didn't know what that meant?

"Maybe I'm not understanding you. You *do* realize that 'putting to sleep' is just a euphemism for killing an animal, don't you?" She tried very hard to keep her voice even when she asked the question.

"Well, 'killing' is a pretty severe term. We just want her to be mercifully put to sleep. No pain, no suffering."

"Ma'am, if you had a heart attack and died in your sleep tonight, you'd have no pain or suffering, but you'd be just as dead as if you'd been hit by a truck."

She saw the woman bristle at this, saw the set of her jaw go forward and her teeth clinch a bit. But she couldn't just let her walk out of the room without forcing her to look at, to say out loud, what it was she was really asking to be done. The woman seemed to believe that if she could call it by some other name, some *nice* name, then she wasn't actually ordering a killing of convenience.

"Could you just do it, please?" she asked, stone faced now.

"Ms. Schultz, I don't mean to be difficult, but since, as you said, this is such a nice little dog, why don't you just get her spayed? Why have her killed, when you could so easily take care of the problem with a simple surgery, instead?"

The woman rolled her eyes and let out a huge, exaggerated sigh. "That's expensive, it takes time that I don't have, and it's painful and traumatic for the poor animal. Why don't *you* just do what you're paid for, and put her to sleep, so she doesn't have to suffer?"

Not normally prone to violence, she was fighting the compulsion to jump across the table and dance on the woman's head. She'd never done it before, but—a first time for everything. Instead, she forced an obviously insincere smile, and replied, "Ms. Schultz, now that you bring up cost, I could set you up with a very low cost spay and neuter clinic right here in town. In fact, I could probably find you a clinic that would do it for free. And you know, we put them under anesthesia when we spay them, so there's no pain until after the surgery, and then very little. Have you ever had children, Ms. Schultz?"

All attempts at congeniality disintegrated with the posing of this question. "Not that it's any of your damn business, but yes, I've had three."

"Well, then you're aware that giving birth is painful, and if this dog has gone through that so many times, the post-op pain of a spaying would be a breeze for her. You say you're worried about trauma to the dog, but what could be more traumatic than being killed in the prime of her life, when she's perfectly healthy?"

Ms. Schultz slammed her wallet down on the table, causing the dog to jump away from her and lean against Genevieve in an automatic response to the threat of violence.

"I want to see the manager of this clinic! I will *not* be insulted just for being humane enough to take care of this problem, instead of dumping her out in the country, like most people would do! And it's not your place to pass judgement on me."

Knowing she was sticking her neck out, she dropped the smile, but used her best soothing voice. At least it soothed animals smaller than the one with the pocketbook.

"I will be glad to find a managing partner for you, but first, let me make you a proposition. If you will sign your dog over to me, I'll have her spayed at my expense, and find her a good home. Your problem is solved, and I won't have to feel guilty about putting down a healthy dog."

"FINE! GREAT! You want the damn dog, take her! Give me the paper and I'll sign her over." She said this with bared, clenched teeth, and Genevieve literally ran to the front desk to grab the paperwork, spilling the rest of the stack on the floor as she rushed back to the examining room to get a signature before the woman could change her mind out of spite.

She smiled as sweetly as possible, trying to make the smile reach her eyes, as she placed the pen and paper on the table in front of whom she now thought of as "The Fiend." Grabbing the pen and paper, Fiend scribbled her name at the bottom, and followed this up by throwing the paper and pen at Genevieve before whirling around and stomping to the front desk. Once there, she stood glaring at the poor receptionist, demanding in her loudest voice to see the lead doctor about his "incompetent, rude, and ignorant bitch of an associate."

The dog, shaking and huddling on the exam table now, pressed up against Genevieve in a bid for protection. She reached down and stroked her head, speaking softly to her, and eventually the shaking stopped.

After a few moments, a calm, masculine voice could be heard coming from the front. But as the woman's voice was raised, Genevieve could hear the change of tone in Dr. Brenner's voice, along with a slight increase in volume.

A lecture on tact was coming, she knew. But the "ignorant bitch" had been a stroke of luck for Genevieve. She'd worked here long enough to know that the managing partner believed in customer service, but would never put up with crude or profane language directed at anyone in his office. She also knew that he didn't believe in killings of convenience.

An hour later, after a mild, half-hearted chastisement, followed by a wink and a slap on the back, she found herself the new owner of a dog that she really didn't need, and probably couldn't keep in her apartment. That was her punishment—she had to take responsibility for the animal she'd saved.

She was also ordered to "take it outside" until she cooled down awhile. As she launched her twentieth ball and heard a satisfying *thunk,* she had to admit she *was* feeling better. This was partly from wallowing in the satisfaction of hearing Dr. Brenner inform the woman loudly, in front of a waiting room full of animal lovers, that although perhaps his associate should have handled things differently, he believed "killings of convenience" were obscene, and he would not now or ever have any part in them. He then advised the woman that he would be glad to forward any medical records she wished to another vet of her choice, since he considered their business together at an end.

The woman had simply glared at him, spun around on her heels and stormed out the door. She tried her best to slam it, but was embarrassingly thwarted by the pneumatic door closer at the top. Immediately after her foiled dramatic exit, the waiting room was completely silent, but then someone started clapping. After a second, the whole room was applauding, and a shout of "Brenner ROCKS," was added to the ovation. Genevieve really loved that man.

She was picking the balls up and putting them back into her bucket, when she saw a fire truck pull into the parking lot. Rushing in the back door, she got to the front desk in time to see a fireman in full uniform, coat covered in soot, walk in the front door carrying a small bundle in his arms. He hurried to the desk and held out the puppy to her when he saw her white coat, asking in a pronounced Boston accent, "Doctor, can you help my little buddy here? We got him out of a house fire and he wasn't breathing at first, but after oxygen, he perked up a tad. I gotta get back to the station, but I'll take responsibility for the little guy."

After saying this, instead of just seeing the white coat, he actually looked at her—creamy skin, large, clear blue eyes, full lips, the face framed by a mass of curly, fire-red hair casually bound up in a high pony tail, with curls escaping in all directions. This remarkable head topped a body that was slender and six feet tall in stocking feet. His next words escaped his lips before he could clamp his mouth shut, and his, "Geeez, you're gorgeous," surprised both of them.

They each gave an embarrassed laugh, then he shook his head and got back to business.

"Sorry—you took me by surprise, there. So, can you take him?"

He realized suddenly that she was staring at his face with an expression close to horror. Great—his first flirt in forever, and he got— horror?

"Ah, of course we'll take the puppy, but I believe you may be in worse shape than your buddy. What is going on with your face?"

His hand flew to his face, and he let out a groan. "Oh,no. It's the soap. The alarm sounded when I was in the shower, and I didn't do too good a job rinsing off." He could feel bumps from his hairline to half way down his forehead, and when he felt his ears, they were covered with bumps too, and painful to touch.

"We've been talking for what, thirty seconds or less? In that time, that rash has spread from just at your hairline to where it is now." She turned to the receptionist and said, "Monica, could you please give the puppy to one of the other doctors, and then go tell the other men on the truck that Mr. aah—"

"Uccello. But please, call me Enzo."

"All right. Could you tell them that Mr. Uccello is going to be a few minutes?"

Monica reached out and took the puppy, and Genevieve ordered, "Mr. Uccello, come around the corner here, take off your hat, hood, and jacket, and follow me. Quick." To argue with her never crossed his mind, and he dutifully removed his helmet and stripped off his hood and jacket. *Maledizione!* His whole scalp was covered with burning, itching bumps. As he rounded the corner, she grabbed his free arm, pulled him into a room with a huge, stainless steel sink, and turned on the cold water.

"Put your head under here, and let me rinse it off. Hurry!"

He dropped his helmet on the floor, and she used the sprayer to hit every inch of his head, neck, and ears with cold water, continuing to spray for a good five minutes. She turned off the faucet then, handed him a towel, and asked one of the vet techs to bring her an ice pack.

"Don't rub your head with the towel, just blot it, then put this ice pack on, but move it around from place to place. Never more than fifteen or twenty minutes in one spot," she ordered.

What a relief. His head still burned like crazy, but so much less than before, and the cold pack felt wonderful. He saw Genevieve rush to the other room and then come back in, digging through her purse while she was walking. She finally found what she was looking for, pulled out a bottle, and looked him sternly. He was staring at her with a half grin on his face, awaiting further orders.

"Okay. What you have is something like a chemical burn, and an allergic reaction to boot. I'm a veterinarian, and it's against the law for me to treat you. But if I come upon an emergency situation, there's no law against my giving first aid, and I consider your noggin an emergency. Are you allergic to any medication, dyes, etc? Are you short of breath? Having trouble swallowing?"

He shook his head.

"All right. I can't prescribe medication or dispense to you as a professional, but as one friend to another, I can share over the counter medication with you. Are you my friend?"

He grabbed his helmet off the floor, held it over his heart and bowed his head. "I, Enzo Uccello, am the best friend you will *ever* have, if you will have me. Ask me for anything, anything, and it's yours. My phone number in particular." Then he gave her a smile, and made Groucho brows.

She laughed in spite of herself. "Okay my friend, I am giving you fifty milligrams of Benadryl out of my purse, *as one friend to another*, so that you can take these at the water fountain just to your left there. Don't drive or do anything dangerous, like fighting fires, because you'll be under the influence with these. They make some people really sleepy. Then you need to go straight to your headquarters and shower in cold water for a long time, to be sure you get every bit of soap residue off the rest of you that wouldn't fit in the sink. And after that you need to see a doctor, because you probably need to be on steroids. Now go, go!"

"Yes ma'am, anything you say!" He turned to the fountain and downed the pills, then turned back and took her hand. "Thank you for saving my life. I'll call back with my info for the puppy as soon as I shower. Bless you, Lady Red." He started to walk out, when she called out to him.

"Mr. Uccello, one more thing."

"Oh please, since we're such good friends, it's gotta be 'Enzo.'"

She smiled and said, "Okay, Enzo. Did you say 'geez' a few minutes ago?"

"Yes ma'am. I didn't say 'Jesus.' 'Geez' is short for 'Gee whiz.' It's just an expression my whole family uses. Old habits die hard, and it's better than what I'm thinking about saying half the time. Why?"

"No reason. Take care of that rash, Enzo."

He made a deep bow, sweeping his helmet out to the side with a flourish, while holding the ice pack on with his other hand. "Anything for you, Principessa."

He stuck his helmet under one arm, swooped up his jacket and hood with the other, and walked out the door to the waiting fire truck. Monica laughed, twirling around in her chair to face Genevieve. "He's *so* cute! I don't know what that means, but I'm sure it's good. Lady Red."

"Don't start! He certainly was a confident little guy, wasn't he?" She laughed again, and gave Monica a playful backhanded slap on the arm when she heaved a big sigh.

Then it was back to business, and she walked into an exam room to see the next patient.

A stab of home sickness had hit her when she'd heard him say "geez," and then saw him do "Groucho brows" at her. That was what her parents always called it when people wiggled their eyebrows up and down. Her adopted sister, Gisella, had even taught one of their dogs to do it. And her mom, her mom's parents, and all of her mom's kids, herself included, had been saying "geez" almost since they'd learned to talk.

#

Ralphie had been sneezing and itching all over, and his worried owner had brought him in for allergy medication to keep him from scratching himself raw. Genevieve gave the owner advice and the dog an injection, handed out the meds, made small talk, and then left the office, this being her half-day. She'd left her new dog in a kennel at work, with plans on spaying her the next day.

Thinking about the incident with the fireman, she realized that after he'd talked to her for a minute or so, his accent had sort of disappeared in her mind. He'd still had it, of course, but it just seemed natural to her ears. Actually, she thought it was sort of cute. He was kind of cute himself, for that matter. Black hair, olive skin, and gorgeous brown eyes with long black lashes. He had what her mom called a "hawk" nose—with a break a little ways from the top of the bridge, where it took a steep dive in direction, rather than lying in a straight plane all the way down.

Without his boots, she figured him to stand about five-five, which didn't lessen his appeal at all. In her work shoes, she stood at least six-one, if not taller, but for once, the difference in their height hadn't crossed her mind while he was flirting. He just did it so well.

#

When she got home, she walked in, immediately kicked off her shoes, and headed for her computer to check her email. Both her parents were big emailers, and she loved getting all the news about everybody on a daily basis. They skyped with her too, at least once a week.

After answering her folks, she browsed through the internet, looking for interesting items. Anything about animals usually caught her eye. Lo and behold, what was this? Somebody had posted a video with the title "Fireman risks it all to save puppy." Could that be Mr. Boston?

She clicked on the title, and there he was, running into a burning building, and coming out carrying the pup he'd handed over to her. The person who'd taken the video had zoomed in on his face as he watched his chief giving oxygen to the little thing, and the look of anxiety mixed with hope that she saw there touched her heart. Then when the puppy started breathing and she saw the happiness and relief in Boston's eyes, she was sold. This was a guy she was going to get to know, one way or another.

CHAPTER THREE

At *least* two weeks off duty. That's what the doctor had said. Not what he'd wanted to hear, but on the other hand, with the way his head felt right now, he thought that if he had to wear a helmet over all these irritated bumps, his skin would probably just slough off and leave him a bloody mess. He called the news in to his captain, and told him he'd be in the next day to pick up some things and bring in his doctor's note with the form for workman's comp.

The Lieutenant had called in one of the off duty guys to drive him to the doctor and then home. He didn't want to send him in a cab, in case his symptoms progressed, and he'd made Jerry take an Epipen along with them, to be on the safe side. When Enzo had been in the shower trying to rinse the rest of the soap off, the Lieutenant had walked in to check on him, seen how bad he looked, and headed straight to the phone to start arranging everything.

When they arrived at his house, he said his thanks to his driver and bud, Jerry, who'd been nice enough to also take him to the pharmacy to fill the prescriptions he'd been given. He went to the door, opened it, and looked back to wave at Jerry, who'd waited to see him in. His first step inside brought the sound of crunching glass.

Great. He'd forgotten all about that. He threw his bags on the counter and swept up the glass from the lamp. Too tired to do anything else, he took one of the pills he'd gotten, and smeared the prescription cream all over his head, back, and everywhere else he felt any bumps or itching. Then he headed straight to his bed and crashed. He hardly ever took medication, and now with the Benadryl on board, the desire to lie down was so overwhelming that he'd had to force himself all the way to his bed. When he'd first walked through the door, he'd seriously considered just curling up on the floor, glass or no glass.

He slept so deeply that when he woke, for a few seconds he had no idea where he was or how he'd gotten there. Then the itching brought it all back to him. *Oh yeah, Rash Man.*

He was still too groggy to get up, so he let his mind wander as he lay looking up at the slowly turning fan over his bed. He wondered how the puppy was doing, but he wondered even more about Lady Red. She seemed to like him. But maybe the smile just went along with the act of mercy she'd performed on him. But she'd shared her own personal stash of Benadryl with him. Would she do that for just anybody? Yeah, probably. But she'd laughed when he flirted, and not a snotty laugh—a kind of "maybe you're not so bad" laugh. Did he dare ask her out, or was she completely out of his league? Vets were doctors, and he figured they made big bucks, so would she look down her nose at a regular guy? He didn't think so, or he wouldn't be attracted to her.

He had to go back and settle the bill, but he didn't want her to see him like this, something straight out of a dermatology text book. He couldn't go today anyway. No car, still feeling groggy after the Benadryl and the injection he'd been given, and covered with slimy cream—-it all boiled down to his being a homebody tonight. He'd decide what to do in the morning, he thought, just before he dropped off again.

##

She'd just finished spaying her new dog, and could tell by the shape of the animal's uterus, that she had given birth quite a few times. If The Fiend was going to have the poor thing killed for it, she shuddered to think of how she might have dealt with the puppies. "Okay, no more wild nights for you, Ms. Lola," she murmured, as she checked the animal's vitals once more before the tech carried her to recovery.

She liked the name "Lola" for her new dog—sounded like a name a reformed vamp might use. Lola had come through surgery without a hitch, as her doctor/new owner knew she would. To think that The Fiend had let the little dog suffer through who knew how many pregnancies and deliveries just because she was too lazy and cheap to have her spayed, and then wanted to have her killed because of it, still made Genevieve's blood boil. Made her need to throw a baseball at something.

After cleaning up, she went to check on the puppy from the fire. All of the vet techs did double duty, taking turns manning the reception area and working the back. Monica was off the desk today, and Genevieve found her sitting in front of one of the cages, cuddling the puppy in her lap. The little guy was nuzzling her hand as she gently rubbed his face, and his tiny tail was wagging so fast that he looked like a wind-up toy.

Monica looked up at her when she walked in, and with a sigh, said "I think I found my new baby."

Genevieve gasped and stared at her, eyes wide and eyebrows up in an unspoken question.

Monica nodded emphatically and smiled. "Yep. I'm sure. He's the one."

Rushing over, Genevieve leaned in and gave her a hug. "I'm so glad for you. And for him, too. It's about time."

A year ago, Monica had lost her nine year old Weimaraner/Poodle/mutt mix to cancer. At thirty, Monica was unmarried, and her animals were everything to her. Frank had been the closest of all of her pets, and her constant companion. He went everywhere with her, even coming to work, where he had the run of the office. He'd been one of those dogs who loved everybody, including other dogs. Even dogs who were normally dog-aggressive would warm up to Frank eventually, and though it couldn't be said that their feline customers *liked* him, at least he was one large dog that none of them seemed afraid of.

He'd slept on his mistress' bed, cuddled with her on the couch when she watched TV, absolutely refused to leave her side whenever she was ill, and lived for rides in the car. She'd taught him all kinds of funny tricks, which he'd perform just to please her, without the need for treats. All of her vacation spots were chosen on the grounds of whether or not the area and the accommodations were pet friendly.

When he'd finally reached the point where she knew she had to put him down and end his suffering, she was so devastated that the whole staff was concerned about her. She'd hired a pet sitter to come and care for her other animals, and then she'd just left town for two weeks, because she couldn't face going home to a house where there was no Frank.

She returned to work after that, but it was months before her usually cheerful personality began to reappear. She still couldn't even think about getting another dog—it would seem like such a betrayal of Frank's memory. But she did ache for that companionship and devotion that had filled her days.

For her to take the plunge and reach out to this little creature, to open her heart again completely, was unexpected and worth shouting about. Genevieve went from room to room announcing the news, and pretty soon the whole staff was gathering around the woman with hugs, congratulations, and words of encouragement.

To one who had never experienced a deep affection for an animal, this moment would have seemed ridiculously dramatic and over the top. But for the people in that office, people who cared enough about animals to dedicate their lives to their well-being, it was as if they were seeing a heart resurrected. Their friend was back, ready to start living again, and there was nothing trivial about that.

The rest of the day went by quickly, with everybody on a high, and even some of their long-time customers were let in on the good news. Genevieve gave Monica one last hug as she walked out the door with her new little guy. Once sure that the office was empty and hers alone, she went to the front desk and looked up the number for Mr. Boston.

It took a long time for someone to answer at the firehouse, and she was just about to hang up and try the cell number, when the Lieutenant finally picked up.

"Station fifty-five. May I help you?"

"Uh, yes, this is Dr. Sayers, at the animal hospital. Would it be possible for me to speak with Mr. Uccello?"

"Dr. Sayers, he's been put on medical leave for two weeks, but your timing is perfect. He just stopped in to pick up a few things, and then he'll be leaving."

"You know, on second thought, could you ask him to wait for me? I'm just down the street from you, and I'd rather speak to him in person. I can be there in five minutes."

"Sure. We'll tie him up, if necessary. How's the pup doing? This isn't bad news, is it?"

"Oh, no sir, it's the best."

She could almost hear the smile in his voice when he answered then.

"Well, that's just fantastic news. But I won't say anything. I'll let you tell him."

"Thank you so much. I'd really like that. Good bye."

The Lieutenant hung up the phone, smiling to himself, and then hollered out, "Uccello! You can't leave yet. Got a visitor coming to see you."

Ten heads, currently bent over plates at the kitchen table, swiveled around at that. "Who's coming to see our Amazing Human Gila Monster?" one of the guys shouted back.

"None of your business, and I wouldn't tell you it's a young female-type animal doctor, even if it was. Because it's none of your business and we all respect personal privacy here at the Fifty-Fifth."

Enzo was just coming out of the sleeping quarters with a couple of books he'd picked up, when he heard the conversation, and suddenly he panicked. He wanted to see that woman again in the worst way, but not like this. Even his grandmother couldn't stand to look at him like this. Not only had the red bumps that were all over his head moved down his forehead almost to his eyebrows, but some of the white cream he was supposed to use was clotted up between the bumps, making him even stranger and nastier looking than when she'd seen him before. *A real lady killer, eh, Uccello?*

He ran into the bathroom to look at himself, and this put him in a state of total despair. Why even worry about it? It was over before it ever began. If he asked for her number looking like this, she'd either laugh at him or run away screaming.

The doorbell rang, and everybody got up to answer the door together, laughing and quietly jostling for a place at the front of the pack. Enzo was at the very back, and too short to see over most of the heads in front of him. He heard her voice, and someone inviting her in, but mercifully, she replied that she'd prefer to speak with him outside, privately.

He finally pushed his way through to the door. "Excuse my brethren here. They're a nosy bunch of idiots, but I still love 'em." He turned back to the men and asked loudly, "So will you EXCUSE US, please?"

There were a few mutters and grumbles, but the herd returned to their grazing as he stepped out from behind the screen and onto the porch. He heard an involuntary gasp as she got a good look at him.

"Oh my gosh, you did get worse, didn't you?"

And then she did the last thing he would've expected her to do. She reached up and *touched* his forehead. "Does it hurt? I've never seen a rash this bad. If you were a dog, we'd probably recommend that you be put down."

"Oh thanks. You're a real morale booster. You and my brethren in there. I was gonna stay and have supper with them, but they said they couldn't eat with me around—spoiled their appetites."

She nodded in agreement. "I can certainly understand. You *are* sort of disgusting looking."

He'd expected distaste, but not disrespect. "Well, thanks again for that encouraging word. Did you have something to tell me, or did you just come to torment a wounded man?" Suddenly, she wasn't so beautiful anymore. He didn't need more tactless, disparaging remarks to brighten his day.

"I actually came for two reasons. One, to tell you that the puppy is doing great, and one of our own staff is adopting him! That dog is going to have the best possible life a dog could have. And two, I wanted to ask you to have dinner with me."

He was mistaken. She was gorgeous.

"Ah, uh, geez, I uh, well, this is a surprise."

Embarrassed now, she took a step back. "Look, I'm sorry. I didn't mean to put you on the spot like this. Forget it. My bad. Oh, and there's no charge for the puppy's care. Bye." She turned around to leave, hoping she'd turned fast enough so that he couldn't see her mortified blush.

He came as close to flying as he ever would when he lunged to grab her arm. "Wait, wait! I didn't mean I didn't want to! I mean, geez, I've been dying to call you, but I didn't know if I stood a chance at getting a date. And I was not too keen on you seeing me looking like this, devoid of my normally devastating good looks and irresistible charm. Aw, you're so cute when you blush. It brings out your eyes."

That made her blush even more, but she laughed in spite of her burning face, and said, "Well? Are we on?"

His hands went to his face as he shook his head. "Where could we go with me looking this way? I don't want to empty out some restaurant. I mean, geez, half the people who see me will think I'm contagious, and the other half will get too nauseated to eat." He looked at her quizzically. "It won't make you lose your appetite to eat with me?"

"You know what I do for a living. I've been up to my elbow in some cow's rear, checking her labor, and wondering at the same time what I'll have for breakfast when I finish."

He grimaced and covered his face with one hand. "Aww, too much information! Now I don't know if *I* can eat with *you* without getting nauseated. You have to promise me, no shop talk."

She smiled and held up one hand. "Okay, I swear, but you do have a point about restaurants. We could order a pizza and go to my apartment. As long as you understand it's *just* for pizza."

He smiled and gave a little bow. "Principessa, I will be on my best behavior."

"You bet you will. So do you want to follow me, or shall I just give you the address?"

"Ah, well…my car's still on the fritz. I took a taxi, so you'd better just give me your address. I'm not sure how long it's gonna take to get another one out here."

She looked at him, shook her head, and laughed. "My gosh, you're just so pitiful! Of course you're not taking a taxi. We'll go in my car and I'll drop you home later. Just promise me not to leave a layer of skin on the upholstery."

"Not to worry—-I only shed my skin in the spring. Let me grab my stuff and I'll be right out."

As she turned to walk to her car, she tried to keep from smiling—could not *believe* she'd just done that. She'd never asked a guy out before—went pretty well, she thought. And now she was having Boston for pizza.

As she'd turned to her car, he'd turned back to the firehouse. He tried to act cool instead of running to the door like he wanted to. He stepped in and all activity stopped. Every face turned towards him. To heck with cool. With a grin on his face, he leaned towards them and half-whispered. "Dinner at her place. Now. She's driving."

Hoots, "All Right's," and "Go Uchi's," filled the room, and half a dozen high fives were offered up. "Would you guys shut up, for Pete's sake, she's gonna hear you!"

He finally made it back to the door with all his stuff, and when he turned to say goodbye to the crew, one of them started whisper-chanting "Uchi, Uchi, Uchi," and the rest of the table crowd gradually joined in. He started laughing, took a bow, blew kisses and walked out. The chanters rushed to the front windows and peeked out between the blinds.

Ernesto sighed. "How does he do it? Five-five, hideous looking disease all over his head, a crazy Boston accent, and he gets a gorgeous, six foot redhead, with big blue eyes and legs that just won't quit, who's a doctor, no less, coming to take him out. Why not me?"

"Don't be too hard on yourself, Ernie. It's the puppy. Women go wild for puppies."

"Then I tell you what. I'm going out right now and get us a mascot. A cute, precious, Dalmatian puppy. He goes with us to all the fires, and we take turns rescuing him. Never know who we might meet."

Rick raised his hands and shook his head. "Hey now, wait a minute. You've got to leave us married guys out of that. My wife ever catches me with a puppy in my hands, she'll know right away, and Hell hath no fury…"

"Yeah, that's what happened with my wife's first husband," Raul chimed in. "She caught him mongrel mongering, and," he snapped his fingers above his head, "it was over."

#

He was trying to get the giggles under control. They'd started from the guys' teasing him, and his nervousness made them worse—so bad that his eyes had started watering. He took a deep breath to compose himself and to get the stupid grin off his face, and then headed down the sidewalk.

Genevieve was waiting in her car, and when she saw his serious face, eyes brimming with tears, she got out of the car and met him. "Are you okay?" she asked, reaching out to touch his shoulder.

That look of genuine concern set him off once more, so he just let himself go, unable to stop long laughing enough to explain. He shook his head, took her arm, and headed back to her car while he tried to stifle himself. He could hear the laughter in the house behind him, and he knew the men were peeking out the curtains and cracking up at what they saw—which kept him going until he got in the car, out of earshot.

By the time she'd gotten back in the driver's seat, she had a pretty good idea what all the laughter was about, having been razzed a few times herself when she'd lived in a dorm. "So those are tears of joy?"

"That's what they are. You're the first Principessa to ever offer me pizza. I should be calling the newspapers."

"Yeah, well, you're the first fireman I've ever invited. I usually do a background check before I let somebody into my apartment. But I saw you on the internet, saving that puppy, and I figured that was a good enough character reference."

"What? That was on the internet?"

"Yes. Don't you know there is *always* somebody around with a cell phone, taking pictures, no matter what you're doing? It seems impossible that there are any unsolved crimes anymore."

As she drove, he leaned back against the car door to face her, studying her while she talked. He was astonished by this turn of events. She was even prettier than he'd remembered. When she became animated as she talked, and her expressions brightened and relaxed, it just added to the attraction.

"So, Boston, tell me about yourself. How'd you end up in San Antonio?"

"Nothing too exciting. I'm single, and I wanted to experience living someplace different, while moving was still uncomplicated. Made a few inquiries online, and here I am."

"So, is your family all in Boston?"

"Yeah, all the ones in this country. My grandparents on both sides came over from Italy. They had actually known each other over there. The four were very close, and decided that if they left the old country together, then at least when they got to the new country, they'd have friends. They sort of pledged their children to each other even before they were born. That kind of thing was going out of style by then, but they did their best to see that their kids spent a lot of time together, and then pushed them to date each other when they got older, and whaddaya know—it worked.

"My parents just sort of rolled their eyes when they first started 'dating.' They figured they'd go out a few times, just to ease the pressure on them from their folks, but they talked about how they weren't real dates. They'd liked each other as friends their whole lives. Knew pretty much everything there was to know about each other's background, their whole childhood, you know? But after about their third date with just the two of them together, really talking, and not just as children, they realized there was more to each other than either had ever imagined. And just like that— they were hooked on each other. They still are."

"What a great story!"

"And what about you, Genny, if I may call you that?"

"Sure. I answer to about anything, as long as it's decent and well-intended. Genny, Gen, Genevieve—all the same to me."

"Lady Red suits you the best, but we'll go with Genny for now. What's your story?"

"I'm Canadian. My folks are American, transplanted to Canada because of some property my dad inherited. He was raised for most of his childhood by his great aunt in England, and visited his parents in the U.S. on holidays. So he has this upper class Brit with a dash of American accent that always has people trying to guess where he's from. My granddad thought he was a phony for years, partly because of the accent, and—well, other things that are just too complicated to get into.

"I went to veterinary school in the U.S., because, like you, I wanted to experience living somewhere else while I was single and *portable*. Got a position here at a clinic to work until I decide if I want to specialize. And I tell you, I did get a change coming to Texas from Canada. The weather here is about as far removed from home as it gets."

"Tell me about it! I think most of the kids in this city think snow is just a legend."

She laughed and nodded. "I do love it here. The people, the city, they kind of grow on you, but I know I'll go home someday. I miss the change of seasons and the beauty. It's beautiful here, in its own way, but not like home."

"Nah, it's never like home. I feel the same way. So what else can you tell me to convince me that I'm safe in your hands, Lady Red?"

"I never said you were. I have a temper, but I usually take it out on a target my dad made for me. I throw baseballs at it. Keeps me from going to prison. Some days I don't even use it. Other days, I need maybe a half-bucket of balls, and some days are two bucket days. People make me crazy sometimes. So watch your step, Boston. I can hit other things besides the target."

"You barely know me, and already with the threats? What have I done to deserve that?"

"Not a thing. Just thought I should give you fair warning. And you did ask. Still want pizza?"

"My whole being is craving it. Wild horses couldn't drag me away, now. Dangerous women intrigue me."

"And *I've* always been intrigued by men with horrible looking rashes all over their heads."

"Seriously?" *That explains everything.*

"No."

He huffed and rolled his eyes. "Geez, don't do that! You really had me scared. I thought I was going to have to leap out of a moving car there for a minute."

"Sorry about that. No, I'm essentially unkinky. And just for future reference, if you do decide to bail, let me know, and I'll stop the car for you. So much more considerate of the street cleaners."

"So why *did* you ask me out, if I may be so bold?"

She didn't answer at first, just scrunched up her face in concentration.

"Don't let this go to your head, but I thought your accent was kind of cute."

"Wait, wait, let me get a pen and write this down."

"You won't need one. It's a short list."

"Dangerous and cruel, too."

"There was just something about your personality that I liked. You're confident without being obnoxious. Or at least I think so, since I don't really know you yet. And of course, the big seller was you saving that puppy and taking responsibility for it. I'd had an experience earlier in the day with someone that seemed to have absolutely no idea that other species are God's creations, too. Compassion is very high on my 'must have' list."

Suddenly, she was embarrassed at saying so much. She risked a glance over at him, and he was leaning back against the car door, smiling as he watched her.

"Wow, for a cruel and dangerous woman, you say some nice stuff."

##

Four months later, after seeing each other almost every day, they were lying in a double hammock in Enzo's back yard, looking at the stars. He'd started to speak several times, but stopped himself. Genevieve kept hearing him take deep breaths for the speech, but with no speech forthcoming, she'd begun to wonder if he'd developed a respiratory problem.

"Are you okay?"

"No, I'm not."

She sat up and looked at him worriedly. "What's wrong?"

He sat up and gently pushed her back down in the hammock, saying "Lie back down. This will be easier if I don't have to look in your eyes."

She lay back down, starting to get a little teary and fighting it for all she was worth. *I can't believe it. He's dumping me. I thought he loved me. I can't believe it.* Not saying a word, she felt anger and sorrow building up as she waited for the worst.

"I'm tired of this. Not of being with you, of course, I'd never get tired of that. But I'm sick to death of not knowing, and worrying if you'll still be in my life next week, or next month, because I can't stand to think of you not being there. So, you wanna get married? 'Cause I don't see my future without you in it, so why waste any more time dating? That's not what I want. I want us to be permanent, and I want to be able to tell everybody that we are formally, legally, spiritually, soulfully, physically, *meta*physically, and every other way, bound to each other for eternity. How's that grab ya?"

She lay there, stark still for a second, then rolled over, grabbed his hair in both hands, and gave him the longest, deepest kiss of his life. Then she rolled back over without saying anything. He was still lying there, smiling.

"Should I take that as a 'grabs me fine?'"

"Quit being such a coward, and come look in my eyes."

He sat up then and looked down at her, and when their eyes met she said, “Yeah, it grabs me just fine.”

Now it was his turn to get teary, and then he started laughing. He grabbed her with both arms to pull her up to him, but instead, managed to flip them out of the hammock and onto the concrete patio.

CHAPTER FOUR

At the emergency room later, while she was being examined for a concussion, Enzo apologized for the thousandth time. The doctor continued checking her pupils without acknowledging him, and when he finished, Genevieve looked at Enzo in exasperation. "I know, I *know*. If you tell me one more time, I'm getting out my baseballs."

"How long were you out, would you say?" Holding her chart, the doctor continued to ignore Enzo's presence, speaking only to her.

Enzo spoke up anyway, because how would she know? "She came to in maybe half a minute. I was afraid to move her, in case her neck was hurt too, but then she came to and wanted to sit up. She was dizzy for about five minutes after that, and I had to kind of help her to the car so we could come here."

The doctor looked at him like he was dirt's filthier brother, then turned back to addresss her. "Does that sound accurate?"

She nodded tiredly. "Yeah, that's right, I think. Since I was out, it's hard to say."

Turning back to Enzo, the doctor paused a moment before he spoke, as if he found it loathsome to address him at all. "I'll need to speak to Genevieve alone for a minute. You can have a seat in the waiting room and we'll call you back in after I get an X-ray and maybe some other tests." His manner brooked no argument, so Enzo leaned around the doctor to reach her, gave her a kiss, said, "I'm right out there if you need me," and left for the lobby.

The next ten minutes were spent with the doctor grilling Genevieve about how she "really" got injured. She repeated her story, explaining that they'd just gotten engaged. The man shook his head sadly and said, "Don't you realize this will only escalate once you're married? If he does this now, what will he do to you once he feels like he owns you?"

She was tired, her head hurt, and she was angry at the inferred accusations that Enzo was a woman beater and that she was someone who would take that kind of abuse. She was sitting on the side of the stretcher, and with her long arms, she reached out, taking the doctor by both shoulders, and drew him to within a few inches of her. Giving him her most intimidating stare, she spoke with an air of finality.

"I appreciate your concern, Doctor, but look into my eyes and know the truth. The truth is that if he had done this to me, *he* would be the one on the stretcher, and a bump on his head would be the *least* of his injuries."

She released him then, and he backed away quickly, looked at her face, and gave a brief nod. "Okay then, let's get that x-ray."

#

Had anyone in the history of the world, ever screwed things up so bad? That's right, propose and then dump her head-first onto a concrete slab. She probably thought a concussion was Italian foreplay. *Maledizione.*

Five hours later, after tests and symptoms established that there was no skull fracture or obvious intracranial bleeding, she was released into his care. He took her straight home. While Lola bounced all over the living room in ecstasy at having Genevieve back, he got her settled on the couch with pillows and blanket when she said she didn't want to go to bed yet.

He started to apologize again, but stopped himself when she gave him the bad eye. "I'm staying over tonight. The doc said I needed to wake you up during the night, to be sure that I *can* wake you up. If you want to stay on the couch, here on the floor is fine with me."

The moment he lay down to show her how fine it was, Lola was all over him, bouncing on and off of his chest and stomach, with her sharp little claws sticking him and her never ending kisses wetting his whole face. He sat up again. "Or not."

She laughed as he got back up to escape the ravages of the four-legged hurricane.

"You know, I think of all the things she's found on this floor, she likes you best."

"I won't say I'm sorry again, since you're in no shape to throw a ball, but I feel terrible that on this night, when we should be celebrating the idea of starting our life together, you're nursing your worst headache ever. And your memories of *me* on this night, will be of wanting to kill me for waking you up and making you count my fingers."

He was sitting on the edge of the couch, and now she reached over and patted his hand. "It could be worse. We could have *both* gotten knocked out, and then who would have driven us to the hospital? Nobody would have believed our stories, then. And we'd have to depend on Lola to keep waking us up." At the sound of her name, the little mammal-on-springs began bouncing up and down again, tongue hanging out and flopping around as she sailed happily through the air.

Genevieve gripped his hand tightly then. "Enzo, are you absolutely sure that this is what you want?"

He looked shocked at the question, that she should doubt his feelings.

"Lady Red, I have never wanted anything so bad in my life. I've never really been in love before—oh I've had 'romances,' and little flings, but what I feel for you is completely different. Now I don't see how I survived without you. Everything is better. *I'm* better. Hey, I know we'll have fights now and then, but I also know that they won't change the way I feel about you. I'm yours, Genny. Forever. If you can believe anything, believe that."

She smiled then, and pulled his head down to hers for a kiss. When he sat back up, she did, too, and moved into a corner of the couch so that she could look at him while she talked.

"Enzo, it's only been a few months, but I trust you more completely than anyone I've ever known, other than my parents. I'm about to entrust you with a family secret that could destroy my family if it ever got out. It would destroy *us*. My parents made all of us swear that no one but our spouses could be told about this. The only reason I'm telling you now, is that I believe with my whole heart that you mean what you say, and that you will be my husband—and I don't want to be married without you knowing about my family. All of my family. You have to swear to me that even if we break up, you will never tell this to anyone else."

He took both of her hands in his and gave them a shake as he looked back at her. "Lady Red, if this is that important to you, then it is to me, too. I swear to never tell a soul. Ever." He kissed her hands and then stared at her, waiting.

"Even if you think I'm crazy."

"Oh, I *know* you're crazy. But that won't change my promise. I gave you my word. That means my honor. And believe it or not, my honor is really important to me. So let me have it, crazy girl."

She told him about her family. She told him everything, from the time her parents had been abducted and how they met on the Elpies' world, to the dogs and cats that had been given telepathy and shared memories with her parents. She told him about her Elpie family—her dad's "brother," and her mom's "sisters," and how she was named after a cat.

He listened with his whole attention, and every once in a while he would ask questions, not derisively, but with respect, in order to clarify certain details in his head.

She told him about her dad's dying from poison after saving his Elpie brother, and about his "refurbishing," as he called it, by the Bluemen. And then she told him about the second time her dad had been killed, when he sacrificed himself for her brother and mom, and how the Bluemen had once again managed to bring him back, though with much more difficulty the second time.

When she'd finished, she looked at him questioningly, waiting for a response.

He just nodded and said, "Whew, that's a relief. I thought this was gonna be something really bad. Aliens? No problem."

Now she was mad. Almost baseball mad. She threw the blanket off of her lap and stood up, just to groan and sit back down when she got dizzy and her head felt like it exploded. "You're not taking this seriously! I can tell, because you don't look shocked, or worried. I'm telling you the truth. This is no time for jokes, Enzo. This is a huge part of my life, and if you can't accept this, then you can't accept me, and we're finished."

He looked aghast at her, and shook his head in denial. "Baby, I *am* serious! *Assolutamente!* I've *always* believed in life on other planets. I mean, how could we be the only ones with any brains in all these solar systems. *That* doesn't make sense to me. I'll admit, your story sounds far-fetched, and if it was anybody but you telling me, I'd probably be trying to get out of here politely, but *rapidamente.* But it's you telling me. If I want to spend the rest of my life with you, then I must believe in you, right? I believe in you, so I believe in your story. One-hundred percent."

Searching his face, looking for any sign of jest or incredulousness, she was finally satisfied that he was telling her the truth. "All right then. Now I am going to show you something that no one outside of my family has ever seen. I was never allowed to see it until I turned twenty-one, and then my oldest brother, Eli, showed my brother Colder and me. My dad doesn't even know that we've seen it.

"We already knew a children's version of it that Eli had told us when we were kids, so that we'd understand what had happened to Dad, and why he was so sick for a while. But Eli thought that we needed to see the disk, to *completely* understand the truth of it, and to understand what kind of people my parents are. And it showed us, too, how much the Elpies really are family to us.

"Are you up for this, Enzo? You'd better have a strong stomach. Every one of us kids ended up vomiting when we saw it, and my brother Jonas did when he *experienced* it. It wasn't just from seeing the blood, but from thinking of the pain and injuries of people we loved. I think this will help cement your belief in my story. I can't watch it again, but I'll give you the disk and you can watch it in my bedroom. I'll stay here until it's over."

She got up cautiously then, retrieved the disk from her desk drawer, and showed him how to activate it. If he hadn't believed her before, he would have then, seeing the reluctance she felt to even pick it up. When she handed it to him, he took it and went into the bedroom and closed the door. She could barely make out the sounds, but it was enough to bring back the images, and when he at last finished and came out, she was depressed and a little sick.

Shaking his head, he walked over, sat beside her, and gathered her into his arms. "Oh, Principessa, I'm so sorry. But—but he is alive now, right? They brought your dad back, and healed your mom's eye?"

She took a deep breath and let out a long, shaky sigh. Smiling, she looked at him and nodded. "That's right. He won. By letting that horrible creature kill him, my dad took his hands away from the knife and fire stick that he had against my mother's ribs and my brother's head. That allowed the Elpies to attack him without risking the fire stick going off, and without his being able to…to take the knives out of my dad fast enough to stab my mom before he went down. When my dad planned that, he didn't know that the Bluemen would be there in time to resuscitate him and heal my mom. He really was expecting to die. And he did. That's what makes it so wrenching and unbelievable.

All the pain and suffering they went through on that day was real, whether they got 'fixed' later or not."

"That took some kinda stones to do what he did. And I'll be marrying into this family? Geez."

She smiled at that. "I showed you this for another reason, Enzo."

"Yeah, and what is that?"

"To prepare you to meet the Bluemen and the Elpies."

"No—get outta here!"

"They come to see my folks at least twice a year, and I'm timing our going for you to meet my family so that we'll be there when their visit occurs. We all try to make it home to see them when they come each time. I'm not telling them that I'm bringing you, because my dad would have a fit, since we're not married yet. Nobody outside of our family knows about them. Well, except for Harvey Washington."

"Oh, Genny, I don't think that's real smart to just show up with me. I don't want them to hate me for barging in."

"You're not barging in— I am. They'll just have to deal with it. Don't worry, it will be fine. They'll love you."

"Why are my palms suddenly sweaty? Does your dad carry a gun?"

"No, he doesn't need to. He's very strong."

"Yeah, and he protects his kids with his life. Move over, I think I need to lie down."

Suddenly, he sat straight up and slapped his forehead. "I forgot! I gotta take you to meet *my* parents! My mom would never forgive me if I didn't bring you home before the wedding, which is…."

"How does eight months sound? That should give us time to make all the arrangements, meet the parents, and get our jobs lined up. One more thing I need to tell you, Enzo."

"After aliens, it's gotta be a bit anticlimactic."

"My parents are wealthy, they live on an estate, and for our wedding present, they'll give us a house on ten acres of it."

Suddenly, he looked disturbed for the first time. "This is a done deal? I don't have any say?"

Looking hurt, she shook her head. "Of course you do. We don't have to live there. I have three brothers, and my parents told us long ago that when we get married, they would build each of us a house and put it on ten acres of the estate, with that parcel of land and the house being put into a deed in our names. That way, they could keep the family close, but everybody would still have their privacy. They realized that all of us might not want to live there, especially at first, but they'll still build each of us a house, deed us that land, and pay our taxes on it every year. They have people to serve as caretakers for any uninhabited homes, so that whenever we come back to visit, we'll have our houses there for us and our children. And we'd never find a more beautiful place to live."

"So what if you never married?"

"We get the same deal when we're thirty, if we're not married by then."

"Geez, Genny, I don't know. I always envisioned providing for my family, or both of us providing, and building a house together. I don't like taking a handout."

She bristled at this. "It's *not* a handout, it's a precious gift, and like I said, we don't have to live there. Anyway, we have time to think about it. Still want me?"

"I'll always want you."

CHAPTER FIVE

Two months later, at the home of Giuseppe and Angelina Uccello.

"And you're telling me it doesn't upset you that we don't know anything about this girl, and suddenly he's engaged?"

Angelina was a petite woman, and at five feet, four inches, she had to look up into Giuseppe's eyes to argue with him. Fortunately, she could shift her eyes the two inches without straining her neck. Her dark hair was interrupted with only a few strands of gray, and her brown eyes could be amazingly fierce.

Recently turned forty-eight, she'd begun to pay the price for her culinary skills with a few unwanted pounds, but she was still an attractive little fire brand. Her Jewish neighbors referred to her as "zaftig." A kinder word for plump, it translated literally as "juicy" or "succulent." Had she known, she would have approved.

Their house, a narrow, modest two story on a street packed tightly with similar houses of different colors, had been in a frenzy of activity all day, and Angelina's irritation and anxiety permeated the atmosphere. She'd been in the kitchen, but now she'd come into the dining room to accost her husband one more time about the topic they'd been discussing for a week.

"Well, *he* knows about her, and *he's* the one who's marrying her! Our son is twenty-eight years old, and for the past five years you've been harping on him. 'Enzo, when are you going to marry some nice girl and give your mama grandbabies, eh? Enzo, what's wrong with you, not enough girls in Boston for you—had to go to Texas? What's the problem, Enzo, not enough girls in Texas to choose from?'

"And now, when he *does* find the girl 'of his dreams,' as he puts it, and brings her all the way to Boston to meet us—now you're upset about it. Angelina, sometimes you're impossible." Seeing the look she gave him then, he would have liked to separate himself from those angry eyes by a lot more distance than his height allowed.

He enjoyed shows about animals, and he'd watched a documentary about mantis shrimp, once. With two club-like appendages on the front of their bodies that move with unbelievably devastating speed and force, they bludgeon their prey and enemies alike. The blow of a mantis shrimp was said to land with the force of a twenty-two caliber bullet.

Ever since seeing that program, when his wife was upset, he could envision her eyes popping out of her head on stalks, clobbering him senseless, and then snapping back into her head. The police would never find the weapon, and she would plead shocked innocence.

Giuseppe had never lacked for imagination, and thus had experienced but a few boring moments in his life.

"Oh, it's so easy for you to be blasé about this. You're not his mother."

He rolled his eyes and raised his hands skyward. "And thank you, Lord, for that! It would have been a gruesome delivery."

Angelina growled something he was sure he was better off not hearing, and stormed out of the room, only to storm back in after she felt the storming out had made her point. She wasn't finished talking by a long shot. Coming through the arch between the living room and dining room, she put her hands on the table and leaned aggressively in his direction.

Giuseppe felt a clubbing coming on. "And what kind of girl gets engaged after only four months of dating? Four months from meeting him!"

"Well, Angie, I would imagine the kind of girl who likes the kind of *guy* who would get engaged four months after meeting her. And that kind of guy happens to be our son, who, as you know, has excellent breeding and character. Besides, she's not a girl. He said that she's twenty-three. That's a woman."

"How can he be sure she's not after his money?" Angelina crossed her arms and challenged her husband to answer *that*.

"Did you not listen to a word he said about her on the phone? She's a veterinarian. I know they don't make much starting out, but eventually, she'll probably earn quite a bit more than him. You don't hear many girls saying, 'Oh, Mama, if I could only marry a rich fireman, we could go and live in his castle.'"

Suddenly, her anger and energy just seeped away, and she seemed to deflate like a week old balloon. She dropped into a chair and put her head in her hands. Now Giuseppe saw her not as a frightening Mantis Shrimp, but more like—-an octopus. A little clingy at times, but intelligent, and soft to the touch.

He walked over and put his hands on her shoulders. "Angie, I know it's hard for a mother to turn her son over to another woman. You worry that nobody's good enough for Enzo. Or maybe you're worried that he'll forget about his mama when he gets married. But you know he'll always honor and love you, and you also know that this moment had to come. We did our job by loving him and raising him to be a fine man. Now it's our job to love the woman he's chosen. That's what cements a family together."

She looked up at him, smiled, and then laid her head against one of his hands, holding the other with her own. "Ah, Giuseppe, you always know the right thing to say to calm me down and make me see reason."

Self-preservation.

"They should be here any minute. Where are the girls?"

"Oh, they're just freshening up, and changing the sheets in the guest rooms, and you notice I used the plural of room?"

"That's fine, Angie."

The "girls" upstairs were Enzo's two younger sisters, Rosemarie, twenty-six, and Althea, twenty-four, both married, with children, but they'd left their families at home to come to the viewing of Enzo's fiancée. Enzo, at five-five, was the tallest of the siblings.

Rosemarie had a perpetually sunny nature, short dark hair, a gentle, sweet face, and was pleasantly plump.

Althea, the baby of the family, had long, straight, bleached blonde hair, a face and personality that brought the word "harpy" to mind, and was thin, with the exception of amazingly large bosoms, whose origin had been in question amongst the family members ever since the miraculous overnight appearance of the weighty pair soon after she turned twenty-one.

But this was Althea, so the question was never put to her. When she was angry, Giuseppe could see the snakes writhing from her head, and knew she was waiting to turn to stone anyone foolish enough to look upon her face.

The doorbell rang, and screams of excitement erupted from the sisters upstairs. Angelina ripped off her apron and threw it on a chair in the kitchen, fluffing her hair and straightening her clothes. "Do I look okay?" she asked Giuseppe in a low and near frantic voice.

"Beautiful as always." *Exactly like you did thirty minutes ago, in fact.*

They opened the door as a couple, with huge, welcoming smiles steam-ironed on their faces, and then they saw her. The smiles turned into gawks, with an accompanying "Oh!" from Angelina. Enzo had told them about her beautiful red hair and startling blue eyes, but had neglected to mention her six foot frame. And today, to show her respect by dressing for the occasion, she wore two inch heels to match her lovely blue dress.

Giuseppe recovered first. The smile returned, and he went forward to embrace his son. Then he turned to embrace Genevieve, but thought better of it for fear of where his face might land. Instead, he backed up and put one arm around her shoulder.

"Come in, come in! We're so happy you're here!"

Angelina snapped out of her trance and slapped the smile back onto her face. She grabbed her son in a hug, and with her back to Genevieve, raised her eyebrows and gave him the "Are you INSANE?" look. Then she turned to Genevieve, took both her hands in hers, gave her the best smile she could fake, under the circumstances, and said "Yes, yes, that's right. We are happy. To see you. Both of you."

The two walked into the house, with Enzo holding tightly to her hand, as if to spare her any embarrassment by making his claim obvious and undeniable. It was at this moment that the sisters appeared at the top of the stairs and got a look at their future in-law. Two *loud* gasps, and an "Oh my—they *do* make everything bigger in Texas."

"And here are my lovely sisters," Enzo said even louder, to cut off their comments.

Attempting to turn the other cheek, even though both were red by this point, Genevieve smiled and tried to make her voice pleasant and gracious sounding. "Hello. I've heard so much about all of you from Enzo. I'm—so happy to finally meet you! And I'm Canadian," she added, looking up at his sisters. *Where are my baseballs when I need them?*

Both sisters hustled down the stairs then, and Rosemarie, who could care less where her face landed, threw her arms around Genevieve and gave her an actually genuine hug. "Welcome to the family, Genny! I knew you had to be special for Enzo to fall for you. He's so picky. Come on in the living room and we can get acquainted before we eat." She took her by the arm then, and led her to the couch. His mom excused herself to return to the kitchen.

The room was pleasant enough: small, painted a very pale yellow, with an odd but comfortably compatible mish-mash of furniture, from older pieces—a wooden rocker and a credenza that appeared to be family heirlooms—to two modern leather couches done in cream and peach, set to face each other. The whole room was brightly lit from the large, open bay windows. As good a place as any to do battle, she supposed.

Fortified by at least this one sincere greeting, Genevieve decided to just be herself. *I'm here for Enzo. I will try and love his family if at all possible. There is nothing to fear. I will not be intimidated. Not much, anyway.*

Althea sat across from her on the other couch, openly staring, Giuseppe noticed. *Like a vulture.* Suddenly she laughed, and said, "Oh, my gosh, look at those feet! What size shoe do you wear, girl?"

"*Althea!*" Enzo and his dad raised their voices together in reprimand.

Genevieve squeezed his hand and gave her head a quick shake. She started to reply with her shoe size, but then decided she wouldn't give his sister another chance to act shocked.

"I wear whatever size fits my feet. I would imagine you do the same." She smiled at her, but her eyes were saying, "Bring it on, *sister*."

Rosemarie was desperate to change the mood of the room. "Whatever size they are, those are great shoes. Just high enough to be dressy and stylish, but low enough for comfort. Now that's a good combination."

Appreciating her attempt at friendliness, Genevieve thanked her and sent a smile that included her eyes. Just then, Angelina stuck her head in and said, "Dinner's almost on the table." When Genevieve rose and offered to help, she smiled and waved her off. "No, no, you're company. You all just sit and enjoy getting to know each other."

Giuseppe glanced at his wife and raised one eyebrow. *Like the pride of lions gets to know the antelope.*

"Enzo, do you think you could come help me with something for a minute?"

"Mom, if you don't mind, I'd rather stay with Gen here, in case she needs protection," he answered, with a pointed glare at Althea.

"Oh, with her size, I'll bet she could take anybody in the room. Come on and help your mother for a minute."

Enzo stood abruptly, feeling embarrassed, protective, angry, and saddened all at the same time. "You know, I think we should just leave. A restaurant's sounding pretty good to me about now."

His mother stepped into the room with a shocked look on her face, and Rosemarie moaned. His dad stood up, shaking his head in apology and reaching out to him, but before anyone else could speak, Genevieve rose to her full height, slowly and purposefully, and pulled on Enzo's hand.

"No. We need to stay. And your mother's right. I *could* take anybody in this room," she said, fixing Althea with her second glare in five minutes. "Go—go talk with your mom." Then she gave him a private little smile and a wink, and said, "I'll be fine. Trust me on that."

Seeing the look in her eyes, he suddenly broke into a grin, and kissed her hand. "Maybe I should stay and protect *them.*" Then he left and followed Angelina into the bedroom.

He closed the door behind them, then leaned back against it and stared at his mother, just waiting. She smiled at first, her pretty face fixed in an innocent expression, and then she dropped the pretense. Sitting down on the green spread of her and Giuseppe's perfectly made bed, she patted the space next to her for him to sit, but he shook his head.

Taking a deep breath, she decided to barge right in. "Enzo, my son…" He knew this was bad news if she started out by staking her claim. "Enzo—granted she has a lovely face, and good teeth, but have you even thought about the repercussions of this?"

"What are you talking about? What repercussions?"

"Well, isn't it obvious? People will be staring at you everywhere you go, laughing behind your back. Whatever possessed you to bring home a giraffe?"

He slammed his hand down on the back of the chair beside him. He would *not* scream at his mother. He would not.

"Yeah, Mom, people do look at us everywhere we go, except that they're usually staring at her, because she just takes over a room when she walks in. Her height and the way she carries herself make her look like a queen. Her mom taught her that. Then people look at her face and see that the queen is beautiful. And if people laugh at us together, it's because they're shaking their heads and wondering what a guy like me had to do to be with a woman like that. It doesn't make me feel small, Mom. It makes me proud. She doesn't make me feel short—I feel ten feet tall when I look in her eyes and see that she loves me, and that she's *proud* to be with me."

She could see by his face that she was losing—had already lost, but made one last bid.

"But—how do you dance?"

"Beautifully." He turned and walked out, closing the door gently behind him.

#

Dinner was delicious. If there was one thing Angelina knew, it was how to cook. Angelina had been taught that on special occasions, the full five-part Italian meal should be enjoyed, and tonight she'd outdone herself. After everyone was seated at the table, she stood before the expectant diners and proudly described the dishes to be served.

For the *antipasto*, the appetizer, they had Prosciutto e Melone, a wonderful combination of Italian ham wrapped around cantaloupe and honeydew melon balls. For the *primi piatti*, the first plate, Angelina had made tortellini filled with ricotta cheese and spinach, with a zesty meat sauce. The *secondi piatti*, the second plate, was steak medallions scaloppini al vino. Genevieve found at least one thing to appreciate about Enzo's mom, in the fact that she refused to buy or eat veal, which normally would have been used with this savory, wine cooked dish.

On the side, they had the *contorno,* of roasted potatoes with rosemary and parmesan, and grilled vegetables with pesto sauce. And if anyone was still able to even move their spoons to their mouths after all of this, the *dolci* was to be a warm chocolate custard with whipped cream, served with biscotti on the side.

While she recited the menu, there were *mmm's* and *ah's* sounded after each description, with an occasional outburst of applause from Giuseppe. Eating was his favorite pastime. Genevieve couldn't help but be impressed by all the work the woman had gone to. *She may want to murder me, but at least I'll die with a happy stomach.*

Giuseppe and Rosemarie made small talk with the couple, and in the silences prompted by the need to chew, Giuseppe studied the pair. *Two antelopes with bandoliers of bullets across their chests and rifles resting on their hooves, watch the lionesses watching them.*

Finally, his mother spoke. "So how did the two of you meet, Genevieve?"

"Enzo rescued a puppy from a fire, and brought it into the veterinary clinic where I was working. And by the way, Mrs. Uccello, everything is amazing. So delicious!"

Angelina smiled and prodded her on. "Yes, but that can't be all. How did you start dating? I mean, did he just fall all over himself the first time he saw you and invite you to dinner, just like that, or what?"

"Actually, Mom, I was having a pretty horrible allergic reaction, she recognized it, gave me first aid and sent me to the doctor. Might have even saved my life, who knows? If I hadn't had some treatment when I did, it might have gotten way worse. As it was, I had bumps all over me for about a month."

"So you asked her on a date out of gratitude?"

He put down his fork and stared at his plate, and then said quietly, "*Basta.* Enough."

Genevieve put a restraining hand on his arm, and smiled. "He didn't ask me out, Mrs. Uccello. When we met, I liked his personality, the little I saw of it. I liked the fact that he brought a puppy in and was willing to foot the bill for its care, even though it wasn't his responsibility. And I *loved* the fact that he risked his life in a burning building to save a helpless animal. That told me a lot about who he was as a person, and I found myself very attracted to that person." Enzo was watching her open-mouthed, in rapt attention.

His mom was listening in tight lipped silence, Rosemarie was nodding her head appreciatively, and Althea had a smug, "I knew it" expression on her face. Giuseppe was smiling broadly. *The female antelope drops to her belly, licks a hoof and raises it to test the wind, then closes one eye and draws a bead with her rifle.*

"I'd never asked a man out before, whatever you might want to believe about me, *Althea,*" she said, looking directly at the smirking sibling, "but I decided not to waste an opportunity to get to know someone like Enzo. So I went to the fire station with the excuse of telling him about the puppy, and I asked him out. And Mrs. Uccello, I have never been sorry for that. Not for one instant."

Giuseppe started laughing, and raised his glass in a toast. "Here's to you, Enzo. I *like* your woman."

Rosemarie raised her glass with a smile, and Althea did too, after a moment, saying, "I'm all for going after what you want."

Angelina hesitated a moment, then with a small, forced smile, she nodded and raised her glass.

After the toast, the meal went a little smoother, with Giuseppe and the sisters telling stories about Enzo as a child, much to his embarrassment and Genevieve's amusement. After Angelina's refusal to let them help with the clean-up, Enzo announced that they were staying at a hotel downtown. He'd already decided that he wasn't going to subject the two of them to the tension that staying over and sharing breakfast would prolong. He'd done his duty and brought his future wife home, she had run the gauntlet, and now they were done. His parents began to protest, but he simply held up his hand and shook his head.

"Well, thank you for a fabulous meal, Mrs. Uccello. Before we go, though, I'd like to speak to the four of you without Enzo."

"No way, Principessa."

She gave him a look, and his dad saw it. *The wolf rolls onto his back and exposes his throat.* Enzo shrugged and left the room, closing the door behind him.

"Why don't we all sit for a minute?" They did as she asked, and sat back down at the table, looking at her curiously.

She sat, too, but since she was the tallest, no one had a problem seeing her, and as she talked, she made sure to turn her head so that she made eye contact with each of them.

The cobra, for all its venom, is helpless against the mongoose as it weaves and turns in its dance of death.

"I don't want to walk out of here with any misunderstandings, Mr. and Mrs. Uccello. I love your son. I see in him everything good, honest, and noble that I've ever wanted in a man. And there's this special Enzo thing that just draws me to him. I feel like—no, I *know* that we are meant to be together. He calls me 'Principessa,' and that's how he makes me feel.

"He's talked about all of you so much, that I feel like I know you. He loves you. But he loves me too, and we're going to make a life together. I *want* to love you like he does. If you don't shut me out, I think, *over time*, that might be possible. In-laws can enrich a marriage wonderfully. *Or* they can put so much tension, stress, and bitterness in the relationship, that they break it completely. And even if they don't destroy it, they can at least erode it so that it could never be as whole and fulfilling as it might be otherwise. I've seen couples where one or the other's family has been completely struck from their lives, because that's the only way the two could be happy together."

The mongoose takes no prisoners.

"I would *never* want that.

"I love Enzo, and that means I want all of him. I want him as the complete, happy, wonderful person he is, and you're all a part of that. He wouldn't be whole without you. I couldn't stand the hurt that shutting you off would cause him. It would be like asking him to cut off an arm for me, and I can't—I won't do that. If you tried to come between us, *you'd* be asking him to cut out part of himself, and he would never be the same. Because he loves me, with all of his incredible heart and soul. And I can guarantee you, all of you," she said, with a glance at Althea, "that nobody will ever love him more than I do."

She stood up then and looked around the room at each of them. "That's it. Nothing more I can say. I hope to see you all at the wedding."

Giuseppe rose abruptly, grabbed her head and pulled it down to plant a kiss on her cheek, and Rosemarie stood and hugged her from the other side. Althea just looked at her, gave a nod and the "OK" sign with her hand. Angelina moved over to her then and said, "You're right. We all want him in one piece. Take care of him. You'll never find anyone better."

Then she pulled her future daughter-in-law over to the side and planted a kiss on her other cheek, and Genevieve got a little misty as she answered, "I know."

CHAPTER SIX

Sixty-three years earlier, in England….

"But Aunt Minerva, why can't I stay here with you? You like me, don't you? Are you mad at me? I like my room, and the staff is so nice, and I get to play with all the animals. Why do I have to go away?"

The crestfallen little boy was looking at her with so much fear, close to panic, and trying desperately not to cry. She could see he felt bewildered, betrayed. It broke her heart, and she almost changed her mind, but she knew it wouldn't be for the best if she let her emotions sway her.

"No, darling, please, come here to Aunt Minerva and let me hold you. I don't just like you. I love you, lad. You can always be sure of that." She reached out to him from her ancient upholstered rocker, and though he walked to her slowly, once she had him in her arms, he leaned into the embrace and threw his arms around her.

His parents, Hannah and Malcom Sayers, were biologists, working in Alaska on a long term assignment, studying the Kodiak bear and wolf populations. After he was born, they'd decided that it would be difficult, but ultimately rewarding to raise him in the woods with them while they did their field work. The idea of his being exposed to nature in all its beauty and raw power every day from a young age was wonderfully attractive in theory, making them feel as if they would be molding him into a more natural human, devoid of all the negative influences and conceits of modern society.

Very soon into their grand endeavor, however, they found that idealism and reality are often far removed from each other. After a very near miss involving an angry bear, Hannah, and their infant son riding papoose-style on her back, the couple felt it necessary to re-evaluate their situation.

They had both worked very hard and long to get this assignment, and both felt an absolute dedication towards the positive impact their study might eventually produce. Neither was willing to return to the city to raise their child alone, while the other continued *their* work with a new partner. The one solution they came up with was to appeal to Hannah's Aunt Minerva in England.

Minerva had been a beautiful and vivacious young woman who had married for love, twice, and had been twice widowed. In both marriages, she had longed and then grieved for children, when multiple miscarriages proved this an unfulfilled dream.

She had begun her adult life with inherited money, and both of her husbands had been exceedingly wealthy. But the wealth she possessed did not change the fact that she was alone. When asked if she might bring up this child for her niece and her husband, she saw only the positives of the situation, and jumped at the chance. He might not be her son, but he would certainly be the next best thing.

The boy was named Simon, which she thought very regrettable, given his last name. His parents had not intended any hardships for him, they swore—they had both just always liked the name. "Simon" sounded strong and wise to their ears, so "Simon" it was. Ah, well, she supposed many innocent children had been saddled with much worse names in the course of history. Perhaps dealing with it would build character.

Fortunately, the baby had adapted to her quickly, and Minerva found an intense happiness in every new day with him. His parents flew over to see him once or twice a year and she insisted on paying their plane fares each time, knowing that they could ill afford to. She could see how it devastated them when they had to say goodbye, but she saw too, how pleased they were that he was thriving under her care.

As Simon grew, he proved to be extremely active, full of energy, curious about everything, and always thrilled to be with other children his age. He was very attached to her, and he loved life on the estate, riding the ponies and wandering about with the grounds keeper, who had taken it upon himself to teach the lad everything he knew. By the time he was five, however, she realized that this life was not enough for him. He needed other boys to be wild and rambunctious with, he needed sports to give him an outlet for all that energy. He needed a well-rounded education and to be taught social graces. He needed to see the world outside of the estate.

Knowing that she was ending an extraordinarily wonderful period of her life, Minerva enrolled Simon into a most prestigious boys' boarding school, and now she had to make him see that it was for the best. But hearing his fear, seeing him fighting back tears, and understanding his feelings of betrayal, she wondered if it had all been a mistake.

She held him close for a few minutes, and then gently pushed him back and patted her knee for him to climb up on, since she could no longer lift him. From what she knew of his father's family, he came from a long line of uncommonly large and strong men, and the boy was already bigger than most children two or three years his senior. He was also very precocious and mature for his age, a result of being in the company of intelligent and well-mannered adults all of his young life, she supposed.

Once he was settled on her knee, he leaned against her, and she rocked him for a while, savoring the feelings of contentment and love that holding this child always brought to her mother's heart. Knowing that this was all about to change was almost more than she could bear.

As she rocked him, she looked around the room, this place where they'd had so many happy times. Her gaze fell first on the massive stone hearth in front of the huge fireplace. With its specially designed vents, the fireplace heated half the lower floor, and the boy had a great affection for it, saying that it was friendly and made him feel at home.

She could see Simon as a toddler, playing there with his toys, and then lying on the rug in front of the fire a year or two later, totally absorbed in a picture book. She saw the tall windows on the other side of the room, with their heavy burgundy curtains and the window seats where he would sit and watch the snow falling for hours. She turned her gaze to the book shelves of burnished wood standing twelve feet high, and saw him climbing the ladder to look at different titles, so curious and fascinated by books even before she'd taught him to read. This house would feel so empty without him. But it was time.

She stopped rocking after ten minutes or so, when she felt the moisture on her shoulder from his silent tears. Gently, she sat him up, keeping one arm around his back and the other across his lap, with her hand tucked around his side. She wanted him to feel held while they spoke.

Before she could begin, the lad voiced the concern that she knew he'd harbored for some time. "Aunt Minerva, is there something about me that people don't like? First my parents sent me to another country to live, and now you're sending me away, too. I thought this was my home now." His eyes filled with tears again, and he sobbed as he said, "I don't know what it is, or I'd try to fix it."

Now she was crying, at the anguish in his voice, in his eyes, that *she* was causing him.

"No, no, no. You are the most wonderful child I could ever imagine, Simon. And your parents feel the same way. It tore them apart to send you to me, because they loved you so much. But that love is what made them send you, because they realized it was too dangerous to keep you with them. They have a perilous job sometimes, and the thought of anything happening to you—-well, they just could never, ever, take that chance. You were too precious to them. There is not a single day that goes by that they don't think about you, and pray for you, and wish they could have you with them."

They'd talked about his parents' reasons for sending him here many times before, and each time he would seem satisfied with her answer. But when he continued to bring it up again, she realized that reason did not often hold sway in a child's heart.

"And Simon, my love, I had longed for a child ever since I can remember. When your parents asked me if I could watch over you for them, it was like a dream come true. I loved you before I even met you, and when I met you, oh my gracious, I thought I held a piece of Heaven in my arms. I couldn't believe that God had finally answered my prayers and given me such a wonderful little bundle, even though you were just on loan from your parents.

"You were the sweetest, best baby, the funniest, cutest toddler, and now you're the smartest, best mannered, the most interesting and wonderful boy in the world. I don't know how I'm going to live without you here in my house and in my arms."

Alarmed at seeing tears running down her cheeks, Simon took her face in both of his hands.

"Please don't cry, Auntie! I'll come see you on holidays, and we can talk on the phone, just like you said. You can bring the dogs inside to keep you company. They'd like that. Don't be sad." Then he kissed her cheek, sat back and gave her a lovely and obviously forced smile.

Well, if he could be stout hearted about it, so could she. With a monumental effort, she sat up straighter and stopped her tears. "That's right! This is not goodbye. We'll be in touch all the time! And you are going to have such a marvelous time with all the other lads! You don't get much company your age here, and I can't give you the sports and teach you all of the wonderful things that you'll learn in a school like this.

"You'll have a grand education that will make you more than ready for the university someday. And I'll just bet you'll be on all the teams, and I will come to every game that I can, to watch you play. You're going to be the happiest boy in the world! Just think—you have people on two different continents who love you, and now you'll have a whole school full of friends. You are one lucky lad!"

That conversation started him thinking that maybe this *would* be fun. Maybe he *would* be great at sports and have a million friends, and still get to see his aunt. He did get lonely for other children his age sometimes, and it would be fun to see some place new. As much as he loved his aunt, she *was* sort of old, and just not fast enough to catch him anymore when they played chase. He used to jump up into her arms when he was little, but Wallace had warned him in private that with him growing so fast, he couldn't jump up like that anymore, because he might make her fall and break her bones. Being able to wrestle with somebody would be pretty great.

One week later, he said goodbye to his aunt and to Wallace, his beloved grounds keeper, and he thought he saw tears in the man's eyes when he knelt down to hug him. He'd already said goodbye to every one of the animals, and even to the fireplace, but he'd saved Wallace and Aunt Minerva for last. As the driver put the car in gear, Simon looked out the window and waved. When his aunt and Wallace waved back, he saw his aunt smiling bravely, with Wallace awkwardly patting her back.

CHAPTER SEVEN

Miserable. The first week at school was miserable. He was in a dormitory with a lot of boys he didn't know, and it was a little on the cold side, with no cheery fireplace to sit in front of and no warm hugs to send him off to bed. The food was okay, but there was nothing like Miss Nancy's scones with clotted cream or her amazing bread pudding.

The headmaster seemed a nice enough sort, but he *had* to put his best face forward, didn't he? He was the one whose appearance and manner had to convince people to leave their children here. So Simon wasn't sure if the man really was who he seemed to be. He was a little shy about talking to the other boys, some of whom he thought were put off by his size. One boy in particular seemed to think that being tall made him a perfect target for teasing.

His aunt had given him a secret weapon though, and so far, it seemed to be working well. She had suspected that he might get teased, for his height as well as his name. She said that when people made fun of you, if you laughed *with* them, it took away their power. They wanted to embarrass others and to make them feel bad about themselves, but it's difficult to *give* offense to someone who refuses to *take* it. The best way to shatter their power to hurt you was to never let their words take root in your heart.

Wallace had talked to him about this too, and had made him memorize a few come backs to put in his arsenal, to use along with the laughter. The boys all seemed to think his name's resemblance to "Simon Says" was funny. On his first day at school, when the boys were seated at dinner and plates of cookies were set on the midline of the long tables, the same annoying boy who joked about his height had said loudly, "Simon Sayers your arms are too long. Simon Sayers no dessert for you." A few of the boys had laughed.

He'd laughed back and replied, "Simon Sayers these arms can get to the cookies before yours can," and reached out, easily grabbing a couple with his large hands. *All* of the boys within earshot had laughed at that. *Thank you, Wallace.*

When he'd lived with his aunt, on cold nights at home she would take him into the huge kitchen and they'd make hot chocolate together, just the two of them. After drinking their fill of the warming, decadent concoction, they would go to the big rocking chair in the den and he'd sit in her lap in front of the fire. With a blanket wrapped around them both, she would rock him to sleep as she told him stories and fables, and shared her wisdom and advice.

It was on one of these nights that she first told him about the heart, and she would mention it often after this. She told him that the heart was a wonderful garden, full of rich soil just waiting for seeds, and that the mind was the gardener. Lots of seeds got planted in the heart, good and bad, and it was the gardener's job to pull the bad seeds up when they'd only just sprouted, before they could take root too deep. It was also the gardener's job to nurture the good seeds and see that they grew. He had to protect them from ice and snow, and to be sure they were exposed to sunlight, and watered when they were thirsty. And when he'd done his best, but the weather was too harsh to let his garden thrive, well, then a good gardener would pray for his plants, and trust that the *great* gardener would see them through.

He was trying his best to be a good gardener at school. Wallace had given him a bit of pesticide to use in his garden, as well. They were all making their beds one morning, when Arthur, the boy who seemed the most amused by his size, walked up to him and asked him loudly, in the hopes of embarrassing him, "Shouldn't you be with the upper classmen? I bet you were too stupid to pass, so here you are, to try again."

A few boys had snickered, but he noticed that most had not. Most had seemed uncomfortable at the obvious spitefulness. He remembered what Wallace had told him, and replied, "Oh, I decided to grow up early so that when I got here, I could teach the ones who couldn't manage to on their own." And then he'd smiled and patted Arthur's back.

The boys who'd been watching the exchange broke out laughing. *Thank you, Wallace.* The only one who didn't laugh was Arthur, who'd looked at Simon with such a seething hostility that it actually startled him. It was just a little tit for tat—nothing to hate someone for. Another boy slapped Simon on the back with a smile, and suddenly, with that slap of approval, he had a good seed growing. In his mind, he picked up the bad seed before it even had a chance to sprout, and tossed it into his basket of weeds.

That day had been a turning point for him. He had seen in the faces of the other boys that many were just like him. They had gardens that needed planting, too. He decided then and there that he would plant only good seeds in other people's gardens. He would try to become a master gardener. That decision, fostered by his aunt's gentle story, would stay with him for the rest of his life, and help, in a large part, to shape the man he would become.

The dorm was still a little cold at night, and he still missed his aunt, and Wallace and the animals, but by the end of the second week he didn't feel lonely anymore. He'd started forcing himself to talk, especially to those boys who seemed most uncomfortable. When they responded, he would try and bring them around to where other boys were gathering, and gradually ease them into the conversation. He'd ease himself in as well, until finally, there were very few boys that he didn't consider friends.

When he first tried this tact, during a break between exercise sessions out in the field, the two boys that he strolled up to seemed a bit taciturn and surprised that he'd stepped in with the other lad. But he found that when he concentrated on someone else instead of himself—-on being a proper gardener, that he lost his shyness. Then his natural friendliness and positive nature made conversation easy and eventually won people over.

In most of the games they played on the field, his size and strength became an advantage, and this helped his self-confidence to the point that he wasn't hesitant about talking with anyone anymore.

He never boasted about his skills, and continued to garden whenever he could. There are not many to whom a compliment or a friendly word is considered an affront, and most people are sorely in need of one or the other—even those who seem happy or confident may be battling weeds just beneath the surface.

The anger Simon had seen in the eyes of Arthur on that fateful day did not abate with time. If anything, it intensified, but the child learned to hide it in order not to appear too surly or ill-natured. He hid it from all but Simon, or so he thought, for he wanted him to feel his enmity. Having come from a loving family, it was difficult for Simon to understand the reason for Arthur's feelings, and he tried more than once to break down the barrier that the boy seemed to have erected between them.

He'd overheard Arthur's parents speaking with him on two different occasions, and had noted not the slightest hint of affection from them. He'd also noticed, as had all the boys, that Arthur's parents rarely came to visit. Simon thought that this lack of positive attention probably had something to do with the way the boy acted. He also reasoned that his own bounty of affection from his aunt and his parents, when they were able to visit, probably stirred resentment, as Arthur saw someone else receiving what he longed for but couldn't have. So he continued to try gardening with Arthur whenever he saw an opening. There were times that he thought he'd made some inroad, until two more incidents cemented the nature of their relationship.

One day during that first year, the boys' science class had been assigned to small groups, with each team responsible for catching a particular type of bug. The insects captured were to be examined and discussed in class later. Since the two had been assigned to the same group, Simon decided to risk a friendly overture.

Many of the boys had nicknames, and it seemed to him a mark of acceptance and friendship when others called him "Si," (as in "sigh"). Some of the monikers awarded were shortened first names, and others had to do with their personal accomplishments or characteristics. There was a "Catch," for one of the boys particularly adroit at that skill, a "Whitey," named for his light blonde hair, and "Sketch," for his propensity for doodling stick figures in class when he was bored.

Thinking it would please the other boy to be included with this sign of camaraderie, Simon, in front of the other boys in the group, called loudly to him, "Hey, Art, there's a beetle just there by your feet."

Instead of seeming pleased, as Simon had hoped he might, Arthur whirled around and yelled angrily, "It's *Arthur,* you great dolt. Arthur is a name of kings." He said this proudly, but unfortunately, the haughty stance he took as he pronounced this, trying to make himself appear as tall as possible, with his chin up, and shoulders back, struck all the other boys as screamingly funny. When they began laughing, first he glared at them, and then he turned his gaze back to Simon, who knew by then that his attempt at being chums had backfired badly. The fury in Arthur's eyes said it all.

#

When the boys were seven, and had just returned from holiday after Christmas, Simon and some of his friends walked out into the court yard in the center of the school. A fountain there contained a large statue of an angel, from the top of whose head spewed streams of water, something that Simon had always found slightly nauseating. There was a pool around the angel's feet, where its cranial eruptions were gathered and then gradually drained away.

As the boys entered the courtyard, their attention was drawn to a small group gathered around Arthur, who was putting something in the pool of the fountain. Simon and the others had started to walk over and check out the goings on, when suddenly they heard a little screech coming from the pool. They all knew then what was happening, and Simon ran over and shoved his way through the group to get to the pool.

There was Arthur, holding a kitten stuffed into a laundry bag, with only its head visible and soaked. It started screeching and mewling pitifully as the boy started to dunk it again. "STOP IT," Simon screamed in outrage.

Arthur looked at him, smiled, and said, "Sod off, Sayers," and continued his downward thrust with the wretched animal.

Before the kitten's head reached the water, however, Simon's hands had hold of the other boy's wrists, and he physically pushed him back from the fountain. "Sketch, get the bag from him," he ordered. The boy he addressed, though having been in the group watching the cruelty, guiltily did as he was told.

"Get your filthy hands off! Wait until my parents hear you laid hands on me!" Arthur looked around frantically for supporters, but now the boys with him were all finding interesting things to look at on the ground, and the boys who had come in with Simon were looking at him as if he were gutter soup.

Simon was outraged. He'd never really wanted to hurt anyone before, but to see that little thing, so frightened and helpless, being tortured for no good reason made him want to hurt Arthur. Instead of hitting him though, he simply stood there, holding the other boy's wrists as he glared at him.

The headmaster, hearing the shouting, had rushed into the courtyard in time to see Simon standing there, his face red, and his hands firmly wrapped around Arthur's wrists. Having observed these boys for the past two years, and seeing the dripping kitten held in Sketch's arms, he had a fair idea of what had gone on.

"Mr. Sayers, you will kindly release Mr. Worthington's wrists. Both of you, in my office. Now. And you," he said, turning to Sketch, "take that kitten to the infirmary and let the nurse have a look at it. And I warn you, Mr. Worthington, there had better be no injuries apparent on it."

Because he knew both students, it wasn't difficult for the headmaster to sort things out in his office. When he asked Arthur if he had put the kitten in the pool, he looked down and refused to answer. Simon wouldn't say what had happened, but when asked directly if *he* had put the kitten in the water, he'd answered, "No! I would *never* do that!" with such vehemence that any doubt Mister Whitman might have had about who had done the deed was permanently put to rest.

Simon was verbally chastised, as a mere formality, for laying hands in a hostile manner on another student, while Arthur's parents were called and advised to pick up their son for an indefinite suspension.

Rather than reacting with shock or shame, his father first asked if the kitten had been killed. When told that it hadn't, he replied that no harm had been done then, and that the whole thing was just a boy's harmless prank and should be treated as such. He flatly refused to come for his son, saying that both he and his wife had some business interests in Sweden, and couldn't cancel their trip on the spur of the moment. When Mister Whitman had insisted, Arthur's father had replied, "We'll see what the board has to say about this," and hung up.

Unfortunately, the senior Mr. Worthington possessed an embarrassing degree of clout with the board, and since the school was always running slightly over budget, his offering of a scandalous amount of money for the incident to be excused was accepted without hesitation. The order for this resolution of the matter was relayed to the headmaster in record time.

Mister Whitman was livid when he was directed thus by the board, but he was getting older, and didn't relish the thought of losing his position at this point in his life. So he swallowed his principles and allowed Arthur to stay. He also called Simon's aunt and explained the whole situation to her, extending his apologies for his inability to act as he felt he should. He then commended her nephew for stepping in, and her for raising him to do so.

Arthur never spoke to Simon again, except in polite conversations that consisted of yeses and no's on his part, when interaction could not be avoided. But once in a while, when he could catch Simon's eye and he felt no one else was watching, he would smile and form his fingers into the shape of a gun, point at him, and pretend to shoot. Then he would whisper or mouth the word, "Someday."

#

When Arthur and Simon were fourteen, one much more troubling incident occurred. There was to be a cycling race with another school, and Simon and several other classmates were entered. Each boy practiced with his own assigned bicycle, so that he would be aware of the unique feel and handling of it when he raced. The bicycles were stored in a special shed that, though not far from the dorms, was hidden from view by a hedge of large shrubs.

The day of the race came, and everyone in the vicinity turned out. It was to be run through the beautiful countryside near the school. This was an area of rolling hills and a slow moving river that was crisscrossed by bridges as it flowed along its meandering course.

As the race commenced, Simon got off to a strong start, and gradually ended up moving into fourth place out of twenty. He kept feeling an unusual vibration coming through the bike, but didn't dare stop to check it, for fear of falling further behind. The pack in the lead had finished about half the course when they rounded a curve and then headed straight downhill towards the third bridge of the day. Just as Simon's bike hit the small bump at the entrance to the bridge, his cycle split in two. The front half veered wildly as he tried to pull it back towards himself in an attempt to balance. With the speed at which they were going however, the effort was futile, and Simon slammed head-first into the railing, doing a flip into the river when the railing broke.

Fortunately, the current was gentle, the water relatively clear, and the bridge low over the water, or they would have lost him, for even wearing a helmet, he was knocked cold when his head hit the railing. There were people everywhere along the route, and his rescuers were in the water almost before he was. They dragged him to shore, where he came to within a minute, gasping and fighting off a Good Samaritan who was determined to give him CPR despite the fact that he didn't need it.

As luck would have it, his Aunt Minerva was there to see him race that day. She'd come close to falling out of the spectator stands when she'd leapt to her feet at the sight of her boy flying through the air to land in the water below. She'd had her driver rush them to the hospital, though Simon kept insisting he was all right. The fact that he'd tried to enter the car through the trunk told her otherwise.

Suffering a concussion, sore neck muscles, and a few abrasions, Simon saw no reason not to return to school. Before she would allow this, however, Minerva went and spoke with the headmaster, demanding an explanation. Were new cycles needed? Were the current devices neglected badly enough to pose a danger to the lives of the students?

The headmaster had already ordered the two sections of the damaged cycle to be brought to his office, along with the cycling coach. When the pieces were examined, at the split, the metal appeared to have been filed through, but only from the bottom, where it wouldn't have been obvious. The top side of the frame had finally torn, due to the stress of supporting the total weight of its rider. Both Minerva and the headmaster immediately suspected Arthur, though it almost defied logic that a fourteen year old would plan and carry out this kind of sabotage.

Sadly, there was no evidence, and when Arthur was called into the office for questioning, not only did he deny having any hand in the affair, but he had the audacity to dare the headmaster to produce proof of his suspicions. Arthur's parents weren't called, since there *was* no proof, even though Whitman was certain in his own mind that somehow the boy was involved.

The child who had once cried at the thought of going to school was now a youth beside himself at the thought of not returning. "Aunt Minerva, you're not serious! You can't make me switch schools now! I'll be graduating in a few years and all my friends are there. I *can't* leave now. You made me go there, and it was the right thing to do. This school is my home, too. *Please, please, don't do this!*"

Seeing his pleading eyes, and the horror with which her idea of switching schools was received, Minerva finally relented. "Simon, my boy, it's very possible that someone tried to do you harm by tampering with your bicycle. You could have easily been badly injured or even killed yesterday. We both know who's behind this, but the headmaster says his hands are tied because there's no proof. No one remembers seeing that boy down by the shed, and of course, prints are worthless, since everyone handles the cycles. I'm afraid of what he might try next."

Ever since he'd found out the cycle had been purposely damaged, Simon had been mulling over the same thing. "Aunt Minerva, I know you told me never to fight in school, or to—"

"Simon, don't say another word. There comes a time when one must take a firm hand. Since the school won't do it, I say that whatever you need to do to put a stop to this, you should do it and know that you have my blessings. I can see those wheels turning in your little broken head. You have a plan, don't you?"

Smiling slyly, he sat up on the couch where he'd been lying. "Don't I always?"

Two days later, he was back at school with the doctor's permission and the stipulation that he avoid contact sports for two weeks. On his return, Simon had a get together with the largest of his friends—six to be exact. After watching Arthur's comings and goings for several days, the group managed to maneuver him into a secluded area by the pond.

Surrounding him, they herded him down to the water and behind some trees. When he tried to get away, two of the boys grabbed his arms, and when he started to call for help, another boy held a wadded sock up to his face and raised his eyebrows. Arthur quickly shook his head and clamped his lips shut.

When they reached a spot they felt was adequately hidden from view, Simon put one hand on the boy's shoulder and bent down to stare into his face. "Arthur, I know what you did. The whole school knows what you did."

"I didn't do *anything*! You've got no proof!" the now terrified boy shouted at him, trying to keep from crying.

Simon shook his head, but otherwise maintained his position. "You're the proof, Arthur. The way you've acted all these years. Some of the other boys said that when I went off that bridge, you laughed and pointed your little gun here," he said, grabbing Arthur's index finger, "and then you pulled the trigger. That's proof enough for me."

He thrust the boy's hand away then and put his face even closer. He was a good four inches taller than Arthur by this point in their lives, and from regularly working out, very well-muscled for a fourteen year old. He'd never really tried intimidation before, but found that in this particular case, he was quite enjoying it.

Making his voice as low and masculine as he could, he began. "Listen to me good, *Arthur*. I've tried to turn the other cheek to your little snide remarks over the years, and your petty pranks, I really have. But you just haven't taken the hint. You haven't grown up at all. I don't intend to let you hurt me or any of my friends *ever again*. I'm not going to pound you into the dirt today. But be aware that if I ever see or suspect you of doing something that might be even slightly harmful to *anyone or anything* again, I will beat you into nothingness. And if anything should happen to me, well, my large friends here are just dying to take up the slack." On cue, as they'd rehearsed, all the other boys leaned forward and tried to look dangerous. "Do you understand?"

Finally losing his attempt at bravery, Arthur nodded his head, wiping tears and snot away with his sleeve. Simon released the boy's shoulder with a little shove. "Now get lost."

Whirling around, Arthur ran faster than Simon would have thought him capable of.

"Beat you into *nothingness?"* Whitey asked with a grin.

"I know, I know. I couldn't think of a better word. I should have written it out and memorized it, like you said. You chaps did all right though, didn't you? You looked very nearly ferocious."

Randall, one of his tall but skinny friends, gave a muscle man pose, flexing his almost nonexistent biceps. "Who would *dare* trifle with these?"

Reggie slapped the back of his head, and then they all started laughing and headed back to the dorm.

Arthur ran straight to the headmaster's office, past his secretary, and flung open his door without knocking or announcing himself. Whitman was calmly working on some papers and barely acknowledged his presence.

"I've been assaulted and threatened!" Arthur screamed at the man, spitting generously with the ferocity of his announcement.

The headmaster looked at him over the top of his glasses without raising his head. "Where's the proof? Do you have evidence?"

Suddenly Arthur knew the terrible truth. He'd been set up. The headmaster knew all about it. He was trapped. He couldn't even call his parents and ask them to sue the school, because they were "bloody well sick of hearing *from* him and *about* him," as they put it, and they might just "slap him into a military school if he kept on mucking around." He let out a little sob, and the tears and snot dripped even more copiously when he saw the slight smile on the headmaster's face.

##

The years went by, and both boys managed to graduate without ever coming to blows or even shouting at one another again. For the most part, the two had avoided each other, and when they couldn't, were polite but aloof, as neither wanted anymore trouble on record. Simon had thought that over time, the hostility would gradually drain away, but at least once or twice a year, all the way to graduation, Arthur would smile and repeat his little shooting gesture.

The headmaster had seen this performance once, when the boys were fourteen, and he'd called Arthur's father, demanding he remove his son and seek counseling, for he could see that this was not a joke for the boy, and feared future violence. The results of his phone call were almost identical to his first call about the kitten.

The gesture did bother Simon, for over the years he'd come to understand that there was real hatred within the other boy. Occasionally he'd actually felt sorry for him, for he didn't know how someone could live with all of that rancor constantly eating at him. At a loss for how to stop it, however, and knowing that reaching out to Arthur would prove futile, he'd tried to ignore it.

The day of graduation came, and the ceremony was stuffy and grand at the same time, as only the English can manage. Everyone was in high spirits, but a little saddened as well. Having lived and gone to school together for so many years, all of them felt like they were leaving home and family, and most of them vowed to keep in touch with each other. Simon wanted that day to be a true celebration, and so decided to make one last effort.

After hugging his aunt and parents, he made his way through the crowd until he found Arthur standing with a few of his friends. Simon took a deep breath, walked up to him and held out his hand in the offer of a handshake. Arthur looked down at his hand, smiled, and moved as if to take his hand, but at the last second, pulled his hand back, pointed his index finger "gun," fired, and said, "Someday, Sayers. Someday."

CHAPTER EIGHT

Present day…

"All right, see you in a bit, then." He gave Bess a quick peck on the lips, and then took off running down the road. This was Simon's ten mile day. Most days, he'd do five miles, but once a week, he liked to do ten, just to keep his stamina up.

Bess had to come in to her gallery today to help prepare for the showing of her new pieces. It was set for four months away, but there were always details to attend to, even this far ahead of time. After helping her with what he could, Simon had wandered around town to kill time while she worked the rest of the morning.

Theirs was a small, picturesque town that drew a number of tourists for that very reason. Artisans of varied mediums had set up shops and galleries, which also drew tourists, which drew restaurants, which drew more people, including locals. A few people actually lived in the town, but most who worked or practiced their arts there lived in the surrounding countryside. Everyone knew Bess and Simon, and both of them appreciated being able to greet people by name when they strolled down the sidewalk.

Just before noon, she decided there was no more she could accomplish today, and called him on his cell. They met at her car, drove to the spot they'd clocked as being ten miles from home, and parted company there, per their usual routine on his ten mile days.

Most of this area to the east side of the road belonged to the grounds of a massive estate that had been owned by the Carmichaels, a lovely old couple who had finally agreed to let their children sell the estate for them, so that they could go to live with them in the U.S. The couple had reached the point where they seldom left the house, and since they lived basically in two or three rooms, it made no sense to maintain the huge staff necessary for managing the castle-sized house and its extensive grounds.

It was agonizing for them in one way, to leave this home where they had lived for sixty happy years together. But they were realists, and on the flip side, it would be a great relief not to have to worry about it anymore. And the prospect of spending their remaining years surrounded by their grandchildren had made the decision to move much easier.

To the west side of the road stood a densely forested area that had never been cultivated or occupied. Simon wasn't sure if it was owned by someone who wanted to save some wilderness, or if it was still government property. He hoped the former, because the government might turn it into a park or who knew what else, and he dreaded the traffic on this beautiful stretch of quiet road if that should happen.

He would miss seeing the Carmichaels on the more and more infrequent occasions when they ventured out. Every month or so, he'd go by just to be neighborly, and to see how they were getting on. Sadly, he had seen how this grand home that had always been such a source of joy for them was slowly becoming a burden.

So he was happy for them when one of their daughters had stopped by and informed the Sayers that her parents were coming to live with her. Their estates bordered each other, and during the last thirty-five years, both families had enjoyed the blessing of good neighbors.

As he rounded a bend, to his surprise, he saw four moving vans and two eighteen-wheelers traveling through the gates of the estate and heading towards the main house. He was taken completely off guard by this development, as he'd heard nothing about the place having been sold already. Wondering at first if he should jog on up to the house and introduce himself, he finally decided to wait until the new owners had a chance to settle in.

He picked up his pace and ran past the gate. A Mercedes was coming down the road towards the estate and as it closed the distance to Simon, it slowed and then came to a stop just in front of him. He saw a window roll down, and he trotted up to see if perhaps someone needed directions. Just before he reached the window, a head poked out.

The head had a dark beard heavily streaked with gray, thinning brown hair that had the look of a recent dye job, and two small blue eyes that Simon recognized in spite of the hair and the years.

"Simon Sayers, it *is* you! My word, you haven't changed much, except for getting old and gray like the rest of us. How have you been?"

He stood speechless for a moment before his brain and manners kicked in.

"Uh, well, Arthur! I've been just fine. And yourself? What brings you to these parts?" He could not bring himself to say it was good to see him. It was taking all his self-control to pretend he wasn't horrified to see him in this *country*, much less near his home.

Arthur smiled charmingly. "Actually, we're neighbors, you and I. I've just bought the Carmichael estate. Moving in this week. I'd been looking for a large wooded piece of land, and my broker informed me that this place had come available. When I began checking out the area and its history and saw that you owned the adjoining property, well, it seemed like destiny. Always thought we'd meet up again someday."

Simon didn't return his smile, and stared hard at the man, trying to decide if this last statement had been some kind of a threat. When he didn't respond, Arthur shook his head with a sad expression on his face.

"Look here, Simon—I know that we had our many differences when we were children, but that's just the point, isn't it? We were children. I think you're aware that I had a rather unhappy childhood, and I'm afraid I acted out because of it. But I've had many, many years of therapy, and when I look back, there are so many things I wish I could go back and change. And one of those things is the way I acted towards you.

"That's one of the reasons I took this place. To start over with you and wipe the old slate clean—or no, just throw the thing away and start with a new one. My therapists have said that's the best thing I can do—make peace with anyone I've wronged in the past. I'm a different person than I was then, and I'd like to be your friend. Think that would be possible?" He held his hand out the window then, with a hopeful look on his face.

Even though Simon found the whole speech very difficult to believe, how could he refuse his hand to someone who was truly trying to change? He wouldn't be the stumbling block in another man's redemption. He held out his hand with a smile. "I think it's entirely possible."

They shook hands, and he thought he saw genuine relief and gratitude on Arthur's face. "That's simply grand. I hope to see you soon."

Arthur had his driver start moving on, and as Simon waved him off, feeling almost warm towards this "new man," Arthur stuck his head out the window again with a smile, and pointing his finger like a gun at Simon, pulled the imaginary trigger.

#

Bess was puttering around in the kitchen, rearranging some crockery on the counters while she sipped her tea.

Puttering was what she did best in the kitchen, since cooking had never been her forte. Fortunately, she had always been aware of this, and her acknowledgement of it had probably saved her marriage as well as her children. They'd never been forced to eat any of her disastrous forays into the culinary arts, and she had become a master at ordering healthy take-out. When the children were living at home, she'd employed a cook to come in once or twice a week and prepare dishes that she could refrigerate and reheat, so that meal time would have a more homey atmosphere, without paper cartons lying everywhere.

Now that it was just her and Simon most of the time, sandwiches, salads, soup, and eggs were the staples. Simon liked to throw every leftover he found into his soups, and she boiled a mean egg. She could also broil a wonderfully flavorful steak on occasion, but a positive outcome when she attempted to was never guaranteed.

Designed for a manor that was expected to host large parties from time to time and could sleep from ten to twenty guests, the kitchen was enormous. Slightly modernized recently, it boasted two almond colored freezers, two matching refrigerators, and a large green and blue tiled island at the center. Bright lighting in stainless fixtures hung above the work spaces, and multicolored Tiffany lamps graced the rest of the room with a softer glow. Oak cabinets covered the walls, and the walk-in pantry could easily house a station wagon. Side by side ovens built into one wall waited silently for someone to appreciate their capabilities. Bess thought the two must miss her parents in between their visits.

A smoothed over slab of oak on four sturdy legs served as the kitchen table, where Simon and Bess usually ate their meals. Its chairs had been made for comfort, with padded seats and backs that curved to fit the body, and arms slightly depressed down the center to cradle their human counterparts. Blues and greens dominated, with a splash of red here and there.

Even though the ovens lay dormant until her parents' visits, something about the room always gave her a sense of warmth and hominess. She supposed it had to do with the fact that children spend so much time eating, and this room held many memories of her family as they were growing up. When she boiled water in the microwave to make tea, Bess liked to linger in the kitchen to drink it with a bite of cheese.

Content with the results of her puttering, she stopped and gazed out the wide window above the sink. This was her favorite view: a long green field fronting a barn with a forest of tall firs towering behind it. Three horses were in the field, and one was rolling in the grass, his legs waving above his stomach as he savored the answer to an itch.

#

His ten mile days always flew by for him as he got into “the zone,” when the pace became automatic, and his whole being was in tune to the rhythm of muscle and lung and heart as they labored together. His mind would empty of everything but the colors that flew by as he ran, and the sounds of his shoes hitting the pavement. But today the distance seemed interminable. He searched for every landmark that told him he was that much closer to home as he stewed and mumbled to himself. His feet felt like lead as he was—running? Slogging would be a better description of what it seemed.

When he finally half staggered through the back door, Bess was just rinsing her cup out in the sink, and she turned to watch him as he bent over, hands on knees, catching his breath. Then he stood up and walked towards her, panting, red-faced, and soaked.

“Eeww—sweaty man!”

He held his arms wide and puckered his lips, making loud kissing noises.

She laughed and pushed him away gingerly with one finger, touching as little liquefied male as possible.

“Come on baby, you know you want it!”

Swatting him with one of her ever-present paint rags, she laughed again and followed him when he turned to the kitchen table and collapsed into a chair.

They'd been married over thirty-five years, and if living with and loving someone for that long weren't enough to cue them in, they also had the gifted telepathy that let them taste each other's moods. If they felt it necessary, they could even taste each other's pain or other physical sensations. But she hardly needed telepathy to tell her something was off today.

He wiped the sweat off of his face and arms with the paper towels she handed him. "I want to know when they changed the roads and made them all uphill. There should have been a memo."

She sat down in a chair on his side of the table and turned it to face him, peering at him with furrowed brow. "Okay, let's see: face redder than usual, bod sweatier, time slower, and I don't feel that post-run mellowness you always exude when you come in. Worry and annoyance are almost oozing out of your ears. What gives, Mr. Stinky?"

He quickly sniffed both pits. "I beg your pardon. Still fresh as a daisy."

Sighing then, all attempts at levity dropped, he leaned back in his chair. With long legs splayed out in front of him and one arm lying on the table, he wadded up the towels one-handed and tossed them to the floor. Over anything else, this small gesture sent her radar up, as Simon was much neater than she was inclined to be, and she'd never seen him throw trash anywhere other than a waste basket.

More than a little concerned now, she leaned over and took his hand. "What is it, Simon?"

He sighed again, and asked, "Do you remember the mean, somewhat 'disturbed' lad that I told you about—the one at boarding school?"

"Yeah, sure. It was Arthur, right? He's the one who said 'Arthur was a name of kings?'"

"Yup. Well, guess who just bought the Carmichaels' place and is moving in today?"

She gasped and sat up straight. "You're kidding me!"

"Nope. He stopped me as I was running by his place and gave me this lovely, earnest sounding speech about how he'd changed and was sorry for the way he'd been in school, and how he wanted to be friends."

"Well, that's a good thing, right?"

"That would be a *wonderful* thing if it were true. He almost had me convinced."

"What changed your mind?"

"When he was driving away, he did this," he said, and repeated the gesture of the shooting gun. "He always said, 'Someday, Sayers.' And today he mentioned that he'd always thought he'd see me again *someday*. I don't know, maybe I'm being paranoid, but it makes me nervous having him on the next property. That gesture was always one of evil intent, and I don't think it's changed at all. Good grief, it's been *fifty years* since we've seen each other. He should have grown up by now.

"Bess, I don't want you running by yourself, and I think you should start locking the doors when you're here alone. I know—we have security cameras, Harvey and Winston in the daytime, and James and Kent at night. But we live on ten thousand acres, and even with the ATVs and Jeeps, there's no way they can prevent someone coming on the property who's determined to, with so many points of entry. You know, I've never felt that we really needed the security that we have, but I hired them thinking it was the responsible thing to do. Now I feel like it's woefully inadequate."

"Do you really think he'd do anything—violent, after all these years? It just seems so crazy. I mean, it's not like you ever injured him, or gave him any other basis for that sort of vendetta."

"I know, I know, but for a grown man to make that kind of gesture—and one that held so much hatefulness when we were young—to do that now makes me think he *is* a little crazy. That frightens me, especially when we have our grandchildren visiting and with Viola Marie and

Duncan living here. And think how often you and Gisella or her mom are here alone. I just realized how helpless the sane and law-abiding are against the insane and criminal. You have to wait for a crime to be committed before you can legally do anything about it.

"That settles it. I'm hiring two more men to work security. I'll talk to James and Kent tonight about getting some recommendations. Will you speak with Gisella and Hiram, and the Allbrights? Just to give them a heads up?"

"Of course." She got up to stand behind his chair, and in spite of the sweat, put her arms around his neck and laid her head on top of his. She remembered that time, so many years ago, when she'd been told of the threat that two criminals posed on the Elpie world. Her sense of well-being and the complete freedom she'd felt had vanished in a heartbeat, and she'd begun to think of the village as a fortress under siege.

That threat had been real, and proven deadly.

CHAPTER NINE

Arthur Worthington was very happy with his new home. Only four months of settling in, and he'd already enjoyed a score of hunts.

A small army of workmen had been employed to set up electric fencing on the property, to surround a long stretch of open field bordered with dense forest on both sides. This was where he held his hunts. Arthur had always gloried in having what others could not, so his favorite hunts were those of protected species. The rarer the animal, the greater the pleasure in killing it, simply because no one else was allowed to.

His employees smuggled, poached, and stole any creature that captured his interest. He would have the animal brought to the warehouse-sized enclosure he'd had built as soon as he'd purchased the property, and after studying the caged victim for a while and maybe teasing it into a frenzy, he would have it released into his hunting corridor. Sometimes he hunted with dogs, and on occasion liked to stand back and watch them finish off the quarry.

Some time ago, he'd enlisted a handler to start breeding foxhounds, blood hounds, Cane Corsos, and Dogo Argentinos together, and he had finally come up with an exceedingly aggressive and fearless dog that had an excellent nose but could work as a sight hunter as well. Though Arthur was thrilled with his living concoctions, he was also afraid of the beasts. When hunting, he always had his handler on site to beat the animals off or to hold them back long enough for him to take aim and finish the quarry with a shot or two. He made a point of using a sound suppressor on whatever gun he chose to use, which was one way he kept the authorities out of his hair. What they didn't know, wouldn't hurt him.

Being able to make his old *friend* Simon nervous was the greatest pleasure provided by his new home. He had no intention of doing bodily harm to the man or his family. Investigations into such efforts might reveal their unhappy history together and cast suspicion his way. But Sayers didn't know this. Arthur was well aware that his mere presence had put a dark cloud over the normally sunny atmosphere of the Sayers' estate.

He'd done a lot of research into the person that Sayers had become, and what always stood out in the articles he'd read was that Simon was above all, a family man. Just knowing that he'd moved into the estate next to his intentionally, with the object of seeing him again, was enough to have him concerned for his family. How pleasant that thought was. Imagining dear Simon fuming and sweating about what he might be planning, and being unable to do one bloody thing about the situation, gave him a lovely rush.

Researching online and asking questions around town had afforded him enough information to allow him to appear at many of the places that Simon's family frequented. He would always make a point to stare fixedly at the group, however small or large, but only when he thought Simon was looking at him. He preferred that the rest of the family not see him in a threatening attitude, so that Simon would bear the burden of paranoia alone. Once Arthur had even walked up to the group to introduce himself, behaving as charmingly as possible, letting only Simon see the predatory look in his eyes.

Any other man who possessed the staggering fortune that Simon Sayers did, might well have arranged for Arthur's disappearance. But he knew Simon well enough to know that he would never do this. Instead, he would stew and stay awake at night worrying about endless, dreadful possibilities.

At one gathering, a fund raiser for Sayers' pet project, the Eli Institute for the Treatment and Research of Chronic

Obstructive Lung Disease, Arthur had spent the whole evening watching Sayers' wife.

She wasn't beautiful, but very striking. Simon himself was six feet, four inches, and his wife, in heels, was only a few inches shorter. She had luxurious, wavy black hair, streaked a bit with gray, and remarkable light brown eyes, almost golden in color. He wasn't sure what it was about her—the way she carried herself, straight and tall, practically gliding around the room in natural looking, easy strides, rather than the comical, short, fearful steps that so many women wearing heels were reduced to—or maybe it was the way she used her eyes. She looked at people straight on when she spoke, seeming to peer right into their minds. When spoken to, she had an almost raptor-like intensity as she strove to absorb each word and every little nuance from the speaker. But perhaps even more arresting was the air of absolute confidence about her that made it difficult to look away when she was in a room. She knew exactly who she was, and made no apologies. As a woman, however, she was really not his type. Too old, for one thing.

He knew that she was sixty-three, and Simon sixty-nine, but both appeared to be in their late forties or early fifties, something that Arthur found particularly galling. He could find no telltale signs of cosmetic surgery on either one of them. Their faces were relaxed and natural in appearance, with nothing tightened or enhanced looking. It must be genetics. He'd had his own wattle removed, pinned up, or whatever it was they'd done, his face lifted, a small amount of collagen injected into his lips, Botox on his brow, and he was considering hair implants. He'd been pleased with the results of his efforts, but knew that there was still a strained quality to his new features.

Arthur Worthington was, however, under the delusion that he had a certain charisma—an animal magnetism that drew women to him, and he felt that this would override any imperfections in his appearance. He thought perhaps it was some masculine essence he put forth, or a special pheromone that caused women to find him irresistible. He conveniently refused to notice that the women who seemingly found him so, were usually not women of quality or character. Arthur *did* draw, like flies, women of a certain mindset, who valued money or status above almost anything and were willing to barter their lives for it.

At sixty-nine, Arthur had been married five times, and was currently divorced. He'd always found himself drawn to beauty, real or artificial, but he'd always become bored easily, as well. His attraction to those five women had lasted a very short time.

Two of them, who had refused his demands for divorce, had tragically suffered fatal "accidents:" one in a car crash, while driving alone along a mountain road one night, and the other while swimming alone off of a secluded beach late in the evening, in an area known for its dangerous riptides.

Even though the latter wife had no history of midnight ocean swims, there had been no evidence of foul play, and so the incident had been ruled an accidental drowning, with the help of a few greased palms. Remarkable how money could expedite the bureaucracy.

"Accidental" deaths might have been the fate of all of his wives, had he not known that three such accidents would be too damning in the eyes of the law, and put him under scrutiny that he could ill afford. Even though he'd almost been caught in his first planned accident, when Simon and he were boys, the thrill of seeing the culmination of his plans when Simon went flying off the bridge on that long ago day had been completely riveting. Since that time, the titillation of choreographing new accidents had proven more addicting than any drug could have.

One wife he'd bought off and the other two had finally decided that no amount of money in the world was worth living with a man as cold, mean-spirited, and occasionally outright vicious as Arthur Worthington, and so had left on their own.

After studying Bess, and the way she and Simon interacted, he soon realized that it would put a knife through the very heart of the man if he could seduce his wife. He doubted that Sayers had ever experienced a betrayal of that magnitude. Just the thought of what he would feel when this happened put a winsome smile on Arthur's face.

He made a point of always approaching Bess in a friendly, charming, and completely non-threatening way whenever the opportunity arose. And it often did, since he had her followed so that her whereabouts could be phoned to him. It would never do to be too obvious or pushy with a woman like that. He would let his personality slowly work its magic over time. Soon, very soon, he would reach out, and by then she would willingly be his.

##

Simon had been so upset about Arthur's appearance in their lives that Bess hesitated to tell him about her frequent chance meetings with the man. She didn't want him to get more uneasy than he already was, and perhaps feel compelled to take drastic actions. Arthur was always the perfect gentleman and never lingered too long after a greeting and momentary small talk. She supposed that in a town this small, they were bound to run into each other occasionally. But after the fourth such meeting in only eight days, she had started feeling uneasy about things, and mentioned it to Simon.

They'd been sitting on the couch together, reading the morning paper, when she folded hers and put it aside to broach the subject. His reaction came as no surprise. At the mention of Arthur's name, he snapped his pages closed loudly, holding them in his lap to listen, and when she told him what had been happening, he threw the paper onto the table.

"And you're *just now* telling me? Bess, this man is dangerous. I know the town isn't that big, but *four times?* That's too many to be coincidence. Maybe I should try and get a Peace Bond."

"On what grounds, Simon? He hasn't been rude to me in any way, and you have no proof of his antagonism towards you. It would just make you look paranoid."

"I could care *less* what it makes me look like. I want him to leave you alone."

"But don't you see? Everything he does is strictly to make you nervous. If you try to take legal steps just because he's spoken to me politely a few times, that will prove to him that he's doing the perfect thing—that he's winning, and making you crazy.

"Because of his seeking me out like he has, if indeed, none of this is by chance, I think—and I may be way off—but I think he's going to start coming on to me. What better way to hurt you than to take away your wife? That would hurt you *and* cause you public humiliation."

He folded his arms and shook his head. "Of course! That would be a crippling blow to any man, but especially to a man who loves his wife."

He leaned across the couch and raised his eyebrows. "Are you terribly tempted? Should I clean my dueling pistols?"

She leaned back and turned her head from side to side, studying him, before finally shaking her head. "You have better hair, so I'll stay."

"Ah, the passion!" They laughed, but it was a strained attempt on both their parts.

"I wanted you to know about this, but—I'd really rather you let me handle it on my own. You know I've done that before without too much difficulty."

He leaned back and smiled. "You *are* excellent at what you do. I remember those incidents rather well. The way you handled things kept me out of a brawl or two, and allowed for the scorned parties to retain a little dignity. A nice touch, that."

In Bess' younger days, there had been a few occasions when men had attempted to put the moves on her, even with Simon present in the room. The first time it had happened, she'd had to repeatedly signal her husband to stay where he was and let her handle it.

At the wedding of a friend, he'd gone to get them drinks, and while he was standing in line he'd noticed a man talking to her and leaning in a bit too far. He'd started towards them angrily, but she'd caught his eye and shaken her head while shaking a finger at him, both gestures unnoticed by her unwelcome suitor. Against his instincts, Simon had nodded and sat himself at a nearby table, where he could step in quickly if he needed to.

Bess had laughed charmingly at the man, never acting offended, and then had walked away towards Simon, leaving Romeo looking slightly embarrassed, but seemingly unscarred. She'd come to Simon's table, given him a quick peck on the lips, thanked him for her drink, and pulled a chair closer to his before sitting down.

"Okay, I give up. What did you say to him?"

She kept a smile on her face, and her eyes *off* of the gentleman in question, so that he wouldn't think he was being talked about. "I acted as if I thought he was joking. As if the whole idea of him coming on to me was so ludicrous that he *must* be joking, and I laughed and applauded his outrageous sense of humor. I prefer that to shooting down someone's ego, and causing bad feelings. When a man knows beyond question that he doesn't stand a chance, he can laugh along, pretend it *was* all a joke, and walk away with his pride intact. It's so much kinder than calling him a sleaze bag."

Now he raised his glass in a toast and bowed his head in respect. "Here's to The Queen of Diplomacy." They clicked their OJ glasses and drank.

After that first time, when a similar instance occurred, he would simply stay nearby and let her take care of the situation in her own way. Each time, his admiration for her tact and kindness increased. He liked a woman who was gracious in victory.

"All right, no Peace Bond, and I won't threaten him with bodily injury, but what about having one of our security men accompany you in town?"

"No, that would be too obvious. I don't want him to know that he's made us uncomfortable. Ignoring a person who's trying to annoy you is the worst thing you could do to him. It makes him seem—inconsequential."

He sighed and chewed his lip for a moment before acquiescing. "Well, all right. For now. But if these meetings increase, I want to know. You shouldn't have to be uncomfortable going about your daily business. Something will have to be done. I just need to figure out what that something is."

CHAPTER TEN

Moving with the rolling rhythm of his six-legged mount, the Elpie had almost fallen asleep more than once. The day was cool, but the large insect he was riding had not drunk for several hours and was heading for water at an uncharacteristically rapid pace. He did nothing to alter its speed or direction. Where he went no longer mattered to him.

A year ago, it would have been a different story. He wouldn't have wanted to go far from home, where his one year old daughter and young wife waited for him. But a freak accident had changed everything. Nothing looked the same, felt the same to him anymore. Colors seemed less brilliant, food had lost its appeal. Even sounds and smells were dulled to match his feelings.

On an outing with some of the other Elpies and their young, his family and he were looking out over the valley from atop a cliff. Because of its spectacular view, this was a favorite meeting place of his tribe. Hundreds of feet below where they stood, a slow moving river transformed into wild rapids that climaxed with majestic grandeur as they spilled over the edge of a waterfall.

He'd been carefully holding his daughter, pointing out landmarks to her, even though he knew her young mind wouldn't understand all his sendings. His wife had taken her from his arms to show the child an animal she'd spotted across the river. He'd heard his daughter chittering happily as he turned and walked back to the group of friends to help lay out the food. He'd heard the chittering, and then a cracking sound and a mental as well as audible shriek from his wife. He'd whirled around just in time to see his wife's hand and foot disappear as she and their daughter fell back with the falling cliff face. The shelf of stone they'd been standing on had broken off and sent his family into the unforgiving rocks and water below.

He could still hear that happy chittering, and then the crack and the shriek. Could still see his wife's hand and foot disappearing over the edge. They'd found their bodies just beyond the foot of the falls that day. He must have gone a little mad, for parts of that day were missing from his mind, and he preferred it that way.

Strange, how a crack in some rock could change the world.

His father Eli, the finest Elpie healer on their world, and his brother, Jonas, the second best healer, could do nothing to ease the pain in his soul, the hole in his heart. At first, he'd tried to be strong and pretend he was still alive inside, but eventually he found it impossible to go through the motions anymore. He'd decided he needed to be on his own, away from the doting concern of his parents, siblings, and well-meaning friends. He would travel until he was able to find some kind of ground between complete desolation and peace.

So he rode away after many palms to his face and the giving of his own palm to the rest of his family. They made him promise to return when he could. He knew it broke his mother's heart to see him leave, but he was helpless to tend to anyone else's when his own heart was a tattered ruin. He'd ridden purposefully away from his village, for had he allowed his insect to take the lead then, it would have returned to its herd. But now, after weeks of rambling, it was lost enough that he could let it wander as it would.

He let his mind wander, just as he did his mount. Not really seeing the land around him, he rode through beautiful fields of green, from where maroon mountains splashed with gold were visible in the distance. His insect had found its sought after stream, and was drinking thirstily, but he barely noticed. His sight was turned inward, and his mind drifted aimlessly. For some reason, Colder, the son of his father's human brother, Simon, kept crossing his mind.

They were the same age, and when he had accompanied Eli to Earth to visit the Sayers, he'd felt an instant connection to Simon's youngest son.

Before his marriage, he'd walked the Sayers' land and sent with his human friend for hours. They each had intense, inquisitive natures, with a little streak of wild running through, and one thing they'd both longed to do was to explore the universe like the Bluemen did. Once he'd found the Elpie female that he wanted to spend his life with, however, and then had a daughter, those dreams they'd shared about adventure didn't seem possible or even that attractive to him anymore.

Now he felt a deep longing to move, to run away to something and somewhere different, where he could feel alive again without seeing the emptiness that his world had held for him since the loss of his family. Here, no matter where he turned, he saw not what was there, but what was *no longer* there.

He needed to start seeing what *was* again. To start looking forward. All the heartache and suffering in the world would not bring back a single moment of the past.

Abruptly, Micah sat straight up. His mount, having finished its drink, reacted to this change in posture and attitude in its rider, and lifted its head. Micah turned the insect and urged it forward at a brisk pace in the direction of the Cold. A stop there, and then hopefully, he would turn homeward for a new beginning.

CHAPTER ELEVEN

Poised on a rock in the middle of the frigid stream, looking for all the world like a green gargoyle, the Colder watched without moving. A calico cat sitting on another rock five feet away, stared intently at the fish swimming just below her. Suddenly, her paw shot out and hooked it, bringing it up to her waiting jaws.

With the fish flopping madly between her teeth, she danced across three stones and then made one final jump to dry land. Another cat, a Siamese cross, was watching her passively, eyes half lidded, waiting to share the meal that he knew was forthcoming. When Genevieve landed and settled down to eat, Boris strolled over and began helping himself.

She growled menacingly at him, but he ignored the warning. This was her fourth fish, and he knew she was already full. Time for him to step up and make sure this creature hadn't died in vain. Hurling mental insults, the calico expressed doubts as to whether breathing air was actually a fitting pastime for him. He ignored this too, relishing the tangy flavor of the flesh as he chewed.

For thirty-eight years, these cats had been together, first as normal felines in an apartment with a woman named Bess, and then as what they were now—animals with enhanced intelligence and the ability to send and receive mental messages from other telepaths like the Colders and the rest of the Elpies.

When the alien Bluemen had abducted Bess and her three cats from a cabin in the woods, they'd studied them and then dropped them on this planet. Their stay was to be temporary, while the Bluemen finished their expected rounds and refueled.

In order for the animals to survive in an alien world, they had needed to stay with their human. To facilitate this, they'd been given Bess' memories as a basis for context when they were endowed with a greater intelligence and language.

Their speech was only telepathic in nature, for true spoken language would have required an altering of their bodies—something the Bluemen did not approve of. When the cats had received a part of Bess into their minds, they'd also experienced the pleasant side effect of having their years prolonged to a human life span.

Surprisingly, when the time came to return to Earth, Boris and Genevieve chose instead to stay on the Elpies' planet, for the boundless freedom and adventure it afforded them. The third cat, Ishmael, had elected to return to Earth with Bess and the others. The ties between humans and animals had become much tighter and infinitely more complicated when they'd been given the enhancement, especially since they shared memories.

Simon, abducted previously, had found his soul mate in Bess on the Elpie world, and they had married upon their return to earth. They'd named their only daughter after Genevieve, and their other children after Simon's Elpie "brother," Eli, one of his sons, Jonas, and one of the Colders who had befriended them in a time of great need. Eli's family, in turn, had named three of their children after their human family.

The felines who'd stayed behind had become a favorite of the Elpies, the dominant native species. The village Elpies lived in a temperate area, with plains and forests. Their cousins, the Colders, Elpies who exhibited some striking environmental adaptations, lived in a different region with a much more challenging climate.

Even though the Colders no longer hunted for food, they still honed their tracking and hunting skills in tournaments each year with competition between the tribes. The fluidity of movement and grace that came naturally to the cats in their stalking modes served as a never ending source of fascination to the Elpies, and the Colders in particular. Elpies still took their meals from the river on occasion, and observing the feline version of fishing had become a popular spectator sport.

Luigi, a Colder, finally stood up, stretched, and then plowed through the freezing water, unperturbed by the temperature. He settled on the ground beside the cats and sent to Genevieve that she was a fine hunter with great skill. She nodded in acknowledgement, and kept eating without looking up, even though she was in immediate danger of throwing up. She could eat only so much at one time, but she wasn't about to let Boris get a whole fish from her. She was addicted to fishing. Boris was addicted to fish, but he'd known he needn't brave the frigid water, for eventually Genevieve's obsession would bring about a surplus of food that even *she* couldn't finish off.

The cats' lives consisted of drifting from village to village, where they were treated like celebrities and fawned on tremendously, by the village Elplings in particular. The feel of their thick, luxurious fur thrilled the Elpie young as they petted their backs and bellies, rubbed under chins and behind ears.

The cats usually entertained the Elplings by pouncing on a dozen or so, and would feign fear and surprise when the Elplings' returned their pounces. Their most famous skill—faked skedaddling, never failed to astound the somewhat awkward Elpies.

Skedaddling was how Bess had described the incredibly frenzied leaping, ricocheting, scrabbling, evasive maneuvers performed by Ishmael once when he'd been asleep and a neighbor's dog had accosted him. The dog was a Chihuahua, but barking in a sleeping cat's ear produced the same results as if he'd been a Doberman, and the little dickens seemed to have understood this on a profound level.

The cats would feign sleep and pretend to be unaware of the horde of Elplings creeping up. The moment that the Elpie young laid hands on them, the two would perform their wildly frenetic acrobatics and speed off into the bushes. The whole village would gather for skedaddling exhibitions, and when the two feline performers strolled back into the village afterwards, it was always to applause, rub downs, and treats. Not a bad life.

Lying back on the snow covered ground, Luigi looked up at a green sky partially covered with clouds. Heavy with snow, the clouds were beautiful, but their burdens could be deadly if the temperature continued to drop. The cats would be heading back into the lower areas soon, where the weather was warmer and more suited to the travel of animals their size. He would stay on, however, for this was his home, and snow was a part of it.

Luigi stood six feet, three inches, and had the green, leathery skin of his Elpie cousins who lived on the plains. The Elpies who'd been born with an aberration for a reptile—fur—had moved to the colder country, and after many years of breeding with others of a similar nature, a random pattern had turned into a specific trait. Colders had fur on their shoulders, fur from above their elbows to their wrists, and from above their knees to their ankles. Black fur epaulettes, arm mufflers and leg warmers.

They also had a strip of very distinctive coarse, black fur that started at the back half of their scalps and ran along their spines all the way to the start of their long tails. The fur on their heads was quill-like in its coarseness, and it would stand upright and even tilt forwards at times of great emotion. Long, silky hair between their six inch toes and on their soles repelled water and kept their feet from freezing. They still looked like giant anoles, as did the other Elpies, but anoles dressed for winter.

After catching and eating several fish himself, Luigi was pleasantly full. He was enjoying watching the clouds, being with friends—just *being*. Taking pleasure in every moment and sensation was very much an Elpie attribute. Life was simple, rich, and sweet for Elpies, and they seldom rushed or worried about anything.

Starting to doze off, he came on alert when someone's sending touched his mind—a barely discernible mental beckoning. Sitting up quickly, he focused on the sending, trying to catch the direction it was coming from.

Abruptly, he scrambled to his feet and began running towards the base of the highlands. The cats had felt *something*, but not being as finely tuned in their minds as one who had lived his whole life as a telepath, they couldn't distinguish the sender. Nor did they care to. Boris was full, and Genevieve had finally grown bored with fishing and eating, and was ready for a nap. They were cats, after all.

Luigi ran as fast as the terrain allowed, leaping over the deeper drifts, for he knew the sender now. It was his friend, Micah. Only fourteen days apart in age, the two had been the best of friends growing up, and whenever the clans of Elpies and Colders had gathered, they could always be found together. Luigi's adoptive father, Barnabas, and Micah's father were close friends, so their frequent visits to each other had always included their sons, making for even closer ties.

Though Luigi seldom worried, he had worried for his friend. Since the deaths of his wife and daughter, it was as if his spirit had withered into something desiccated and empty. Physically, he had declined as well, losing weight, often forgetting to eat, and avoiding sleep for fear of the wrenching dreams that waited for him there.

Micah would dream that this sad reality *was* the dream. When he woke, for the first few moments, he would know such joy and relief to think that his family was alive—that it had all been a terrible nightmare. But as wakefulness brought him back to the real world, his brief respite from grief would be shattered and he would suffer the loss all over again. He found this repeated denial of his family's salvation to be intolerable. Endless nights of this had made him dread sleeping, and without sleep, his body and nerves functioned in a brittle state.

Luigi had heard that Micah had left to go wandering, to try and settle his soul alone. For a time, he'd considered trying to find him, so that his wanderings would be with a companion to ease his loneliness. But Barnabas had convinced him that Micah would be better left to his own time of healing. To receive a sending from him now made his heart glad for his friend, for he sensed an optimism that had long been missing from his soul.

Micah didn't call for him by name, for Elpies had never used names before the human, Simon, had come to live with them. Elpies had no need for names, for they had no spoken language, and the configurations of each mind's sendings spoke its identity clearly. But Simon, being human, had been at a loss, and had asked the Elpies for permission to name them, so that he could differentiate between them in his mind.

They'd considered their naming to be an amusing experiment, and though they couldn't say the names themselves, they could send their memories of the way the humans pronounced them. Over the years, it had become a custom among many of the reptilians who fondly remembered their friendship with the humans, to give their offspring human names. They would never use them when sending to each other and would never hear them spoken, other than on the CD of names that the Sayers had sent to them to choose from.

Luigi and Micah were among the few Elpies who traveled to Earth from time to time, so their names were much more than ceremonial, as far as the humans who used them were concerned.

Luigi moved steadily in the clumsy looking but mile-eating lope of the Elpies. Broken by the weight of the snow, tree branches lay submerged beneath the white blanket. Like deadly snakes hidden within the leaves on a forest floor, they waited, ready to wound or even kill the unwary runner. Sharp rocks and holes shrouded by the snow were ever present as well, but he was a Colder, and he knew the telltale signs to look for to keep himself out of danger. Using his strong back legs to bound over the larger rocks, he twice lost his footing and rolled a ways downhill, only to jump back up and continue his quest.

At last he saw him in the distance. When Luigi called to him with his mind, Micah looked up and spotted him. With a chirp of happy surprise, he jumped off of his shivering mount and charged up the hill towards his friend. Just before their bodies met, they leapt through the air to slam into each other and go crashing to the ground, wrestling, punching, kicking and shoving one another like the Elplings they'd once been together. They might not have an oral language, but their chittering and yelps filled the air with unmistakable celebration.

Finally, battered, exhausted, and happy, they fell apart to lie back on the ground, laughing and panting with exertion. After catching their breath, they sat up to lean forward and touch foreheads, and to put their palms on each other's faces as tradition required. Then they collapsed again onto the cold ground.

The emotions that most human friends could never bring themselves to verbalize, for fear of appearing *overly* demonstrative or loving, and thereby risking rejection, were expressed freely between Elpies, with no risk of misinterpretation. Their minds opened to one another like windows, allowing the thoughts and feelings of each to be seen clearly, and understood without question.

Eventually their thoughts drifted to recent days, and though Luigi tasted the pain in his friend's heart, he also caught the hope in a future that he wanted Luigi to be a part of. Micah knew Luigi's wandering spirit, and that he was not yet attached to one female, nor yearning to start a family.

It wasn't that Luigi didn't love his family. It wasn't that he didn't care for Elplings. He just didn't care for them in his own tent for very long at a time. Since coming to live with his foster parents at a young age, he'd lived most of his life in a tent full of other Elplings, for Barnabas and Isabel were a favorite uncle and aunt within the huge community of cousins in the village. As a young one, he'd enjoyed the usually happy chaos this entailed, but as he'd gotten older, he'd often longed to be out on his own, away from this beloved horde.

He'd taken to wandering far afield, exploring anything different or new, and he often traveled with Boris and Genevieve. He loved watching them hunt—the way their joints seemed to automatically know exactly how far to lower their bodies in order to remain hidden, and how they could stop in mid-stride and maintain that position indefinitely if they believed that movement might give them away.

Traveling with the two, Luigi was always welcomed in the villages, as any Elpie would be. All Elpies viewed each other as relatives, even if they'd never met, and hospitality in any village was a given.

Now it appeared that his wandering days on this planet had come to an end, for what Micah suggested was far more appealing. The Bluemen had sent to Micah and Colder, his human friend, that someday they hoped to form an interplanetary research team, with different species adding their special skills and insights to make their ventures onto distant planets more stimulating and fruitful. Sven, the Leader of the Blueman ship that ferried Elpies to and from their visits with the Sayers family, had thought that Elpie crewmen would be particularly good additions, due to their empathic as well as telepathic skills.

Why not now? Micah sent that their visit should take place in three days, giving both of them time to say goodbye to their families and make it to the rendezvous area. For their visit to Earth, the Bluemen usually had enough fuel to transport Luigi's father, Barnabas, Eli, and his three wives, one of which was Dulcie, Micah's birth mother. On this trip, however, Micah knew that two of Eli's wives, Ruth and Martha, would not be going, because one of his half-sisters was about to lay her third egg, and the two wanted to be with her. That would leave two extra spaces for Luigi and him.

Luigi had to consider the idea of space exploration for all of two seconds before he leapt to his feet and started racing for home. He promised to meet Micah in three days, hopefully to convince the Bluemen to act on their previous suggestion.

Micah returned to his beast, but instead of mounting the insect, signaled for it to follow him. Energized now, he loped away towards his village, feeling hope in a heart that had been empty of it far too long.

CHAPTER TWELVE

Ask anyone who has pets—cats and dogs especially. They will say that there's nothing more destructive than a bored animal.

For any large carnivore on the planet, the giant insects kept in herds by the Elpies were the natural choice for prey. The creatures possessed tiny brains and acted accordingly. The main protein source for the Elpies, they also acted as beasts of burden. Their sturdy hides were cured and employed extensively by the tribes, for everything from tent making to bedding. Being empaths, the Elpies never abused the creatures, and as a result, they were trusting and even affectionate when they could focus long enough to form an attachment to someone.

The size of small horses, covered with fur and possessing four eyes and six legs, they lived in large herds. Individuals often wandered away from the main body of beasts and became lost if not noticed immediately by their herdsmen. They wandered away, not from curiosity about lands unknown, or the desire for better pastures, but because they were too stupid to lift their heads from time to time when they were grazing, and would simply follow the next mouthful of grass until the rest of the herd was out of sight.

The lioness had only been on the planet for about a year, but already she was restless. The insects were good eating, but so easy to hunt and bring down that there was little running or stalking involved, and little exercise required to find the next escapee when her hunger returned. She was a young lioness, with no one to play with, no difficult hunts, and unfortunately in possession of a great deal of excess energy. In other words, she was bored.

When the Bluemen picked up wild animals to study, they occasionally dropped them off on the Elpies' world due to fuel constraints, rather than taking them back to their home planets. They did this infrequently, for fear of changing the balance of nature on the planet, and when they did leave a specimen, it was rendered sterile before the drop-off. The animals were given a smattering of telepathy—just enough to allow the Elpies to have a bit of influence over them through communication.

Sometimes when she was very bored, the lioness would watch the local Elpies or Colders, and occasionally she would stalk them. She wasn't hungry, but *was* interested in playing with prey that actually had the brain capacity to run or put up a fight. The Bluemen had put a suggestion in her mind before they dropped her off, that Elpies were terrible tasting, and very frightening.

She *had* been very frightened of them in the beginning, but as curiosity and boredom got the better of her and she began to watch the two-legged lizards, her fear had gradually dulled. The other part of the Bluemen's suggestion remained with her, however, and she harbored no desire to taste their flesh.

Today she'd been watching the furred lizard as he interacted first with the small lions, and then with the newly arrived lizard. When he began to run away from the other and travel alone, she trotted parallel to him from within the forest as he bounded across the clearings, heading uphill towards his home.

Racing up the mountain, Luigi avoided the many submerged branches, rocks, and other common hazards, but as he attempted to jump over one fallen log, his right foot hit a short broken branch protruding from it. When that contact set the log rolling, his feet flew up and he landed on the back of his shoulders. The steepness of the incline didn't allow for his fall to stop there, however, and he began a backward somersault that turned into a tumbling, bouncing, sliding descent down the mountain, ending with an unintentional but impressive cannonball into the half-frozen river below.

He hit the water hard, and plunged down several feet below the surface. It took him a second to figure out which way was up, but then he swam to the top and broke the surface with minimal effort. The current was strong here, but there were plenty of handholds with all the reeds along the banks, and the occasional half-submerged boulder to brace his feet against. He didn't have any *severe* pain, so he assumed he had no fractures. Grabbing a handful of reeds, he started to pull himself to the bank when he heard a low growl. Looking through the curtain of green, he saw something that froze him worse than the water.

The lioness had seen him tumbling down the hill, the motion making him an irresistible target, especially with the squeaks and grunts of pain erupting with each bounce. She hadn't been fast enough to catch him in motion, and when he'd gone barreling out to splash down in the river, she thought she'd lost him.

Frustrated, she'd stalked along the bank until she saw movement in the reeds. There he was—her new toy. She didn't want to get into the river here, even though she could swim. It was too deep, the current too swift for her liking, and the water too icy to stay in long. So she sat and waited for her toy to come to her.

He could see her eyes, wide with anticipation. Releasing his grip on the reeds, he let himself float farther downstream, but the lioness trotted along the bank, parallel to his position. He couldn't make for the other side, where the water was shallower, because a thin layer of ice had formed over the top, extending to the middle of the river, and it was too fragile to support his weight. If he tried to take hold of the ice, it would snap off in his hands, and what was worse, the current there might drag him under the frozen layer to an area where it was too thick to break through to the surface, and he would drown.

He grabbed onto the closest reed, but stayed neck deep in the water. Every time he tried getting closer to the bank, the lioness started into the water to meet him. Several times, he tried the same move and drifted farther downstream, but the big cat always kept perfect pace with him. He tried sending to the animal that he was friendly, not a threat, and very bad tasting. If lions had a sense of humor, she would have laughed. She *knew* by his fear that he was no threat, and she wasn't hungry. She had no need of a friend. She just wanted something to play with.

The only thing left for him to try was to broadcast a sending for help. He was too far from the village to reach it with his mind, but there were always Colders out and about, foraging, gathering firewood, working with the herds, or just wandering. He concentrated on sending and tried to ignore his increasingly numb fingers and toes.

Finally, the lioness became annoyed and decided to go in after him. If she did that, he was finished, because he was too cold to control his muscles well enough to swim out of reach. He tried once more to send a cry for help, and then he watched as his death approached. He saw her wiggle her back end just as he'd seen the cats do when they prepared to jump, and he heard, grossly magnified, that same clicking of teeth as came from the cats when they zeroed in on their prey.

He remembered watching them toy with the small rodents they'd caught, throwing them up in the air and then batting them away with their paws, only to run after them and grab them once more in their teeth, to fling them upwards again and start the game over. Sometimes he hadn't been able to stand the cruelty anymore and had taken the pitiful creatures away and snapped their necks to end their suffering. He remembered, too, the crunch of their little skulls between the cats' teeth. He wondered which would command his attention more—the pain or the sound of his skull breaking between those huge jaws.

He decided to let go of the reeds and let himself drift away down the river. Drowning couldn't be a worse death than being eaten alive. But to his horror, he could no longer control his hands. They were locked in place around the reeds, and his legs and feet were too numb to push himself farther out.

Suddenly, two small masses of fur came streaking across the bank and over the lioness' back. She leapt up, twisting around in alarm, only to see the small lions staring at her from twenty feet away.

Boris and Genevieve, catching their friend's sending for help, had run to see what was happening. This big cat was obviously eager for action, so they decided to invite her to play.

"You go first. We'll take turns," Genevieve sent. To her surprise, Boris agreed.

"Okay, but if I die, I'm coming back to haunt you. Just so you know."

He ran to within a few yards of the lioness, just out of reach of her claws, and then raced back and stopped, staring at her.

She'd forgotten her toy in the water. These were her kind, almost, and they were daring her to catch them. Running forward, she roared and then lunged at Boris, but he was too agile for her and scooted away. Then Genevieve came from the other side and ran over the lioness' back, shoving off as hard as she could to be sure to land out of reach.

The lioness twisted around and then threw herself onto her back. She rolled onto her side, reaching out and pawing the air in Genevieve's direction, in an obvious plea for her to come back and play. Genevieve looked at Luigi, shaking badly, his color almost turquoise, and ran back to the lioness. Instead of going near her paws, she ran at her tail and batted it around until the animal sat up and swiped at her, and then she leapt straight up in the air, twisting around to change her direction in a *real* skedaddling.

Luigi was shivering uncontrollably, and starting to feel heavy with exhaustion. His position shifted slightly, and he saw the reeds he was holding onto starting to bend. If they bent too far, he could slide off with the current, and he was past his ability to swim. Just as despair was sweeping over him, he felt a faint sending reaching out to pin down his location. He started concentrating, but even his sending felt weak. The cats had felt it too, however, and they both started sending to the would-be rescuer.

Boris ran in, bounced off the lioness' stomach, and bounded away. She rolled in his direction now and reached out with her paws again. So far so good, but both cats knew that this playfulness wouldn't last long. Boredom would set in if she couldn't actually catch something, and as neither cat was into self-sacrifice, things could still end badly for Luigi.

They heard a crashing sound then, and saw Barnabas come plowing through the trees. He ripped a branch off a rotting log just before exiting the wood, and then ran straight for the huge animal.

When she saw him coming, she jumped to her feet and started running towards him, but stopped short when she saw that he wasn't slowing his charge as he neared her. She leaned back with her front legs, and put her haunches on the ground, opening her mouth wide in a roar that ended in a snarl.

Just five feet from her, Barnabas finally leaned back, planted his heels, and jerked to a stop. He raised his club, opened his mouth wide in a hiss, and sent all of his stiff mane pointing forward at the lioness. He stared at her menacingly, throwing his ferocity like a spear into the mind of the big cat.

She lunged forward, barely taking her haunches off the ground, stretching out to swipe at him with her huge claws, but he parried and batted her paw away painfully with his branch.

Shocked, she yowled with pain and anger and lunged again, only to have her paw knocked away once more. She was so much larger, and he was thin and leathery, with only his arm and leg fur to protect him from her claws and teeth. This was wrong. He should be easy prey. He should be afraid. But something kept insisting in her mind that this creature was fearsome—that *she* should be afraid. Her paw was hurting, and she felt confused and angry, and then he lunged at her, hissing and bombarding her mind with fury from his own.

She'd had enough. Annoyance, pain, and confusion, combined with that touch of unreasonable fear, made her too unsure to continue the battle, so she roared once more, turned, and loped away.

Luigi had seen it all. The lioness was gone, and he could come out of the water. But he was so sleepy, and he could see the reeds as they bent down into the water. He watched his frozen, clutching hands slide off and felt himself drift away.

As soon as the lioness turned and began her retreat, Barnabas rushed down to the reeds that he'd seen Luigi clinging to. He fought his way through the nearer reeds to reach the spot and—Luigi was gone.

Panicking, he shoved his arms under the water in all directions, but he felt nothing, and he knew then that the river had taken his son. Pulling out of the reeds and into the main current, he held on with one hand as he looked downstream, but he saw no trace.

What he did see, were six other Colders who had been downstream with their nets when they'd heard Luigi's call for help. They'd been rushing towards him when they saw him slide off the reeds and sink down into the water. He was still upstream from them, so they'd fought their way as far as they dared towards the other side, stretching their nets between them and holding onto a rope they'd tied to a tree to keep themselves from being swept away. They'd knotted another rope and tossed it over the ice to catch between two boulders in the river, to give them an anchorage from the opposite side.

One of them suddenly pulled his side of the net taut and sent to the others to pull him in. As three of them pulled the rope and the nets towards the bank, two more made their way out, anchored by a third rope, to try and help the Colder struggling with something in his net.

Paralyzed with fear for his son, and unable to help from where he was, Barnabas stood and watched as one of the Colders reached down and brought Luigi's head above the water. Whirling back towards the bank then, Barnabas pulled and pushed his way back through the reeds, to clamber up the side and run down the shore towards Luigi.

They had him out of the water now and laid out on the bank. His skin was turquoise in color and he wasn't breathing. One of the Colders went down on his hands and knees and arched his spine, and three others lifted Luigi's limp body and slung him face down across the first Colder's back. His upper body was hanging over the side of the Colder, and the others slowly pulled his legs, dragging him back towards them until Luigi's upper chest was touching the Colder's arched back. Barnabas arrived and lent his hands as they performed the same maneuver three more times, and each time they saw more water fall from his mouth. With the fifth attempt, there was a gush of water, and they heard Luigi gasp.

They lifted him then, laid him on his back, and pressed on his belly. He coughed and then turned and vomited out water. There was a commotion from behind them, and Barnabas' wife, Isabel, pushed her way through to her son. He halfway opened his eyes when she sent to him, but she perceived no coherent thoughts before he closed them again.

One of the Colders was starting a fire to the side of them, and Isabel slid off the rolled up hides tied to her back. She hurriedly spread one out, and they laid Luigi in the center of it. She lay down on one side of him and Barnabas lay on the other. They reached across him to clasp forearms so that Luigi was wedged tightly between the two, and then the other two hides were laid over them.

The other Colders dragged the hides next to the fire, and then set about making a carrying sling out of their nets.

They had to get him to the healer's village. If they could warm Luigi up enough and keep him breathing, they could carry the three in the sling. He'd breathed in water, and though they could hopefully keep him alive for a while, the water in his lungs would eventually kill him if something wasn't done.

When Luigi was very young, a virulent but short-lived virus had swept through the Colder village where he lived. Barnabas and Isabel were close friends with his parents, and when they had both come down with the virus, Isabel and her husband had come to their tent to care for them, since Luigi was too young to be of any help.

On that terrible night when both of his parents had succumbed, Isabel and Barnabas had taken the child into their arms and sent that he was now their son. Overcome with grief and the fear of being alone, Luigi had clung to them and believed in their sendings.

Barnabas and Isabel had been older than his parents, and all of their children were grown, but their tent was always filled with grandchildren, cousins, nieces, and nephews, so Luigi had never lacked for playmates. Soon, the resilience of youth had brought his spirit back. Smart, loving, and hardworking, Luigi fit into their lives so seamlessly, that after a short time they ceased to think of him as their adopted son.

The two Colders looked at each other across his chest, and prayed to the Maker that Luigi, their son, would survive.

CHAPTER THIRTEEN

Long before the Elpie village was in sight, Eli, the medicine Elpie, and four other males appeared coming over a rise, running and leading eight galloping insects behind them. Two of the eight were tied side by side, with a sling rigged between them that was braced to keep the insects from crushing the passenger within.

As soon as they'd come into sending range, all of the Colders had begun reaching out with their minds in sync. The receiving village Elpies had hurriedly roped the herd insects and harnessed up Eli's sling before heading out. Elpies could run as fast as the insects could gallop over uneven terrain, but they knew that the Colders they were going to meet would be exhausted from bearing Luigi and his parents these many miles.

When the two groups met, Eli went straight to Luigi to assess the situation, and the hiss that escaped him when he saw their son frightened his worried parents. Luigi was going in and out of consciousness, but Eli managed to get a small ball of herbs down his throat before turning to Barnabas and Isabel. They'd been hoping for a sending of reassurance that their son would be fine after Eli's ministrations, but after a quick listen to his lungs and heart, he sent only that they needed to get him to the village.

It had been a very long ride for the couple, between their muscles cramping horribly and the jostling of the sling causing nausea and headaches. They could feel Luigi warming between the two of them, but they could also hear his labored breathing. The Colders raised their transformed nets to place their passengers within Eli's insect harnessed sling, and then gratefully mounted the other insects to make for the village.

When they carried the sling into the healer's tent and laid it atop Eli's raised platform of hides, he wasted no time. Isabel and Barnabas rolled off of the platform on their own, but had to be helped to stand. Eli pushed more balls of compressed herbs down Luigi's throat, and began placing warm packs that Micah had prepared for him. Raising his head and chest with hides, they covered his body with the packs and held a steaming bowl of herbs beneath his nose.

The steam had the desired effect, and Luigi began moving his head back and forth to get away from the noxious odor. Then he started coughing, and Eli looked at his parents and nodded.

After a few hours, his shivering stopped, he was staying awake for longer periods, and his sendings had become coherent. Aware enough now to have the blanks in his memories filled in by his father, Luigi reached out with his mind to thank the Colders who had risked themselves to save him, and then used their nets and muscles to bring him to Eli's village. His parents had promised to thank Boris and Genevieve when next they saw them.

With his friend seemingly improved, Micah decided to tell Luigi's parents and his own about their plan for asking the Bluemen to take them on as crew members.

His announcement was a beacon of hope for Eli. It had taken the group one day to get to the village, and in two more days, the Bluemen would come. If the Bluemen accepted the two as crew, then they would heal Luigi of any problems that Eli could not, for there was no guarantee that his condition wouldn't worsen.

Before he'd known about Micah's plans, he had hoped to convince the Bluemen to work their magic on Luigi. Because the lioness had been brought to this planet by the Bluemen, Eli assumed that they would feel somewhat responsible for his near fatal mishap. Over the years, Eli had come to know the Bluemen well—Sven in particular, and he knew that there was kindness in them. They would *want* to heal Luigi, so they would try and let themselves be persuaded.

#

The next morning Luigi was more alert, and coughing, but his breathing was strained. Barnabas and Isabel stayed by his side so that he would feel their presence and be able to send with them when he was awake.

Still astounded by his father's courage, Luigi sent to Barnabas to ask him how he'd made the lioness leave. He'd seen him frighten off other large animals before by facing them down this way, but never anything as huge and fierce as a lion. When he'd watched him from the river, running *towards* the huge animal, instead of away from her, as good sense would warrant, he'd feared that Barnabas would be killed.

His father answered that he'd thrown a sending of ferocity into the lioness' mind. *He* had to believe that he was fiercer and more dangerous than the lioness in order to make her believe it. And since it was his son whose life was at stake, he had more reason to be fierce.

Luigi believed him, but he didn't think he'd ever be able to pull the same thing off, no matter how much he loved someone. He couldn't make himself believe that his teeth were longer, or his claws sharper than that huge cat's. It was a skill he needed to practice. The worrisome issue was how to test his progress. How would he know when he'd practiced enough to avoid being someone's supper? He drifted off to sleep again thinking about ferocity and being eaten.

By nightfall, the young Colder was running a fever and sending incoherently. His pulse had gone up again, and his breaths were loud, with a rattling sound to them. These were symptoms that Eli had feared might develop, and he only hoped that he could keep Luigi alive long enough for the Bluemen to save him.

CHAPTER FOURTEEN

Right on schedule, the Bluemen stepped down from the ship and began walking towards the village. Seeing Eli and Barnabas running towards them, they felt the agitation and urgency in their minds, and changed their walk to a run.

When Elpies and Bluemen met, Eli immediately launched into an explanation of the situation. He ended by sending that despite his efforts, Luigi was in danger of dying if the Bluemen refused to take action. He stopped sending then, and along with Barnabas, stood silently staring at the Bluemen, with faces and minds begging an affirmative answer. Eli had planned, out of courtesy, to wait for their decision on taking the two young Elpies as crew, instead of asking for a healing straightaway, but he feared Luigi had no time for such niceties now.

Sven glanced over at Luca. They both knew the protocol concerning healings. They could use their medical equipment to help or heal other species only if Bluemen were responsible for an injury or illness, or if a current study subject was in danger.

"If Luigi was frightened by the lion that *we* left, and he was rushing to see *us,* then clearly, we were involved in two factors contributing to his injury. Good enough?"

Sven nodded. "Good enough."

Both knew, if up for review, these factors might not be enough to justify a medical intervention, but in the field they were allowed to use their own judgement. Hopefully, it would escape scrutiny. Their natures were prone towards mercy.

They both sent agreement to the Elpies, whose relief and gratitude were so obvious in their faces and posture that no sendings were necessary. They urged the Bluemen into a run then, for Luigi's condition had worsened so much in the past few hours that they'd begun to fear the Bluemen might come too late.

The young Colder's temp had spiked, and he was moving constantly with the relentless aching of fever. Occasionally he would thrash about, sending incoherently, and then would suddenly lie still and grow pale. When he breathed they could hear the gurgling in his chest from across the tent.

When the Bluemen arrived at the tent and saw the stricken Colder, Luca heard his labored breathing, and sent to Sven that their intervention was indeed necessary. He laid a disk on his chest and Luigi appeared to evaporate. His mother let out a frightened chirp at the sight, even though she knew he'd just been transported to the ship. The disappearance of a son was something no mother would find easy to witness.

Sven stayed to speak with the others, but Luca returned to the ship to oversee Luigi's treatment, after reassuring his parents that the healing would be simple and rapid with the ship's machines. He would be well by morning. The Elpies and Colders sent their deepest thanks to Luca before he placed the disk on his own chest and disappeared.

Sven readily agreed to take the lioness off the planet, and apologized for the danger she had put them in. He'd not anticipated the lioness being able to overcome the suggestion to fear the Elpies.

#

Eli's medicine tent was much larger than the regular Elpie lodging. With a domed roof, the hide covered structure had space for a raised bed, and a separate area with a bed raised even higher, where he could set bones and perform minor surgeries. The lighting was much brighter in the tent as well, with windows cut high in the hides of the dome to let sunlight through, and torches set all about the interior, with carefully thinned and treated hides attached in frames to focus their light.

A pile of hides stood off to one side, to be used as the healer saw fit. There was a cook fire and a separate smaller fire pit for preparing medicines, and a long work table where wooden bowls full of herbs were carefully set out and organized. Racks of drying plants hung on both sides of the table. The tent had also been made large enough to allow as many as eight Elpies to sleep there, for the families of those who were gravely ill generally desired to stay by their sides as Eli worked to save them.

With Luigi out of their hands, the group sat and exchanged pleasantries, asking about family members and recent goings on in the village. Barnabas and Isabel stayed out of most of the sendings. The tension of the past few days of fearing for their son's life had left them emotionally drained and barely capable of polite, insignificant sendings. Now they felt only overwhelming relief. They leaned back against a pile of hides together, leaving their minds open to each other in quiet celebration.

Micah finally broke into the casual sendings and asked if Sven's idea of having a interspecies exploration team could start now, with Luigi and himself as the Elpie contingent.

Sven considered the request only momentarily before consenting. "Very well. But there is one stipulation. Are you willing to wear clothes? In good conscience, I could not allow you off the ship in possibly hostile environments without protective clothing."

Ecstatic now, Micah had no hesitation. After all, in the rocky country, they wore foot protection, and when visiting the Colders in winter, they wore coats if the weather was severe. He agreed for himself *and* Luigi.

Sven was actually enthused about this development. The team had been his idea, and he thought that these two young Elpies would make a very positive beginning. And as a bonus, there was also the fact that by Luigi's becoming a team member, his healing was no longer a protocol issue.

A few minutes after departure time had been settled, Sven surprised everyone by reaching out towards an approaching Blueman that none recognized. When this new alien entered the tent it became obvious to all, through the character of the sendings, that he was a she.

Sven put one arm around the shoulder of this new visitor, and drew her over to him. "I would like to introduce my daughter Sadie to all of you." Like the Elpies, the Bluemen took human names when on these excursions, as a courtesy to the humans. Their true names, along with their entire language, were unintelligible to humans and Elpies alike.

She was a mere seven feet tall, and had huge, beautiful violet eyes like her mother. Her skin was a very pale blue, offsetting the color of her eyes. She had her mother's ears as well. Large, bat-like ears to the human eye, but to Sven, they were magnificently shaped. When they tilted and turned in the direction of sound, he was always reminded of his first meeting with her mother, and how her ears had taken his breath away. He still could lose himself in watching them, at times.

She half-bowed to the group, who rose as one and offered her their palms in polite welcome. She attempted to do the same at first, but stopped at the awkwardness that huge hands and fingers caused. Eli caught her discomfort and sent that she shouldn't worry—she would get used to their ways in time.

When cordially questioned about herself, Sadie responded with a sending. "I'm going to be a ship's leader one day, like my mother and father. I've finished the first round of my leadership training, and now I'll spend several spans traveling, to learn under the direction of my assigned ship's leaders."

She stopped explaining at this point, not wanting to appear boastful. Her aptitude for leadership had been the highest in her group, so she had been assigned to work under the two leaders who were considered her planet's best—Sven and Cleo, her parents. All present could feel the pride pouring off of Sven at the accomplishments and obvious character of his daughter.

After a meal had been offered and politely consumed by Sven and Sadie, the two left to spend the night on the ship. Elpies and Colders stretched out together in family groups and tried to sleep. Dulcie, Micah's birth mother, put out her hand and laid it on his arm tenderly. She sent a gentle question to her son: Was this what he truly wanted? Was running from his grief again going to help him?

He put his other hand on top of hers, and sent to her that he knew he'd been running. But everywhere he ran on this planet, he only missed his wife and child more, for part of his heart still expected to see them, still felt that they should be out there waiting for him to return. He'd thought that leaving his village, his home, would help him heal. But he'd come to realize that this whole planet was his home, and the emptiness was always there before him.

Going on this ship would take him away. Nothing about the ship or his future destinations spoke to him of home, and so he would not subconsciously be looking for his family to appear. Yes, it was running, but he was running *to* something this time—a new life where he was just Micah, not Micah the widower, or Micah the childless father. The wounds in his heart would never disappear, but redefining his life could help the scar tissue form. He could live with scars, but he'd reached the end of his ability to live with the pain of open wounds.

Dulcie sent her love and her hope for him, and then rolled over to leave him to his thoughts. Eli had already sent to his son that he thought it might be a good thing for him to leave, though he would miss him, and his mothers would grieve over his absence. All of his mothers.

#

Once the great wash of relief began to subside, Isabel began thinking about her son's new plan, and she was becoming more and more agitated. She was tossing back and forth on their bed of hides, and Barnabas knew her mind was in turmoil. How long would it be between visits home? What kind of dangers might he be facing? Had he considered that? A few hours ago, she had worried about him surviving the day, and now, even before he was healed, she learned that Luigi was leaving the planet to walk into new, unknown perils. Unacceptable.

Feeling her anger and worry, Barnabas let her simmer for a while, and then he moved closer to her and rested a hand across her waist. He sent that whatever they felt about their son, he was a grown Colder, and he would make his own choices. She could send her opinions to him, but she must accept his decision. Although he had a few of the same concerns as his wife, Barnabas thought the joining with the Bluemen a fine idea.

Isabel balked at this, but he sent that now was the perfect time in Luigi's life for an adventure. In Barnabas' younger, single days, if the offer had been made to him, he would've accepted it gladly. If there was danger—well, danger was a part of life. Isabel was still unhappy, but her mood was bolstered a little by Barnabas' enthusiasm, and she moved closer as she lay awake and waited for her son to return to them, alive and healthy once more.

CHAPTER FIFTEEN

Screams encircled their home, along with the sound of frantic footfalls and the constant barking of their faithful golden mutt, Madelyn. After turning off the lights in the room to keep from being seen, Gisella and her husband, Hiram, dared only to peek through a slit in the blinds. The hideous beast had appeared suddenly, its origin a mystery. All they knew for certain was that it was after their children, and they were forbidden to intervene.

Eight year old Aluin, the second Eli's youngest, had a paper bag over his head, with construction paper horns and fangs pasted on, and was snarling in menace as he chased his twelve year old sister, Simone, and Hiram and Gisella's eight year old son, Duncan Thomas, around the outside of the house. Viola Marie, their oldest, and at fifteen, the heir apparent to all teenage wisdom, or so she believed, was busily making her own monster. With the help of an old fright wig and make-up, she intended on sneaking up behind the current monster and scaring the bejeebers out of him.

The Elpies and Bluemen were coming tomorrow, which meant that the Sayers offspring were coming home for the reunion. Gisella, the Sayers' adopted daughter, her husband, and their two children lived in their home a hundred or so yards from the main house. A physical therapist, she had a lavishly equipped practice, compliments of Simon and Bess, set up in another building on the grounds of the estate.

These reunions were always the best times of the year for everyone in the family, with Bess' parents coming to stay, along with Eli, Babette, and their boisterous brood. Even though Viola Marie was a teenager, God help them, during these visits she let herself be a kid again, without the teenage self-consciousness and overwhelming need to appear cool that normally governed her life. Free of these constraints, she threw herself whole-heartedly into the tradition of happy lunacy always in progress when the cousins congregated.

Gisella's adoptive brother, Eli, named of course, after Simon's "brother," the Elpie Eli, had wasted no time after his marriage to his sweet Babette from Quebec. He loved kids and was great with them, so Babette had obligingly delivered five children in close succession. Although every child had been planned for and was dearly loved, after number five, Babette had announced to her happy husband that their doctors had appointments to see both of them—him for a vasectomy, and her for a tubal. She wanted no mistakes, no accidents. She *was* going to have her body back and functioning normally once more.

Because he loved her more than life itself, and because sweet Babette promised to get a knife from the kitchen and perform the procedure herself, if he refused, Eli consented quickly to her demands, and settled on five children. He was secretly relieved that it was her idea, and that *he* hadn't been forced to raise the issue. Sometimes the noise level in their home threatened his hearing as well as his sanity, and he'd wondered how many more little ones they could harbor without his going completely deaf and slightly mad.

#

Hiram and Gisella loved to spy on the kids while they were playing. Watching their children in their own element, happy and laughing with their cousins, had become an addictive pleasure for the two.

When they heard Viola coming down the stairs, they quickly turned the lights on and pretended to be reading the paper. Their daughter, resplendent in a fright wig that stood out a whole foot around her head and sported plastic spiders that peeked through the tangled locks, black leotards and black sweatshirt, with face and neck done a sickly green, blood red lipstick smeared around her mouth, and fluorescent plastic fangs, ran down the stairs and headed for the back door, but stopped when her hand hit the knob. She purposefully let go of the knob, turned around, and marched over to stand in front of her parents in the kitchen.

"Mom, Dad," she began, with the classic teenage all-knowing and long-suffering expression—difficult to achieve wearing plastic fangs and a fright wig—"you need to be told. I promithed the otherth I wouldn't, but—we've known about your thpying for yearth now."

The two at the table did their best to look confused.

Though the fangs gave her a pronounced lisp, she continued in a dignified manner. "At firtht it made uth mad, and then we thought it wath funny, and then we thort of thought it wath cute, but now, well, it'th thort of pathetic, with you two trying to live vicariouthly through your children. I'm thorry, but it had to be thaid. If you want to watch, for goodneth thake, jutht open the blindth."

She sighed then, rolled her eyes, and ran out the back door. Her parents looked at each other in surprise, then burst out laughing, and as commanded, opened the blinds. The kids were still circling the house, running and screaming in feigned terror, with Madelyn running behind the creature and nipping at the seat of his jeans. Viola hid behind one of the bushes, and as soon as the bag headed monster passed her, she jumped out and ran after him. Oblivious to her pursuit, due to his own roaring and the screams of the others, he was taken unawares when she grabbed him from behind and lifted him off his feet. He screamed in surprise at first, and when he turned his head enough to get a look at his captor, he screamed in fear.

The other kids turned around at the change in noise coming from behind, and when they took in the scene, they ran back, laughing and screaming. Viola was laughing as she dumped her prize on the ground.

Hiram and Gisella were actually happy about being found out. The show was decidedly better with the blinds wide open.

Aluin, or "Al," as he liked to be called when he was visiting, much to his parents' amusement and his French grandmother's horror, had stopped screaming after his initial fright. Now he was trying to laugh like a good sport instead of yelling at his older cousin for turning the tables on him. But the annoyance he felt was quickly forgotten when Viola gave him back his dropped monster head and grabbed his hand to form a creature tag team.

#

In the Sayers' kitchen, Bess' parents, Sarah and Angus McPhinney, were busy preparing a massive late lunch, already starting some of the prep work, even though the meal was hours away. Sarah had always been and ever would be the baking chef, with her double fudge caramel macaroons still drawing aliens from several galaxies. But Angus, in his retirement, had taken up cooking partly because he liked to eat, partly because he enjoyed spending time with Sarah, and partly because he'd discovered that, in his words, he was "pretty damn good at it."

With normally just the two of them in the house, Bess and Simon tended to eat sparingly and on the healthy side. So when his in-laws visited, Simon was always in lipid heaven for the duration of their stay. Sarah and Angus would officially take over the kitchen, and cook huge, *wonderful,* horribly unhealthy and gloriously delicious meals.

Feeling guilty about their always working so much when they visited, Bess had sat her parents down one day to talk to them about letting her have catered meals brought in for the gatherings. Neither Angus nor Sarah would hear of it. Angus said he *liked* cooking for a big group, and Sarah shared their philosophy on the matter.

For Angus and her, it was like a performance. All that backstage preparation, the sweat and nervousness of trying to get every detail attended to, and then, at last, the curtains opened to "oohs" and "aahs," and the producers would bask in the satisfaction of seeing their show devoured with passion and fervor.

Elsie, the Sayers' large brown mutt, was very much in favor of keeping things the way they were. She liked to linger under the table in the kitchen during the McPhinneys' creative sessions, just in case something dropped on the floor, accidentally or otherwise—the "otherwise" usually accompanied by a wink from Angus or sly smile from Sarah.

When the Bluemen had let the dogs keep Simon's memories, along with telepathy, the dogs, like the cats who had Bess' memories, had also received human life spans. But they were still dogs, with dogs' more sensitive digestive systems. Madelyn and Elsie were treated with the same respect as any other family member, except in that one area, because the vet had warned the Sayers that "human" food was very unhealthy for dogs.

Both Bess and Simon occasionally cheated and slipped a piece of bacon or part of a burger to them, but that was only occasionally, and there was only the two of them. On these gatherings, there were usually seventeen people to occasionally cheat and slip them something incredible that Angus or Sarah had whipped up. While neither canine had ever had to be hospitalized after a visit, both would have confessed, if asked, to an occasional extended grass eating and barfing session brought on by this long awaited but forbidden cornucopia.

Simon was his in-laws' biggest fan, and he gave himself over to lard lust with gleeful abandon. He'd eat bacon, sausage, biscuits and gravy, eggs, and hash browns for breakfast every morning, or sometimes it was pancakes with eggs cooked to order, home fries, Canadian bacon, and frozen blueberries with cream that turned into an icy slush which froze and delighted the tongue.

Because the breakfasts were so huge, people were left to scrounge for themselves if they wanted anything before supper, which was always served on the early side. Today, because of Bess' showing tonight, they were having a very late lunch instead of supper. The menu was going to be Angus' incredible chicken-fried steak with creamed gravy, mashed potatoes, and a mix of green beans, corn, and tomatoes, all fresh from the nearby farmers' market. Sarah was making yeast rolls, and dessert was to be cherry-peach cobbler with whipped cream.

Walking into the kitchen, Simon saw Angus oiling and cleaning the most gigantic cast iron skillet he'd ever seen. He put both hands on his father-in-law's shoulders and began working out a few kinks as he peered over at his work-in-progress. "Good grief, Angus, are you cooking or preparing for war? How can you even lift that thing?"

Angus chuckled and hefted the skillet up in the air with one hand. "Just because my muscles don't bulge out of my clothes, doesn't mean they're not there, bub."

"With all the deliciously deadly ingredients in your masterpieces, I've always considered your frying pan a lethal weapon. But you should have a license for that thing. I didn't know they could even make pans that huge. It's—gargantuan!"

Angus lovingly rubbed his other hand around the outside of the skillet and laid it reverently back on the stove. "Thing of beauty, isn't it?"

Simon slapped his back. "That it is."

Wandering over to Sarah, who was busy making multiple batches of macaroons for the Elpie and Bluemen visitors, he leaned down to put his head on her shoulder from behind, and gave her a hug. She laughed, and Simon looked over at Angus.

"Mind if I make time with your woman?"

Angus looked back, put his hand on his chin and screwed up his mouth as if in deep consideration, then turned back to his skillet with a wave of his hand in Simon's direction. "Nah, take her. Just have her back in time to make the cobbler."

In less than a second, the side of Angus' face was festooned with double fudge caramel batter, compliments of Sarah's spatula. He calmly wiped his face, licked his fingers, and winked at her. "Damn, but I love a feisty woman in the kitchen!"

This was followed by giggling and threats, flying food, name calling and laughter, and Simon left the kitchen feeling blessed to have these people in his life and in his home.

#

That one. No, this one. Maybe the other one… Pacing back and forth, Bess changed her mind for the hundredth time about what she was going to wear at the showing of her new group of paintings. Why did she do this? Was anyone going to like or dislike a painting because of what she was wearing? And after she chose the dress, she'd obsess on the earrings for a while. This was so stupid. She'd decided a week ago what to wear so that she wouldn't do this to herself again. But here she was, same as always, with her usual pre-show jitters, second guessing herself about everything from the paintings she'd done and the paintings she'd chosen to show, to the wine they'd serve, and the shoes she'd wear.

"Come in," she shouted, in a none-too-friendly tone when she heard a gentle knock on the door. A few moments later a hand came through a small opening in the door, waving a white flag, or in this case, a T-shirt from the hamper. She sighed, and slumped down on the edge of the bed.

"I'm so sorry. Didn't mean to snap. Come in, friendly stranger."

A head full of straight black hair followed the arm through, and she jumped up to give a hug to her thirty-one year old son. "Jonas! I didn't even know you'd gotten here! Oh, honey, it's so good to see you!"

"Hey, Mom, good to see you, too. Going through your pre-show ritual, I see."

"Oh, geez, you mean you know? It's not my own secret ceremony?"

"Mom, you've done this as long as I can remember. You're all cool and relaxed about a new showing until about eight hours before, and then you go bonkers and take everything out of your closet to try on, and experiment with thirty different hair styles, and then you pour out all your earrings—"

"Okay, okay, I get it. You know. Anyway, you're just the distraction I needed. Let me look at you!" She put him at arm's length and studied his face. His golden-brown eyes, so much like her own, studied hers in turn. "Have you grown anymore? You look a little tired. Handsome, as always, of course, but a little tired. Long drive?"

"Yeah, and it's been a long month. I was so ready for this break. And no, I haven't grown. I think I was done at twenty-five, Mom. Six-five is it for me."

He flopped down across the bed onto his stomach, like he used to do when he was a kid. Picking up a cobalt blue dress that had been thrown in a pile with five others of assorted hues, he studied it a moment and then held it up for her to take. "This one. This is a great color on you." Scooting over to the edge of the bed then, he hung his head over the side, and with one arm, shuffled through her box of earrings. "And these earrings with this necklace." Then he looked across the room and simply pointed at a pair of shoes lying sideways in the pile she'd made while trying to decide about tonight.

"There, all the decisions are made; everything else is out of your hands, so you can chill out. Oh, and wear your hair in a twist. Perfect for that dress. See? All done. Now come on downstairs and relax."

Sitting across from him in a chair, she smiled, thinking about how well he knew her. Of all her sons, he understood her best. Eli had her artist's eye for colors and detail, and her passion for putting the world he saw onto canvas. But Jonas was the most like her in looks and temperament, and with the ill-fated trip to the Bluemen's planet, they had been through more together than any of her other children.

She took a deep breath, slapped her thighs, and stood up, no longer nervous. "I don't know how you do that, but geez, I wish you still lived at home. You're right about the dress. You're right about the earrings and shoes, too. That's actually the ensemble I picked out for myself a week ago. Plus, you said the magic words—'It's out of my hands.' Just coming to grips with the idea that everything is already set in stone and there's nothing more I can do, is remarkably liberating. So let's go downstairs and steal a macaroon."

##

The ordeal on the Bluemen's planet had changed Jonas and impacted everything he'd done thereafter, at least in some small way. Almost being killed himself, seeing his mother brutalized and his father murdered—that horrible feeling of helplessness was something he was determined to never experience again. When he'd returned home and stepped off that ship, a different Jonas had walked away.

He was never a teenager after that—not really. How could he be? Everything was more serious, more intense for him. Flirting was no longer a priority. Pretty girls hadn't even made him nervous anymore.

His parents meant more to him than they ever had before, not just because he'd nearly lost them, but because he'd come to know them on a different and deeper level.

There were so many facets of their personalities he'd never seen as a child, and he'd finally realized what his parents meant to each other as Bess and Simon, rather than simply Mom and Dad. Above all, he'd come to understand how much he meant to them, and what they were willing to sacrifice to save him.

When he was a boy, his dad had insisted that all of the kids take some kind of martial arts lessons. He'd stressed that he didn't care if they ever got awards, or even went far enough in the disciplines to earn any belts. What he wanted them to learn was that there was always *something* they could do to defend themselves. But when that huge Blueman had come into their apartment and attacked them, his efforts to defend his mom had been useless, as if he were using a paper sword against the real thing. And no martial arts meant diddly against a gun, or in his case, a fire-stick that could be shot from a distance.

He came home determined to find a weapon and become proficient with it. He hated guns, and was terrified that if he kept one, some kid might get hold of it with fatal consequences. He'd seen that on the news so many times that he doubted he'd ever keep one in his house. He'd been really good with a sling shot when he was younger, so he kept a huge one in his apartment, along with a can of ball bearings.

He'd also taken up archery, and he'd become highly skilled with a bow. Like his dad, all of the Sayers boys were exceptionally strong, even without working out, and he had excellent vision. He didn't hunt, but he used hunting points for his arrows, and he practiced not against targets, but against trees, branches, hillsides—anything nonliving, and soft enough for an arrow to penetrate. His favorite targets were branches or logs floating in the water, so he could practice on moving objects. He wasn't sure why it made him feel more in control to have this skill—he didn't carry his bow and quiver with him when he walked downtown alone after his late shift, and if anyone broke into his apartment in the middle of the night, his ball bearings and slingshot would be faster and more effective. But knowing he had the bow and could use it gave him a sense of security. It was not exactly fear that motivated him, but the resolution to never be in another's control again.

Sometimes when he came home for these twice a year visitations, he and Genevieve would go out together, and she'd throw balls while he shot arrows. They'd had some pretty deep conversations during those times, strange to say. He'd promised if the world got overrun by zombies, as every other sci-fi movie out there predicted, that he'd come over with his bow and arrow, and she'd sworn to come to his apartment and throw balls at his burglars.

##

He followed his mom downstairs, and heard the back door opening just as he reached the first floor. A loud voice came booming out of the kitchen. "Is that my little brother's footsteps I hear?" Then the voice was followed by a huge body barreling into the den. Jonas' laugh turned into a squeak as he was scooped up and hugged tightly by his oldest brother, Eli.

When it had become apparent that Eli was going to keep growing past his high school years, he'd become more serious about lifting weights and over all conditioning. If he was going to be unusually tall, he wanted his body to be proportionate, instead of just having a long, skinny frame and a big head, like an olive on a toothpick. In high school, he'd started packing on muscle simply because of hormonal changes, but already at six feet, four inches by his junior year, he'd still felt he looked as if he were made up of arms, legs, and a head.

He'd continued growing through college, until finally topping out at six feet, eight inches. His final height made him especially glad he'd started conditioning, for now, instead of a "bean pole" or a "stick," people most often equated him with a Viking.

The musculature in his arms was pronounced, but not grotesque in size. Since he valued endurance and stamina, something he'd been taught by his father, he ran. Except for his extra four inches, and slightly bigger muscles, he could have been mistaken for a younger Simon. With light brown hair, usually sun streaked, Simon's pale green eyes, black lashes and brows, he never failed to attract female attention in public.

Eli's most endearing qualities, however, had nothing to do with his appearance. What had won Babette's heart and the hearts of most who knew him, were his intelligence, modesty, kindness, and unaffected friendliness.

He barely noticed the female attention he garnered. *Never* would he have classified himself as *hot* or a *hunk,* the words most often bandied about by women who eyed him from a distance. The very idea of the words embarrassed him, and he wouldn't be caught dead in a muscle shirt.

In his mind, he was just a guy, a husband, and a dad. Totally devoted to Babette, his beautiful, black haired, blue eyed pixie of a wife, whom he dwarfed, he was happy to be at her command. As he had been since their first date.

"Dude, it has been a thousand years since I laid eyes on you! You missed the last one of these, and I tell ya, it just wasn't the same without you, man. It's so good to see you!" Jonas had just gotten his breath back when his brother grabbed him up and hugged him again.

"Hey, you're staying at our house with the kids and me." Eli and Babette had accepted Simon and Bess' gift of ten acres and a house when they were married, and though they lived in Quebec, they kept enough clothes and necessities in the house here that they seldom needed to pack much of anything when they came to visit. Simon also maintained a jeep at their house for when they were tooling around the estate.

"Babette's mom was having surgery, so she wanted to stay and help her out afterwards. It's just Aluin, Simone and me. The other three kids had hockey, gymnastics, and Jiu Jitsu practices that none of them wanted to miss, because everybody has tournaments or meets coming up. Can you imagine it, bro? That they'd give up communing with our awesome aliens just so they could go for lessons? Unreal. That's the world we live in now, I guess. So, anyway, we got plenty of room, and you and I can talk all night catching up."

Jonas never thought a lot about his brother when he was away, but now, looking at his big, affectionate smile, he wondered, as always, how he could miss somebody so much and not even know it. "Sounds great to me, Eli. I just dumped my bags and bow in the living room when I came in. We can lug them to your house after we visit with the folks for a while."

"All right! Hey, have you seen Grandma and Gramps yet?"

"Yeah, when I first got here. I can't even think about them without salivating."

"Same here! When I look at Grandma, I can smell chocolate, caramel, and coconut, and when I see Gramps, I can just feel my arteries clogging up. Let's go see 'em again before we hit the living room. We never get to talk with them that much when they're in their cooking routine."

Sarah had flour up to her elbows and some on her nose, when Eli snuck up behind her, grabbed her around the waist to lift her off her feet, and bent his neck around to kiss her cheek. His lips never met flesh, however, for she screamed when he picked her up, and slapped a wad of dough over her shoulder, catching him square on the mouth, and sending a cloud of flour to cover his face. He let go of her on contact with the unborn roll, and now he was coughing and snorting from the flour, and blinking furiously to try and get it out of his eyes.

"Geez, Grandma, you coulda just told me to stop," he sputtered, trying to wipe his eyes, and getting more flour in them in the process.

Jonas and Angus were laughing, but Sarah was visibly upset. "Oh, no, Eli, I'm so sorry, honey, I—well, you startled me, and that was just a reaction. Didn't even know I was going to do it until it was done. Here, let me help you." She tried wiping his face, but since she had dough stuck to her fingers, she only succeeded in adding spats of it to his already floured head. She winced when she saw the sticky little globules she'd just added to his eyebrows. He took her wrists, gently pushing them back in her direction.

"No, it's okay, Grandma, I got it, I got it. Don't help me anymore, please. My fault."

Seeing Angus' giant skillet, Jonas laughed. "Hey, man, you're just lucky you didn't scare Grandpa. Let me guess, Gramps—you frying up Moby Dick for supper? Couldn't you find anything bigger to cook with?"

Angus smiled proudly. "Feast your eyes on this baby, kiddoes. I can cook four steaks at a time, or use it to bake a whole pan of biscuits. Plus," he added, hefting it in the air with one hand and twisting his wrist to twirl the pan by its handle, "I just like the feel of it. It molds to my hand like it was made for me."

"We love you, Gramps, and that's why I have to tell you that you need help, and the sooner the better. Cast iron fixations are the hardest to treat, you know."

"No therapy will ever come between me and my pan, boy," he said, and kissed the bottom of it, looking at Jonas with one eyebrow raised as he did.

"You're so warped, Gramps. But you can really cook, so you can stay." He kissed the top of his grandfather's head, and then walked out of the kitchen, grabbing Eli, who was still wiping his face with the wet towel Sarah had given him. Leading him towards the bathroom by his arm, he said, "Come on, guy. They play too rough for us in there. Let's go flush out your eyes in the bathroom." Then over his shoulder, "We'll come see you two again when you're not armed."

Jonas doubled back into the kitchen and grabbed a bowl to use for the flushing, and then headed to the bathroom again. The two had just started the process, when there was a knock at the door. He heard his parents rushing in that direction, and smiled to himself, thinking about all the squeals and hugs that would accompany Genevieve's arrival.

Bess opened the door and Simon crowded in behind her to receive their daughter. They both had their arms half-raised in preparation for the hugs, when they saw Enzo standing beside her. They stopped for a split second, open-mouthed and staring.

Genevieve leapt into the void, pulling Enzo forward. "Mom, Dad, I'd like you to meet Enzo Uccello, my fiancé."

Their mouths dropped a little further open, but neither drooled. Elsie shoved her head out between their legs and started panting. They were so stunned that they were only half aware of the little dog Genevieve was holding. Then Bess came to herself, and screamed, "Your fiancé? Oh my gosh! Well come in, come in!" She took Enzo by the arm and ushered him into the living room. Simon put his arm out to stop Genevieve from going in, and said, "We'll be there in a minute. I just need to give my girl a hug and have a word first."

He stepped out onto the porch and Genevieve let Lola down so she could run into the house before Simon closed the door behind him. He took his daughter's arm with one hand and stared down into her face incredulously. "Are you out of your mind? You know the Bluemen and the Elpies will be here tomorrow! He can't see them!"

She'd been prepared for this reaction from him. "Dad, did you not hear what I said? Enzo is my fiancé. We're getting married. Spouses get told about our extended family. And yeah, it's good to see you, too, Dad."

He gave an exasperated sigh, grabbed her quickly in a bear hug, and then pushed her back to look in her face again as he continued. "A fiancé is *not* the same as a spouse. You could break up tomorrow, and then he might tell everybody he knows, just to get even with you. And then what? We never see our friends, our *family* again, because people will be watching us? Good Lord, Genevieve, what were you thinking?"

So agitated that he couldn't stay still any longer, Simon began pacing back and forth on the porch. Genevieve rushed after him and grabbed his hand.

"Dad, stop it! How many guys have I ever brought home? None. How many times have I ever professed to be in love? None. Dad, I am ridiculously careful with my heart. I've never even used that four letter word about anyone outside of our family, before. And you're right, we're not married yet, but there is no chance, period, that we won't be. And I wanted you all, Elpies and Bluemen included, to meet him, so that the next time they visit us, they could maybe attend our wedding, which I'd very much like to have here."

He'd stopped pacing when she grabbed his hand, but now he was shaking his head. "How long have you even known this man? It couldn't be that long."

"How long had you and Mom known each other when you got married?"

"I'm not even sure, but that was entirely different."

"Why, Dad? Why were your feelings about each other more genuine than ours? If anything, yours should have been in question—you were the only adult, non-homicidal humans on the planet. Enzo and I had lots of humans to choose from, and we chose each other."

"How do you know he's not after your money?"

"In the first place, Dad, *I* asked *him* out. He had no idea of my background. And then when I did tell him, I think it actually put him off a little."

"Oh, our money's not good enough for him?"

"No, it's not that. He's just always pictured himself providing for his family. Money is not an issue for him *or* for me."

"What does he do for a living?"

"He's a firefighter."

"And you're willing to chance that you'll be raising your children alone? He risks his life every day. And a fireman's risk of cancer is so much greater than the average—"

"Let me tell you right now," she broke in fiercely, "that I would rather have one year, one month, one day with him, than fifty years with someone else. You don't know him, but Dad, he has such a good soul. Next to you, he's the finest man I've ever known. He's smart, and kind, and loyal—"

"But he's so short."

Now *she* started pacing in frustration. "I can't believe this. We just got through an ordeal with *his* parents, and his family was upset because I'm tall. He said his mother asked him how he could bring home a giraffe."

"WHAT? How dare they call you names! What kind of people *are* they? You're the most beautiful woman I've ever seen, not counting your mother, of course. They'd be damn lucky to have you in their family." He was seething now, and she realized it might not have been wise to spew the whole story out like that.

"Wait—she didn't say it to my face. She said it in private to him, like you're talking to me, telling me he's short, as if that's some horrible affliction. He only told me about the 'giraffe' thing later because it was so stupid that it was funny. He told her that he was proud to be with me, proud that a beautiful woman like me loved him."

"Now I understand. You're a status symbol to him. I've heard that some short men only go for tall women—it makes them feel powerful."

Exploding with a cross between a growl and a shriek, she grabbed both of his arms with her hands and said furiously, "Stop it, Dad! My gosh, you're so determined to make something bad out of whatever I tell you."

Just then the door opened, and Enzo stuck his head out. "Everything okay out here?" he asked, with what he hoped was an ingratiating smile.

Simon reached over, grabbed the door handle and said, "Everything's just peachy," then pulled the door closed in his face, with Enzo drawing his head back just in time to save his nose.

Genevieve gasped. "That was sooo *rude!*"

"How do you know how he'll react when he sees the aliens? He might be scared out of his mind."

"He's already seen them. I showed him the disk."

"You did what? I didn't even know *you'd* seen it. That disk is so—personal. And horrendous. How did you get it, and why on Earth did you show it to an outsider?"

"Eli showed Colder and me the disk when I turned twenty-one. He knew you wouldn't want him to show us, because it was so—well, you said it—horrendous. But he showed us so that we would really know and understand what Mom and Jonas had suffered, how they fought for each other, and what you did to save your family. We'd been told when we were younger, but as we got older and sort of forgot about it, it just became a story. Seeing the disk—that was a whole different thing. And I didn't show it to an outsider. I didn't show Enzo until after we got engaged. I wanted him to know what kind of a man my father was." She looked down then, deflated, tired of fighting, and at a loss for words to make him understand.

Simon saw the tears welling in her eyes, and was suddenly ashamed and full of remorse for making his wonderful daughter cry for telling him the most exciting news of her life. He sighed and stepped forwards to envelop her in his arms, and she sank against his chest. He laid his head on top of hers.

"Oh sweetheart, I'm sorry. I just want what's best for you and the family. And our friends. If you love him, I'm sure we will, too. Eventually. But—how do you dance?"

She pushed away from him and laughed now in exasperation. "I'm going inside to introduce Enzo to the rest of the family. Coming?"

By the time Genevieve and Simon stepped into the living room, her fiancé had already been classified as such, and introduced to Eli and Jonas. The nervous young man had been given a huge, smothering hug by Eli, and a sincere welcome and handshake from Jonas. Eli advised that they not inform Angus and Sarah until her hands were flourless and doughless, and Angus was not in possession of his frying pan, lest their surprise and exuberance at the announcement cause an unintended tragedy.

Since she'd been allowed inside, Lola had been bouncing and running all over the living room and everyone in it. Suddenly in a sea of giants, including a giant dog, she was focusing on being distracted. Running from one person to the next, licking any hand she could jump up far enough to reach, and then bouncing into and out of Bess' lap, once it was available, her attention finally settled on *the dog.*

The dog was amazing. She sensed friendliness and a maternal nature in the huge animal, and she'd helped herself to quite a few rear end sniffs, but couldn't manage to get her attention.

Elsie had been sniffing poor Enzo frantically, since hearing that he was marrying Genevieve. He kept trying to politely push her away from his crotch, until Bess finally intervened and physically pulled her away, excusing her manners. "I'm very sorry. She's just so excited about the news that she wants to get to know you really fast." Blushing, she tried again. "That came out wrong, I know, but there's just no way to explain it—in a polite way if—I mean, it's polite if you're a dog—I think, but if you're not—"

Elsie asked Bess to express her sincerest apologies, and to tell him she thought he had a wonderful smell, but when Bess hesitantly translated this last part, Enzo was even more embarrassed than before.

He decided that changing the subject quickly was his only refuge. "If I remember this right, you all can understand what she 'sends' to you, and she can understand what everybody's saying, correct?" Bess and Genevieve nodded.

"Uhhh—Elsie, would you consider it rude of me to pet you, since you're sort of not really a dog? I mean, yes you are, but you're—"

Elsie stopped him by planting a huge paw on his knee and shoving her head up under one of his hands. He jerked back in surprise, then smiled and began stroking her head, scratching behind her ears, and then, oh my, rubbing her whole ear. She sent to Bess to tell him that he *really* knew how to pet a dog, and then turned her head over so that he could get the other ear.

As if by magic, Lola appeared in Enzo's lap, staring and panting in Elsie's face. She didn't mind sharing, but if the big one was going to get attention from *her* man, she could at least acknowledge her. Elsie reared her head back, startled, and then sent excitedly to Bess. "Can we keep her? I haven't been around a regular dog in forever, and she's so cute! Please, Bess. Madelyn and I will take her under our wings and make sure she doesn't mess anywhere, and you know, show her how things work here. We'd be great role models!"

Genevieve saw the conversation going on between her mom and Elsie, and seized the opportunity.

"Uh, Mom, Dad, I was hoping that we might leave Lola here with you until the wedding. I didn't intentionally get a dog—if I hadn't taken her, this witch that owned her was going to have her put down, so I didn't have a choice. She's so sweet, and I know that Elsie and Madelyn would be great with her.

"She'd have a ball running loose around here, with the other dogs to keep her out of trouble and the kids to play with, because she's super high energy. The way my schedule is right now, she's stuck in my apartment for long hours at a time, and keeping a dog like that crated all day is like having her in jail. We'd take her with us after the honeymoon, if it's okay for her to stay until then."

Simon looked at Bess for her approval and she nodded. Simon shrugged, not willing to take his attention off the other matter at hand. "Yeah, sure. Elsie looks like she's all for it."

Elsie jumped up, wiggling all over with excitement, and sent to Lola, "Come on, I'll show you around and introduce you to everybody! Madelyn's going to love you!"

Then she ran for the back door, only to look behind her and see Lola still sitting in Enzo's lap. She was looking at Elsie hopefully, turning her head from side to side, trying to figure out what it was she wanted. Sighing, Elsie turned around and walked back to the little dog. It had been a long time since she'd been around a dog without telepathy. This was going to be a challenge.

She gave a short bark at Lola and did a play bow, and that did the trick. The little dynamo sprang off of Enzo's lap and began bouncing and yipping around Elsie, who caught herself thinking, to her shame, *was I ever that dumb?*

This time when Elsie ran out, Lola followed, and attention in the room was once again fixed on the new human in their midst.

They all sat and made small talk for a while, with Bess excited and bubbly, and Simon smiling fixedly, but with a faraway look in his eyes. Bess left in a few minutes and returned with her parents, gluten free and panless for the announcement. Sarah screamed of course, and hugged and kissed her granddaughter and future grandson-in-law. Angus said, "Well it's about time, girlie!" and gave Enzo a hard slap on the back, followed by a handshake. Five minutes later, they made their excuses and headed back to their domain.

After those last introductions, Simon stood up and said unnecessarily loudly, "Well, let's go get your bags and get everybody settled in. Genny, we've got your old room ready for you, and Enzo, there's plenty of room for you at Eli's house."

Genevieve started to say something, but she caught a look and a small head shake from Enzo, and closed her mouth. Her brothers grabbed his things and Jonas' bags and bow, and her dad took her bags.

"Hey, I'll see you later, Lady Red," Enzo said quietly, giving her a quick kiss before he headed out the door with Eli and Jonas on either side.

Simon looked at Genevieve, chin down and eyebrows raised. "Lady Red?"

"Don't even start."

CHAPTER SIXTEEN

Putting her clothes up in the closet of her old room always made Genevieve a little homesick. She'd had a wonderful childhood, and this room had been a big part of it. It had started out as her nursery, changed into a toddler's paradise, rolled over into a little girl's pretend castle and sometimes jungle, transformed into a teenager's realm, and then into the study and refuge of a young adult. When she stopped and looked around the room, every color peeking out from beneath the zillion other colors painted over it, every mark on the wall or nick in the closet door held some memory for her.

She'd felt a little of this when she went away to college, and felt it even more when she'd graduated from vet school and set out to make her way on her own. But now, knowing that she was going to make a new life, a new family, with a new identity—even a new name—she felt that lonely ache stronger than ever before.

There were no doubts as to her course. Enzo and she were meant to be together. She knew this, and was thrilled with the idea of starting a home, of joining her life with his. But that meant the ultimate cord cutting. She could never be a girl again, and for some reason, that filled her with an unreasonable sadness.

"Genevieve, you in there?"

"Come in, Mom."

When Bess came through the door and shut it behind her, Genevieve turned from her closet, walked over, leaned her head against her shoulder, and put her arms around her waist. "At exactly the right time, as always. Oh, Mom, I feel so—I don't know—sad. Ridiculous, isn't it?"

She took her hand then and led her to the bed. Bess already knew the drill. She crawled up onto the big bed, and sat against the headboard, pulling one of the pillows out from beneath the covers and putting it in her lap. Genevieve crawled in after and laid her head on the pillow, letting her mood hold reign. Her mother stroked her hair and hummed, as she had when her daughter was a small child, and all the other times since, when she'd been sad or frightened.

They stayed this way for a time, with neither speaking until Bess quit humming and asked, "Are you afraid?"

Genevieve had been almost dozing, hypnotized by the gentle rhythm of her mother's hand on her hair, and the soft hum of her voice—the familiar, comforting ritual. Rolling onto her back so she could look up into Bess' face, she shook her head. "No, not scared. It's just this deep melancholy about leaving home, leaving childhood, leaving—this," she answered, as she drew her mom's hand to her face and rubbed her cheek against it.

"It's addlepated, I know. Oh my gosh, that was a Dad-word, wasn't it?" She gave a little laugh, remembering all the times she'd heard him say that. Maybe using it now was just another way of hanging onto home.

"I haven't been a child for quite a few years now, and I have my own apartment, my own career. But I guess somewhere in the back of my mind, there's this little girl who feels like she's just playing at being a grown-up, and who thinks she can come back home if she needs to be a child again. Here's my old room, just waiting for me. Sounds mental, doesn't it? When I started looking around today, I realized that when I marry Enzo, that's it. This won't be my room anymore. Childhood, girlhood—it's all really, really over. Forever. And even though I want to marry him more than anything in the world, saying goodbye to that part of me is—wrenching."

Bess held her hand, treasuring the feel of it, knowing that *she* was saying goodbye, as well. "I don't think you're addlepated *or* mental. And you know your father would be deeply honored to know you used his word." She gave a little laugh as she stroked her daughter's hair.

"Every young bride goes through this, at least a little. When you see a girl crying before or after her wedding, it's not always because of the beauty or meaning of the ceremony. Sometimes she's crying because she realizes that who she was just changed forever. She's going to be someone new, and she feels the loss at having to say goodbye to the girl she was before, in the life that came before."

"How did you know I needed you just now? How have you always known?"

Bess held a few strands of Genevieve's hair in her hand, studying the color while she thought about how to answer. Then she laid the strands back into place and combed them in with her fingers as she gazed down at her daughter. "You know that your dad and I have had telepathy with each other, the animals, the Bluemen and the Elpies, since the Bluemen picked us up, way before you were born. When we came back to Earth, we found that we were more attuned to other people, and once we became parents, that mental connection just naturally became the strongest with our children. When you're close by, I can feel when you're upset, so I come to you.

"But it's more than that. You're my child, and I'm bound to all of my children by a thread that runs through my soul and back into theirs. I feel for you. Eventually, all of you have to cut the cord, but no one can sever that thread. As long as I'm alive, Genevieve, there will be a pillow for my lap when you feel sad or troubled. Relationships change over the years, but we are forever a part of each other, and I will always be there for you.

"Do you remember when you were a child, how when I slept, I'd just be out cold? A tree could fall on the house, and I'd still be sleeping. And yet, if one of you had a bad dream, or was sick—one little whimper and I'd be instantly awake. That's a mom thing, and I pray someday you'll learn that firsthand."

Holding her mother's hand and rubbing it between her own two, as she'd done as a child, she looked into her memories. "I remember that so well. Waking up in the middle of the night with a fever, or a bad dream, too scared to even move, and all of a sudden, I'd see your silhouette in the doorway. Seeing you there was so overwhelming—this huge sense of relief would hit me, and I knew that everything would be okay. Because you were there. I love you, Mom."

Now they both got a little teary, and that made them start giggling when they reached for a tissue at the same time. Genevieve got up to go blow her nose and wash her face, and then she came back to the bed and leaned against an end post to face her mom.

Bess stared back expectantly. "So—tell me about him."

"Well, first of all—and I know this will be important for you to hear—he says 'geez.'"

Bess clapped her hands, gave a short scream, and laughed. "It was meant to be!"

She laughed with her mom for a minute, and then Genevieve turned serious again.

"Oh Mom, he's who I would have made up if I'd tried to invent a man for myself. He's gentle and kind, intelligent and funny, interested in and enthusiastic about almost everything—he really *lives* every day of his life. He listens to me, respects me, and believes in me. And at the risk of appearing shallow, I am very attracted to him, physically, too. He has the smoothest skin, the most gorgeous eyes, and I love his big, strong nose."

"Just like your father's. I always liked his nose, too."

"Yeah, I guess it is like his, now that you mention it. And he's just so naturally masculine and strong. Confident without ever being overbearing. Never tries to be macho, because he doesn't need to. When people look at him, some just see that he's kind of short. What they don't see, is that he is solid muscle. And whoa, can he kiss. When he—"

"Okay, remember, you're talking to your mother, here."

She "tsked" at her mom and continued. "I was just going to say that when he holds me, I feel so—right. Like the world could fall apart, but as long as he's got me, I'll be okay. We'll be okay. I feel like in his arms is where I'm meant to be. Yes, I'm independent, and I love being a vet, but—where Enzo is—that's my *place* in this world now. Geez, I know how schmaltzy this sounds, but—"

"No, it sounds real. I've always felt that way about your dad. I can still remember feeling that for the first time, too. I'm so happy that you found each other. Some people go their whole lives without ever finding the person who can make that place for them.

"When we were on the Elpie's planet, and your father was dying from the poison—when I saw his life slipping away, I felt mine diminishing right along with his. I had been so determined to return to Earth before, but on those last days in the medicine tent, when I knew that I was going to lose him, Earth didn't matter anymore, because it would never feel like my home without him in it. Then when the Bluemen brought him back, and I was in his arms again, I knew *that* was where my home was. Where it still is. So I understand exactly what you mean, honey, and I couldn't be happier for you."

Bess held her arms open then, and her daughter came and filled them, as she had so many times before.

##

After Enzo and the brothers drove up to the house, Eli jumped out of the jeep, reached over, grabbed both bags and led the way to the door. The handle was a lever rather than a nob. Eli turned to the other two and ordered, "Prepare to be amazed. Only one of my many unique talents." He backed up to the door and pressed the lever down with one glute. When it unlatched, Eli gave a little bow and pushed the door open with his hip.

Jonas raised his eyebrows and nodded in appreciation. "Wow, Eli, I never knew you had such a talented butt! You don't want to start using it for everything though—you could lose the use of your hands."

"You might be right—it would simplify my life to start using my hands again. The hardest thing has been writing checks." Jonas laughed, and Eli pretended to hold something out in front and to the side of him, scrunching his face in concentration, jiggling his buns around slightly as he peered into the invisible glass. "I have to use a mirror, and people always think I'm dancing. I gotta tell 'em, 'Nope, just paying bills.'"

Enzo laughed and shook his head. Yeah, he was gonna fit right in.

#

Seeing Eli's house was an adventure in itself for Enzo. It was a two story natural stone house, with only a few logs thrown in here and there for decoration and to make peaks for the large A-frame windows at the front and back of the second story. It had an almost medieval flavor to the outside of it, much like the main house, and the inside was a satisfying mix of modern and rustic furnishings. The rich browns and golds, subtle beiges and soft blues blended gracefully in the living room, giving a feeling of warmth and welcome when one walked through the door. With three bedrooms upstairs and three down, there was plenty of room for when Eli's whole wild crew was present.

Enzo was instantly mesmerized with his first look at Eli's paintings, which claimed most of the walls in the house. He put his bags down in the room that Eli pointed to as his, but after seeing the painting in his room, he couldn't focus on anything else until he'd seen them all.

With Eli's permission, he went from one wall to the next, studying each land or seascape. The colors, detail, and depth in each of them drew him in. He could almost feel the wind on his face and the grass under his feet. The aroma of wheat fields under a hot summer sun, and the sounds of waves lapping at the shore or crashing on the rocks flooded his senses. He felt alive with anticipation at the sight of a coming storm; could smell the rain lying ominously in dark clouds on the canvas.

When he was studying the last painting in the living room, he felt Eli watching him and turned to look at him. Eli was standing and leaning against the back of the couch with a huge smile on his face.

"Enzo, you can't imagine what it does for an artist to watch someone drink in his work the way you've been doing. You know, it's always nice to get a good review from a critic, but that's not why I paint. People like you are the ones who make me feel like a success. You were there, weren't you? You were *in* those paintings for a while."

"Oh man, Eli, I'm blown away! These are the kind of paintings that speak to me—the ones that can take me somewhere. These are just—extraordinary. Gen told me you were really good, but I had no idea that you could do this kind of work.

"You're right about where I was." He looked around him and started pointing to the different pictures on the walls as he talked about each one. "I've just walked through fields and forests and I've been to the ocean. I felt the sun on my back, and heard the wind moving through the leaves. It's like—I could smell the water and feel that cold spray on my face when those waves broke on the rocks. Yeah—I was there."

Eli never stopped smiling while Enzo was talking to him, and when he finished, he walked over, slapped him on the back, and squeezed his shoulder with one hand. "Thank you for that, guy. Knowing that you see what I tried to put on canvas—that's the best payday in the world for me."

He left him then and went into the kitchen, and Enzo returned to his room to unpack. He and Jonas were just getting settled into their rooms when the pounding started on the front door.

"Little pigs, little pigs, let me come in, or I'll huff and I'll puff and I'll—"

Eli threw the front door open, grabbed his brother by the front of his shirt, and launched him into the living room. "*What* will you do, you little turd brain?"

Enzo had stuck his head out of his room when the banging started, but after seeing the entrance and what ensued, he wasn't quite sure what to do. Jonas saw the look on his face, and laughed. "Not to worry. Here, 'turd brain' translates to 'beloved brother,' when Eli says it. A holdover from when we were kids. That's his tender side shining through."

Then Jonas ran out into the room and jumped onto his little but bigger brother's back, laughing as Colder spun around, trying to dislodge him. His baby brother had affronted him with the audacity to outgrow him by one inch. At six-feet, six inches, Colder was also two inches taller than his dad, which made the insult wider spread and thus not as hurtful.

Laughing and yelling, Colder finally threw himself on the couch, landing on Jonas and making him say, "Give!" before letting him up. Eli plopped down next to them on the couch, and grabbing his youngest brother's head in one arm, gave it a squeeze before punching him painfully but fondly on the arm.

All three brothers were laughing and shoving each other when Colder suddenly noticed Enzo standing there watching. He extricated himself from the mob, stood up, and held out his hand. "Hey, sorry, I didn't mean to ignore you. I'm Colder, the youngest and most maligned but obviously the most handsome and intelligent of the Sayers brothers. And who might you be?"

Enzo stepped forward and shook hands, then looked at the other brothers for a cue. "Hey Colder. I'm Enzo Uccello, and I'm uh… have you seen Genevieve yet?"

Genevieve had talked a lot about Colder. They were the closest in age, just a year apart, and being much younger than the other siblings, the two had naturally become each other's playmates, confidants, and friends when they were growing up together. They were more like twins than just siblings, able to finish each other's sentences, and often knowing the other's moods and thoughts, unasked. Enzo thought for sure that Genevieve would want to give him the news herself.

"He's Genny's *betrothed*!" Jonas said, batting his eyes, with his fingers clasped beneath his chin coquettishly.

Colder froze, and looked at Eli. "What did he say?"

"You heard him, bro. Genevieve's going to marry Mr. Uccello."

Looking down at him, Colder asked, "For real? This isn't just one of my brothers' stupid jokes?"

Now Enzo was getting annoyed. "Yeah, it's *for real*. She's got the ring to prove it. Problem?"

"Uh, well, no, of course not. I'm just shocked. I mean, I'm just surprised. She's so…and you're kind of …"

"It's been mentioned before, but—not a problem for us. Is it for you?"

Well, hell yes, since she never even bothered to call me and tell me about you.

"No, not at all. I mean, shoot, if you two don't care, why should I? Welcome to the family, Enzo!" He gave him a man hug then, replete with hard slaps on the back and a punch on the arm, and Enzo breathed a sigh of relief.

##

Aluin and Simone were staying over at their cousins' house, so the three brothers and soon-to-be brother cracked open some beers and sodas and sat around the horseshoe shaped couch in the living room, catching up and getting to know each other. Without conscious thought, the brothers arranged themselves on one side of the couch, with Enzo on the other, across from them.

As usual, after a few minutes, Eli felt compelled to organize, and had them take turns telling about themselves.

"Okay, I'll go first," he began.

"Just like always. First outta the womb, first to get married, first to clean his and everybody else's plate."

Eli rolled his eyes, refusing to look at Jonas, and shook his head at Enzo.

"Jealousy is such an unbecoming emotion, don't you think? Just ignore anything that might fall from the mouth of Bean Butt over there, and we can continue in a civilized manner."

Bean Butt reached over Colder and punched Eli's arm, almost making him spill his Coke.

"Hey, watch the furniture, guy! Acting like some kind of animal… Well, anyway, I am the illustrious Eli Aloysius Sayers, sometimes called 'Eli the second,' or 'Eli two,' when the Elpies are here, since I'm named after the Elpie that my dad always talks about as his brother. But don't be alarmed, nothing kinky going on with their parents—it's strictly a male-bonding thing."

Colder snorted beer when Eli said that, and then he recovered and gave him a shove. Which was like pushing a wall.

"And please ignore my other brother's swinish behavior. Normally we make him eat and drink outside. It's bad enough when he snorts beer, but when he gets to eating fast and snorts mashed potatoes, man, it gets ugly…"

"Just tell your story, Number Two. You know, that name really suits you."

"Anyway, I'm thirty-four, and I live in Quebec with my five fantastic kids and my beautiful—"

"And he does mean beautiful."

"Yeah, like freakin' gorgeous. We think he must have spiked her drinks. For years. We used to always call her 'Eli's sweet Babette,' cuz she just always is, you know. Until we found out that after their fifth kid, she offered to perform a vasectomy on him for free, without anesthetic, if he didn't make an appointment for one."

"Ouch."

"Yeah, don't ever argue with a woman holding a butcher knife. It was just a prop for emphasis, of course. Just to make her point, no pun intended. And it really did make me understand the urgency of the matter. I am officially whipped and clipped."

Colder snorted beer again when he laughed, and his brothers made pig noises at him.

"As I was about to say—- I live with the kids and my beautiful wife, Babette."

After saying her name, he reached over to the lamp table, picked up a framed picture of his family, and stood up to hand it to Enzo.

He took the picture and studied it a few seconds. "Wow. You weren't kidding. She *is* beautiful. And that's a great looking bunch of kids. You're a lucky man."

Eli accepted the picture back and got serious for a moment, studying the faces in the frame. "Thanks. Yeah, I am." Then he took up his elder brother air again and continued.

"I'm an artist. I like land and seascapes, as you've noticed, but I do portraits on commission for money, and sometimes I even do local fairs, because I'm pretty good at speed painting and I get a kick out of it. I'll be having a showing soon in Ottawa, and hopefully that will lead to other things. I show my stuff through a few galleries around the country, and word of mouth and the internet have done me pretty well. I know my mom could help me by promoting my paintings through her gallery, but this is something I have to do on my own, and she respects that. And my youngest male sibling lied to you, obviously, since as you can see, I'm the handsomest, and as you can tell from my eloquence, by far the most intelligent of the male Sayers offspring."

"Okay, enough out of you." Colder reached over and jerked an imaginary microphone out of Eli's hand and held it up to his mouth.

"Hi, I'm Colder Malcolm Sayers. Now, I know, you're thinking, 'who is Malcolm colder than?' But that's okay. I was named after an Elpie, too—well, a Colder actually—who is now known as 'Barnabas,' but that's a long story that you can ask Genny to tell you. I guess if my dad can live with a name like 'Simon Sayers,' for all these years, I can deal with 'Colder.' I'm twenty-four, I have a degree in Business, but I don't know why—I guess it just seemed the easiest thing, since I have no idea what I want to do when I grow up. I have a good head for business, but hate the idea of running one. I am currently working for a landscaper, because I love being outdoors, I have a good eye for detail, and I can help him with the business part. I'm also amazingly skilled with a shovel and pick ax.

"I love to ski, snowboard, have dabbled in Tae Kwon Do and Jiu Jitsu, but was too lazy and uninterested to excel at either, used to like to play chess, but got tired of getting beat by a cat. I hope to someday find some sort of profession that I can feel enthused about enough to pursue. I am currently not involved with anyone."

The brothers on both sides of him said "aawww" at this, and patted his back. Jonas handed him a box of Kleenex.

"I'm a year older than Genevieve, and we've always been super close. She usually calls me two or three times a week and tells me all about everything she's been doing. And I gotta say, I am extremely pissed and concerned that she never told me about you."

Eli sat up and turned to look Colder in the face, while Jonas put one hand on Colder's shoulder and stammered out an apology to Enzo. Eli started doing the same, while Colder just sat and glared at their guest.

"No, no, let him talk, please. Now's the time to air everything, and get it out of the way before the wedding." Enzo patted the air with both hands, motioning for the other brothers to sit back and let Colder go.

"No offense, but I think maybe she didn't tell me because you're so—well, sorry, but you're short and she's tall and that's just weird to think of you two together. Or maybe she didn't tell me because there's something about you that she thinks she needs to hide from the family. You're Italian. Are you involved with the Cosa Nostra or something?"

"Ah geez, Colder, you make us all look stupid! For cryin' out loud!" Jonas was embarrassed to even be related to him, after that question. Eli just moaned and shook his head apologetically at Enzo. To their surprise, Enzo laughed.

"No, I am not. And contrary to popular opinion, not all Italian-Americans are connected to the Mafia. And yes, I'm short and Gen is tall. But when I look at your sister, Colder, I don't see tall. I see amazing. I see beautiful, and brilliant. I see this glow coming from her that I need in my life. I see a spirit that reaches me like none other, and I see a hand that I want to hold in mine while we grow old together. I believe she understands what I see in her, and her soul responds to it."

The three brothers stared at him in silence for a few seconds, until Eli started clapping and shouting, "GOOD ANSWER, GOOD ANSWER!" and then Jonas got into it, started whistling, and stood to reach across the room to give Enzo a high five.

Colder pursed his lips and looked around the room, trying to think of something wrong in what he'd just heard. He couldn't. But—who talked like that? He noticed they were all staring at him, waiting for his response. Geez, what was he supposed to say to that?

"Okay, okay, *Shakespeare*, so you love each other. But—how are you supposed to dance?"

His brothers started pushing him from both sides and calling him the usual names.

Enzo held up his hands again, and when they were quiet, he answered, "I don't get why, but everybody seems obsessed with how we dance. Why? You gonna go dancing with us? You planning on dancing *with us*? *With me?* Whadda *you* care how we dance?"

Jonas piped in, with "Yeah, whadda *you* care?"and gave Colder a little shove. Eli echoed him from the other side, also with a slight shove for emphasis.

Colder sighed, feeling like a pinball, bouncing between the two brothers, knowing he was outclassed and outnumbered.

"All right! Enough about the height thing, already. But why hasn't she called me?"

Enzo sat forward, rested his elbows on his knees, and laced his fingers together. He looked at Colder and asked, "You really wanna know?"

"Yeah, I want to know."

"Okay. Well, first of all, since we started dating, we've seen each other every day after work, and whenever we have days off, we try to take them together. So she hasn't had a lot of time to call you. It's always late by the time she'd have a chance, and she probably didn't want to wake you."

"Ah, that's bull. She's woken me up at all hours of the morning and night when she's been upset or happy about something."

"The other reason is—she used to share everything with you. Now she shares everything with me. She's been afraid you'll feel like she's deserting you, and hate me for it. Or turn against her. And she loves you so much, Colder, that she can't face that. She said you've always been like her other half, and she's terrified of losing you."

"She told you that?" Colder asked, his voice a near whisper. His heart sank as he thought of Genevieve being afraid to call him, afraid to tell him, afraid that he'd reject her out of stupid jealousy.

"Yeah, she did. And she'll be furious with me for telling you, because I know she wanted to have some time alone with you to talk about it first. But there it is. Please, don't tell her I told you. I only told you because—-you asked."

Colder looked down, subdued. Now his brothers each had a hand on one of his shoulders, giving him little shakes of comfort and commiseration.

"Will you guys stop it—I'm getting motion sickness!"

His brothers dropped their hands quickly and sat back.

"I want to tell you that's BS, too, but I guess maybe I'm acting just like she expected me to. I was hurt that she hadn't been calling me like she used to. And really hurt that I wasn't the first one to know that she was serious about somebody. I should've been the first to know that she was engaged. I *did* feel deserted. I *am* a little jealous." He waved his hands palms forward suddenly, shaking his head and saying, "No, no, not jealous *like that*—that's not what I meant—there was never anything like that between Genny and me!" The two other brothers gasped at the thought, and started voicing their denials loudly, as well.

"Hey guys, it's okay, I never thought that. Chill, chill."

With a sigh of relief, and still red in the face, Colder continued. "It's like you said, she goes to you now with her problems, her good news. That's how it's supposed to be when you find—" He looked at Eli and Jonas, and then all three brothers said together, "The One."

They laughed, and Jonas explained, "That's what our folks have always said when they're talking about our future spouses. Especially our mom. She always says you'll know when you find 'The One.'"

Colder's voice got quiet again. "I guess she just didn't know how to tell me that I had to step down from my place in her life."

Eli leaned sideways against him, and said comfortingly, "Everybody's expendable, dude."

He started to get angry, but then looked at Eli's face and laughed instead, punching his arm.

Enzo leaned further forward and looked Colder in the eyes. "Hey, I want you to know something. It would kill Genevieve, and I mean it—it would kill her inside if you turned away from her. And that would kill me. So from the bottom of my heart, I tell you that I want you to be a major part of our lives together. I won't mind if she calls you about stuff, and if you have to wake us up in the middle of the night because you need to talk to her—I'm okay with that. Anytime you want to drop by, and that goes for all of you—just do it. She loves you, and that means, like it or not, you bunch of clowns, I gotta love you too."

All of the brothers were moved by his speech, which embarrassed the heck out of all of them except Eli, who actually got a little misty.

Enzo stood up and the others followed suit. He held out his hand to Colder. "Brothers?" he asked.

Colder slapped away his hand and gave him a man-hug, and then the other two joined in, with the compulsory back pounding. Finally, with nearly simultaneous sighs, they took their seats, their sodas and beers, and began again.

"My turn," Jonas said.

"My name is Jonas Angus Sayers, I am thirty-one, and sadly, at six foot-five, the shortest of the Sayers brothers, but one inch taller than my dad." Cheers all around.

"Thank you, thank you for that. I have a degree in engineering, but like my younger and obviously dumber brother, graduated thinking, 'Why am I here?'

"Not to brag, but we all have pretty high IQ's, and all of our lives, we just expected to go to college and get a degree in something. But unfortunately, that 'something' didn't appeal to either of us. I mean, I've always been a whiz at math. I love numbers—they just work for me. But the idea of being a math teacher, or an accountant, or business major bores me crazy, and I just can't picture myself as a physicist or astronomer. Engineering didn't do it for me either. So now I'm thinking about going to med school.

"I heard about Genevieve showing you the disk. That kind of shocked me, because besides being *verboten*, it's also extremely personal. That whole experience really changed me. Changed the way I thought. The way I felt about so many things, and especially about my parents. About the Elpies and Bluemen, too. It's like—well, like we really did become family by helping each other survive. Lots of things happened on that trip that aren't on the disk.

"It also left me feeling like I needed to do something important with my life. I don't mean important as in somebody famous is important, but somebody who makes a difference in people's lives, or even in just one person's life. Maybe that means giving to a charity, or working with the Red Cross, or something like that. I don't know. But I know I haven't found my calling yet. I know that I will, someday. I just hope I'm not too old to *answer* the call by the time I find out what it is."

He laughed at that, but realized that the rest of the guys had been listening intently—his brothers were looking at him as if they were starting to understand him for the first time.

"Well, geez, that was heavy. Anyway, what I'm doing right now is helping out as a research assistant in a lab. My dad got me interested in that by taking me with him lots of times to the institute he founded. They're working on COPD—chronic obstructive pulmonary diseases. I mean, yeah, that could be really rewarding if I got into it big time, and went back to school. But I'm just not sure at this point. That's it for me. Oh, and I can knock a mosquito out of the air at fifty paces with an arrow."

"He's lying! He can't hit 'em if they're farther than forty."

"Okay, *Brother Enzo,* tell all."

Leaning back on his side of the couch, Enzo began. "Well, of course, I'll start with what you were all wondering. My name is Enzo Andres Uccello, and I am five-feet, five inches and twenty-eight years old. I'm a firefighter. Always wanted to be a firefighter, from the time I was a little boy. And not to brag, but I too, have a rather high IQ— something I really wish had never been tested, because when my parents were informed, in their minds, I immediately became the future doctor or lawyer in the family.

"I scored really high on the MCAT, which I'm sure you all know, but just in case, is the test you have to take to see if you even qualify for med school. My parents were ecstatic. My mom would stay up into the wee hours looking at brochures for medical schools. I almost caved and started to go for it, but in the end, I couldn't do it. I think that was the worst moment of my life—telling my parents that I wanted to be a fireman. Not that they don't respect firefighters. But they had it so deep in their minds and hearts that I'd be rich and famous, that when I told them I was going to follow *my* dream, it just about crushed them. But, they love me, so they got over it. Mostly. Sort of.

"I'm from Boston—can ya tell? I decided I wanted to work some place really different and experience living in a new environment while I was young and single and it was easy to move. That's how I ended up in San Antonio, and meeting your sister. Let's see…I speak Italian, and I can understand a lot of Spanish because of it. Ummm, I took Jiu Jitsu lessons for years, and I'm pretty good at it.

"I like to do almost anything outdoors. I'll play any game I get a chance to, as long as somebody will explain the rules to me first, but I never gamble for money. And I don't drink because I saw several friends get into alcohol early in their lives, along with some other stuff, and it ruined them. Utterly, totally ruined them. Turned me off of it completely. So I just don't.

"Oh, and one of my passions is Chess. Aside from winning your sister's hand, probably my life's greatest achievement so far is—get ready for this, guys—last week, I Beat The Cat!"

He was expecting exuberant congratulations and appropriate awe, since he knew from conversations with Genevieve that the whole family played, and anybody who played knew about the "Beat the Cat Chess Web." He was holding out his arms, palms up, big smile on his wide open mouth, waiting to accept the onslaught of praise and wonder, but nothing happened.

For a moment, the three sat there staring at him, incomprehension on their faces. Then slowly, their heads turned to look at each other, and grins began to form.

Eli put his Coke on the table and leaned forward. "Are you being straight, man?"

"Sure I am. Why would I make up something like that? I've been trying to beat him since I was eight years old." He chuckled and shook his head, thinking back. "When I was a kid, I'd always picture this real cat sitting at a chess board and moving the pieces out there somewhere, playing against me. I thought that was the coolest thing."

The brothers' grins were getting bigger. Colder spoke up then. "I am highly impressed, dude. That cat is the reason I quit playing. I got tired of losing every time, and it seemed like each time I played him, he beat me quicker, the smug little bastard."

Eli nudged Colder with his elbow. "Whoa, bro, I think you're channeling Dad." The brothers chuckled at that, as did Enzo, just to be sociable, even though he didn't get it.

Enzo nodded. "It was like that with me for a lot of years, and then I started getting mad about it and tried to quit for a while. But I kid you not—and this will make me sound sort of obsessive, I realize—I would wake up in the middle of the night, dreaming about chess moves. I'd get up and write them down, and some of them weren't too bad, in theory. I just couldn't back off—it became one of my life's missions to find a way to beat him. I even started reading books on chess."

Jonas yawned and patted his mouth. "Wheee, that must have been exciting."

"You'd be surprised."

"Yeah, I would."

"Well, anyway, it's been taking him longer and longer to beat me the past few years, and last week I finally did it. I won. I still can't believe it. Except for Gen, you guys are the first people I've told. I don't wanna *sound* like I'm bragging, but geez, I wanna brag so bad, I can't stand it. It's just hard to introduce it into a conversation, you know? Like, 'Yes ma'am, the fire's out, and we're checking now to try and find the source of the fire—you know, what started it. And by the way, did I tell you that I beat 'The Cat?'"

They all laughed, and he continued. "It's such a relief to tell you guys—I thought I was going to have to hire somebody to listen to me brag. Like—maybe take a two hour taxi ride, where I've got a captive audience in the poor driver, or maybe I could go to confession where the priest *has* to listen to you. I could confess to the sin of pride, and then expound on the amazing accomplishment that I'm so proud of. And I'm not even Catholic—but he still has to listen, doesn't he? Do you think taking out an ad in the New York Times would be—"

"I think we get the picture, Enzo," Colder broke in.

"Speaking of cats," Eli said, "have you met Ishmael?"

"No, and I'm dying to. I've met Elsie, but she's the only animal, so far. That was a trip—talking to her and having her answer through Genevieve. Just getting me primed to meet the other members of your family."

Eli faced his brothers then, and said, "Yeah, speaking of *cats,* Mom said she's been really worried about Ishmael. For about *a week,* he's been off his feed, and you know how he loves to eat. Yup, started about *a week ago.* She says he's been moping around, doesn't want to *play* and you know he loves to *play*." Wink, nudge, Groucho brows. "He won't discuss the problem with her, and Mom said she's never seen him this depressed. She's even thinking about getting dad to trap him so they can take him to the vet by force, since that's the only way he'll go." Then to Enzo, "How much has our sister told you about Ishmael?"

"Just that he's a real character. Jokes around, kind of a smart ass. That your dad calls him a 'cheeky little bastard,' and it suits him perfectly. But if he's really depressed, and he has human intelligence, a regular vet probably couldn't do anything for him. Wouldn't he need a shrink?"

"Good thinking! I think I'll tell mom that, before she convinces Dad to do something regrettable. I don't think Ishmael would ever forgive either of them if they forced him to the vet's."

Colder stood up then. "Well, *brothers,* it's been real, but I'd like to get a few winks before lunch. Hey, you're all going to Mom's showing tonight, right?"

"Natch."

"Great. Eli, is it okay with you if I bunk here?"

"Wouldn't have it any other way. I just assumed you were planning on it. And this is perfect—I got three fewer kids than usual, so I got three extra beds. Grab a bed and make yourself at home. I'm gonna take a snooze myself. I need to rest my mastication muscles for the evening's repast."

"Aah, quit talking dirty and go to bed."

CHAPTER SEVENTEEN

Intent on getting the last seeds out of the feeder, the bird didn't notice the squirrel trying to scale the pole for the fourth time. Bess had put Squirrel Away on the pole, and no matter how the determined animal approached it, the result was the same. He'd take a flying leap and grab on half-way up the pole, just to slide down again.

Ishmael was watching from the bushes. He knew the furry little rat was unaware of his presence. All he had to do was to time his move for when the thing was in the air, in mid-leap. Crouching down, his rear end began moving slightly, back and forth, winding up for the spring, and his teeth began to chatter in anticipation. The squirrel made its leap, and the cat threw himself through the air, claws outstretched to hook his prey. But with the frenzied, uncanny grace and speed that squirrels possess, his victim saw movement and twisted in mid-air to land on the ground and shoot up a tree faster than the cat could recover.

Damn. He stopped running and yawned, then pretended that he was in this particular spot because it looked like a good place to groom himself. No one was watching him, but this was standard post-screw-up procedure. Never let them think you missed. He washed for a few minutes to make it look believable, and then walked away, so annoyed he could hardly keep from hissing at the grass under his feet.

It was bad enough that he'd never been able to catch one of those demon-spawned rodents, even though they were everywhere. But the other defeat never left his mind. He couldn't stop thinking about the web. Somebody beat him. How was that possible?

With only a few exceptions in the past thirty-four years—and he considered those exceptions flukes, maybe caused by solar flares, or holes in the ozone—he had always come out on top. This guy must be some kind of genius. Or mutant. Or alien. That's right! This could be one of Sarah's macaroon monsters from far, far away, come to humiliate the puny Earthlings with a demonstration of its alien intelligence! But probably not.

For a week, he hadn't been able to think of much else. Maybe he was losing it. Or just getting old. But since he'd been given a human life span, and he'd been only a few years old at the time, he was only in his thirties, in human age. Did they get senile that young? And now he was questioning himself like a human. Before he'd been given Bess' memories to help him understand language, he'd never questioned himself. Why would he? He was a cat, so what was there to ask about? Cats knew everything they needed to.

He'd never been this perturbed and morose. He didn't know how it had happened, but he couldn't make himself even look at the chess screen now. His nerves were so taut that everything made him jump, and when he slept he kept dreaming of that final move, and the horrible realization that he'd lost.

He had to stop this. It was idiotic and annoyingly human. He was, after all, a cat, and he needed to show a little class. He wouldn't be ruled by ridiculous human insecurities. Probably a pound lighter already, since he'd lost his appetite as well, he felt the weight loss. It made him feel unhealthy, and that made him even more irritable. His fur wasn't as sleek as usual, because cats groom the most after they eat. When he didn't eat, he got sloppy and he looked it. That was it. No more. He would eat supper and groom himself back to his former glory, and forget about Chess. Stupid *human* game.

Madelyn had already sent to him about Genevieve's announcement. Home from the States, engaged, and he hadn't even checked out her intended yet. Elsie sent that he smelled like a good one, and her nose was usually right, but really, he was supposed to take a crotch sniff as a character reference?

For a dog, Elsie was okay. And after all these years together, he almost considered her a friend, though he'd never admit it. But dogs were often idiots. They couldn't help it. Sometimes people were, too. So he'd better check this guy out for himself. It was the least he could do for one of the kids. If this one was a loser, better she find out now than later. He'd give him the once over at supper, run a few tests. Give his verdict. They might not like it, but he knew they'd appreciate it in the end.

CHAPTER EIGHTEEN

She couldn't get over his behavior. Simon was usually so friendly and welcoming to people, but today he was acting like a snitty old curmudgeon. Most unbecoming. She started to say something, but then decided to wait. Maybe he'd work it out on his own.

Going through his socks, he couldn't find the exact pair he wanted, and after rummaging through the drawer several times, he let out a muted roar, pulled the drawer out of the dresser, and angrily dumped its whole contents onto the bed. Classic toddler behavior in a sixty-nine year old. And for his finale, he started picking up each pair, pulling them apart to minutely examine the toes, and the socks deemed unworthy were then thrown to the far corners of the room.

"Where are the *damned black ones* with the *little foxes* on the big toe? I need *that* pair!" His face was red, and he was almost shouting.

"I threw them away. They had holes in the heel."

"You did *what?* What right did you have to touch my socks?" he asked loudly, glaring at her.

She slowly turned her body to face him, put her hands on her hips, and raised her eyebrows. She kept her voice calm, but the challenge was clear. "The right that being the one who *always* puts them away *gives* me." Then with obvious annoyance, "What is your problem, Simon?" She picked a pair of socks up from the floor and tossed it over her shoulder without looking. "My gosh, you're acting like a spoiled brat! Who cares what socks you wear? Nobody sees them anyway."

"*I care!* I'll know that…I'll know that the socks that would have worked best…" he began, but the longer he talked, the more asinine he sounded, even to himself. He'd never cared about his socks before and he didn't particularly now, either.

"Are you done? Is it safe to talk to you?"

He looked down at all the socks on the bed, swept them to the floor with one arm, and then sat on the bed to let his himself fall back on it, his arms flung out to either side. Letting out a huge sigh, he said in a barely discernable voice, "Sorry."

She launched herself onto the bed to stretch out beside him, but on her belly, so she could look at him while they talked. The bouncing of the bed when she landed only served to irritate him more. "Positivity" could be highly overrated at times, he thought.

Raising herself on her elbows, she peered down into his face, which showed her that he was still in full-on-crabby-mode. At least she had him down in bed, where they communicated the best.

She'd often wondered why that was, since it had nothing to do with sex. Somehow, when they were lying down, stretched out together, their defenses toppled and the world seemed to narrow to include just the two of them. Or maybe it was because their closeness made them speak quietly, and the quiet made them listen closer. Whatever the reason—it worked for them. Most of the major decisions in their life together had been made in bed.

"Okay, Simon, this has nothing to do with your socks and we both know it. You're still upset about Genevieve getting engaged, aren't you?"

"Aren't you?"

"No, I'm happy for her. Simon, she loves him, and there's something about the way he looks at her and really listens when she talks—like he just assumes that whatever she has to say matters—that tells me he values her. The whole package. I think they're a wonderful match."

"But—but—he's so short!"

"So what? Does being a behemoth make a man a good catch?"

"Excuse me? Are you referring to me?"

"No. You're only five inches taller than me. She's seven inches taller than him. Being tall doesn't make her any less feminine, and being short doesn't make him any less masculine. But why am I telling you this? You know that. This is still about losing your daughter."

"But—how will they dance?" he demanded crossly, as if this were a pressing issue.

She laughed and slapped him on the chest. "That's their problem, isn't it? You don't care about that. Maybe they don't even go dancing. I don't seem to recall our daughter ever pining away about missing any dance, do you?"

He didn't answer, but instead, seemed to be studying the light fixture on the ceiling with intense concentration. That task finished, he went straightaway into checking the seams on the hem of the comforter they were lying on, pulling it up from the side of the bed and running over it carefully with one finger as he peered at it. When he couldn't stall any longer, he looked back at the ceiling instead of at Bess.

"But why didn't she tell us about him? I just feel so…so blindsided. Almost betrayed," he added vehemently, throwing one hand straight up in anger with those last words, but then letting it fall slowly, palm up, in a gesture of frustration. "I know these days it doesn't happen much, but I'd always pictured myself screening her dates and culling out the bad seeds before she even left the house with them."

Bess looked down at him and shook her head when he finally met her eyes. "That would all be well and good if she weren't an adult, and she was still living in our house. But she's flown the coop, honey. That's it. We're chickless. She's already out of our hands. The last thing we want to do is to put a wedge between her and her future, and the way it looks to me, he's her future."

He was back to looking at the ceiling and now he was gesturing his annoyance with both hands. "She still should have called us, or emailed us. Good grief, we email all the time, and what about all the texting? She could have told us *something.*" Then his tone changed from anger to hurt, as his voice lost volume. "We weren't important enough for her to bother telling us about this little matter?"

"Simon, do you remember that couple we met at the gallery years ago—Stan and Louise?" He nodded. "Well, they'd been trying for years to have a baby, and when she finally conceived, it was the biggest, most wonderful news of their lives together, but they didn't tell anyone, not even their folks, until she was about five months along."

"And your point is?"

"The reason they didn't tell anybody was because it was so profoundly important to them. They wanted to keep it to themselves, and cherish the news until they were sure the pregnancy would come to term, so that if it didn't, they wouldn't have to explain to everybody and put themselves through that pain over and over again. And they also said they didn't want to 'jinx' it by talking about it before they knew everything was going to work out."

He gave her a longsuffering look. "I feel an analogy coming on."

She ignored that and continued. "I think maybe Genevieve felt the same way about falling for Enzo. She's never been in love before. Coming to that point in your life—meeting that person that you can finally say those words about, and actually consider spending your whole life with— geez, what could be more personal than that? And you don't want to talk about it all starry-eyed, and then have everything bottom out on you. How embarrassing and painful would that be? Besides, that way she wouldn't have to deal with all your crap about his being short until they were too attached for your interference."

This last was said with a poke to his ribs. He rolled his eyes and sighed. "Have I ever told you how I hate it when you're all—wise? And even worse, when you're right?"

She smiled down at him. "Only almost every time. Which is quite a lot, since I am. Usually. You know who you remind me of when you're grousing about Enzo?"

"Don't say it. Don't you dare." He sat up now, shaking a finger at her, as she opened her mouth wide in an exaggerated beginning.

"Just like my d—" He clamped one hand over her mouth and took her down to the mattress, with her saying a muffled "--ad" through his hand. He loomed over her threateningly, still covering her mouth.

"I'm going to take my hand away slowly now, if you promise you won't say those words. If you do, the gag and duct tape come out. Are you going to be quiet?"

She did her best to look frightened, and held up both hands in surrender.

"All right. Behave yourself and nobody gets hurt. Just remember, behemoths don't mess around." He took his hand off slowly, and she lay there with her lips pressed firmly together.

"There, isn't that better?"

"MY DAD, MY DAD, MY DAD," she screamed, and rolled to the other side of the bed, but not fast enough to get away. He grabbed her arm and pulled her back down, clamping his hand over her mouth again. He put his face a few inches above hers.

"Such horrible words from those lovely lips. I hate you." Then he let go of her mouth and said, "I love you," and kissed her.

"You lied," she said, when he came up for air. "Behemoths do too mess around."

Just then there was a knock on the door, and Genevieve called out, "Is everything okay in there?"

Simon pushed himself up on his forearms and Bess gave him a quick peck before answering. "Everything's fine, sweetheart. We were just discussing behemoths, and things got a little heated. Everything's okay."

There was silence from the other side of the door while their daughter tried to process this information, and then they heard, "Whatever," and her footsteps moving down the hall.

CHAPTER NINETEEN

The cognac was perfect. He'd just cleaned up after another hunt. Unfortunately, this victim had only been a tiger, and tigers were depressingly easy to come by. He didn't even bother having the heads mounted anymore. But the hunt had provided him with the necessary rush he frequently needed to get through the day. Only after a killing did he feel fulfilled and able to relax. That's when a cognac tasted best.

Resting his feet on an ottoman, he thought about tonight. He'd decided to go uninvited to Bess Sayers' showing of her new body of work. A good number of the townsfolk were invited, and he knew the Sayers wouldn't be so rude as to have him booted out. Even if they wanted to, it would make too much of a scene, and ruin the evening

Bess had made a name for herself with her paintings, but he found her work unexceptional. There certainly was no accounting for tastes, but if she could make a fortune with those trivial pieces, he supposed she should be considered a success, of sorts. He liked successful women. For a while.

He thought tonight would be an excellent time to make his move. He had slowly gotten her used to seeing him as a courteous, nonthreatening gentleman who admired her from afar.

He could picture the scene as it would play out tonight. She would have had a few drinks, perhaps, and feel heady with the compliments and all the sucking up rampant at these types of occasions. Simon would probably be bored and inattentive, after having been to who knew how many of these interminable affairs.

Then *he* would appear, handsome and dashing, and give her the type of attention that he knew women craved. The idea of propositioning her with her husband in the room was most appealing. They could arrange a tryst, and then later, after it was over, he would arrange for someone to "spill the beans" to Simon.

The man would be devastated, and even more so when Arthur casually threw his precious wife away, as a mere evening's dalliance. Intriguing as she was, he really had no interest in her. He preferred young, blonde, and bosomy, and sadly, Mrs. Sayers was none of those things. He smiled as he thought of Simon being humbled; at the look he would have on his face and the pain he'd feel in his very soul when he heard the news.

My, the cognac was tasting better all the time.

CHAPTER TWENTY

At three-thirty sharp, lunch was served. Or *lupper,* as the kids called it, when it fell between lunch and supper time. Although Bess couldn't convince her parents not to cook for the whole tribe, she had no problem at all in convincing them to let her have people in to do the clean-up. Once the food was on, Sarah and Angus could relax for the day and spend some quality time *with* the family, instead of just feeding them. Bess could only do this until the Elpies arrived, however, and then the whole family would pitch in after dinner.

She hadn't been raised wealthy, and neither she nor the rest of the family had ever put much stock in formality. Meals were self-served in the kitchen, buffet-style, out of the pots on the stove and from bowls and plates on the island. Ishmael was eating his food in the corner of the kitchen, trying to decide when he should introduce himself to the newcomer, when the mass of humans milling about convinced him that later would prevent his premature death by trampling.

When they seated themselves at the long table in the dining room, Simon insisted on sitting next to Enzo, making everyone *but* Enzo, a bit uneasy. The four kids were seated across and down the table from him, and the two eight year olds stared openly. The girls, at twelve and fifteen, had better manners and would only glance up surreptitiously when they thought they could do so without being noticed. None had met him yet, and none had been told of the height disparity between him and their aunt.

Instead of sitting beside their men, Bess and Genevieve had both chosen to sit across from them, in order to keep an eye on Simon, and to more easily converse with Enzo. Hiram and Gisella were between their daughter and son. Once all were seated, Angus said grace, and everybody dug in. The expected "ohs," "oohs," and "aahs" exploded spontaneously from nearly every mouth, and even Simon seemed distracted from his previous negativity.

Nobody spoke for the first five minutes or so, other than to compliment the chefs, and then out of the blue, Aluin blurted out, "Wow, for a grown-up man, you're pretty short!"

"*ALUIN!*" his father exclaimed.

Enzo just laughed, and held up his hand to prevent Eli from taking his son outside for a talk on manners. He never minded statements like that from children.

"As a matter of fact, I am."

Viola took on a scholarly attitude and proceeded to enlighten the boy. "Aluin, a lot of famous people in history were short. Napoleon was short, and—"

"*And* he was a megalomaniac," Simon added.

"Dad!" Genevieve glared over at him.

"*Simon…*" Bess' radar was up now.

With a look of total innocence, he took a bite of steak and spoke around it. "I'm just giving some historical background."

Enzo nodded at Simon in feigned appreciation. "I like history. In fact, Aluin, history tells us about a lot of great people who were considered short. Like Alexander the Great, Mahatma Gandhi, Ben-Gurion, Martin Luther King, Jr., Beethoven, Isaac Newton—"

"Had your little 'short list' all prepared did you?" Simon interjected, to the glares of his daughter and wife.

"Oh, I've had that down since junior high. There are *so many* names on the list, that kids would get bored with listening and decide to drop the whole 'short' thing. Came in remarkably handy."

"Good for you," Simon said, sullenly.

Hiram reached for the salt and pepper, focusing his eyes on Simon rather than Enzo as he spoke. "That was very mature thinking for a kid that age. There'd be a lot less violence in public schools these days if more people would react with their brains, like you did, instead of their fists. Your parents must have been proud of you for that."

"Well, since I'm taller than my mom, and my dad's only an inch taller than me—"

"No way!" shouted Duncan in disbelief.

Then he jerked around to look at Gisella, saying, "Hey, Mom, watch your feet! You kicked me really hard just now." She smiled up at the table and then turned to her son with eyes wide and lips sealed, staring until he finally got the message.

"What I meant was—that's really interesting." Once he understood the kick was a warning, he realized he'd better think about his wording if he ever wanted to use that leg again.

"Both my parents had years of experience with people who liked to embarrass and bully. My dad always had some great comebacks, but he also taught me that it was better not to get nasty." He looked at Simon as he continued. "Because sometimes the people who harassed you were just *really ignorant*, and after they got to know you, you might end up being friends."

Gisella subtly patted her son's arm and gave him a slight nod. "What a commendable outlook. Your father must be a very wise man."

"He has his moments."

After sitting through an entire minute which seemed like hours of his dad's stares, Aluin spoke up again. "Uh, I'm sorry I was rude. I didn't mean that short people were wimps or anything. Sir," he added at the last, when Eli's eyebrows shot up expectantly.

"Whoa," he answered, laughing again. "I'm not used to having anybody 'sir' me."

"That's because they can't tell you're a grown-up," Simon remarked quietly. The three brothers stared open mouthed at their dad, and then started cracking up, shaking their heads, but their sister and mother were not amused.

"Sorry," he mumbled.

Bess slammed her napkin down on the table, and started to stand, but Enzo shook his head and pleaded with his eyes for her to sit.

"Please, Mrs. Sayers—"

"Bess."

"Thank you, Bess. I appreciate it, but you don't need to protect me from Simon." He turned to him, and asked, "If I may call you Simon?"

"Be my guest." *In another country, preferably.*

"Thanks, Simon. I'm not sure why you have a bee up your—in your bonnet, but I imagine that it's partly because you had no warning, and it's a big shock, thinking about losing your daughter. Which of course, you won't be. You'll just have a new son that doesn't eat as much." That won an appreciative smile from Genevieve and a thumbs up from Eli.

Knowing that he looked like a complete jackass, but trying not to, Simon smiled at Enzo and nodded his head graciously. "Wonderful. You know I've just been teasing you to make you feel like part of the family."

Jonas "tsked" loudly and huffed, shaking his head at him for trying such a lame excuse. Genevieve continued to glare at him and he didn't dare meet Bess' eyes.

Tired of these less than subtle attacks on Enzo, Genevieve decided to take matters into her own hands and go on the offensive.

"Speaking of *not* being a wimp, Aluin, did you know that Enzo is a firefighter?"

"No! Really, Mr—"

"Enzo, please."

"No kidding, Enzo? Wow, you must be really brave. Will you tell us some stories after we eat?"

"Sure, be happy to."

"And on those lines, Enzo had been thinking at one time of becoming a smoke jumper, one of those firefighters who parachute into areas with forest fires, to try and put them out."

"No way! That's wicked dangerous!"

"Yes way, and he looked up the physical requirements and started training for them. One of those is that they have to run three miles in mountainous terrain, in under forty-five minutes, carrying forty-five pound packs on their backs. And he did that, every time he had a day off from his regular job." She turned to look at her father. "Do you think you could do that, Dad?"

He wiped his mouth daintily with his napkin. "Don't know. Never tried it. Maybe if I trained for it—"

"Sure he could do it," Enzo broke in. "Look at the shape he's in!" He reached over and started to squeeze Simon's bicep, but at the look he received from him, he dropped his hand and continued. "And you said he runs ten miles once a week. Pretty impressive there, guy!"

Guy? He smiled tightly and nodded his head.

"Are you always this agreeable?" he asked Enzo, with a smile.

"Try to be."

He looked at Genevieve. "And you *like* that?"

"I *love* that," she answered, glaring thermonuclear warheads at him.

Twelve year old Simone got her courage up and said, "Enzo, I love your accent. I think it's really cute." The brothers "oohed" at that, making the poor child blush and sink into her chair a little.

"Yeah, I think your accent's pretty funky," Duncan chimed in.

Enzo laughed and grinned at each of them. "Hey, thanks. You know, I think your Grandpa Simon's accent is pretty cute and funky, too." Now it was Bess' turn to snort milk up her nose, and that set all the kids to laughing.

Simon fumed but kept his peace. Temporarily.

They made it all the way to dessert without Simon or the children saying anything else obnoxious. The diners had their cobbler with whipped cream in front of them, chowing down happily. With the sounds of everybody eating, he thought he could get by with it, but after his previous comments, all ears were tuned to anything that came out of his mouth.

With his head bowed over his cobbler, and eyes glued to his spoon full of whipped cream, Simon leaned closer to Enzo, and half-whispered, "If you hurt my daughter, I'll kill you."

Angus spit whipped cream on the table and then started laughing for all he was worth, and the various cries of "DAD, SIMON, Whoa, Dad, Chill out, Dad, *Oh, Simon,*" and, "I can't believe Grandpa just said that!" sounded around the table.

One last time, Enzo held up his hand for peace as he looked across at Genevieve, who had her hands covering her eyes, shaking her head and moaning, "Mom, do something!"

Everyone got quiet, as he slowly put his napkin down and stood up to face Simon.

In a broad, sweeping gesture, he threw his right arm out and swung it back around, slapping his hand over his heart and holding it there. He looked down at the red-faced man in front of him, and in his most dramatic voice, solemnly declared, "Simon, if I hurt your daughter, I'd have to kill *myself*."

Silence for a moment and then Eli began pounding on the table, and all three brothers shouted in unison, "GOOD ANSWER, GOOD ANSWER!"

Simon looked at him and said quietly, "That was the *right* answer."

Genevieve looked at Enzo with shining eyes, and just nodded. Then she looked at her dad and did the same, but in a shorter version and with an entirely different meaning, as her mom put her arm around her shoulders.

Completely out of ammunition, and feeling like a caricature of the "evil in-law," Simon was about to stand up and excuse himself, when Colder held up his hand to stop him. He announced loudly, to be sure his voice carried into the kitchen, "Hey everybody, he didn't want to brag about it, but guess what? Enzo beat 'The Cat' last week!"

A weird, ascending mewling noise, quickly reaching a crescendo in a yowl, came from the direction of the kitchen, and a wild black mass of fur, with every single hair sticking straight out, came bouncing into the dining room on tiptoe to ricochet off walls and windows, spitting, hissing, running the length of the room and back, and then skedaddling out the back door.

The humans in the room screamed and jerked back in their chairs at the spectacular surprise performance, but the apparition disappeared before they could react much more.

Enzo stood up so fast that his chair fell over. "*Che cavolo!* What *was* that?"

Jonas laughed and tilted his head at him. "You should know, dude, you've been playing him since you were eight."

"What?"

"Enzo, that was 'The Cat.'"

##

"Ishmael!"

"Uh, hello, Mr. Cat, Sir?" Enzo and Genevieve had been looking for him for over an hour. "Genny, you're not putting me on? That was really 'The Cat?'"

"I kid you not. And as you could probably tell by that little display, he doesn't seem to be taking defeat well."

"*That's* what they were talking about. Your brothers, whom I like a lot, by the way, were saying that he hasn't been eating well or sleeping for the past week. I guess I'm the cause of that."

"Well, geez, don't feel guilty about it. Somebody was going to beat him sooner or later. At least this way, he won't have to wonder about who it was. He can hate you in person."

"Thanks. Hey, what is that there, under the bird feeder?"

Ishmael had no idea why he'd finally settled here, at the spot of his latest humiliation. Maybe he was just a closet masochist. Watching with half-lidded eyes as Genevieve and Enzo approached him, he decided not to sulk, but to meet this head on. He walked towards Enzo and just before reaching him, turned his back to his leg, with his tail straight up in the air. Genevieve saw his tail twitch, and screamed, "NO!" lunging over to shove him off target in the nick of time.

Now he'd sulk. He sat down with his back to them.

Not used to talking with cats, Enzo stood there until Genevieve gave him a little nudge forward. He took the hint, walked around to face Ishmael, and then sat on the ground in front of him.

He shook his head, holding one hand against his chest. "Mr. Cat, I cannot believe you would want to pee on my leg. I'm your greatest admirer! For the last twenty years, I have tried to beat you. I've stayed up all night thinking of how I could do it. When I was in high school, I'd be trying to study for tests, and chess moves would start taking over my brain. Beating you became one of my life's ambitions. You just—well, geez, you don't know what an honor it is for me to meet you."

Ishmael looked at Genevieve and sent, "What's wrong with his mouth?"

"Nothing. He's from Boston. They all talk like that."

He looked at her intently, just to build the suspense, and then sent, "Why?"

"They just do. Drop it."

"What?"

"I'm just answering him. He thought your mouth was injured. I explained about Boston."

"Oh man, this is too weird."

"You'll get used to it."

"So, Mr. Cat—"

"Call him Ishmael."

"I was just trying to show my respect, Gen."

"I know that, but he thinks it's peculiar. Don't give him anything to pick on."

She looked from Enzo to Ishmael, at an untranslated sending, and retorted "Yes, you would."

"Is he done 'talking' to you? May I continue?"

"Sure."

"Well, Mr. Ishmael—"

"Enzo!"

"Okay, okay. Well, Ishmael, here's how it goes. You're an icon to me. Greatest player ever, taking on the whole world, any comers, all from your home screen, forever shrouded in mystery. You are the epitome of cool, man. Just because I beat you one time, doesn't mean you've been humiliated. Far from it—you've inspired me to hone my skills and study, and strive to be my best. The greatest players make the greatest teachers. You've made me thirst for greatness."

Genevieve started laughing, and he looked at her for translation. "He thinks you're laying it on a little thick, but gets the idea. He sort of forgives you and wants you to go away now."

Feeling suddenly chilled, he realized he'd been sweating. "Oh boy, that's a relief. I couldn't stand to think I'd made an enemy of 'The Cat,' after all these years of idolizing him." He started to get to his feet, but instead turned back to Ishmael and held up one hand. "High five, buddy?"

The only move Ishmael made in response was to look at Genevieve to translate.

Genevieve looked at Enzo and gave an apologetic smile as she relayed, "In your dreams."

CHAPTER TWENTY-ONE

"Before we walk out of this room, Simon, I want your word of honor that you are done, finished, over, with *all* of this garbage. I thought you'd resigned yourself to the situation. And I don't care *what* the situation is, I will *not* sit idly by and watch you try to humiliate or bully a guest in this house. You should be ashamed of yourself. I've always admired the fact that you were a gentleman, but tonight you shamed both of us with your behavior.

"Genevieve told me some of the things his family said to her, and I was thinking what a relief it must be for her to know that *her* family would never act like that."

Bess was furious, especially since Enzo had rushed out after Ishmael, and Genevieve had rushed after him before Simon could make a formal apology. What would he think of them? It was enough that he knew they had regular visits from aliens, had named his fiancée after a cat, and their other children after lizard people. But for him to think they were *rude*?

"One good thing came out of your little performance this afternoon—we got to witness first-hand how much class *he* has. At the same time that I was feeling ashamed of you, I was feeling proud of *him* for the way he handled himself."

Simon sat in a chair in their bedroom, head down, his hands clasped in front of him, taking it all in silence.

"Well? No response? No plea of innocence?"

He sighed and looked up at her. "I have nothing to say, because I have no excuse. You're right. I shamed all of us. I thought I'd resigned myself too, but the minute I saw him, all the irritation and hurt came back, and I just wanted to get him out of there—out of here. When I'd say something, I could hear myself, and how awful I was being, but I just couldn't stop. He really must think I'm a horrible person. No way would they ever want to live in a house on the estate now, with him dreading being around me even for a meal. I'm so sorry."

Seeing him looking truly beaten and remorseful, she couldn't stay angry with him. Or at least not *as* angry. The impulse to comfort him was too ingrained. She walked over and put her hands on his shoulders. "Simon, you're the best man I've ever known, and I want Enzo to see *that* man. And you know your daughter wants that even more. I think she's been hurt much worse by this than he has. She believes, or *did* believe, before dinner, that you're a great man, and she's always been so proud of you. For her to bring her future husband here to meet us, and have you act like this—well, I'm sure she's sorry they came. I know she's crushed, embarrassed, and terribly disappointed in you. I only hope you can regain her respect. You need to go and apologize to both of them. Individually."

He took one of her hands, kissed it, and then stood up and headed for the door.

"Wish me luck. If I'm not back in two hours, I've decided to do the honorable thing and jump in the river."

Bess looked at him with a hint of a smile. "And if you haven't accomplished your mission by then, I'll be on the bank to hand you an anvil."

As he walked down the hall to Genevieve's room, he thought about the fact that he'd already apologized twice—once at the door and once at the table, and obviously, he hadn't been sincere either time. Well, three's the charm. This time his apology would come from the heart. He knocked on her door and announced himself, and she took her sweet time before telling him to come in.

She was sitting on her bed, her back against the headboard, looking at him expectantly. Raised eyebrows, lips in a tight line. He closed the door behind him, pulled up a chair from her vanity, straddled it, and sat down in front of her. She said nothing, waiting for him to start. He cleared his throat and looked around the room for a second before finally getting up the courage to speak to this clearly hostile audience.

"There are no words to excuse the way I've behaved. I was so stunned at the news that you were engaged, and upset and hurt that you hadn't told us anything about him—that you hadn't shared that part of your life with us—that I just flew off at the mouth and behaved like an absolute boor. I know that I embarrassed you. I was incredibly rude to your fiancé, who also happens to be our guest. I just love you so much, and I felt that I didn't have a chance to guide or protect you or any of those things that fathers are supposed to do when suitors come for their daughters. And part of it, if I'm really honest with myself, I guess, is that—I know I'm losing you. Please forgive me."

He was suddenly so embarrassed about everything that he couldn't even look at her. He had a mental picture of himself, could hear the words he'd said—how ridiculous, petty, and small he'd sounded. He felt his face burning at the memory.

She saw him turn red as he put his head down to avoid her eyes, and like her mom, was a sucker for remorse. She crawled across the bed and then stood up on her knees in front of him, putting her hands on his shoulders, just like her mom had done.

"Oh, Daddy. You were such an enormous jerk. But I guess I sort of understand. Doesn't mean you're *excused* for being hateful, but you're forgiven."

Then they both leaned forward, and as they hugged, the only thought in his mind was, *She called me "Daddy."*

#

The door to Eli's was opened with his first knock. It was Jonas, and after one look at his father's expression, he nodded his head knowingly. "Come in. I'll go get him, and the rest of us will take off for a while."

"Thanks."

Jonas quietly went to his brothers' rooms first, and he heard him say softly, "It's Dad. Let's split for a few." No discussion. None was needed. When his sons passed him as they went out the door, Colder gave him a pat on the back and Jonas punched his arm. Eli went a little further, and whispered, "He's a good guy, Dad. Let him know the *real* you. Love you."

His vision went a little blurry for a second, and he shook his head to clear it, wondering how he'd ended up with such great kids. Enzo came out then, and Simon asked, "Can we sit?"

He nodded silently and took a place on the couch, with Simon facing him from the other side.

He looked at this young man who was going to be family for the rest of his life, and again, he was almost too ashamed to speak. His face reddened, and he opened his mouth to start, but to his surprise, Enzo spoke first.

"Hey, Simon. Well—by the look on your face, I assume you're here to apologize, and by the color of your face, I presume you're really embarrassed about everything. And you should be, 'cause you were a real shit."

Simon was slightly taken aback by that, but since it was true, he didn't argue.

"*But,* since my family acted the same way with Gen, I guess this was just our trial by fire. The one thing this ought to prove to you though, is that I love her, because if I didn't, I would have gotten up and walked out. I've heard little wisecracks about my height my whole adult life, and though they don't intimidate me, they do make me think less of the person spouting them.

"But with you I don't feel that way. I know that even though, yes, you were a shit, the bottom line is—you're afraid for your daughter, because you really don't know me from Adam, and you're also rocked by the sudden idea of losing her."

He needn't have worried about finding the right words. He'd just sit here and let this guy do all the talking—he'd nod his head sincerely a couple of times, and maybe not have to speak at all.

"You know, Simon, I want to be a dad someday. And now, when I look at Genevieve, I can see our children in my mind. I see a little girl that looks like her, or maybe like Bess, and a little guy that takes after me. And when I look at that little girl, and put myself in your position, with some Bozo from out of the blue walking in my house and saying, 'By the way, I'm marrying your daughter,' well, I think I might have reacted the same as you. Maybe I'd be an even bigger shit, though I don't know how that would be possible.

"The other reason I can't *not* respect you, is that Genny showed me the disk—something I won't ever forget. And I tell you now, Simon, father of Genevieve, that I will love my family the way that you love yours. Whatever it takes, for the rest of my life, I will love your daughter like that, and our children, *your* grandchildren, will have a father who will always give everything he's got—even himself, to protect them."

Hearing that, every fear and misgiving he'd had, vanished in a heartbeat. When he looked at the person across from him, he actually *saw* him: the man that his daughter loved, his soon to be son-in-law and father of his future grandchildren. And he could see by his eyes that he'd meant every word he said.

They sat and stared at each other and then they stood, met mid-room, and shook hands. When they parted, Simon nodded and said quietly, "I couldn't ask for more than that."

CHAPTER TWENTY-TWO

"Okay, I guess I'm finally ready."

Simon looked up the stairs at her voice, and inhaled sharply. She could still wow him after all these years. Cobalt blue dress with three-quarter sleeves, of a material with just a hint of iridescence, a scooped neck to accentuate the contrast to her fair skin, and sparkles of dark blue on her chest and at her ears. The dress was slightly snug at the waist and hips, and flowing from the mid-thigh into a slight flair that allowed for a feminine swirl of material a few inches above her ankles. Her dark, wavy hair was done up in a simple twist, with a few strands loosened to float alongside her amber eyes and high cheekbones. She wore only mascara to accentuate her eyes, but her lips, which she usually left bare, tonight were a rich, deep burgundy.

He smiled as he watched her descend, and when she reached the bottom, he held out his hand for hers. When she took it, he looked her up and down one more time appreciatively, and shook his head. "Simply stunning."

Letting out an embarrassed little laugh, she flushed with pleasure. Then she took note of him: dressed in a black tux, trim, tall, his broad shoulders accentuated by his jacket, big smile above a strong jaw. "Mmm-mmm, Mr. Sayers, very nice. I was wondering—if you're not busy after the showing tonight—"

The door opened, and Enzo and the brothers walked in. "Wow, Mom, you look gorgeous!" Colder exclaimed. Then, "Ooh, Dad, right out of GQ!" Simon held out his arms and twirled around for the admiring crowd, while Bess beamed at the compliments.

The brothers all had on their best suits, but Enzo had rented a tux, since Genevieve had told him she was going formal for the night. He was the last to enter, and when he saw the two, his eyes went wide and he threw his hands up in the air. "Oh, mama mia, what a vision! I was struck speechless there for a millisecond. Oh, and you look beautiful too, Bess."

They all laughed, and everyone in the room could tell by the quality of Simon's laugh, that something had changed. There was no more hostility or tension in his voice—and could there actually be—a little warmth? When Bess heard that, she felt such relief that she kissed Simon lightly on the lips, sending to him how happy it made her to feel the change. Then she turned around and gave a hug and peck on the cheek to "all of her handsome sons," and included Enzo, to his great delight.

Genevieve appeared at the top of the stairs, in a forest green, cowl necked, sleeveless gown of a flowing, satiny material. It clung to every curve until just past the waist, and then fell loosely, almost to her ankles, skirt rippling like water with every little movement. Part of her wild red curls were piled high near the back of her head, with half of her hair hanging loose in a fiery mass to a few inches below her shoulders. She looked like a Grecian statue.

Everyone heard a gasp, and then, "Oh, Principessa! Cosi bella!" They were all a little surprised by the emotion in Enzo's voice. When Bess and Simon saw how affected he was by the sight of their daughter in her gown, they turned to each other and nodded. Oh yeah, he was "The One."

Gliding down the stairs, Genevieve saw his look, and basked in it. Then she returned the same, as she beheld him in a tux for the first time. He went to the foot of the stairs and held out his hand for hers. When she gave it, he bowed and kissed it, saying, "Just beautiful," as he stood back up.

"Well, I don't know about everybody else, but suddenly, I'm feeling a little nauseated," Colder proclaimed loudly. His brothers started laughing and his mom slapped the top of his head. Gently, of course. For a slap.

Genevieve looked a little embarrassed, but Enzo laughed and said loudly, "Jealousy rears its ugly head!

Someday you too, may have a beauty to grace your side, Colder. But I doubt it." Laughter, arm punches. Enzo thought it amazing that a day starting out like this one had turned into one of his best ever.

Simon clapped his hands and went into command mode. "Okay, is everybody ready to roll? Genevieve and Enzo, you ride with us, guys, you're going in Eli's car, and all the kids are riding with Hiram and Gisella, right? Oh, and Genevieve, Elsie sent not to worry about Lola. She's going to hang with her while she's here. Let's get moving, then."

##

The rest of the family stayed behind, for various reasons of their own.

They loved their daughter dearly, and had always been impressed with her talent, but there were only so many of these "hoity-toity" affairs they could take. When they'd come back to the house from their fourth showing, many years ago, after complimenting Bess on her organization, presentation, and the quality of her work, Angus had announced that he'd rather be eaten alive by raccoons than go to another showing. Sarah had smiled sweetly, but nodded her head in agreement.

Knowing her father, Bess had been expecting this announcement for some time, though she'd been hoping for kinder wording. She'd only invited her parents when they were staying with them, and then only because she'd have felt rude in not doing so. She was fully aware that the showings were not their idea of fun. Not hers either, for that matter, but something she had to go through for the sake of her business. She customarily invited a few other artists to exhibit their work along with hers, and she knew that they were counting on these showings to give their careers a boost, as well.

Gisella's "real" parents, Viola and Tom Allbright, who served as caretakers and managers of the estate, were in the United States visiting family for a month, and catching up with all they had left behind in order to reunite with their "daughter," thirty-five years before.

Ishmael, sadly, had no interest in art. The dogs stayed home because it was too difficult to explain to guests why the two would go from picture to picture, as if they were studying form and style, and then would turn and stare at each other as if mentally discussing the same. Which they were. Lola would only have been able to see ankles, and sniffing was the only art form she understood. Truth be told, they were happy to stay home with Angus and Sarah, where they would be the recipients of numerous forbidden treats.

##

The evening had been going even better than she'd hoped. There was a larger turnout than usual, and a wealthy financier who had come twice before was to be in attendance. He was building himself a mansion and was looking for paintings to complement each room. He'd come to two previous showings, and had purchased two paintings each time. When he'd accepted her invitation for this showing, he'd hinted that he might be interested in a much larger purchase if she'd done anything new that appealed to him. When she saw him walk in, she gave a little gasp of excitement. Simon put a hand on her shoulder and whispered, "Three's the charm."

Simon and the rest of the family didn't usually stay with Bess during these occasions, so that she'd be free to welcome her guests and speak with potential buyers and those who simply admired her work. Wandering about, the brothers and their dad would spend the evening eating, tasting the wine, admiring the different works displayed, and greeting the friends and acquaintances who attended.

Occasionally, Jonas and Colder, the latter in particular, would spy an unattached young woman and strike up a conversation, hopefully ending with an exchange of phone numbers.

The children loved these events because, according to Duncan, they always had "fantastic snackers."' Because she knew they looked forward so to them, Bess made sure the "snackers" that were served were always kid-friendly. After scarfing as many as they could, the youngsters were allowed to go upstairs to play cards in the comfortably furnished sitting room just off the second floor gallery.

He'd been having a pleasant talk with one of his friends from town, when Simon saw Arthur Worthington step through the door. He lost track of the conversation instantly, and with his apologies, excused himself and headed over to greet his old "friend."

Arthur saw him coming, and met him with a smile and an extended hand. Simon shook his hand, but couldn't quite force a smile. "Arthur, I didn't know you liked art. In fact, I didn't even know you'd been invited tonight," he said quietly.

Shaking his head and looking apologetic, Arthur returned, in a much louder voice, "I must ask your forgiveness, Simon. You're correct. There was no invitation extended to me, but as I see your wife about town quite often, and we always have such pleasant conversations, I was sure she wouldn't mind if I attended."

Still gripping his hand after the shake, and holding Arthur's elbow with his other hand, just in case he needed to escort him out the door, he looked up and saw Bess watching them worriedly. She gave a small smile and nodded. Knowing that any kind of row or unpleasantness would ruin the evening for her, he nodded back and released his hold on the other man.

"Well, Arthur, I'm sure you're right. Make yourself at home. You'll be welcome as long as you behave yourself." Simon gave him a toothy smile then, which Arthur correctly interpreted as a snarl, slapped his arm a tiny bit too hard, and walked away.

Seething, Arthur managed to keep an almost pleasant expression on his face as he watched Simon stroll across the room. That bastard, talking to him like he might to a naughty child. Well, he'd see who was smiling at the end of the evening. *Ah, there she is. Goodness yes, normally striking, but tonight, gorgeous. Could she really be in her sixties?*

He wandered over to the painting she was standing beside, and pretended to study it while she explained the variation of colors to a young couple who'd stopped to admire the piece. When the two finally thanked her and walked on to the next exhibit, he quickly took their place.

"Ah, Bess, what a delight you are tonight. I knew you were lovely, but I never realized what a beauty you were." He reached down then, took her hand, and gallantly kissed the back of it. She shook her head and laughed, and saw Simon staring at them with raised eyebrows.

Jonas was the first of the brothers to notice Arthur, and he signaled the others over. "Hey guys, don't look now, but isn't that the dude that Dad warned us about? Don't be obvious, just glance over to your right, near the door to the next room, and don't look at the same time."

Both turned together to stare at the man, and then looked back at Jonas. "Yeah, that's him."

"*Geez*, you guys are about a subtle as a moose in heat! Look at Dad, trying to be all cool and not stare, but he's watching, too. Come on. Let's go give him some moral support."

Bess was politely making small talk with Arthur, but she was getting more and more annoyed. She had no illusions as to his intentions, and assumed that he wanted to seduce her, not because he found her attractive, but to humiliate her husband. Being married was rather a big deal for her, and she thought it insulting to be hit on by someone who knew that she was.

If she believed that a man was truly attracted to her, then she felt a little sorry for the misguided person, and tried to be as gentle as possible in her rejection of his attentions. But this narcissistic creep—he didn't deserve a soft landing. However, the last thing she wanted tonight was a bar room brawl, and by the looks of her husband and three sons across the room, she knew it wouldn't take much to start one.

Eli sidled up to his dad, put an arm around his shoulders and smiled, trying to look like he was having a pleasant conversation as he said quietly, still smiling, "Dad, I think that guy is hitting on Mom!" The other brothers smiled at him as they nodded their agreement. Looking at his sons, it occurred to Simon that they must appear to be a gathering of lunatics—all of them with big smiles and crazy eyes, nodding continuously together, at seemingly nothing in particular. On second thought, they looked more like a collection of happy dashboard bobble heads.

"All right, everybody drop the smiles. Now. And the nodding. Just talk to me as if we're having a normal conversation."

Colder stared at him, wide eyed. "But Dad, he *kissed her hand.* Are you going to just stand there?"

"Ah, my son, my son—you know so little about the world. Let me enlighten you. For one thing, kissing a lady's hand is considered only polite in some high society gatherings in Europe. Secondly, your mother is in control of the situation. That's not to say I'm not monitoring it.

"Dear Arthur is trying to get your mother to have an affair with him."

"What?" the three almost shouted in unison. Several heads turned in their direction, and Simon rolled his eyes and mouthed, "Hold it down!"

"Why aren't you doing anything about it?" Jonas whispered.

"Look, lads, you may or may not have noticed, since she's your mother, but my wife is a very attractive woman, and this is not the first time in our married life that some lothario has tried to make time with her. But she doesn't like to make a scene, and rightly so, especially tonight.

"This—person, would like nothing better than to have me, or one of you, go over and make a big to-do, resulting in him looking like the innocent victim and ruining this night for your mom. His whole purpose in being here is to try and humiliate and damage me by going through the woman I love. If I made a move right now, I'd just be playing into his hands.

"Your mother is aware of all this and she'd much rather handle it herself, in a gentler manner. Her standard maneuver is to pretend that what the amorous twit is saying to her is so ridiculous that it must be a joke, thereby letting the rejected buffoon grab what's left of his dignity by laughing along with her. It's a thing of beauty to watch. Your mother really is an artist.

"Now, just be subtle and only glance over occasionally. And don't worry. She knows we're watching, and if she wants me, she only has to nod."

Bess saw her three sons "subtly" staring at them, and was praying that Simon had them under control. Arthur had his back to them and didn't realize the unarmed forces had arrived.

After chatting for a few minutes, he took a step closer to her, and she saw all four of her men stand up straighter. She stepped back, and Arthur half whispered to her, "Bess, you're wasted with that man. You and I are so alike. We talk so easily—we communicate on such a deep level. You know you're feeling it too—that we should be together."

She looked into his eyes, putting a gentle hand on his chest. And broke out laughing.

"Arthur, you are so funny! For a minute there, I thought you were serious and I'd have to have you committed! In all our conversations, you never let me see this side of you. What a sense of humor, you crazy guy!" She laughed harder then, and said, "Wait 'til I tell Simon!

He could use a good laugh!" She gave Simon a nod then, and he strolled over with their sons in tow.

She continued to laugh, a little louder now, and she said between laughs, "Oh, Simon, come here, wait 'til you hear this. You never told me that Arthur was such a crack up!"

Arthur gave her a tight smile. "Excuse me, I must be leaving. So glad I could give you a chuckle." Turning on his heels then, he headed for another area of the room, hearing Bess calling him back so that she could share the hilarity with Simon. He refused to leave the gallery just yet, though, and let Simon think they'd run him off.

When he reached her side, Bess gave Simon a little kiss of greeting, and slid her arm through his, making sure she continued laughing while she told him what Arthur had said. Simon smiled, laughed loudly, and waited to catch the other man's eye. As soon as Arthur glanced up, he smiled and gave him a wink, as if to say, "Good one!"

Arthur was considering making his way to the door, when Genevieve and Enzo stepped in from the next room. He'd heard about the Sayers' daughter, but he'd never seen her. *She makes her mother look like a shriveled old crow. What a beauty!*

Then a wonderful thought came to him. What if he took his daughter instead of his wife? That would crush Sayers almost as badly—maybe even worse. Who was that short man with her? No matter. These young things were easily swept off their feet by older, experienced men. This would be a pleasure, and almost too easy to be sporting.

#

An old friend put a hand on Genevieve's shoulder, and after the two had hugged and she'd introduced Enzo, she stayed to chat while he wandered over to shoot the breeze with her brothers. While Enzo was walking in their direction, Arthur was slowly moving across the room towards Genevieve.

Colder saw what was happening, and punched Eli and then his dad, saying quietly, "Slime alert, slime alert!"

Arthur waited politely beside Genevieve, looking at a painting, but obviously wanting to speak with her. The young woman talking to her took the hint, and excused herself to allow the next person a chance at conversation.

Turning towards him, at first she didn't know who he was, until his accent gave him away. She resigned herself to being polite as he introduced himself and began chatting.

Enzo had just reached the brothers, when Eli leaned towards him. "Hey man, guess who's chatting up your woman." He whirled around, and then laughed quietly.

"Aah, that's okay. I don't feel too threatened by old geezers."

"No, seriously. I'll bet you ten bucks he makes a play for her. He just hit on Mom and now he's trying for Genevieve. He's the guy we told you about."

Enzo started in that direction, but Simon caught his arm. "No, Enzo, wait. I find this as distasteful as you do, believe me, but we don't need to make a scene. Bess coached her daughter on her technique for losing unwanted suitors years ago. Although comparing temperaments, I would imagine Genevieve isn't always as kind hearted in the practice of those techniques. This should be interesting. Just relax and watch her work.

"She has five men just thirty feet away to defend her honor, if need be, but my guess is she could defend it by herself without any help."

He stood with her family and watched, instead of going over and destroying the old man, as he felt like doing. That *was* a sort of Neanderthal approach, Enzo realized, so he decided to be civilized and wait for Genevieve's performance.

Once again, Arthur's back was to the rest of the family. After polite introductions, he began talking about his time in Europe, and some of the places he'd been. Bored, annoyed, and suspicious of his motives, Genevieve was trying to keep smiling. But her feet were hurting from standing in one place, and she finally decided she needed to cut off the conversation and launch her getaway. As she began to make her goodbyes, the mood of Arthur's words changed abruptly.

"Who is that short gentleman that you were talking to, if I may ask?"

"That's Enzo Uccello, my fiancé."

Now it was Arthur's turn to laugh. "You can't be serious? He looks like a little boy next to you!" Then he stepped closer. "You could do so much better. A beauty like you—you move like a queen, and you should be seen with someone that could treat you like one. Someone like me, perhaps." He thought he was at his finest at that moment. He could feel himself exuding virile, electric charm—the pheromones in the air were probably overwhelming the hapless young thing. She didn't stand a chance.

As she looked down at him, she thought about her mom, and how she'd said to be kind and let men like this down easily. Pretend it was a joke. Let them leave with dignity. But this guy was a sleazoid, and he'd insulted Enzo. And he was too damn old to be hitting on her.

She laughed loudly, and said, "Oh, Mr. Worthington, I never knew you were such a hoot! My mom said you went to school with my dad. That must make you what, sixty-eight, sixty-nine? Wow, almost *seventy*! How time flies, eh?" She made eye contact with Enzo, and in a moment, he was at her side.

Arthur's eyes had gone hostile when she'd mentioned his age. What was the point of the dye, the surgery, the chemicals, if people went around blurting out your age? Was she really that clueless, or just a little bitch?

When Enzo walked up and put an arm around her waist, she said, "Enzo, I'd like you to meet Arthur Worthington, one of my dad's *really old* school chums."

He took his arm from around her waist, and grabbed the other man's hand with a hard slap. "Hey, Artie, glad to meet ya!" he said loudly. "Any friend of Simon's is a friend of mine. Man, you two do go way back, like about a hundred years, huh?" He laughed as he shook hands, but Worthington pulled his hand away sharply, and said heatedly, "It's *Arthur*."

"Oh, yeah I heard. Sorry. It's just that 'Artie' suits you so well. Say Art, do you bowl? You know, we might *have* to call you Arthur at the alley, 'cause there's so many Arties already. Arthurs just naturally gravitate towards bowling, I guess. But then, you probably already know that, eh? Probably own your own ball and shoes, I bet."

Shaking his head, Arthur glared at both of them. "Excuse me, but I have to go." Then he turned and walked away. Enzo hollered after him, "Artie, wait, I didn't get your number! We're getting a new league together in a week, and we thought it'd be nice to have a senior citizen on each team." Without answering, Arthur walked out the door.

Enzo put his arm back around Genevieve's waist, and she whispered, giggling, "You're an evil genius!"

He grinned first at her, and then at her brothers, who each gave him a secretive high five upon his return to the fold. Simon bent his head down to look him in the eye. "If she doesn't marry you, we'll adopt you." Bess leaned over and kissed his cheek. And just like that, he was family.

CHAPTER TWENTY-THREE

Standing in front of the gallery, waiting for his chauffer to come for him may have been embarrassing, but it gave him an alibi. He made sure to be very visible to the guests inside, many of whom had heard Enzo calling after him, and whose gazes followed him out the door as they wondered what was going on.

He slipped his Bluetooth on so that his phone call was not so obvious. Those bitches—trying to act innocent while humiliating him. The whole family was worthless, and none of them had a clue as to what he was capable of. He had quite a variety of people at his disposal, and very few of them operated under a code of ethics.

After making his call, he made a second, and arranged for a car to be waiting in a hidden location for the recipient of his first. As he put his phone away, he nodded to himself with a look of grim satisfaction. The Sayers might not all make it home tonight. Then again they might, but either way, their evening would be at least as unpleasant as his had been.

CHAPTER TWENTY-FOUR

They shut the gallery down at half past eleven. Bess was ecstatic. She'd sold seven paintings to the financier she'd hoped to see there, and five others to individuals. This was the most successful showing she'd ever had, and the other artists sharing the evening with her had also done well. If it hadn't been for the "Arthur Incident," everything would have been perfect, but even that had gone fairly well, she thought.

As she said goodnight to her other children and grandchildren, Simon warmed up the SUV, an Acura MDX, and Genevieve and Enzo climbed in with him. After all the goodbyes, Bess got in and immediately took off her shoes. *What a relief. Heels were really not made for human feet.*

She heard the click of a seatbelt from the back, and fastened her own. Her youngest was twenty-three years old, but Bess' ears were still attuned to the sound of seatbelts being secured, and her brain counted the clicks automatically.

"Enzo, I only heard one seatbelt clicking back there."

"Oh, sorry, Bess. I just forgot. I always do buckle up, honest."

"He really does, Mom, I'm his witness." Genevieve reached over for his hand. "If you didn't, you'd have to learn while you're here. All of us were brainwashed from an early age, and coerced as well. Mom and Dad will *not* move the car until everybody has their seatbelts on. Seriously. If you refused, we'd end up sitting here all night."

"Yes," Simon added, "it's true. Angus calls us 'seatbelt Nazis.' With affection, of course."

Simon turned so he could face all of them. "I must say, I am extremely proud of everyone's performances tonight. And Enzo! Ah, Enzo, the 'Artie' business was magnificent. And the bowling alley bit was staggering in its brilliance!"

Enzo smiled and acknowledged the praise with a little bow of his head.

Reaching across the seat, Simon squeezed Bess' hand. "I'm really happy that things went so well for you—you deserved tonight.

"By the way, did you happen to notice your three sons watching when 'Artie' was hitting on you? They were chomping at the bit to go defend your honor. In fact, all of them were encouraging me to attack, but I insisted we were too civilized for that. Anyway, I thought you'd like to know that you had not one, but four knights in shining armor at your disposal tonight."

He pulled out of the parking lot and headed for the highway. She smiled and turned towards him. "I saw. And I have to admit, it felt pretty nice."

They talked a while longer, and then the three passengers got quiet. It had been a long day, and soon the smooth ride and quiet hum of the engine lulled them into pleasant dozing. Simon glanced over occasionally at the light shimmering off the lake, at Bess leaning back in her seat asleep, breathing softly and evenly, and then in the mirror at Genevieve, eyes closed, but smiling, and holding Enzo's hand. The tranquility and warmth of the moment made Simon want to memorize and hold it in his mind for as long as he could—a little island of peace that he might visit at will.

When he glanced back again at his daughter, his rearview mirror caught the headlights of a vehicle coming up fast behind him from around a curve. Even more alarming than the vehicle's speed, was that it was swerving from one side of the road to the other. Wonderful. Just what they needed—an intoxicated moron driving too fast on a winding road at night.

He slowed and tried to stay as far to the side as possible, hoping the imbecile would get annoyed at his speed and pass him, but driving next to a drop-off didn't allow a large margin of safety for moving over. The vehicle, a big Toyota Land Cruiser, sped up to pass, and he breathed a sigh of relief. At the last second though, just as they were entering a curve, instead of passing, the Toyota put on a bigger burst of speed, and rammed the back left side of the Acura, sending it hurtling off the edge of the road.

He felt the impact and automatically reached out for Bess, as he shouted, "LOOK OUT!" He heard her scream, and saw Genevieve's face in the mirror, eyes wide with fear and disbelief. She threw her arms up to cover her face, just as Enzo reached an arm out in front of her in a futile attempt at protection.

They were airborne for a few seconds before the car slammed down, barreling and bouncing on for twenty yards more before glancing off a tree and hitting a dip that flipped it over. It skidded on its roof a dozen yards or so before coming to rest upside down, only a few feet from the edge of the lake.

All of the airbags had deployed, and the seatbelts had held.

There was no sound at first, except for the slow spinning and scraping of the wheels above their feet. That slight noise and the taste of blood in his mouth brought Simon around, as his stunned brain tried to remember what had just happened. Suddenly it came back to him, and he almost panicked when he found himself upside down, with a semi-conscious Bess hanging next to him. He reached up and got his seatbelt off, dumping himself onto his head and neck, despite trying to catch himself on his arms. With his height, at least there was barely any distance to fall. He could see Bess breathing and coming to, but the roof was partially caved in, and he couldn't get a good look at the back seat.

"Genevieve, Enzo! Are you okay? Genevieve!"

He heard the most wonderful sound in the world, then—a groan. A groan, coming from his *living* daughter.

"I'm okay—I guess. Enzo—ENZO! Dad, he's not waking up! ENZO!"

"Hold on, honey, I'll be there, but I've got to get your mom out. See if you can get out of your seatbelt."

He tried opening his door, but it was jammed solid. He reached over to Bess, who was looking around now, confused, but conscious, at least. "Bess, love, it's okay. We've had an accident and the car flipped. Hold still and I'll get you down."

Suddenly, she became fully alert and shouted, "The kids! Genevieve, Enzo!"

"Genevieve's okay. Let me get you down."

He twisted around until he lay flat on his back and then pushed himself with his feet against the door of the car, sliding his body until he was lying on the ceiling of the SUV, directly beneath Bess. He had to shove her upwards by both shoulders to get underneath, and this allowed enough slack on the belt to slip her right arm out. She reached down and braced herself against his chest when he let go of her right shoulder to stretch his left arm up and unbuckle her. As the straps released, he shoved his right hand under her neck, pushing her head forward enough to keep her from falling straight on top of it. His left hand supported her back and pushed her body towards the dash, so that she ended up in a slouched, almost sitting position on his chest.

They could hear Genevieve crying and saying Enzo's name, begging him to wake up. Bess pulled the handle and Simon shoved the door open on the front passenger's side, enabling her to swing her feet around, slide off of him and out onto the plowed up dirt. As soon as she was free, he pulled himself out with a hand on each side of the door frame, then almost passed out when he stood up. Genevieve was yelling now, "Dad, *help* him!"

"I'm coming, baby, I'm coming!"

Bess was trying to get the door open on Genevieve's side, and Simon was staggering around to Enzo's, when they saw lights above them and heard Eli screaming, "MOM, DAD! GENEVIEVE!"

"WE'RE DOWN HERE! COME DOWN, WE NEED HELP WITH ENZO!"

He heard Eli shout to the others, "They're alive! Call 911, Jonas! Colder, come on, we gotta get down there!"

Simon had one foot on the door frame, and was pulling with both hands on the bent door, but couldn't budge it. He heard pebbles and rocks rolling down the hill then, as Eli and Colder scrambled towards them.

"We need to get him out! I can't open the door!"

Eli grabbed him by the shoulders, pulled him away from the car and pushed him down gently. "Dad, you're bleeding. Just sit, and let us get this. Mom? You okay? Gen?"

Bess and Genevieve answered, both screaming for him to get to Enzo.

When he'd seen they were going off the road after Simon had shouted, Enzo had thrown his right arm out to try and protect Genevieve, but the impact of landing and bouncing down the hill threw his arm back towards him, and when the vehicle flipped, his forearm ended up across his throat. When the car slammed onto its roof, towards the center of the car on Enzo's side, an area of rock jutting above the soil had partially caved it in. This part of the ceiling, thrust up now between Enzo and Genevieve, was pressing against his elbow, preventing him from moving his arm away from his throat, and another protrusion of ceiling behind him, was pushing his head forward, so that his airway was being cut off against his own arm.

Bess kept several small pillows in the back seat for the grandchildren, and Enzo had folded one and stuck it behind his head when he'd first gotten into the car. The pillow didn't help his current situation any, but had at least cushioned his head against the ceiling.

Genevieve could reach his seatbelt to disconnect it, but with his head in the position it was, she feared that if she freed him to drop down, it might break his neck or crush his trachea against his arm. By lying down on the ceiling, she could just get her arm around the caved in area enough to push against his forehead, to try and open his airway a mere fraction of an inch. When she'd first pushed his head back, the tiny increase in oxygen had revived him enough that he'd tried pulling his head back on his own as he gasped for air. With her arm through the opening, she couldn't see him, and had to work blind, but she could feel that his attempts to move his head and breathe were becoming fewer and weaker. They were losing the battle.

Eli aimed his flashlight at Enzo, and when the light hit him, it only took a second to see what was happening. "Colder, go on the other side and find something to try and shove the ceiling back out, or to pull it back towards the center and away from him. I'll work from this side."

Colder ran to the nearest tree and began pulling a branch off of it, breaking and twisting it until it came away. He pulled Bess out of the car, and then crawled in beside Genevieve to try and force the metal back by putting all his weight and muscle on the branch he'd set against it. As he strained and pushed, he could hear his sister crying and pleading with Enzo between sobs. "Come on, Enzo, breathe for me. Come on, don't you give up on me, Uccello! Come on, breathe, again, come on, come on—"

There wasn't room for two people to grasp the door handle, so Eli positioned himself, prayed for strength, roared, and started pulling. Simon watched in awe as gradually the door opened the tiniest bit, and the jammed metal screeched in protest. He jumped up, and grabbing a small rock, crammed it into the opening to keep it from closing back. Eli, face almost purple, took another breath, roared, and pulled again. Simon looked around until he found a broken branch, and shoving it into the opening, threw all his weight against the other end to try and pry the door open further, as Eli pulled again.

Suddenly, Jonas was there with a tire iron, and with the three of them pulling and prying, they were finally able to get the door open enough for Eli to get through. He put his feet on the ceiling, placed his back against the car seat, and pushed upwards, until the pressure against Enzo's head and neck let up just enough for Simon to put one arm through. Once in, he was able support Enzo's neck and brace it so that Genevieve could release the belt. Eli hooked an arm around Enzo's waist, and as soon as the seatbelt opened, he moved sideways, lifting him far enough away from the protruding ceiling to lay him down on the curve of his back. Eli backed all the way out then, his position making it impossible to get a good enough grip on the unconscious man to move him further without injuring him. When he stepped onto the dirt he backed up as fast as he could, to make room for Simon and Jonas as they reached in together and pulled Enzo out.

The other three came running around from the other side, just as they laid him on his back in the dirt and Jonas tilted his head back to open his airway. His face was swollen, with a bluish tinge, and at first, nothing happened. Jonas was getting ready to start CPR, when Enzo gave a huge gasp, followed by another and another. He coughed then, and opened his eyes. Genevieve threw herself to her knees beside him. He looked at them dully, but when he felt her hands all over his face and realized she was sobbing, he patted her back with his good arm, looked at his rescuers, and gave them a weak smile. "Never a dull moment," he rasped.

#

They air lifted Enzo, with Genevieve beside him, because the EMT's feared that laryngeal swelling might block off his airway, necessitating a tracheotomy to be performed en route. With help, the others were able to walk back to the base of the drop-off, where they were brought up to the road with safety harnesses and then taken to the hospital by ambulance.

The Sayers were all diagnosed with mild concussions, abrasions and contusions. Simon was the only one needing stitches—sixteen, to be exact—on the right side of his head.

Enzo's concussion was more serious, but still not as bad as it might have been. The doctor told him that his height had saved him. If he'd been taller, either his head would have been crushed when the rocks caved in the ceiling, or his neck would have broken. His neck was swollen and horribly bruised in the front *and* back, but thus far, no tracheotomy had been necessary. His right shoulder was dislocated, and his right elbow swollen, abraded, and bruised. They had him hooked up to IV's and oxygen, with cold packs to his neck, elbow, and shoulder to reduce the swelling.

When Genevieve was released and finally able to see him again, she had to fight back the tears and panic all over again at the sight of him, so helpless and battered looking. The pain medication was allowing him to drift in and out, but he heard her and squeezed her hand when she said his name.

The others were all released by six a.m., but they kept Enzo longer, and no one wanted to leave without him. A few hours later, when they were sure his breathing was stable, and his vitals and neuro checks satisfactory, they released him against medical advice, per his insistence, with a neck brace and his right arm in a sling. He had steadfastly refused to let his parents be called, saying it would only worry them unnecessarily. He'd tell them about it after he got home.

Jonas had called Hiram, and he'd driven Angus and Sarah to the hospital to wait with their grandsons for the rest of their family. Eli's back and head were bothering him, so Colder drove his car to take the brothers, Genevieve, and Enzo home, while Simon and Bess rode with Hiram, Angus, and Sarah.

The brothers and their dad had given their statements to the police already. Eli had wanted to grab a cup of coffee before starting the long drive home last night, so by the time they'd stopped to buy one and gotten back on the road, their car had ended up a ways behind their parents' SUV. The black Land Cruiser had passed them, weaving crazily. They'd sped up to try and get a license number, but the plates had been obscured with mud, and the windows were tinted, so they never got a look at the driver or the tags.

What they all believed, however, was that this was *not* an accident. They had seen the vehicle overtake the Acura, and assumed the driver would pass it, just as it had passed their car. But suddenly, the driver of the Cruiser had ceased all pretense of not being in control, speeding up at a curve and skillfully propelling the Acura over the edge with one powerful hit, while managing to keep the Cruiser on the road. As soon as the Acura was airborne, the Cruiser had sped up and taken off without a hint of the previous weaving.

They told the police about the incident at the showing, and Simon explained his history with Worthington. The police said they'd check into it, but in his heart, Simon knew that would come to nothing. If Arthur Worthington had orchestrated this accident, then he would have been smart enough to leave no trail leading back to him.

Simon remembered how he'd been so visible waiting for his chauffeur, and had been picked up directly outside of the front doors, so that all would see him depart in his Mercedes. He'd thought it odd at the time, that the man wouldn't want to remain out of sight of the crowd after being embarrassed in front of them. It made him sick to think that someone's petty antipathy for him might have cost the lives of his wife, his daughter, and the man she loved.

He would be paying "Artie" a visit, and very soon.

CHAPTER TWENTY-FIVE

When the family at last arrived home, the four crash victims were already feeling the increase in soreness they'd been warned to expect in another twenty-four hours. Eli's headache had ratcheted down to dull instead of throbbing, and after eight-hundred milligrams of Ibuprofen, his back was feeling better, too. His neck muscles were tender, and his arms felt beaten up, but otherwise, he thought he'd live.

When Bess walked in the back door, Lola leapt towards her to get her attention. Elsie caught the little dog in midair, with her jaws around her neck. Bess cried out, but Elsie sent, "It's okay. I'm just teaching her manners."

Amazing, the impact that teeth around the neck could have. Elsie held Lola dangling from her mouth for a few moments, just to let her get the idea, and then gently put her on the ground. The pint-sized ball of energy sat herself down on landing and looked up at Elsie for further instructions. This was not the way she had envisioned passing on her wisdom, but—whatever worked.

Because of the concussions, all were instructed to have family members wake them every few hours during an extended sleep, to be sure they *could* be awakened.

Genevieve insisted on sleeping at Eli's house so that she could watch Enzo. She was still shaken at the thought of how close she'd come to losing him. Colder said he'd wake both of them after a few hours.

Enzo was trying to be positive and upbeat, but any movement sent shooting pains through his neck and up into his head. The ugly bruise across his whole neck, his swollen face, the reddened eyes from broken blood vessels, and the hoarseness in his voice belied his feigned cheerfulness. The doctors had told him that if he'd stayed trapped only a few minutes more, he probably would have died or been left with brain damage from lack of oxygen.

Only Genevieve's efforts had managed to keep him alive long enough to get him out of the car. Enzo joked about it, but Genevieve knew that he was as rattled as she was about how close he'd come to dying.

#

Looking at his back in the mirror, and the dark bruising that covered his spine six inches across and down to just above his waist, Eli didn't notice that Genevieve and Enzo had come into his room. When he caught movement in his peripheral vision, he started, and grabbed for his shirt when he saw Genevieve.

"Oh, please, it's not like I've never seen you in a bathing suit! Oh my gosh, your poor back! And how's your head?"

"Geez, this is nothing. I'm going to be tender for a while, but no biggie. And my headache's settling down. How are you two feeling? You breathing okay, buddy?"

"Yeah, I just feel like I have the beginnings of a sore throat—you know, it feels swollen and tender. But mainly how I feel is thankful that we're all alive, and that nobody got hurt bad. Which is why we invaded your privacy here—I wanted to thank you for saving my life."

Pulling his shirt back on with a little groan, Eli popped his head out of the neck and smiled. "Hey, all of us had a hand in that."

"I know, and I've already thanked them, but your dad and the others all said the same thing. That nobody could have cracked that door in time, or forced the seat up far enough to get me out of there, except for you. There was only room enough for one person at a time to work on those two things and your dad said he couldn't even budge the door. He's not exactly a featherweight, and I know he's got more muscle than Colder or Jonas. He said that you came and sat him down and just took over, and he felt like he was watching a miracle when he saw that door crack open."

Shaking his head, Eli pointed his thumb upwards. "Maybe there *was* some of that. All I know is, I prayed and pulled from the outside and when I got inside, I prayed and pushed. But when I saw you through that window, Enzo—man, I was scared to death. I thought you were out of time. Didn't want to lose my new brother before I even got to know him."

Unexpectedly, he threw his arms wide in an exaggerated gesture and stepped in to wrap his arms around him in a quick, gentle hug. He laughed as if he were joking, but the huskiness in his voice revealed a different meaning when he added, "I'm just really happy you're still with us."

Surprised and touched, Enzo wrapped his good arm around the big man in return, and replied sincerely, "Me too, Eli."

They backed away from each other, and then Genevieve slid her arms around her brother, with her head tight against his chest. "You know you've always been my hero, don't you Eli? Well, you and Dad. This just seals the deal. You saved Enzo's life, and he's my life now, so you saved mine, too. I can never thank you enough for that. I love you, big brother."

He leaned his head down on top of hers as he tightened his embrace a bit. "Love you too, Bean Butt."

#

Going into his room, he was about to crawl into bed, but stepped back in surprise at the large golden dog sitting there watching him. "Ah, Genny, could you come in here, please?"

Rushing through the door, she reached out for him, afraid that he'd worsened, but he shook his head, or rather, his whole body, wincing, and pointed towards the dog. "If she's one of yours, I'm going to need a translator."

When she saw Genevieve, Madelyn stepped to the edge of the bed, wagging her tail and opening her mouth in what Enzo would have sworn was a smile. Genevieve rushed over to give her a hug, and then started tousling the hair around her face and neck. "Oh, Maddie, I hadn't even seen you yet! Where have you been?"

Looking down, shame-faced, the dog sent, "I'm sorry. I've been busy with the children, and then there was this squirrel in the back yard at lunch time, and I—"

"Oh, that doesn't matter now. It's just wonderful to see you! What are you doing in here?"

"Elsie sent me what happened, so I'm here to watch him," she sent, nodding towards Enzo. "He smells a little more frail right now than the rest of you, so I'm going to keep an eye and a nose on him while he sleeps. Tell him not to worry—I'll get off the bed. But Genny—he smells like a good one. You did well."

Enzo watched in fascination as the dog sent to Genevieve. Except for the fact that Madelyn's mouth wasn't moving—if you didn't count panting—they looked like they were having a casual conversation. This was so surreal—the whole thing: getting engaged and almost getting killed, beating and meeting "The Cat," having a sentient dog in his room to watch over him, and this evening, he was to meet aliens from two different planets. He'd had no idea when he'd said yes to pizza with a gorgeous redhead, what a wild ride she'd be taking him on.

"She just wants to watch you while you sleep, since you were injured the worst. And she likes the way you smell. She thinks you're a 'good one.'"

He laughed in embarrassment. "Yeah? And she hasn't even smelled my crotch yet! Maybe we could bypass that part of the introduction." He reached over and scratched behind her ears, and she melted into his hands. "Hey, Madelyn. Good to meet you and I appreciate your watching out for me." He turned around to Genevieve then to put his arm around her, and felt the room start to spin. "Gen—I gotta lie down. Like right now."

She threw the covers back and guided him as he more or less collapsed onto the bed, and she saw he'd turned pale and was shaking a little. Grabbing a second pillow, she helped him sit up and pushed it under his head. "They said you'd probably breathe better, and it would help prevent more swelling if you slept with your head and chest elevated."

He took his collar off then, saying there was no way he could sleep with it on. Colder came in carrying an extra couple of pillows to help get Enzo comfortable, and they put one across his chest so he could use it to rest his chin on. Genevieve put the other under his elbow, and then took off his sling. She kissed him, and his eyes were closed almost before she stood up. After running a hand across his forehead, she went around and climbed onto the other side of the bed.

"Love you, Lady Red," she heard him whisper, and she reached out her hand to take his.

"Love you, too, Boston."

Jumping off the bed and onto a chaise lounge so that she was level with Enzo, Madelyn sent Genevieve, "Don't worry—let yourself sleep. He'll be fine. I'll see to it."

"I know you will, Maddy. Thanks. You're a great dog."

##

As exhausted as he was, Simon couldn't sleep until he talked with the insurance company and then with the police again, who of course, could do nothing. Going into his office, he took out his phone and made some calls, and then wrote a letter, put it in an envelope, addressed and sealed it. He went to their room to be sure Bess was settled into bed, and then he got into their other car and drove to Arthur's.

#

When he rang the doorbell, a butler opened the door and ushered him in, and then went to announce his presence. At once, Arthur came out of his study in long strides, with a concerned look on his face. Reaching out with both hands, he took Simon's shoulders and peered at him.

"Oh, thank God you're all okay! The police came by and told me about what happened! They said that your daughter's young man was nearly killed. How dreadful! Please, come in and have a seat."

He led him into his study, a room full of dark wood, heavy leather chairs, and a massive desk. Simon tiredly sat himself in a chair directly in front of the desk, and Arthur sat behind it, as if conducting an interview rather than talking with a friend.

"Can I get you anything?"

"Actually, I would appreciate a glass of cold water."

"Of course. Hinson, would you be so kind?"

The other man bowed slightly and left the room, returning in less than a minute with a glass full of ice water. He pulled a small table over to rest beside their guest, and placed the glass on it. Waving a hand and nodding to dismiss him, Arthur leaned forward in his chair, with his hands clasped on his desk.

"What can I do for you, Simon?"

He took a long drink of water before answering—he hadn't realized how thirsty he was, and how exhausted. Putting the water down, he looked back up at Arthur calmly. "I know the police questioned you about what happened, and came up with nothing, as I knew they would."

"Yes, well, I left a good bit earlier than you, so I'm afraid I saw nothing. I'd do anything I could to help, but I don't know what that would be."

Simon sighed and leaned back in his chair. "I'm too tired to draw this out, Arthur. So let's just cut the crap and get to it. This was no accident. We were run off the road and my family could easily have been killed. My daughter's fiancé very nearly was. I believe you paid someone to do this."

Arthur gasped in shock at the notion, with a little more drama than even he thought was warranted, but he felt sure that Simon was probably wearing a wire, hoping to get a gloating confession. "How could you think that I'd do something so horrible and violent? Yes, we've had our problems in the past, but they *are* in the past. Surely you must realize that."

Now Simon rose from his chair, put his hands flat on the edge of the desk, and leaned menacingly towards Arthur. "This is the only warning you'll get. If I had solid proof—if I knew with absolute certainty that it was you who tried to take out my family last night, I'd kill you right now with my bare hands."

Shoving his chair back away from Simon as far as he could get without standing, he didn't have to fake his surprise. "See here, Simon, you can't talk to me that way! I've done nothing wrong. You're out of your mind if you think I'd do something like that, even if I wanted to. I'm no fool. If I wanted to harm you or your family, I'd try to hurt you financially, in some legal fashion, not do something as crass and obviously risky as this. I'm no murderer. I'll admit, I really *don't* like you, but I had resigned myself to trying to get along. I even went to the showing last night as a gesture of good will."

Feeling a little shaky, Simon sat back down. He could almost believe the man. He wanted to—wanted to believe that this whole nightmare was just some freaky coincidence that would never happen again. But he wasn't that naive.

"If I'm wrong about all of this, you have my sincerest apologies, Arthur. But I don't think I am. I know that you could easily hire someone to do just about whatever you want. But I have money, too, and I will do anything—" he leaned forward in his chair and stared at Arthur with death in his eyes—"*anything* to protect my family. You will be watched. My family will be watched. And if anything should happen to any of us—well, you should pray that nothing does, because orders have been left with instructions about what should happen next. *Déjà vu.*

"I'm aware that you have contacts all over the world. But I have *friends* in as many places. Over the years, there have been thousands of people treated for free at the Institute I founded. Some of those people would have died, or lost their children or spouses if they hadn't been treated there. Many of those people were dirt poor. But some were powerful in ways you can only imagine. Some were unsavory in character, but we would never hold that against their children. All over the world, Arthur, there are people who have sworn their undying gratitude to me for what the Institute did for them. They owe me nothing, and yet it's a point of honor for many, that if the time should come, they would do anything to repay what they see as their debt to me.

"You have associates, Arthur. They will work with you or for you, as long as you're channeling money or favors to them. But if you should disappear off the face of the Earth, they wouldn't care, and they wouldn't hold any deal you may have made with them as a sacred trust to be upheld.

"But as I mentioned, my friends will feel differently. If I should disappear, they will know your name. They will find you, wherever you go. Particularly this man. It's a matter of honor." He'd written one name on a sheet of paper and he laid it on Arthur's desk

Arthur reached for the paper, read the name, and blanched. Now he *was* afraid. *Deja vu.* He'd always assumed that Mr. Play-By-The-Book Sayers would be too law abiding and civilized to resort to any retaliation. But apparently he'd been wrong. Sayers did have as much or more money than him, and he could arrange an "accident" as easily as Arthur himself could.

He stood up suddenly, and with quavering voice, almost shouted, "This entire conversation was unnecessary, as I had no part in what happened last night. I find your whole tone offensive, and certainly your accusations. I'd like you to leave now."

Simon stood slowly, trying not to wince as all his muscles protested their earlier treatment. "I'll be happy to do that. The police are aware of our history now, and they'll be watching your activities as well. Just remember what I said. Two can play your game."

Then he turned and walked out, unsatisfied, but too tired to press the issue further. He had said what he'd come to say, and Arthur had heard him clearly, he could tell by the look on his face. He could see uncertainty blossoming up behind those vicious little eyes, as he realized that the fire he'd lit might blow back to consume him. These were not idle threats. Simon had never been more serious.

CHAPTER TWENTY-SIX

"Stop fidgeting!" An exasperated Mona reset the dials again. She'd always enjoyed running the suit fabricator, getting the material to fit perfectly on each crew member—it was a satisfying challenge. There were hundreds of different measurements that the machine needed to take on a non-moving body in order to achieve that flawless fit that would protect the wearer and provide comfort as well. But she'd never tried to fit anyone like Luigi before.

Although he'd been skittish about stepping into the machine, Micah had managed to remain still for the time it took to get his measurements. Luigi, however, was impossible. He'd agreed to wear a uniform, and yet the simple act of stepping into the machine and being enclosed for a short time seemed to throw him into a near panic.

First he'd refused entirely. When Micah had reminded him of the promise they'd made in order to be allowed on the team, however, he'd reluctantly stepped in. The hatch to the machine was closed, but his head was out in the open, so Micah and Mona thought that claustrophobia wouldn't be an issue. But Luigi complained that he was itching, and tried to scratch, and the machine had to be stopped and reset. Then he complained of a cramp in his leg. Then he sent that the machine was too tight and he couldn't breathe. Mona had almost decided to use another machine to immobilize and render him unconscious, when the measurements finally concluded.

Usually very patient with other species, she opened the hatch crossly and sent, "Get out."

The two Elpies left the room in a rush. When on a ship in space, and a seven foot crew member tells a body to leave, he should leave and be quick about it. They'd only been on the ship a few days, but they were already restless to get to Earth and approach Colder about coming with them. They'd explored just about every inch of the ship and each had spent an inordinate amount of time in the bath tank, looking out at the galaxy as they soaked in warm water, inevitably drifting off to sleep.

Having to wake them up in the tub was getting tiresome and embarrassing for Eli and Barnabas. The two would have woken up on their own eventually, but other crew members wanted to use the tub. Their fathers felt that their inconveniencing the rest of the ship reflected poorly on their upbringing.

When they'd begun to drive everyone crazy, Sven had sent to Micah and Luigi, expressing his doubts as to their aptitude for prolonged space travel. But they'd sworn to calm down and get adjusted. They were just anxious to get to Earth, they'd sent him.

A few minutes after their fitting, Mona sent for them to come back to the room they'd been in. She handed them their suits, explaining some of the features. Excited to take this next step in becoming crew members, the Elpies lost their enthusiasm almost immediately when they tried putting their suits on.

The suits were made to cover the whole body, including their tails. To get into the skintight uniforms, they had to start with the pencil thin ends of their tails and work gradually upwards, and then stretch the suits down to stick their long toes and feet in. Trying to don full-body panty hose would have been simpler. It seemed undoable until they figured out how to help each other.

When they proudly came out into the sitting area, Eli and Barnabas turned to them and stared for a second before breaking into wheezy, huffing laughter, annoying and humiliating their offspring. The two males had just started getting control of themselves when Dulcie walked in, took one look, and started laughing.

Elpies didn't *wear* clothes, except for the occasional coat in severe weather, and foot coverings over rocky ground, so seeing an Elpie in any kind of clothes would have struck them as odd. But these clinging, silver suits—the most amusing aspect was their tails being covered—or no, it was really funnier to see Luigi's mane outlined along his spine. No, no, the funniest thing was their feet, with their long toes sparkling in the silver material—

Elpies were by nature a compassionate species, but they offered no mercy on this day, and when one of the three would stop laughing, another would start all over again.

Not wanting to go to their cabins, which were too small for any extended stay, the two resigned themselves to enduring the uncharitable mirth of their relatives. Luigi threw himself into a seat by the window and stared out, and Micah did the same on the other side of the ship.

After a half hour or so of sullen, hurt feelings permeating the atmosphere, Dulcie began to feel guilty about abrading the pair's pride. She ambled over to where Micah was sitting, laid her long fingers on his shoulders from behind, and sent her apologies for laughing. But when she sent him a mental image of himself and Luigi walking out in their new silver skins, he broke into laughter himself. He sent the image to Luigi, and after a moment, he was laughing too. Once they were in on the joke, they no longer found it offensive.

After getting a good look at themselves in Dulcie's memory, the two intrepid explorers-to-be decided that looking ridiculous was something they could deal with for a life of adventure. They'd be landing on Earth in a few hours, and they both hoped that Colder would feel the same.

CHAPTER TWENTY-SEVEN

It was almost eleven-thirty a.m. when Simon got home. He stopped at the guardhouse and asked Harvey to ride with him to the house for a talk. Winston nodded that he had things covered, so Harvey stepped out and climbed into the front seat.

Harvey Washington was a huge man that could have passed for one of the Sayers, with his broad smile and big nose, if not for the fact that he was black. He'd been a Navy Seal in his younger days, and when he left the military, he'd gone to work for a private security company in the Middle East, operating in many of the hot spots at one time or another.

He'd been planning on getting out of the business, because he missed his family and realized that even if he survived each new assignment, which was doubtful, he would never be there to tuck his children in at night. They knew him mostly through the computer, where he'd chat with them in the evenings before they went to bed. Why have children if you weren't going to be there for them? On the rare days that he was home, he was like a favorite uncle. They loved him, but they saw their mom as the real parent. And they were right.

Then he'd gotten the news that his daughter was sick. Really sick. She'd been born with lung problems, and the cost of medication was one of the reasons he did what he did for a living. The pay was good. But when Eunice told him about Rebecca, he could see that she was scared, and his wife was the toughest woman he knew.

Rebecca had been doing so well, and then she'd caught a simple upper respiratory infection at school. Things had gone from bad to worse quickly, and though she was in the hospital, she wasn't improving. She was only seven years old, already fragile, and Eunice said she looked weaker every day.

He'd been in the middle of an assignment that was supposed to end with a big bonus and a leave to go back home for a while—in four months. He'd told his boss he had to leave, and when the man protested, he'd just walked away. When he came home jobless and without the bonus they'd counted on, he thought he'd made it just in time to see his daughter die—she looked that bad.

But his wife had been referred by their doctor to the Eli Institute, as a place that might possibly offer some hope. It was in Canada, and they were Americans in Arizona, so it was doubtful they would be accepted in time, but at this point, their doctor thought they had to try. Eunice emailed the Institute, and her message had been relayed to someone named Simon. There was always a waiting list to get into the place, but when Simon had called her back, and Eunice had told him how poorly Rebecca was doing, he'd requested her permission to discuss her case with their physicians.

The next day, this Simon person had called her again on her cell, and said they had a bed waiting for Rebecca at the Institute. When she balked, suddenly realizing that the expense of flying all of them to Canada was impossible, he'd told her not to worry, that private transport had been arranged for, due to the urgency of Rebecca's case. Accommodations had also been provided for the family, free of charge, in a house near the Institute.

The pilot was a volunteer for the hospital. His wife had been in a similar situation to Rebecca's many years ago, he told them, at a time when he'd had some severe financial reversals. When they'd applied for treatment at the hospital, she'd been taken in and treated at no cost, and even their transportation had been provided for. His wife had recovered, and now that he was back on his feet financially, this was his way of giving back.

When they'd landed, a car driven by another volunteer had been waiting to take them straight to the hospital, and Rebecca was taken in immediately instead of having to go through the lengthy admission process they'd been dreading. The whole experience had been mind-numbing for Harvey and Eunice. They'd felt more like VIPs than a charity case.

For the first week, they hadn't known if their daughter would survive, but then the new treatment and medication she received at the Institute gradually started working the miracle they'd been praying for. This Simon guy had come to see them every day when Rebecca was at her worst: sitting with them, talking to them, even praying with him. They'd thought he was a social worker for two weeks, until one day when they'd asked a nurse what days he had off. She'd laughed and told them "any days he wants."

Then she'd informed them that he'd built the Institute with inherited money, and was constantly raising funds for it. He was chairman of the board that ran the hospital, and he often made decisions about emergency placements like theirs.

Rebecca recovered after a six week long battle, and to see her talking and laughing again without having to struggle for air was simply astounding to her parents. But now the worries set in about going home. They knew that bills were coming due and that the hospital at home would be expecting some kind of payment plan to be set up. Harvey had no job, and Eunice needed to be home with Rebecca and the other children.

A few days before they were to leave the Institute, Simon had asked to speak with Harvey in his office. He'd told him that he'd checked out his background and thought that he was just the sort of man he was looking for to become the head of security on his estate, and had offered him the job. It came with a housing allowance, along with a salary he wouldn't have dared ask for, a sign-on bonus, and relocation pay. Then, six months into the job, the hospital in the states notified him that the remainder of Rebecca's bill had been paid by an anonymous source. Simon would never admit to the deed, insisting on changing the subject whenever Harvey tried to ask him about it.

That was ten years ago, and he'd never looked back, never had one day of regret. The Sayers—all of the Sayers—had treated him like family from the beginning, and he was the only person outside of the family who knew about the Elpies and Bluemen. He saw Simon not just as an employer, but as a father figure, and Simon cared about and believed in him enough to trust him with the lives of his family and friends.

As they rode towards the house in silence, Harvey had been thinking back on all of this. About how much he owed, and yes, loved this man. He knew that he and his family had almost been killed last night, possibly intentionally, and when he saw the stitches and bruising on the side of his head, and the cuts and scrapes on his arms, he felt an indignant, smoldering rage at their being victimized.

They parked near the kitchen and entered the house through there. Bess was at the table, drinking a cup of coffee, and he was shocked when he saw her. The bruises were starting to show, and she had large ones on both upper arms. The right side of her face was swollen and discolored, and her bottom lip was cut and puffy. Normally vivacious and buoyant, now she looked drained, haggard, and exhausted.

When she saw them come in the door, she greeted him warmly, and got up to give him a hug, but caught herself halfway to standing, when the pain in her back and sides caught her by surprise. Simon made a move towards the table, thinking she was going to fall, but she held up her hand to stop him. "No, no, I'm okay. I just didn't realize that everything was going to hurt when I moved. Just took me by surprise. Every time I sit for a few minutes, I find out where the new sore spots are when I stand up." She gave a little laugh. "I've never felt my age before, but geez, I'm feeling it today."

Standing up all the way, her eyes got wide and she blew out a big breath. "There! Ta da! Okay, Harvey, stay right where you are. I should make it over there in about half an hour." She laughed again and started walking towards him, moving like an old woman.

He took two big strides and met her open arms so that she wouldn't have to walk any farther. When he hugged her gently in return, he looked over her shoulder and saw Simon shaking his head, his face a mask of concern, changing quickly to anger. The set in his jaw changed, and his eyes narrowed.

"I hate that lately we only see each other at the gate, and there's never time to talk. You and Eunice, and the kids of course—in a few weeks, after our visitors have left—you could come over after your shift and the family could meet you here for dinner. My folks are going to stay another five weeks, and you know how my dad loves to sabotage the health of friends and family. One delicious dinner won't do you in."

"I don't even have to ask her. Even if Eunice didn't love you, any time she gets a chance to eat somebody else's cooking, she's there."

"Great! I'll give her a call. It probably won't be until the end of the week, though. There are so many loose ends we have to tie up with this situation."

"Fine, fine."

"Sweetheart, Harvey and I were just going into my study for a talk. You still have lots of time before our visitors get here tonight. Why don't you take some Ibuprofen and rest a bit more?"

She nodded and started to turn away, but then looked at him again. "You're the one that hasn't had any sleep, and no offense intended, but you're looking pretty gruesome. Why don't *you* take some IB's and come to bed when Harvey and you are done?"

He leaned in and kissed her gently on the forehead, letting his lips linger there a moment, then held both of her shoulders as he looked into her eyes. "There are things that need taking care of so that what happened last night will never happen again."

A little frightened now, she looked at Harvey questioningly, and then back at him. "Simon, I know you're angry—we all are. But please be careful. What are you—"

"Bess, I intend to do whatever I need to. We'll talk about it later. Right now Harvey and I have to make some plans. It'll be all right. Don't worry." He kissed her forehead again, then motioned towards his office with his head. Bess sighed and walked away as the two disappeared into the other room and closed the door.

"Have a seat, Harvey." As the other man started to sit, Simon let down his calm facade and slammed his fist on the credenza behind his desk. Harvey froze and stared at him. He'd never seen this gentle man truly angry.

Simon closed his eyes, took some deep breaths for control, and then addressed him in a quiet, intense voice. "Do you know what it's like for me to see my wife bruised and hurting, and to know that the person who orchestrated this attack will face no consequences for it? He tried to have my family killed. Because of a vendetta against me.

"I know that you understand what it's like to almost lose your daughter. I could have lost mine last night, and again, because of one man's hatred *for me.* And the man she wants to marry almost died right in front of her. I want to kill the person who did this, but I can't. Because I don't know with absolute certainty that he's responsible. Even though I know it in here," he said with a snarl as he thumped his chest.

He took another breath, staring straight ahead, and then looked back at his friend. "I'm sorry, Harvey. This isn't doing anybody any good. I need to stay calm and work this out."

"So you think Worthington's responsible for last night?" he asked, as he went ahead and sat down.

"Oh yes. He tried hitting on Bess last night at the gallery, and when she quietly rejected him, he tried hitting on—can you believe it—Genevieve. She shot him down less gently than her mother did. Then the crowning blow was when Enzo, her fiancé, got into the act and—oh, well, you get the picture. All of that was an attempt to get back at me, by targeting the women I love. When they spurned him, he left and made a show of leaving, to be sure everyone saw him. The more I think about that, the more I think it was so he'd have witnesses for an alibi."

"Simon, let me take care of this. I owe you—"

"No, Harvey, you don't. And that is the last thing I want. What would your family do if you did something rash to protect us? Would you want your children to grow up visiting their father in prison?"

"Of course not, but Simon—"

"No," he said forcefully. "And we need to get something straight right now. You owe me nothing. I know that you're grateful for the care your daughter received, and you should be, but not to me.

"I've told you our story. You know that I died from poison once, and the worst part of it was the feeling of slowly suffocating—of never being able to get enough air no matter what I did. When I was brought back by the Bluemen, the first thing I was conscious of was how absolutely glorious it felt to be able to breathe again. That experience made me think about all the people, and children especially, who suffer from respiratory problems their whole lives.

"I have been phenomenally blessed in my life, Harvey. All this money—I inherited a massive fortune that I did nothing to deserve. I used some of that money to build the Institute. People have treated me like a saint because of that, but I didn't sacrifice anything for it. All the continuous funding is done through donations from thousands of people all over the world. It's been my *privilege* to be a part of the things that go on there. I'm no doctor or researcher. Being on the board and seeing the difference the Institute has made in people's lives—that's more than I could ever ask for.

"Seeing your child come into the Institute on the brink of death, and being able to see her walk out with the rest of your family—that was *your* gift *to me*," he said, pointing to Harvey and then at himself, emphatically. "I got to share that victory with you, and I didn't have to suffer what all of you did to earn it.

"So now that we have that settled—I know that I probably didn't change your feelings. Over the years, I've learned to cherish your friendship, your honesty and loyalty. And I also appreciate your body of knowledge, your skills, and your connections. Today, I am going to ask you to be a part of something in order to safeguard my family. I'm going to take advantage of your misguided sense of debt and ask you to help me."

Harvey leaned forward in his chair and said earnestly, "Anything, Simon. I would do anything you needed to have done. I don't just owe you. I care about all of you, too. You're family to me, and a man has to protect his family."

They looked at each other without speaking, and then Simon nodded. "All right."

"I'm entrusting you with several jobs. First of all, I want you to go shopping. I made a few calls earlier to some banking associates of mine, and I've opened up a special account for business purposes. You are entitled to sign for whatever amount you need to spend, as head of my security. This account will also let you draw cash, in case you need to purchase anything not commonly found on the open market, and I leave those 'special' purchases completely at your discretion.

"You know I inherited wealth. But I also inherited a very good financial brain, and I've managed to turn that initial wealth into an unbelievable fortune. So you don't need to check with me about how much you can spend. You know security. I don't.

"I also want you to hire people to follow Arthur. Switch them out often, so that he can never be sure of who they are, but let him notice them watching him occasionally. He needs to believe that my threats weren't idle. Buy drones to fly over his place. Update all the security cameras. Any kind of surveillance equipment you need. And update your weapons in the guardhouse—whatever you need to do.

"Hire men—I want only individuals that you know personally. Men who have been soldiers, Harvey, that you can trust to be discreet and honorable, but who won't balk if they need to fight for my family. However many you think necessary. Give them housing allowances so that they can be close by. Hopefully, none will ever have to come here when my children and their families are visiting, except for maybe six to be here on a regular basis. The others—I'll put them on retainers, with the understanding that should you call them, they need to drop everything and get here at a moment's notice. You can have drills or practices, whatever, when we don't have the kids or our visitors here. Do you know enough men to take care of this? You know my retainer will be a generous one."

"That shouldn't be a problem, Simon."

"This last chore—I hope you never need to perform it. If I should die by any 'accidental' means, or if I die of natural causes and then any of my family meets with an 'accident' while Arthur is still living, I need for you to deliver this envelope for me." He reached across the desk and placed it into Harvey's outstretched hand. "You must have nothing to do with this man. Just deliver the envelope and say it's from me. When he reads it, he'll know what to do."

Harvey saw the name on the envelope and whistled, then looked at Simon in surprise.

"I know, I know. Three years ago, he came to the Institute with his youngest son. I had no idea who the man was, but his child was very bad off. We treated him and made arrangements for housing, much as we did for you and your family. The boy's doctors had as good as written him off for a lost cause before he came here. Our staff finally tried some experimental treatment on the child that was ultimately successful.

"You know that we don't charge our patients here, regardless of their finances. Patients are treated according to what they need, and not how much they can pay for.

"When the child was eventually well enough to go home, his father was exceedingly grateful, and wanted to make a huge donation to the Institute, but as you know, we don't take donations from ex-patients. That would make it appear that this is expected when anyone of means is treated here, and we don't operate like that. Often we receive large gifts from relatives of ex-patients, or friends, and those we accept.

"At any rate, this father told me it was urgent that we speak in my office alone before he left with his son. When we met, he told me that if I ever needed anything done, any kind of favor, regardless of how big or whether it was legal or not, that I should present one of his cards to his staff and they would immediately get the message to him. He said he expected no favor in return, and I was not obligated in any way to him.

"Honor demanded that he repay me for the life that was given back to him, he said. I basically told him what I just told you about that, but he simply waved my explanation off. He gave me three cards with his name and phone number on them. A favor for each one. I tried to give them back, but he told me to keep them, because often the most law-abiding people run into problems that can't be dealt with by the law.

"I've kept the cards—don't know why, really. I never expected to need them—to use them.

"When he left, I began doing research on the man, and couldn't believe everything I read. You're obviously familiar with the name."

"Simon, do you really believe there might be another attempt on your lives?"

"I hope not. When I spoke with Arthur today, I told him that he'd be watched, and that I had friends that—well, could cause accidents too. I basically told him if any more accidents occurred, that something very unpleasant would happen to him. Should the subject come up between us again, I want my statement to be true. Unfortunately, I am the world's worst liar.

"And I want to be sure that if he should manage to kill me, he would *never* be able to harm my family or anyone else, for that matter, ever again.

"Do not look in the envelope, Harvey. If you should have to deliver it someday, simply call the number on one of those cards and follow the instructions you're given. You can't be held accountable for delivering an envelope whose contents you know nothing about.

"You know that on the Bluemen's planet I almost lost Bess and Jonas. Last night I almost lost Bess and Genevieve, along with the man she loves. Both times I was helpless to protect them. That will never be the case again. Harvey, you're the only man in the world I would trust with this—with the lives of my family. You're the only man outside my family that I've ever told about the Elpies and Bluemen. If you want to say no to me about any of this, you can walk away right now and simply pretend we never had this talk. I'll manage this in another way, with no hard feelings between us. I would still value you as an employee and cherish you as a dear friend."

Harvey stood up and held his hand out across the desk. Simon reached back and grasped it with both of his.

"You said it was your privilege to help my family. Well, now it's my privilege to help yours."

CHAPTER TWENTY-EIGHT

He thought everything that had happened would keep him awake, but when he finally downed some Ibuprofen and crawled into bed next to Bess, all that had happened put him to sleep instead, with a profound and overpowering exhaustion.

She felt Simon lie down next to her, so she turned towards him, moved closer, and reached out to touch him. Too sore to even have their arms around each other, they went to sleep holding hands. He could hear her soft, even breathing, and with their hands entwined and resting against his chest, she could feel the beat of his heart. Those life signs blended rhythms in a quiet duet that lent peace to both souls—proof that despite the odds, their song continued.

##

After a deep sleep of unremembered dreams, Bess woke up four hours later. There had been a brief wake up snuffle from Elsie, but Bess had checked on Simon, thanked her, and gone immediately back to sleep. She didn't know what woke her up this time, at first, but then she realized it was the wonderful aromas coming from the kitchen.

Suddenly, she was famished. Intending to throw her legs off the side of the bed and force the rest of her body to follow suit, she was caught short when her movement sent stabbing pains everywhere, with the worst in her ribs.

This was absurd. She had to get up sooner or later, and the longer she stayed in bed, the worse she was going to hurt when she rose. Taking a deep breath, she forced herself to sit up. What should have been a one-step sit up, however, became a several-stepper, as her sore ribs forced her to carefully slide her legs off the bed and then push herself upright with her arms.

Sounds from the other side of the bed told her that Simon was having his own struggles. She heard a surprised exclamation on his first attempt at rising, so she assumed he was working on his own several-stepper technique.

Five minutes later, they were both on their feet, hunched over, holding their arms out away from their bodies as they shuffled and hobbled around the room, with little moans and groans accompanying their movements. As they passed each other, going in opposite directions, they glanced in the dresser mirror at the same time. Their eyes met in the mirror, and suddenly they were giggling.

They ended up sitting on the edge of the bed, leaning into one another as they laughed painfully, holding their sore ribs. Abruptly, Bess' giggles turned into tears. She shook her head, and wiped her face with the back of a forearm, annoyed with herself.

"Sorry. I just thought—as we were laughing together at the way we look, doddering around like the oldest couple in the world—that we're just so lucky to still *be* a couple, to still have Genevieve and Enzo. I want them to be a doddering old couple together someday, and they almost lost that chance last night."

He put an arm around her gently, and they sat in silence until she straightened up with a groan.

"Let's go eat. I want to scarf down a huge meal with our family, and drink wine and laugh together. Race you to the bathroom."

They both groaned, easing and levering themselves to their feet, and doddered away to start their lives again.

##

Everyone except Enzo showed up for dinner at seven-thirty, when calls went out from Angus. Sarah had fixed a plate of mashed potatoes, a bowl of cream of chicken soup, and some left over pudding for Enzo, and a regular meal in plastic carriers for Genevieve to take back to the house with her for the both of them

Another amazing, delicious, fat-laden meal downed, and then most drifted back to their rooms to wait for eleven p.m., when they'd greet their friends at the landing area.

After giving them a little time to get settled after supper, Simon and Bess climbed into their jeep and drove out to Eli's house for a talk. They could tell by the noise that the kids were there. As soon as they stepped out of their jeep, the front door banged open, and several voices began yelling, "Grandpa and Grandma! Grandpa Si and Grandma Bess are here!" followed by another shout of, "DO *NOT* JUMP ON THEM!" from Eli.

Thankfully, Eli barreled out the door after them to enforce his edict before the rambunctious little herd destroyed his parents. The kids were used to climbing and jumping all over Simon, and if they were lucky, he'd toss them up in the air. He couldn't toss Viola anymore, but being a teenager now, she wouldn't have allowed it anyway. Today, and for a while, he wouldn't be tossing anything except Ibuprofen, but he hated disappointing his grandkids.

She didn't toss, but ordinarily Bess did an excellent twirl, catching the kids under their arms and swinging them around in a circle. Right now, even thinking about it hurt her ribs.

Eli had explained everything to the kids, and when he shouted that little reminder, they'd all come to a screeching halt just before reaching their grandparents. Both were already grimacing and tensing in expectation of the pain the children's greetings would inflict.

Aluin gently took Simon's hand, and Simone took Bess.' The girl looked up at their faces with concern, and Aluin blurted out, "Hey, Grandpa and Grandma, relax, we're not gonna hurt you. Dad told us everybody is really sore, so we had to be tender with you and couldn't act like little savages."

"Why, that's very considerate of you. And he's right. I don't think I could handle even little savages today."

Viola took Simon's other hand, and the three led them into the house, with Duncan following behind, patting both their backs to comfort them. Eli held the door open and they all traipsed inside.

The kids took them over to twin loungers, sat them down, pulled the levers to put their feet up, and brought pillows out for each. Since Viola was the oldest, she did the honors and kissed them both on top of their heads.

Bess beamed at the royal treatment the kids were dishing out. "Wow, I could get used to this. Hey, Eli, tell me if you're renting out any rooms. I might just come and stay for a week or so, with service like this."

Simone giggled, and then without touching them, she stood between their chairs and put her arms a few inches over their chests in virtual hugs. "We love you, Grandma and Grandpa, and we're so glad you're okay."

Simon pulled her in with one arm, wincing a little, and kissed her forehead. "Thank you. Love you too, sweetheart."

With her ribs killing her, Bess couldn't quite manage the same reciprocation. "Virtual hug back at you, baby."

Colder came in with a big smile and gave them each a glass of water with ice, a straw, and a little umbrella. They laughed at that—Colder must have gotten the umbrellas from the main house. Bess always bought them for parties, claiming they made people happy, so after the disastrous visit to the Bluemen's planet fifteen years ago, the nine year old Colder had supplied everyone who seemed in need, with glasses of ice water fortified with straws and umbrellas. Since then, it had turned into a family tradition. If anybody was hurt, sick, or upset, somebody else was bound to show up with a glass of ice water containing the obligatory straw and umbrella.

Looking at them worriedly, Colder checked out the stitches on Simon's head and the cut and swelling on Bess' lip. Then he returned to Colder mode. "Dad, next time you do this, can you give me a little advance warning? I'm running out of umbrellas."

Simon looked over at Enzo and Genevieve sitting on the couch with their feet propped up on an ottoman, watching TV, and they both raised their glasses to him, each replete with a straw and umbrella. Eli cleared his throat and held up his identical drink. Simon and Bess laughed again and sat back, sipping their water.

He didn't want to stare, but he couldn't keep from looking at Enzo, who'd taken off the neck brace, and was trying to support his head with just his good hand for a while. The bruising on his neck had spread out, and looked especially huge since the blood had oozed downward beneath the skin, sending the purple discoloration all the way into the top of his chest. His face was a little more swollen, and the pain and difficulty he had swallowing were obvious. He was trying gamely to smile and chat, despite his hoarseness, but he looked miserable. Simon eased gently into his mind, to taste his pain, and was horrified at how badly he was hurting.

Genevieve sat beside him, rubbing his arm absentmindedly. There were bruises on her arms and a large abrasion on her face. She looked sad and very subdued.

"So—how are you all doing?" They all sort of mumbled or shrugged "Okay," which he knew meant "lousy."

"Enzo, if you don't mind me saying, you look like crap."

The kids laughed and Simon heard "Grandpa!" from three different directions. Duncan said, "Geez, Grandpa, I thought you liked him now. He said you weren't acting like a shit anymore."

Bess almost spit out her water as she choked back a laugh. Simon raised his eyebrows at Enzo, who just smirked and shrugged his shoulders, wincing as he paid for the gesture. "Well, he's right, I'm not, and don't repeat that anymore, you little toot. What I'm saying is that I'm concerned about him. He doesn't look like he feels very well."

"That's not what it sounded like, Grandpa. Sounded like you called him a name."

A "tsk" and an exasperated sigh erupted from Viola. "Oh Duncan, sometimes you're just so—young—and ignorant! I'll explain it to him later, Grandpa."

Jonas said seriously, "Yeah, Duncan, quit being so—young! And don't sass your Grandpa. He's just a poor, achy old man, and you should be nice to him. You'll be old and decrepit someday, too."

Simon sent over a glare. "As will you. Even sooner."

"Seriously, Enzo, how are you doing? You look like you ought to be hospitalized—we should never have let you sign yourself out."

"No, Simon. I'm just beat up. Same as everybody else."

Genevieve shook her head and said quietly, "Everybody else didn't nearly die."

"Come on, Genny. I'm okay. Simon, I appreciate your concern, but I've got pain meds, muscle relaxants with anti-inflammatories, and that's really all they could give me for this if I *was* in the hospital. And there's this gorgeous redheaded nurse here looking after me. I'm trying to get her number." He squeezed Genevieve's hand and made Groucho brows, but he couldn't get more that a pat on the arm in response. "A couple of days and I'll be my usual charming self."

Putting his drink down, Simon looked over at where the kids were playing Monopoly. "Hey, you Monopoly tycoons, do you think you could go in the other room for just a bit while I talk to your elders? It will only take a minute."

They sighed and rolled their eyes, but mumbled "Okay," and left the room. Jonas closed the door after them and looked back at Simon. Genevieve turned off the TV, and Eli came out of the kitchen with a towel over his shoulder, and sat on a bar stool.

"I wanted to talk to you all about last night. I think we all agree that what occurred was no accident. But you needn't be afraid for yourselves or the children. I've taken steps to see that nothing like that will ever happen again.

"I also wanted to apologize to you all, and especially you, Enzo, for everything. First of all, for acting like an ass, and secondly, because you were victimized because of someone's absurd grudge against me. I can't tell you how sorry I am about what happened.

"I had a talk with Arthur this morning." A collective gasp sounded around the room.

"I told him that I knew he was responsible, and that I've arranged for severe repercussions if anything else happens. He believed me, and he should, because it's true."

"What repercussions, Dad?"

"It's better that you don't know. What you don't know can't be held against you in court. I'm only telling you this so you'll understand that you can feel safe here. I'm also beefing up security, with extra men, better weapons and equipment, and I'm having Arthur watched."

There was silence in the room. It was too frightening and foreign to think about any of this being necessary.

Bess looked around at them sadly. "He won't tell me, either. About the 'repercussions.'"

"Because this is my decision, and mine alone. My responsibility. Sometimes the law can't or won't protect you, and you have no choice but to go on the offensive. I'll do whatever I deem necessary to protect this family. That settles the matter—I won't discuss it any further.

"On a higher note, your mother and I wanted to tell our sons that we are so *stupendously* proud of you three for coming to the rescue last night. Each of you had a part in it, and you did everything exactly right. You acted with intelligence and determination, and kept your heads in a crisis. Thank you for saving our newest family member."

Enzo raised his glass. "Here, here."

"And Genevieve, the doctor told us that you kept Enzo alive in that car. You're all just—amazing."

Serious for once, Colder put his glass down and looked at the four of them, making eye contact with each one as he spoke. "We're just so thankful we were there, and that we still have all of you with us. After seeing your car go flying off that embankment, we weren't sure any of you would be.

"And Enzo, I think we all sort of think of you as family already, even though you turned out to be a redneck." Raspberries and boos were heard from several sectors. He grinned and continued. "But you already know how we feel, because *you* got an umbrella, too."

Enzo held up his water and gave a body nod, and Genevieve smiled for the first time all day.

TWENTY-NINE

The brothers had set up folding chairs in the field for the four crash victims, with a couple of pillows for Enzo to rest his neck on. At eleven p.m. the estate's entire population sat in silent anticipation, with the exception of Enzo, who was so excited that he couldn't stop talking.

His hoarse whispers were so constant, that they'd started the kids giggling. Just when they'd think he was finally wound down, the raspy sounds would start up again, and so would the giggles.

"So will they be upset that I'm here? Ya know, since we didn't tell them—"

"No, they'll be fine with it."

"Good, good.

"What do they look like?"

"Enzo, you saw them on the disk. You said you'd never forget seeing that. You forgot already?"

"No, no, that's right, that's right.

"Will they think I'm weird because I'm not tall like the rest of you?"

"They could care less, and they've seen lots of shorter men, I'm sure."

"Yeah, but have they met any?"

"Probably."

"Will they shake hands?"

"I don't know."

"Well, I need to know to prepare myself. Are their hands slimy? Do they feel creepy? Will they try and get in my head, I mean, like, should I try and shield my brain or anything?"

"Enzo, what could you possibly have in your brain that they would want?"

"That was harsh."

"Sorry, but you need to stop talking."

"Why?"

"I don't know, but I'm trying really hard to think of a reason. There must be one."

Suddenly, there was a pressure in the air, and then the ship was in front of them. There were no lights or fanfare, just a large, triangular ship. Enzo stared at the hatch, unable to believe that this was really happening—that aliens were about to step out. No one spoke or moved, and a few held their breaths in suspense.

When the hatch opened, the Elpies jumped out and ran towards their friends, as they always did, but stopped suddenly when they saw that Simon and Bess were getting up slowly, instead of running to meet them. They sent their questions and tasted their pain, and changed their running into a trot.

Instead of the usual back pounding hugs, the Elpies gently encircled Simon and Bess with their arms, then turned to Genevieve and gave the uninjured side of her face their palms. That is, the elder Elpies.

The two younger were jumping and chittering, pounding the brothers on their backs, and throwing Colder back and forth between them. He was laughing and whooping, and then all the kids and the other brothers got in on the fun, until bodies were flying through the air and rolling around on the ground. They were very careful to catch the children when they threw them, but the brothers were on their own. Genevieve saw Enzo watching them enviously.

She squeezed his hand and bumped his shoulder. "Hey, don't forget—we're getting married, so you'll be seeing stuff like this every six months for the rest of our lives, I hope. You'll get your chance to be crazy with aliens."

He smiled at her, and gave a body nod. "Yeah, I forget that sometimes, Principessa. The rest of our lives together. Even with all we've gone through, that part of it still doesn't seem real sometimes. I like being surprised by the thought of it."

Then the Bluemen stepped out of the ship, and Enzo was rendered speechless—a miracle in itself. Seeing them on the disk had not begun to prepare him for being confronted by seven to eight feet tall Bluemen.

Bess spoke up and announced, "Everybody, I'd like to introduce the newcomer to our family. This is Genevieve's fiancé, Enzo Uccello."

All eyes turned to him, and he was bombarded with the strange sensation of gentle fingers weaving through his mind. Sven's daughter walked up to him and put what looked like a gun to his head. On instinct, he jerked away painfully at her touch, but Genevieve grabbed his arm.

"Hey, be cool, Enzo. She wants to know if you want to be gifted with the ability to send and receive language from them, and mental images from the Elpies. She can do it with that thing in her hand. It doesn't hurt, and it is so cool. You *have* to do it."

"Whoa, are you kidding me? Heck yeah, I want to be gifted. Go for it!" Sadie put the instrument to his head, and then lowered it. "Okay, I'm ready! I'm ready!" When nothing happened, he looked questioningly at Genevieve.

"It's done already. You can talk to them out loud, and they'll get the translations in their minds, and they talk to you with their minds. But you can also send to them, by focusing your thoughts towards that Blueperson. It takes a little more time with the Elpies. They'll get you, but it will take a while for you to completely get them, since they think and send more with pictures and feelings. Gets to be second nature after a while, and you'll find yourself filling in the blanks, so don't worry about it. They're empaths, by the way, so be sure you keep a nice attitude. Oh, and since Eli, that is, Eli the first, is a healer, don't be surprised if he tries to make you feel better. Just go with it. He'd never do anything to hurt you."

Sadie started to walk away before he thanked her, and on reflex he leapt after her to catch her arm. The sudden movement sent jolts of pain shooting down his neck and back, so excruciating that the shock and magnitude of them took him over, and he jerked to a stop, frozen in place. All the Elpies felt his pain, and every one of them instantly turned and reached out to him with a soothing.

It was as if a velvet shield was laid across the knife-like sensations—the pain was still there, but it was blunted, and his mind was put at ease despite the discomfort. He could tell where each soothing was coming from, and there was so much compassion thrust at him at once, that suddenly his eyes were wet. He looked at each of them and said "Thank you." The words were minimal but the emotion behind them was not, and they were well received.

Able to move then, he straightened up slowly, and instead of racing after her, as he'd started to do, this time he tried sending to Sadie. He was elated when his efforts were rewarded by her turning to him and sending, "You're welcome. And it's nice to meet you, too."

The brothers came over to Enzo then, pulling Micah and Luigi along with them. When Jonas introduced Luigi, Enzo's eyes lit up. "Luigi? Ay, Paesano!" He grabbed Luigi's arm and started speaking Italian. Since Elpies understood not words, but the meaning behind the words, the language was irrelevant. The other humans in the group watched as Enzo emphasized almost every other word with one handed gestures, injuries nearly forgotten. The two strolled off together, with Enzo spouting rapid fire Italian. Happy to go with the flow of his new friend's enthusiasm, Luigi nodded, resting one clawed hand on Enzo's uninjured shoulder as they walked a short way and then headed back to the group, like old friends reunited.

Genevieve couldn't stop smiling. Enzo was back. She knew how hard he'd been trying not to let his injuries overwhelm him; not to complain. But he'd been in so much pain since the crash, that his emotions, his movements, energy—everything about him had been dulled and subdued, and it broke her heart to see him like that.

All of a sudden, the effervescence was back, and that energy that nearly crackled off of him at times was there again. When she looked around, her whole family was smiling at him, and she realized that they'd felt it, too. They hadn't realized what was missing until that spirit in him came back. Some people were just meant to be happy, and they couldn't help but affect the people around them.

Then it was Sven's turn to introduce his daughter to the group. The pride and love he felt for her were obvious when he sent her name and why she was with him. He considered these humans his friends, but the depth of affection he felt from them and the warmth in their welcome of his child still surprised him.

With introductions out of the way, the group turned and headed for the house. Sarah's hot cookies were waiting.

##

Although it didn't stop them from eating macaroons, the Elpies' moods were very dark when they received the sendings about what had occurred the night before, and Sven and his crew were concerned as well.

Simon would have loved for Sven to just zap Arthur away, or do a mental adjustment and turn him into a normal person. But he didn't request either, since he knew the Bluemen's hands were tied by their protocol. They had no part in the situation, so they couldn't interfere.

When Gisella was a child and the Bluemen had intervened to save her life, their excuse had been that they were saving their subject who was in danger at the time of their contact with her. That reasoning included their dealing with the people who were a threat to her at that moment. The same could be said for their rescue of Madelyn and Elsie, and the Bluemen's "suggestions" that were given to those involved in their brutalization. They'd helped the other dogs present by lumping them together in the current situation.

In actuality, their contacts with Gisella and the dogs had been initiated *because* of the danger and stress their instruments had shown as they followed the readings of their brain patterns. The Bluepeople's protective feelings towards their subjects were not discussed as such, but their actions often proved them.

Simon's problem with Arthur was long standing, and the crash had occurred when the Bluemen weren't in contact. Had it happened when the Bluemen were present, or reaching out to Simon or his family, they would have been free to act.

#

It seemed to Eli that someone was always trying to kill his brother, and he couldn't fathom why. There was so much goodness in Simon—why would anyone want to destroy that?

Stuffing two macaroons into his mouth, he chewed as he made the rounds of the crash victims. He politely sent for permission from each before feeling their sore muscles with his long, leathery fingers. It was a peculiar sensation, but oddly comforting. He reached in his pouch then, and brought out four little brown balls of compressed herbs, giving one to each of them with the instructions to chew and swallow.

Enzo looked suspiciously at his dose, but when he saw the others pop them into their mouths, he couldn't look the wuss, so he did the same. It was easily the most disgusting thing he'd ever tasted, and he had to fight not to gag when it hit his tongue.

But five minutes later, the soreness all over began easing, and he could talk, swallow, and move his head with the least pain he'd had since the crash. He looked across the room at Eli the first, a six foot lizard, sitting on the sofa across the room from a seven and a half foot blue alien with bat ears and seven fingers, eating cookies and holding china tea cups, and the funny thing was, it didn't seem strange anymore.

He reached out to Eli with his mind, and—AMAZING—it worked! Eli looked up politely, and Enzo sent him his most sincere thanks for caring enough to lessen his pain. The pain was diminished to the point that even his breathing was improved.

In his mind, he felt satisfaction radiating off of Eli, and then received a mental picture of the swelling in his throat and trachea gradually subsiding. He realized then that whatever he'd been given must have brought down the edema—that was why his breathing was better. He gave Eli a smile, bowed his head in thanks, and then looked around the room at the other three crash victims. Every one of them seemed to be moving easier. Their faces showed less tension, too—an unconscious reaction to the decrease in pain.

Simon was deep in mental conversation with the Blueman Leader. "Sven, I know that you can take no action on what happened, because of your protocol."

"Thank you for understanding, Simon. You are our friends and it pains us to see you in any kind of peril, but we can only do so much without losing our ship."

"You know I'd never want that to happen. But…I was wondering if I could ask a favor of you—*only* if you can manage it without getting yourselves in trouble."

"Go ahead and ask. We can listen without endangering our commissions."

"Well—I wonder if you could somehow probe Worthington's memory and tell me if I'm correct in assuming he was responsible for our 'accident.' I feel sure of it, but have no proof. I've made arrangements so that if anything should happen to me or my family, he will face severe consequences—consequences I would not want an innocent man to suffer.

"I thought, since you wouldn't be changing him or his surroundings by doing this, that maybe you could manage a probe without specifically breaking protocol."

Simon watched intently while Sven looked at the other Bluepeople in the living room, telepathically discussing the situation with each. Their discussion lasted a good ten minutes, and then Sven sent to Simon, "It will be done."

Sven rose, and snagging ten more cookies on his way out, left the house.

#

Sarah was in her element standing by the seven huge platters of cookies, smiling, asking if anyone needed more macaroons, milk, coffee, or tea. She never sat during these cookie fests, but served and watched, instead. Nothing was as gratifying to her as seeing people really enjoy her cooking, and nobody enjoyed her cookies like aliens.

Mona was the ship's one permanent female member, and Sarah liked watching her the best. The Bluepeople had long slits for mouths, with only the females having a tiny puffiness that served as lips. Mona would pick up a cookie, open her mouth slightly, and slide the whole thing in. Then she'd sit up straight, close her eyes, and taste—simply taste, with her whole being, it seemed like to Sarah. Her jaws barely moved, and Sarah assumed she was chewing very, very slowly. Then she would swallow and open her eyes with a look of ecstasy and longing fulfilled. Even if nobody else ate Sarah's cookies, watching Mona would have made all the effort worthwhile for her. That was one alien who knew how to appreciate a cookie.

#

The macaroons lasted until the wee hours of the morn, and then everyone turned in except for Simon. He was too excited at seeing the Elpies again, and too anxious about what Sven would tell him. The herbs that Eli had given him made him feel so much better that it was even comfortable sitting and reading again, so he picked up a book that he hadn't touched for a while, and settled into a recliner to wait.

If was four a.m. before Simon was roused from sleep, the book having long since dropped from his hands. Seven fingers rested on his shoulder, and Sven was looking down at him, sending to him before he could even sit upright.

"You were wise to make arrangements. Worthington did call for your vehicle to be attacked, and had another vehicle hidden for the driver to switch into after forcing you off the road."

Simon felt the fury rise in him at the news, but Sven held him down effortlessly when he tried to sit up. "Wait, my friend. I understand your anger—I have family, too. But I also saw in Worthington's mind that the threats you made to him were taken seriously. He is afraid, and that fear will keep him from attempting anything else. I know you desire vengeance. But Simon—no one was killed. If you act now, you would be tried for murder, and we couldn't help you.

"You already have your vengeance, in the fear that haunts his mind constantly. He's even considering moving away. I think you could easily kill him if the accident had just happened, but you're no murderer, and killing him now would eat away at your soul. You want to protect your family—then you must consider the damage you would be doing to them if your actions caused them to suffer the loss of their husband and father. You've done what needed to be done. Now let it rest."

Looking into those huge eyes, and knowing that the mind behind them was looking into his own, he felt ashamed at his desire to kill. Sven was right. About everything. At least now though, he knew that if something should happen, his arrangements would not be sentencing an innocent man. He wondered if Arthur had ever been innocent.

Gripping Sven's wrist, he looked at him and nodded. "Thank you for finding the truth, Sven, and for telling me not just the truth, but the way to handle it. I've been so… so sick and enraged about the whole thing, and every time I look at the brace on Enzo's neck, or see Bess wince when she tries to stand. When I see the abrasion on the face of my daughter, and how depressed she is now…

"You should have seen her, Sven, when she was asleep in the backseat, just moments before the crash. She was so beautiful, so happy and peaceful holding the hand of the man she's chosen. And now it's ruined—the wonderful time she'd hoped to show him—meeting her family and all of you. Now, besides being injured herself, she feels terrible that he was almost killed, and is suffering so much pain as a result of coming here."

Sven took his hand away, and let Simon sit up. "The rest of the crew was discussing that—the pain and the injuries you sustained. We believe that while we're here interacting with you—as the higher species, it might be considered reasonable for us to deal with a current problem. After all, you were sitting for a period, waiting for us to land, and I feel sure that this increased your pain."

Simon nodded, starting to smile.

"And when Sadie gave telepathic and language enhancement to Enzo, he *obviously* reinjured himself as he tried to catch and thank her. That would make us responsible for his increase in pain, in which case, we should—"

Simon grabbed the closest of Sven's three hands, and grasped it tightly between his own two. "I know what you're doing. You don't have to explain to me. Thank you. Thank you so very much."

#

Simon woke Bess up and told her to put a robe on and come with him for a wonderful surprise. She blearily followed him to the jeep, and then into Eli's house, using their master key.

Genevieve had told them she'd be sleeping in Enzo's room to watch him, and he'd left it at that. He hadn't wanted to wake anyone else up, but he felt he should knock. After a few moments, they heard footsteps. Genevieve opened the door a crack, then all the way when she saw it was him. "Dad? Mom? What's going on? Is everything okay?"

"More than okay. Wake Enzo up and come with us."

"Dad, he's finally asleep. He's hardly slept through a whole hour at a time since the accident, he's been in so much pain. I mean, he hasn't said it, but I can tell. He can't ever get comfortable. I hate to—"

"How would you like for all of his pain to stop?"

"What are you ta—" With a gasp, her eyes went wide and she whispered, "The Bluemen? Are they going to heal him? Like—completely?"

"They're going to heal all four of us! Come on, wake him up."

"Oh, Daddy," she squealed, and stood on her toes to kiss his cheek.

"Enzo, wake up, honey, we're going to get repaired!"

She called me "Daddy."

#

They were amazed at how quick their healings were. It took only fifteen minutes for all three Sayers combined. It took forty for Enzo. The difference in the time required to heal his injuries and theirs made them even more aware of how much worse the damage to his body had been.

When he came out of the room after being worked on, he was one giant Enzo smile. "Bellissimo! What a beautiful thing it is, not to hurt! And I can toss this thing!" he shouted, as he threw his neck brace in the air. Genevieve laughed and ran to him, folding him into her arms for a kiss that made her parents blush and look away. Then she seemed to realize where she was, and who she was in front of, and she jerked back, straightening up suddenly.

"Sorry. It's just so good to see him 'right' again. And both of you, too."

Though all helped when needed, Luca Pacioli was the Blueman who served as the major medical personnel on the ship. When he walked out behind Enzo, the humans began bombarding him with their thanks. He nodded his head once, and they could feel his smile.

CHAPTER THIRTY

Mona and her husband, Maurice, were going over with Sven what they'd found out from Arthur Worthington's memory. "Should we tell Simon that he was responsible for the deaths of two of his wives?"

"No. Never. That might push him to take matters into his own hands, as he started to do tonight. He might not suffer any guilt if he killed him for that, but he most certainly would be destroyed by the very law that failed those unfortunate women."

"We couldn't somehow let the law know about those murders?"

"Not without ignoring our directives. We've already gone around them twice in one day, with the delving and the healings. We can't tell The Seated that these women were our subjects, or that we *had* to act. They're already dead. Even if they *were* our subjects, we'd be told that help was no longer possible for them. How many murders of one kind or another take place every day on planets that we visit? We can't step in on all of them, as much as we'd like to."

Maurice walked to the other side of the room in frustration, looking out the windows of the ship, as if an answer lay out there. "But we have no guarantee that this creature won't ever attack the Sayers again. What if he slowly loses his fear, or what if his vile nature overcomes it, and he decides he's willing to pay the price, just to do harm to this family?"

Mona walked over to him, and put one of her arms across his shoulders. "I feel the same about the Sayers—I want to protect them. But how could we justify it?"

Sven folded his three arms and looked at Maurice. "At least we've helped to warn Simon. And he's a man of considerable means. He's sent Harvey Washington out to buy safeguards and weapons."

"How insane, that this man of peace has had to fight for those he loves twice before, and prepares to do so a third time. It makes me sad for him and his family. It makes me sad for all humans."

##

The brothers woke to the smell of coffee. Eli was up first, and he wandered into the kitchen to see Genevieve sitting at the table with her feet up on a chair, reading the paper and drinking a cup of the wonderful smelling brew. Enzo was sitting on the other side of the table, holding a cup below his nose with both hands, taking in the aroma.

Waving sleepily to them, Eli said, "Hey. Up early, huh? Your neck keep you aw—Hey! Where's your neck brace? Where's your sling? And why are you smiling like that?"

Enzo jumped up and did a little dance, and then pulled Genevieve to her feet to dance with him, laughing the whole time. Eli started laughing at the two. "Whoa, were Eli the Elpie's little brown pills that good? Geez, Enzo, your bruise is gone! And that skinned place on your face is gone, too, Genny! How did that—the Bluemen? Like they did with Mom and Dad, and Jonas?"

Enzo danced over, pulled him down, and planted a big kiss on the top of his head. "You know it, my almost big brother! And I cannot even begin to tell you what a wonder it is to feel good again! Your mom is fine now, and even that humongous cut on your dad's head is healed, with no scar even, if you can believe it! Oh, man, I wish we could go parade our nearly perfect bodies in front of that *stronzo* that set us up."

Genevieve turned her head to the side and narrowed her eyes at him. "What do you mean, *nearly* perfect? Speak for yourself, Uccello."

"Oh, *scusa*, Principessa." He danced over to her and kissed her on the lips and danced back to Eli, with arms open wide, making a huge pucker.

Eli held out his hands to stop him. "So, Enzo, does this mean I can punch your arm again?"

"Of course, *if you can catch me!"* Sometimes short was a good thing, he thought, as he ran under Eli's arms and out the front door with a bang of the screen, whooping and laughing. Eli stormed after him, his weight causing resounding thuds through the living room, and his "YAA HAA, I'M COMING FOR YOU!" at the top of his lungs finally rousing the other two brothers from their beds.

Jonas came stumbling out of his room in his shorts, and Colder appeared in a slightly more disheveled state, moments after. "What is it? What's happening? Was that Eli? Who's hurt? Oh no, is it Enzo?" came out of both mouths simultaneously—almost the same words, but not in the same order.

Genevieve smiled, and then broke into a laugh. "Look out the door."

Before they could reach the door, it flew open, and Enzo came bursting through with Eli on his heels. He thought he'd escaped, when one long arm grabbed him around the waist, picked him up off the ground, and slammed him onto his back on the couch. Colder and Jonas both screamed at the sight and then screamed at Eli together, jumping on him, grabbing his arms and trying unsuccessfully to pull them back.

"STOP IT ELI! ARE YOU CRAZY? YOU'RE GONNA KILL HIM! Enzo, are you okay? What's wrong with you, Eli?"

Genevieve had never seen either of them so shaken. Colder was close to tears, thinking he was watching his brother murder a friend. Then Jonas and he realized that both attacker *and* attackee were laughing. She finally took mercy on them.

"The Bluemen healed all of us last night with their machines. Completely healed us!"

Now Eli was tickling Enzo, who was screaming "UNCLE" to no avail. The other two looked in wonder at Genevieve. Colder walked over to her and rubbed his hand over her face, her skin smooth and healthy where she'd had that huge, ugly abrasion just hours before. She smiled at him, and he grabbed her, hugged her, and kissed the top of her head. "Oh Gen, I'm so happy for both of you. I was so scared that Enzo might be permanently screwed up."

She teared up a little and nodded. "Me too, Colder. Just seeing him running around and roughhousing, acting like his usual crazy self—I can't tell you what that means to me. I could die right now and I—"

He put his hand over her mouth. "Uh, considering all that's happened, don't say that out loud. Don't even think it, okay?"

She put her head on his chest and hugged him tight. "Okay."

Jonas had jumped in now, and he was tickling Eli, who was even more ticklish than Enzo, and the three screamed and laughed and finally fell off the couch, too tired and out of breath to move. Suddenly, Enzo said "Hey!" and crawled in a rush over to where Eli was slumped on the floor, leaning against the couch. "Hey, big guy, what's wrong?"

They all looked to see Eli with his head down, covering his face. When he took his hands away, tears were streaming from his eyes. "I'm just so happy everybody's okay!"

The rest of them started laughing then, except for Genevieve, who came over and sat on the floor next to Eli. She took one of his big hands, stood up on her knees and kissed his forehead. He reached over and tousled her hair. Then everyone got quiet when he raised his hands and shrugged his shoulders.

"I know, I know. Yep, this is the Eli who never, ever cried when he was a kid. You coulda cut off both arms, and

I wouldn't have cried. I think I must have stored up the tears, ya know? This all started when I saw the disk—when I saw Jonas beat up, and Mom looking dead, and then watched Dad dying. Something just cracked inside of me. I could hardly stop crying then, and it just didn't seem important to me anymore—not crying."

He looked at Jonas. "And then when you came home, I was so happy to see all of you alive, and so shook up to see Dad looking like he was almost dead, that the tears practically shot out of my face. Ever since then, when I really get emotional, the tears just come, man, and I don't even care.

"Sometimes I'll be looking at my kids and one of them will say something cute, or I'll think about how special they are and how much I love them, and my eyes just fill up. They tease me no end about it, of course. You know the way we call kisses on the forehead 'Dad kisses?' Well, watery eyes are 'Dad eyes,' in our house.

"You should've seen me when our babies were born. Oh, geez, with the first one, the doctor threatened to have me taken out of the room, I was sobbing so loud. I was quieter after that, but otherwise, it was the same with all five. You never get used to it.

"But especially with the first one—here was my beautiful Babette, pushing this grapefruit sized head out of her—"

"No, no, stop, man, don't talk about that! Oh, that's so sick, Eli!" Jonas was almost gagging, and Colder was holding his arms out, shaking his palms at Eli, a horrified look on his face.

"Oh, you guys—you think that now, but when it's your *own* baby—oh man, it's just the most incredible thing in the world to watch. It's so *earthy* and *real*. I'd look at Babette straining, and pushing—"

The other two brothers were shaking their heads, and Colder had his hands over his ears.

"—and all I could think about was what kind of courage it took to grow a whole baby inside of her body, shoving her internal organs all over the place and knowing that she'd eventually have to push something the size of a watermelon—"

Colder left the room in a rush, and Jonas was looking a little green.

"—out of her tiny body, and bring a child that we made together, into the world. She takes a deep breath and gives that final push and all of a sudden, there it is, this big head! Then the rest of the baby sort of pops out after the doctor pulls one shoulder free, and this big gush of fluid right after, like a baby Tsunami! The doctor holds the baby up, and there's this thick, pulsing cord coming from its navel, pulsing with Babette's blood that she's been supplying the baby with—whoa, what a wild concept that is! And then they hand me the scissors, and I feel this 'scrunch' as I cut—"

Jonas excused himself to get some air.

"—to separate the baby from Babette, and make *our* child part of the world outside of her. This amazing little body that's still covered with that greasy white stuff, and blood, and it hits me that this is Babette's blood. Her labor, her battle wounds."

Eli was starting to tear up again. "It's just so freaking beautiful!"

Genevieve put her arm around him and handed him a tissue. "Geez, this feels familiar," he laughed, and she rubbed his back and smiled.

"Yeah, seems I remember starting to supply people with tissue and back rubs about the time you started crying."

He nodded and blew his nose, getting himself under control. "Enzo, we've known each other such a short time, but I already think of you as a brother, guy. You're just that sort of person. And I can see that what's between you and my sister is the real thing.

"Jonas and Colder and I had been talking, and we were all really afraid that you were forever bummed. Neck injuries, even if you didn't break a bone—you know, they don't always heal perfect. We were thinking you might have to quit being a fireman, and you've wanted that your whole life. And all the sports stuff you like—this injury made everything seem so iffy. You know, when the Elpies landed and we were horsing around with them, I glanced up and saw you looking at us, like you'd have given anything to be able to do that. Man, I just felt so bad for you.

"So here you are, running and charging around, and—and—and I'm able to pound on you and have you pound back—all of a sudden I felt so grateful and overwhelmed and happy for you, that I just—"

Enzo stood up on his knees, took the back of Eli's head in his hands, bent it down so that their foreheads met, and said softly, "Dio mio, I love this family."

CHAPTER THIRTY-ONE

It took an hour for Enzo to work up the courage to approach the Bluemen about working their healing magic on Eli. Everyone had forgotten about the strain to his back and arms, since he wasn't one of the victims and because he was tough enough not to show what he was feeling.

The only reason Enzo remembered it was that after their wild romp outside and then their emotional moment sitting on the floor, when Eli tried to get to his feet, he saw him wince and have to change positions so that he could use the couch to push up on. Then when he'd started to stand up straight, the pain had caught him half way to upright. After freezing for a second, he'd had to move in slow motion for the next half of the journey. Having just experienced those knife-like jolts of pain himself, watching Eli move told him the whole story.

The way he'd run around outside, no one would've believed he had any problem, but backs were like that. A person could lift two-hundred pounds, no sweat, and then the next day become almost paralyzed with pain after reaching across the table for the salt shaker. Enzo had seen a lot of guys pay the price for heroics, and it was usually within the next few days.

Without even discussing the issue, Luca went into the medical room and readied the machine. Then came the big problem—convincing Eli to go. He was embarrassed, of all things, thinking he'd be making a fuss about something that he should deal with himself. Fortunately, when the first Eli and Barnabas saw him arguing with Enzo and Genevieve, they came over and inserted themselves into the middle of the issue.

When the two walked up to the group, all conversation ceased, so the first Eli enquired politely about their disagreement. Enzo explained the situation, and afterwards,

Eli the first, with the second Eli's permission, gently felt along his arms, then lifted his shirt to look and feel along his spine.

He seemed so gentle and kind as he turned Eli the second around and began sending to him, that the other two were shocked to see Eli jolted back as if slapped when he received the sending. He straightened himself then and stood with his head bowed, nodding like a mischievous child receiving a scolding. When they finished sending, Eli the first patted the second on the cheek, and walked away.

The big Colder, Barnabas, stayed for a second, staring at him. The row of stiff hairs on his head began tilting forward and he thumped Eli on the top of the head. Then he turned to follow the other Elpie. The three of them watched him go, and then Genevieve and Enzo looked back at their Eli. He was blushing like crazy.

Genevieve put her hand on his arm and peered up at his face. "Geez, what did Eli send to you?"

He raised his head and straightened up, took a deep breath and blew it out.

"Well, you know Elpies don't use words, but they sure know how to get their messages across. I guess I could roughly translate. Um—he sent that my muscles were injured, and my back might never be the same as it once was, and that I'd have to be a freakin' lunatic to turn down this chance." He paused for a second and nodded to himself in agreement. "He also sent that it was an insult to everybody who'd ever been injured and was desperate for healing, to have a chance for it and turn away. Then he sent that I could choose to be made whole again or I could be a freakin' idiot, and pay for it with pain and disability for the rest of my life." He paused again and gave a short laugh. "Then he finished up by sending that I was a fine young man."

"What did Barnabas send to you?"

His blush came back, and he gave an embarrassed laugh. "Uh, Colders aren't quite as subtle and kind as village

Elpies are, you know. Um, the closest translation that I would be willing to repeat in front of a lady is—well, he sent me a mental picture of something and told me not to be one.

"So—do we go straight to the ship, or make an appointment?"

#

Luca motioned Eli into the room, and he was back out in twenty minutes, tearing up big time. Again. He kept reaching back to Luca and shaking one of his hands, then patting this arm and then that one, thanking him over and over. Finally, Luca patted his shoulder, and putting a huge hand on his back, gently shoved him towards the door.

Enzo and Genevieve got the hint, and taking Eli by the arms, they ushered him quickly off the ship. When they got outside, Eli was looking at his arms, smiling and shaking his head. "Oh, man, Eli was right. I'd have to be a freakin' lunatic to pass this up! I didn't realize how the pain was affecting me until it all stopped. This is just incredible! I've had little twinges in my back since college—don't even remember what from—but it's all good now. But Gen, Enzo—Luca sent that there was a little tiny growth on my spine that wasn't causing any symptoms yet, but would soon, so he decided to eliminate that while he was in there."

"What did he say the growth was?"

"I asked him several times, but all he'd send to me was that he was taking care of it, and I didn't have to worry about it ever again. And that I shouldn't mention it. He said he was going to do something to make sure it never came back. Now I'll always wonder if he didn't save my life in there today. Thank you both for pushing me to do this. I gotta thank the other Eli, too. And *maybe* Barnabas. But that's just a maybe."

He leaned over and gave Genevieve a kiss on the cheek, punched Enzo on the arm, and then started running towards the main house. He did a forward flip, landing on his feet, and hollered back at them. "Haven't been able to do that in years!"

#

When Colder walked with Micah and Luigi through the back door into the kitchen, Bess was sitting at the table with Sarah and Dulcie, drinking tea, and Angus was in the living room talking with Simon. Dulcie had watched with total concentration as Sarah baked cookies, macaroons, a pie, and yeast rolls, and she'd focused with even greater intensity on eating samples of each. Now she was reacquainting herself with the pleasures of caffeine, as she sat and sent with Bess and her mom.

Colder gave his mom and grandma a peck on the cheek and a quick palm to Dulcie's face. Micah and Luigi politely gave the palm to everyone's face and then stepped back and let Colder talk.

"Uh, Mom, Grandma, I'd like to get the family together for a little talk. It's nothing bad. In fact, it's something spectacular! The others are coming over from Eli's and the Bluemen's ship, and Hiram and Gisella are bringing the kids. The Elpies already know, but they're coming too. Can we go into the living room?"

Well, well, she thought. It was a surprise, of course, and Simon would probably be ticked off that one more of their kids had decided to get married without them even having been informed that he was dating someone special. But he was a grown man, and he didn't need their permission for anything.

By the time they'd finished off the dregs of their tea and come into the living room, everyone was gathered. Colder had warned the Elpies and Bluemen that his parents might make a little bit of a scene, along with Jonas, due to their horrendous experiences off planet. His mom and grandma might cry, thinking of him being millions of miles away, where they couldn't talk to or see him. And his dad, geez, he wasn't looking forward to that. But he'd assured the others that he could handle everything and it would all be settled down by the time they were ready to leave.

He looked around at all those faces, and realized that all of these people loved him. More than just his mom and grandma might be arguing for him to stay. He stood tall and swallowed, his mouth suddenly dry, and began.

"Everybody, I have an amazing announcement! The Bluemen and Luigi and Micah have invited me to be on their crew—an interspecies crew to study and explore the universe. They're going to give all of us a one week's trial to see if we like it and if they think we're suited for space exploration. We leave tomorrow."

There were raised eyebrows, and "whoas" and "wows" around the room, but Colder didn't see anyone that looked upset. He looked closely at his mom—not a tear. In fact, she was smiling. Then his dad stood up and came over to clap him on the back and give him a hug.

"That's fantastic, son! What an opportunity! Are you already packed? Anything you need?"

Before he could answer, his mom came over and hugged him. "Oh, honey, I'm so happy for you! You'll have a great time, I'm sure. Exploring all those planets, meeting new species. I can't wait to hear your stories!"

He stepped back from them, a half-smile on his lips, but confusion in his eyes. "I thought you'd be upset, or worried. Try to convince me not to go—"

His dad looked at him in surprise. "Why on Earth would we do such a thing? How many people in the world get to experience something like this?"

He lost his smile completely, now. "But you know, this could be really dangerous. I mean, we have no idea what could be out there on hostile planets and—"

His grandpa had heard that, and stuck his two bits in. "Anything worse than what you've got living next door to you? You know that bastard tried to kill you. Well, not you personally, but only because you weren't in the car with your dad. Talk about a hostile planet! You'll probably be safer in space."

"But I'll be millions of miles away!"

His mother laughed and shook her head. "Colder, you're only going for a week! You go a month sometimes without coming home to visit. And a million miles away or fifty, makes no difference to the people you leave at home. Gone is gone. Looks the same from this side. If you decide to do this permanently, maybe I'll feel a little different, but your dad's right—what an adventure!"

He was suddenly feeling less enthusiastic about the whole thing. He'd been expecting to have to fight his way out of here amidst tears and pleas for him to stay. But they were almost packing his bags and shoving him out the door. Didn't anybody care that he could get killed out there?

Eli the second came up and gave him a bear hug, then slapped him on the back.

"Whoa, my brother, the explorer! Way to go, dude! If I didn't have the wife and munchkins, I'd be begging you to take me, too!"

Colder looked at him in irritation. "I thought *you'd* cry, at least."

"Why? You're just gonna be gone for a week. I think I can live that long without you, since I normally only see you every few months anyway. I'm happy for you, but—you know, it's just not something that makes me super emotional. Sorry, bro."

"What if the ship crashed?" he asked, still slightly offended at the joviality his departure elicited.

Sven sent to the room that the last crash was several hundred years ago, with no fatalities.

"Great! Okay! Fine! I'll go then!" He turned around and stormed out of the room, leaving everyone confused. Simon looked at Bess, shaking his head and shrugging his shoulders. "All right, I give up. What did we say?"

She shook her head resignedly. "Who knows? This is Colder."

Simon's cell rang, and he answered, with everyone still in attendance. At first they were sending and talking with each other, but eventually they all stopped listening to anything but Simon's conversation.

"Well, yes, if—if you think it's necessary. All right. One for everybody in the family? They come in children's sizes? I'm not sure we'll ever—all right, maybe a few. NO! NO BAZOOKA. NO ROCKET LAUNCHER! Harvey, do you even know how to drive a tank? No, I have no idea whether generic is okay. Do you know how much noise those would make? Are you expecting an invasion by sea? We just have a lake!"

This went on for a good ten minutes, and when he was finished, he hung up the phone with a worried look on his face. Then he noticed that everyone was staring at him. "That was Harvey. He really loves to shop."

##

Harvey really loved to shop. He still had lots of contacts in the military and security fields, and they had hooked him up with a guy who could get him just about anything he wanted, legal or not. If he were ever going to hyperventilate, it would have been now, as he looked around the massive hanger, situated on an old abandoned private airstrip.

Never having been told to "spend whatever he needed to" before, he was having the time of his life. The guy who managed the place was walking behind him with a clipboard, not suggesting anything or trying to make a sale, just walking and waiting for him to hone in on something—he'd seen the look in Harvey's eyes. He wanted it all.

In his mind, he was trying to bring up scenarios where certain items he was seeing might be needed. He had a wonderful imagination, and he could think of a scenario to justify almost everything here. Good thing he'd made the call to Simon. He'd gotten just a little carried away, and his boss had brought him back down to Earth. When he stood back and looked at the situation, he could see where they might never really *need* a tank, unless they were declaring full out war. But it was on sale, this week only! How could he pass up a sweet deal like that? And the best thing about this place? They delivered! No extra charge!

He'd already ordered Kevlar vests for everybody in the family, including Bess' parents, the new fiancé, Babette, all the kids and dogs, but couldn't find one to fit the cat. But since the cat was all black, he could walk outside at night and practically disappear. So he'd better tell them if there was trouble after dark, to quick, throw the cat outside.

He'd ordered Tasers, stun guns and automatic weapons for all the security guys and Tasers to keep inside the house for the family to use. He had night gear, complete with night vision goggles, and camo gear for all of the humans, including the kids. He'd even picked out a few thirty foot lines of coiled fast rope—the kind that soldiers used to slide down on from helicopters. They had grenades on sale—buy ten, get two free, but sadly, Simon had nixed those, too. Who knew when they'd go on sale again?

They had terrific drones, heat sensing cameras, and knives out the wazoo. He could *live* in this place!

There were tracking devices for cars, in case they needed to follow the crazy guy next door, and tiny ones that could be put on or *in* a human. He ordered a few of those, too. Every time he thought about that SOB trying to kill Simon and his wife and daughter, and oh yeah, the fiancé, his blood started to boil, and he thought about just going against Simon's wishes and taking care of the guy himself. It wouldn't be murder, it would be public service. But his boss was right about one thing—if they caught him, it would be awful on his family. And if they didn't catch him, they might try and blame it on Simon, since the police knew the two had bad blood between them.

He'd bought jamming devices and anti-jamming devices. He would have bought more weaponry, but he'd run out of scenarios that didn't include helicopters and anti-aircraft missiles. Simon had said no to the scuba gear and spear guns, too. He knew in his heart that he was right, but it still hurt.

The coolest thing he was doing, though, was hiking up the security system. He'd actually been working on that for some time—he just hadn't told Simon yet. The working budget Simon gave him every month had been more than enough for what he'd been doing. Now there would be motion detectors on every section of fence surrounding the whole estate, and motion detectors and camera surveillance on every house on the property. He'd put in some extra cameras on the grounds too, and done the work there himself, because of the aliens. And if they needed to, he could flip one switch and light up all the occupied areas of the estate.

On the way home from the hangar/mall, he was so high about the day's business, that he started thinking about doing this full time. If he weren't so attached to the Sayers, he might try and find a job as a personal shopper. Simon was going to be out of his mind when he saw all this stuff.

##

"I must have been out of my mind, giving an unlimited account to Harvey. He's a wonderful person, but good grief, you should see the collection of weapons we have in the storehouse, now. At least he asked me before he bought the tank."

Bess was on her knees in Simon's herb garden, weeding and planting some new seedlings he'd bought online, and Dulcie was helping her. Simon had been showing the first Eli some of his experiments with his plants, and Eli was giving him a few tips. They'd been interrupted when Harvey had called Simon to come and look at the truck load of weaponry and doo-dads that had just been delivered.

"Well, you did tell him to do whatever he deemed necessary. Does it make you feel any better, having all that stuff here?"

"Actually, yes it does, a little. I do like the extra camera monitoring, and the motion detectors on the fence. You know, one minute, I feel like I've just jumped the gun and gone overboard. But that's only because we don't have the pain and marks anymore to remind us that we might have all been killed. The next minute, I feel like I should have done something much more personal the day I went over there."

She didn't get up or look at him after that last statement, but she stopped what she was doing and stared at the ground in anger. "That would have been to protect us? And we would have all been so much better off with you in prison, or dead? That's crazier than the bazooka, and you know it. Either one of those endings would have ruined all of our lives. Don't even *talk* like that around me."

"All right—you're right. It would have been stupid." He picked up another plant and Eli was examining the leaves on it when they saw Harvey drive by with a huge grin on his face, waving to all of them.

"You should have seen Harvey. He was practically glowing, he was so excited and proud of everything he'd bought. If I wasn't such a macho man, I'd say he was very nearly adorable."

Bess got off of her knees slowly; they stiffened up faster these days. As she and Dulcie were walking over to Eli and Simon, her hair drifted across her face in the breeze. When a few strands stuck to her lip, she reached up automatically to pull them away, forgetting that her gloves were covered with soil and mud. A little chunk of mud got deposited on the inside of her lip, and she started spitting and wiping her tongue on her shirt, "Eeww, no telling what was in that!"

Simon gave her a lascivious smile and Groucho brows. "I love it when you talk dirty."

She cracked up and swatted his shoulder with a muddy glove. "I bet you've been saving that line for a hundred years, just praying an opportunity would present itself."

"Why do you think I always ask you to help me?"

The Elpies didn't get it, but no matter. They enjoyed hearing their friends being happy, and human laughter was so strange sounding that they always ended up laughing at the laughter.

Bess leaned back and stretched. "I don't know about you three, but I could really use a walk to limber up, and a dip in the lake sounds pretty good, too."

"We can't skinny dip. The kids and grandkids are down there, and they'd all need therapy."

"We've got to wash these clothes anyway, so why not just wash them while we're in them?" The Elpies loved to swim, and their eagerness at the suggestion made her case.

The leaves rustled in the breeze as the four strolled down the path, most of which was shaded by overlapping branches of the trees on either side. The air felt soft as it slipped across their skin, and a lovely fragrance from the Milkweed blooms drifted in and out on the zephyr. More than just the hikers were attracted by the scent. Visible through the trees, the fields were covered with butterflies of a dozen different types and colors, dipping down and fluttering delicately from blossom to blossom, all coming to partake of their favorite food.

They could hear the racket before they ever saw the lake. Colder had apparently gotten over his snit, and Jonas was there, too, trying to coax Sadie into the water.

Bluepeople weren't natural swimmers, but at seven feet, she had plenty of wading opportunities.

Having had four kids in their house for days, Hiram and Gisella had snuck off in a canoe for a little peace and quiet, or as much as was possible, on the other side of the lake.

A giant air cushion close to shore was taking center stage. Tied to a huge old tree overlooking the water was a rope swing, and everyone was taking turns climbing up, swinging out on it and letting go, trying to land on the cushion. The second Eli ordered all the kids to sit around the edges before he swung, so that when he landed in the middle, they'd all go flying off into the water. Laughter, screams, and shouts left no doubt as to the location of the lake.

The rowdiest of all the revelers was Enzo. Though he hadn't voiced his fears, he'd wondered if he would ever have this kind of freedom of motion again. After the crash, even breathing had hurt his whole neck, throat, and the back of his head. The tiniest movement could be agonizing and without warning, with pains shooting down his back and up his neck. It had been hard for him to imagine ever being completely devoid of pain again, and he couldn't stomach the thought of being one of those unfortunate people who lived from one pain pill to the next. He'd even contemplated whether or not he should break off the engagement. Did he really want to force the woman he loved to live with someone she hadn't known about? Someone who would never again be that guy she'd fallen for?

He hadn't spoken those thoughts to Genevieve because he knew she was already worried about him, and it wouldn't help to add his anxiety to her own. He'd also kept quiet because she would have killed him dead if he'd mentioned those last thoughts. But now, to feel all his muscles and joints working like they were supposed to, strong and solid, and without pain—all he wanted now was to be wild and crazy as only the young and sound of body can be.

He'd stripped off his shirt as soon as they'd rounded the bend and come into view of the lake, and then he'd run to the bank and dived in fearlessly. They all knew he was broad shouldered for his height, but most were surprised at how well built he was. He'd had to put on a good bit of muscle for the physical requirements needed to try out for the Hot Shots, and even though he'd changed his mind about joining them, he liked feeling strong and had kept up the conditioning.

He felt their eyes on him as he jumped out of the tree without the aid of the swing, whooping and somersaulting into the water. He felt their eyes again when he picked up Genevieve and tossed her into the water, jumping in after her and kissing her soundly when they both came up for air. When he would feel someone watching, and look up, invariably he'd see a smile, a look of relief, or one of contentment. It seemed that everyone there understood how close he'd come to losing all of this, and they were silently celebrating with him.

When Eli the first and Dulcie saw the cushion, they looked at each other and took off at a run, charging over to the ladder on the tree to clamber up and wait their turns. They looked around for Barnabas to join them, but he was asleep in the grass under the shade of that same big tree, having been climbing and jumping all morning.

Splashing around in the shallows, Elsie was lapping up water when she spotted Colder stretched out on a towel on the bank. He was almost dry, and looked as if he was about to doze off. The dog went into deeper water to be sure her fur was thoroughly soaked before she trotted over to where he lay with his eyes closed. She gently stepped over his head with her two front feet, careful not to wake him, and then lowered herself to lie on his face. He tried sitting up in a rush, but with a hundred and ten pounds on his face, he had to struggle to get his hands under her belly to shove her off before he died of fur inhalation.

She went completely limp on him to make it harder, but when he finally managed to throw her off, spitting and yelling, she jumped to her feet, and as a parting gift, did her all-time best shake off onto him while he was trying to stand. He scrambled to his feet and lunged for her, but four feet are always better than two, and she beat him back to the lake easily. He hadn't planned on going into the lake again, but now he had to wash off all the fur stuck to his face. He ran into the water yelling furiously, "Elsie, you stupid dog! Geez! I've even got fur in my eyes!"

"So get your mom to brush you sometime. Works for me!" she sent. Now she was behind him in the shallow water, and when he turned around to try and grab her again, one look at her open mouthed, tongue lolling, happy dog face took all the mad out of him. So instead of going for blood, he settled for a game of chase.

Madelyn was doing her retrieving thing with the balls and water toys that Gisella and Hiram had brought for her, and when she'd get tired, she'd flop down next to Barnabas until she got her next burst of energy. Then she'd grab a toy and go accost someone with it, until he or she finally surrendered and began throwing it for her again.

Barely audible with all the yelling and laughter, was an almost continuous yapping. Lola was running back and forth along the shore, barking at anything that caught her attention. A kid! Yap yap! A tree! Yap yap! A ripple! Yap yap yap! Every few minutes, she'd take a running leap into the water, swim out to someone and then swim back. The only time she wasn't yapping was when she swimming or panting, recovering from the yapping. *Never* had she experienced this much freedom or this much activity to satisfy her incredible energy. Lola was one happy dog.

Simon took his shirt off, and Bess just waded in with everything but her shoes on. To say the water was chilly was like saying Godzilla was on the large side, but the kids were moving so fast that it wasn't a problem for them. Simon, however, had never loved frigid water, and after half an hour of lazy swimming, he convinced Bess to join him on the air cushion to dry off in the sun. They'd just stretched out on the sides, out of the way of the jumpers, when they heard their eldest son scream, "This one's for you, Mom and Dad." Two second later he landed, and Mom and Dad were back in the lake.

The Elpies must have swung and jumped a hundred times. Or at least it seemed like that to Bess and Simon. After several hours, everyone else except Barnabas had been happily exhausted and headed back to the main house for food and dry clothes, but the first Eli and Dulcie were still swinging and jumping. Swinging and jumping. Swinging and jumping.

"Are you getting sleepy, too, or is it just me?" They were stretched out on lawn chairs, watching the Elpies, and trying to be good hosts, but geez, would they ever get tired?

Simon scratched his back and let out a sigh. "Oh, I could go for a nap. But what I could really get into is some dry clothes. I'm tired of being soggy."

"Oh, sweetheart, you're getting older, but you're not soggy yet."

"I'd chuckle, but I'm too cold. And I don't want to encourage you."

"What do you think—would it be too rude to tell them to wrap it up? I'm getting hungry, too."

He sat up suddenly. "That's it! Food! They're always ready to eat!" He sent the message that supper was waiting, and within a minute, the five were on the path back to the house.

While they were walking, Eli began to send to the two of them. It turned out that Simon wasn't the only one wanting to be sure that Genevieve's choice was a good one. Eli fessed up that he had committed the gravest breach in Elpie etiquette. When he'd first touched Enzo to examine his injuries, he had delved into his mind. Both the humans and Barnabas were taken aback by this admission, and Eli apologized for his lack of manners when he saw their shock. He sent that their daughter was precious to his family too, and he had to be sure there were no hidden dangers to her within this man. The Elpies had learned through harsh experience that some humans were just—bad.

He stopped sending then, while Bess and Simon waited anxiously to hear what he'd discovered. They waited for a full minute, but no more sendings were forthcoming.

"Well?" Simon asked in irritation. Then he felt Eli's mental smile and knew he was withholding the scoop just to annoy him. He shoved him off the path, laughing.

"You are one evil reptile. Get back up here and tell."

As Eli climbed back onto the path, Simon reached down to give him a hand up. Taking the offered hand, he used it to swing Simon around to go flying off the road. That was always Simon's mistake. He kept forgetting how strong Elpies were. Eli stood on the edge of the road, waiting patiently for Simon to trudge back up the small embankment and resume his position before he began to send.

The first thing he sent had Bess laughing and pointing at Simon while she cackled. He just stared at him when Eli sent that he had found Simon's twin. Even his sons were not so much like him in their souls as was this man.

The second sending made Bess reach for Simon's hand. Eli sent that he believed their daughter had found the man she was meant to be with, because Enzo's love for her had become the most important thing in his life. Even more impressive though, to Eli, was that because of this love, the young man had made the *intellectual* choice to dedicate himself to being a good and honorable husband and father, like his own father before him, and like Simon. And then Eli sent that he didn't need to touch Genevieve's mind to see that Enzo made her happy.

Bess stopped walking to give Eli her thanks and a hug, and Simon put an arm around his neck and planted a kiss on the top of his head. They knew by now, as well as they *could* know, that Enzo was a good man, but to hear it from someone that could look into his soul was a wonderful affirmation for two parents who loved their daughter.

CHAPTER THIRTY-TWO

Not another one! Worthington wasn't going to believe him. It sounded like some lame excuse, but it was the truth. Every time Milt sent a drone out to take pictures of the Sayers' place, it would fly just fine until it reached their property, and then it would short out and crash, like a mosquito hitting a bug zapper.

The boss had been asking for pictures, and Milt had stalled for as long as he could, but he was going to have to tell him. Maybe one of Sayers' security guys was sitting out there watching him, poised for action with some kind of super electronics that could take down his drones. Whatever the case, it was going to be a real treat to tell Worthington.

Gathering up the pieces of wreckage from where they lay looking like dead birds thrown haphazardly along the property line, he looked to see if he could spy anybody in the field or hiding up in a tree, but—nothing.

The Bluemen never took chances when they could help it, and since the first time they'd come to the Sayers,' they'd cloaked the area to prevent detection by low flying planes or choppers, and more recently they'd set up a force field to handle drones. They activated the cloaking and force fields only when Bluepeople or Elpies were present. Anyone flying overhead would see an image emitted over the estate. Their ship was cloaked even without this, but they didn't want to run the risk of having one of the Elpies or themselves seen, and they weren't concerned about the consternation caused by any drone flyer's loss.

#

"What? This is it? All that money spent, and I get pictures from *your phone* of the front gate? I have a phone, too, Milton. If that's all you can do for me, I'll just get rid of you and buy a better phone."

"You want to fire me?" *Oh please, please, yes.*

"Who said anything about firing you? I said 'get rid of you.' I assume you know the difference."

Sitting at his desk, sipping his cognac, Worthington was enjoying watching the man squirm. He knew that he'd wanted to leave his employ for some time now, because things had gotten too violent for his taste. He'd heard that the man was more than a little upset to find that once you worked for Arthur Worthington, you became a lifetime employee. However short a life that might be. His employees had seen too much, knew too much, to ever risk setting them loose. As long as they were in cahoots with him, they wouldn't be talking to anyone because they were just as guilty as he was.

"I don't know why it happens, but there's nothing I can do with the drones. The Sayers have to have some kind of force field or something else that—"

"Don't be an idiot. Force fields? Covering how many square miles? Not even Sayers has that much money, and nobody has that technology. You've been reading too much science fiction."

He leaned back in his chair and took another drink, holding the glass up afterwards to study the color of the liquid. "You know, Milton, this vintage is a masterpiece. Abominably expensive, but worth every penny, because you see, I'm used to getting what I want. And I want pictures of that estate and of *them*. Did you know Sayers is having me followed?"

"Well, I'd heard that you thought that—"

Worthington stood up abruptly and threw his glass, shattering it against the fireplace as he turned to shout at Milton "THOUGHT? THOUGHT? You think I don't *know* what I've seen? Just because the imbeciles I have working for me can't pin down who they are, doesn't mean they're not there. He uses different people all the time, and they let me see them watching me and then disappear when I have my people go after them.

"I don't care how you do it, but I want pictures of where the Sayers go, what they do, when they go to sleep and when they rise. I'm not finished with my neighbors just yet. Do you understand?"

"Yes sir." He understood that being "gotten rid of," resulted in a permanent state of being, and he'd better think of something soon if he wanted to avoid it.

CHAPTER THIRTY-THREE

On the way back to the house, they passed the road that led to the second Eli's. Genevieve and Enzo were gathering up fallen limbs and branches with the three brothers and Eli's brood for a bonfire and marshmallow roast they'd planned later in the week.

"Hey, Enzo, wait up a minute!"

Hearing Simon flag him down, Enzo turned, then put down his load of branches and dusted his hands off on his jeans to walk over and meet him, with Genevieve close behind. Simon came jogging up to him, and when Enzo stopped, Simon took him by both shoulders, held him at arm's length to look into his eyes for a moment, then pulled him to his chest and gave him a man-hug with back slaps. Enzo stepped back and looked at him in surprise, waiting for some word of explanation. Simon turned around to trot back, thought better of it, came back, grabbed Enzo's head with both hands, and planted a kiss on the top of it, then took off again without a word.

He stood there confused, as he watched Simon jogging back to the others. Finally he called out, "Hey, what was that all about?"

Without turning around, Simon waved and yelled, "Something that had to be done, that's all."

Jerking his head around, he raised his eyebrows at Genevieve. "What was *that*?"

She shrugged her shoulders. "Beats me. But that's the way he always kisses his kids. Either there or on the forehead, so I'd say it's a very good sign. Dad can be pretty—*effusive*, at times. When he's really happy or proud, or—sometimes he'll just be looking at us when we're all together, and all of a sudden, he has to come kiss us on the head. You know, that's the same thing that Eli was talking about when he gets 'Dad eyes,' from looking at his kids.

Must run in the family. My mom does it too, but my dad's just so much bigger that it startles you more when he ambushes you."

"Yeah, it is a bit startling. But nice. My dad gets that way, but his thing is a shoulder shake. He'll come up and turn you around, put his hands on your shoulders, and just shake them while he nods at you and looks into your eyes. Never says a word, just shakes, stares and nods, but you always understand that it's 'a moment.' Still—pump your mom about it. My bet is, she knows."

An hour later, after everybody had showered and gotten into dry clothes, the family was all congregated in the kitchen. Simon was the last to come down, because he'd had to take a call from the Institute—just a few minor details he'd forgotten to wrap up before he'd left on vacation, but it had taken a while to get them settled.

From the top of the stairs, he heard everyone in the kitchen suddenly break into laughter and exclamations of shock. Half way down the steps, the laughter turned into "aawws." By the time he got into the kitchen, everybody had their plates half full, and their conversations finished. Meaning to ask what had been so funny, he forgot instantly when the sight of food wiped everything else from his mind. He greeted Sarah with a kiss, Angus with a back slap and both with lavish thanks when he surveyed the feast they'd laid out.

It wasn't until dessert that Enzo finally brought up the subject. With a mouth full of cherry pie shoved into one cheek, he asked, "So Simon, if I'm your twin, does that make Genevieve my niece?"

The whole table erupted in laughter, as Simon put down his fork and stared at Bess. "Someone has a big mouth, *Bess*."

She looked up, eyes wide in feigned innocence. "Why, whatever do you mean, dear?"

Jonas looked at his dad with a confused expression. "Why do you think it was Mom that told us? It could have been—yeah, it was Mom."

Enzo nodded and pointed with his fork for emphasis. "You know, that's how I really met Gen. I walked into the clinic with that puppy, and she takes one look, runs out and says, 'Dad?'" Everybody cracked up again.

Even Simon was fighting back a laugh now, which only encouraged Enzo. "And by the way, I didn't know how to say this, but I guess I just need to come right out with it. Please—quit borrowing my clothes. And my shoes. I didn't bring enough for both of us."

Bess stifled a laugh and then looked at Enzo sternly. "Enzo, you really should have told me it was you the other night before we—"

"*Mom*! Geez, it's bad enough that Dad goes around kissing on my fiancé, but you too?"

When everybody had stopped laughing, Simon, putting on a stern face, stood up and looked around the table at all of them. Everything got very quiet, and Bess figured her joke had maybe pushed him a little too far, even though she thought it hilarious.

"If my loose-lipped wife told you about that, I assume she must have told you about what else Eli sent to us." Everybody nodded silently at him. "Then I think you should all share a toast with me to Genevieve's good fortune, and Enzo's good taste." He raised his glass and the room erupted with applause, laughter, and the clinking of glass.

##

Late that evening, Bess and Simon walked over to Eli's house and knocked on the door. Enzo answered this time. When he saw Simon, he hollered over his shoulder, "It's just my brother. Oh, and I see he brought his loose-lipped lover!"

Simon shook his head and rolled his eyes. "Don't push it kid. Hey, could you ask Colder to come out here, please?"

"Sure, bro," he smirked, and went in to get him.

Refusing to look at her, Simon stared straight ahead as he spoke. "You realize we're never going to hear the end of this, don't you?"

"It was just too funny not to share. I almost snorted milk at the table."

"Ever the lady."

Colder came out, and both of them noticed that he seemed a little down. Bess hooked an arm through his, and Simon put an arm around his shoulders. "Let's take a walk."

They traveled a ways in silence, with his parents hoping that he'd broach the subject of his earlier behavior. When he didn't, Bess finally spoke up.

"Colder, what happened this morning? You made an announcement that you were all excited about, and when we were happy for you, it made you angry. So what's up? I've thought about it, and now I think that maybe you're not really sure you want to go. You were ambivalent about it and wanted us to try and stop you—to make that decision for you. But you're an adult, and if you tell us you're going to do something, we'll try and support you."

Giving a big sigh, Colder thought about stopping the walk so he could face them as he talked, but decided he'd rather not have to look at them. He didn't really want to see their disappointment.

"I'm sorry. I know I acted like a dip wad this morning, and stupid and rude to boot, but hey, what's new? Part of it was that I was expecting everybody to be worried or afraid for me. When nobody was—well, I guess I was a little hurt. But maybe you're right, and I did want you to say no to something I wasn't sure about, and then I wouldn't have to feel responsible for passing up an amazing opportunity. Maybe I'm afraid I'll be lousy at this, too. I know both of you are probably wondering if I'll ever get serious and grow up. I'm wondering about that, myself."

Simon squeezed his shoulder and shook his head. "I have to be honest with you, Colder. When you made that announcement, I thought it would be a chance for you to experience something incredible. You've been around aliens for most of your life, but you've never seen other worlds. The sad part about it is not being able to tell anybody, and that's always been a frustrating constraint for this family. But you could share your adventures with us.

"I was hoping, too, that you might find something out there that stirred you, something you could feel a passion for to help you gain some direction in your life. But—still in the spirit of honesty—I figured that a week was all you'd be able to take. Not because anything is lacking in you—just the opposite. It's because you have so much energy, and you love the outdoors. You've always hated sitting around or being cooped up, and there's so much of that on a ship. It just about drove us crazy on the way to the Bluemen's planet.

"On the other hand, if you were a crew member, they'd probably train you to do something useful during the voyages. You can't know until you give it a shot. I'm not worried because the Bluemen are super safety conscious, and I know they'll watch out for the new crew members.

"I don't want you to think we're disappointed in you for not having a goal right now. If you were just sitting on your tush in the house, watching TV all day—that would be a disappointment. But you've gotten a degree, you're supporting yourself, you have your own apartment—those are all actions of a responsible adult.

"We don't see you as a child or a deadbeat. It's hard to figure out what you want to do with the rest of your life. We understand that. You've still got time. And if you don't want to go tomorrow, you don't need us to tell you. It's for you to tell them. Whatever you decide is fine with us."

Now he did stop, and turned to his parents. He looked from one to the other and then gave them a smile of relief as he shook his head.

"You don't realize how much it means to know you're not disappointed in me. I may be a grown man, but you two are still the people that I want to impress with my accomplishments, if I ever *have* any."

"You've had plenty and you'll have plenty more. But honey," Bess said, "you have to promise me something before you get on that ship."

"What?"

"Promise me that you'll marry within your species."

Colder laughed, and backed up to look in her face. "Don't worry, Mom. I love our friends, but I don't have fantasies about lovely green skin or dream about blue maidens with bat ears. You can trust me on this."

When they got back to the house, Simon turned to face him, still with a hand on one shoulder. "So are you going in the morning?"

Colder looked at both of them and smiled. "Yeah. I wouldn't miss it for the world."

##

Little did they know that Sven had made the same request of his daughter, only more in the form of a command, a little earlier in the day. He'd seen how Jonas had been talking with Sadie on the shore, splashing water on her, trying to get her to play, and how she'd seemed pleased with the attention. He remembered when they'd had dinner with the humans on their planet, and how Luca's sixteen year old daughter had shamelessly landed a kiss on Jonas, quite to his surprise and that of everyone else in the room.

"Sadie, do you like Jonas?"

"Yes, he's been very nice to me."

"I mean, do you *like* Jonas. Does he make your heart go pitty-pat?"

"What do you mean by that, Father?"

"It's something that Bess told me about, before I met your mother. Your mother gave me the sensation of cardiac malfunctioning when I first spoke with her. She still does, at times."

Looking first confused and then shocked, Sadie looked at his chest and then back at his face. "She hurts you? Deliberately?"

"No, no. It's a physiological response to someone who stirs great emotion in you."

She steadied herself and then refocused on Sven's question, pondering what he'd said. And then gasped. "You thought that I was attracted—that I was pitty-patting for Jonas?"

"Remember what I told you about Luca's daughter at the dinner we had with them?"

"Oh, Father… I find Jonas very kind and caring. He senses that I'm shy, and he was trying very hard to include me today, as a good host should. I appreciated his efforts and I will always think of him as a friend. But Father, he's not even our *species*. How could I ever—we couldn't even—I would *never*—"

"Very good. I just needed to be sure. I want no complications on the ship, *or* in your life."

She gave a little shudder of revulsion, and said, "That's one thing I can promise you. I'm acquainted with their cat, too, but I'd never—"

"Good. I think that's enough talk."

##

At seven a.m. the next morning, after an enormous breakfast that his grandparents had been up since four preparing, Colder Malcolm Sayers said goodbye to each one of his family members as if he were leaving forever. It just seemed like the thing to do when he was going millions of miles away.

Everyone looked happy for him, and sent him off with smiles, hugs, and kisses, but right before he got to his oldest brother, Eli suddenly turned away, and when he turned back to Colder, he had tears in his eyes. Seeing that emotion warmed his heart. To know he would truly be missed by his family, his brother.

He grabbed Eli and hugged him tightly. "Thanks, Eli. Don't worry, I'll be back soon."

Eli nodded and smiled bravely, and then waved as he watched the hatch closing. As the ship lifted off, Jonas stuck an elbow in his ribs. "What was that you just put in your eyes?"

"Artificial tears. I just couldn't get worked up enough to give him any real ones. But it seemed important to him that somebody shed a few when he left. So—hey, we do what we gotta do."

He felt pressure against his leg, and saw Elsie leaning on him and looking up as she sent to him. "You're a good brother, Eli."

Smiling down at that earnest face, he patted her head and scratched behind her ears. "And you're a great dog."

CHAPTER THIRTY-FOUR

Colder looked out the window at his friends and family below and the thought that he was leaving everyone and everything he'd ever loved came crushing down on him. Okay, so it was only for a week, but still…being millions of miles away versus hundreds made a difference to him, even if it didn't to anybody else. The ship hovered twelve feet above the ground for about five seconds—just long enough to get one last panoramic view of his family, and then he was looking down at a vast landscape. The landscape changed to clouds, and then to a planet. After a few more seconds, his world was lost to view, and he was suddenly very lonely.

Looking around the room, he saw that Luigi and Micah were no longer with him. Terrific—millions of miles from home, and the two friends who'd convinced him to come on this trip in the first place weren't even around. He didn't feel comfortable wandering through the ship by himself— didn't even know if it was allowed.

With an enormous sigh, he flopped back into his seat and leaned his head against a window to look at the planets they were passing. He should be fascinated, he knew, but the idea that he was in space was so unreal to him that he felt like he was looking at a movie, and he'd never found this part of the movie particularly interesting. Going from nervous to lonely, from lonely to bored and lonely, he quickly slid into lonely, bored, and morose.

A portal slid open, and in walked Luigi and Micah with their suits on. When they'd come to visit on Earth, the Bluemen hadn't required that they wear them, but once on the ship, the suits were obligatory. Colder was just starting to chuckle at the sight of their pointy tail coverings, when Mona came out and sent that it was his turn to be fitted. Luigi and Micah nodded their heads and sent mental smiles.

Relieved that at least this fitting would run smoothly, Mona instructed him to disrobe and get into the measuring chamber. Colder found it interesting, but uncomfortably personal. In only a few minutes, she let him go back to the main room, and then called him back to change into his suit soon afterwards.

Silver and very snug, the suit was nevertheless pretty easy to put on. When he asked to see a mirror, Mona directed him to look at his reflection on the shiny side of the bath chamber door.

Whoa, he looked *good*! The silver set off his honey colored hair, blue eyes, and slightly rosy cheeks, and the snugness of the suit showed off his physique. All dressed up and nowhere to show it off. No human women for millions of miles, and when he did see one again, he couldn't wear the suit. No one would ever even know how hot he looked. Just his luck.

When he walked back into the main room, the Elpies started pointing and laughing at him, sending that the uniform covered *his* tail, too.

#

The first thing the two showed him on the ship, of course, was the huge tub with the view of the stars. They had him stripped down and in the tub within five minutes, warning him that he'd go to sleep, and promising they'd be back to wake him up soon, since humans were more prone to pruning up in water than any species they knew.

As he sank down into the liquid warmth and looked out onto the stars spread out before him, he thought that yeah, maybe he could get used to this. The next thing he knew, Luigi was thunking his arm to wake him up

When he was dressed, they took him to the cabin assigned to him, and geez, it was pretty small. The built-in bunk was plenty big, since it had to accommodate seven to eight footers, but the rest of the room was just big enough for a very small built-in compartment for clothes, and the Blueman version of a chair. No frills.

Luigi and Micah weren't that excited about the rest of the ship anymore, but it was still fun for them to show the ropes to Colder. They dragged him to a room with chairs and large flat slats on pedestals that he assumed were tables, since the food simulators were in there.

Ah, the food. Especially after a week of his grandparents' sumptuous feasts, the food on the ship was worse than bad. Very little flavor, and the textures were so strange that some things he just couldn't choke down. Not surprisingly, Micah and Luigi thought the food was great.

The room that all three of them loved was a sort of lounge, with huge pillows in a wild variety of colors and shapes. These were thrown about on carpet of a midnight blue, velvety material, several inches thick. Lighted from within, the walls suffused the chamber in a warm, relaxing glow. When the two entered the room with him for the first time, after the bland look of the rest of the ship, Colder was astounded and grateful. Finally, some color!

As his eyes drifted from one hue to the next, he was startled to see Sadie nestled into a mound of pillows, reading. She had on a robe that was a mosaic of bright pinks, subtle mauves, and blues, and with her light blue skin, she'd just blended in with the rest of the room until he'd actually focused on her.

"Oh, Sadie, hey! Uh, do you mind if we join you?"

She nodded and gestured to the pillows in her vicinity. He was looking to Micah and Luigi for clues on decorum, but he needn't have bothered. The two took running leaps, twisting around in the air to land on their backs and bounce off the cushions, and then twisting in the air again to land on their bellies on the carpet, startling Sadie and sending pillows flying. They started laughing until they sensed that they had disturbed the Bluegirl, and then they jumped up and began sending embarrassed apologies.

Gesturing with her three hands for them to be seated again, she accepted their apologies graciously. Then she explained that she wasn't used to such exuberant, undisciplined behavior on the ship. They rightly took this as a courteous reprimand, and expressed their determination to act in a more mature manner.

Colder sat down a few feet away from her, and asked politely, "What are you reading? I mean, if it's okay to ask."

He thought that maybe she smiled at him, but with Bluemouths, it was hard to tell. Her sending had a hint of a smile in it. "I'm reading a play about the days when The Rebirth was taking place on our planet. It's very interesting to see how my people went from trying to deny their feelings, to being able to express them and form bonds."

"So—your dad mentioned—oh, sorry, do you have less formal names for your parents, like 'dad' or 'mom?'"

"We do, but I would normally never use them on the ship. When here, I am officially my father's trainee, not just his daughter. He can show no partiality to me."

"Oh yeah, I guess not. Well, anyway, he mentioned that you're only fourteen."

"That's true."

"When my family was on your planet fifteen years ago, they met Luca Pacioli's daughter. Jonas said she was sixteen and acted like a typical sixteen year old on Earth. But you're two years younger, and you're so mature. I feel like I'm speaking with an adult."

Tilting her head down shyly, her smile came through in her sending again. "Thank you for saying that. On our planet, age is not as indicative of maturity and intelligence as it is on yours. I too, have heard of that dinner with your family, and I was appalled at the actions of Luca's daughter. I hope you wouldn't expect the same behavior from me."

"Oh, no, hey, I was just saying how different you act from her. And my family wasn't appalled. They thought it was funny—you know, something a teenage girl on Earth might do, if she was a little on the wild side. They weren't insulted or anything."

"And Jonas?"

"He was *certainly* taken by surprise, but he was flattered, sort of."

"I'm glad he wasn't offended. It was very unfitting for her to do such a thing, even if he had been a Blueman."

"So…what does fourteen years mean in your world?"

He noticed that her light blue skin darkened slightly, almost like a blush in a human, when she seemed a little embarrassed or uneasy. It was becoming on her, setting off her huge violet eyes that were really very pretty—something he'd never have thought he'd say when describing a Blueperson.

"On my planet, determination and desire have much to do with how a person ages. The young Blueperson we've spoken of had not set any goals for herself, so her mindset was still immature and uncontrolled. I have wanted to be a ship's leader since I was very young, which is natural, considering that both my parents are leaders. My brother and I have accompanied my parents in their ships on a very frequent basis for most of our lives.

"Because of my determination and what I've achieved in education and experience thus far, I'm considered an adult. Are you considered an adult?"

He bridled a little at that question, but made himself see reason. She was just asking him the same thing he'd asked her, and it was a fair question. After all, she'd only seen him playing around at his parents' place. "Yes, I'm twenty-four, and that's an adult. I have a degree, which is education that allows me to accomplish certain things that—that—"

"That you've always wanted to do?" she prompted.

"The problem is, Sadie, that I don't really know what I want to do."

She looked down quickly, as if she were ashamed for him, and that one movement triggered first embarrassment, then irritation.

He got to his feet quickly, excused himself, and was turning to go, when she reached out and caught his wrist.

"Oh, please, I'm sorry if I offended you! It was not my intention. Please, stay. It's so nice to have someone to talk to."

There he went, acting like a jerk again. He hated himself for reacting like that—so ready to be defensive. It made him look pretty rude about half the time. His parents had taught him better manners than that. He turned around to look at her, and her violet eyes were pleading with him in a way that any species would recognize.

Looking over at his buddies, he saw that both of them, having full bellies, were sound asleep, stretched out on the thick carpet and snoring softly. He shrugged his shoulders and sat back down.

"No, I'm the one who should apologize. I know you didn't mean any offense, so I shouldn't have taken any. I just thought you looked like you were shocked at my lack of ambition, like I was substandard or something."

"No, no. I just—you seemed embarrassed and I didn't know how to respond to that. My conversations with humans have been very limited. I don't have any idea what life is like for you on Earth, or what is expected of the young or the adult. I'm as curious about your life as you are about mine. Please understand that I would never intentionally offend you, so if I say something wrong—you can correct me and I won't do it again."

She was so sincere, he couldn't help but smile, and he held out his hand for a shake. She slapped it, and he laughed. Then she seemed embarrassed again. "Whoa, time out. We need to establish a couple of things if we're going to be friends, and I'd really like for us to." She said nothing, but nodded, with her eyes cast downward.

"Please, Sadie, look at me." She looked up and he continued. "Well, in the first place, you don't ever need to feel shy around me. Humans laugh a lot. Dumb stuff strikes us funny. We don't mean offense. I laughed because I put my hand out for a handshake. That's a human custom that can be a greeting. But it also means that two people are agreeing on something—like, to do something the same way. Okay, hold out your hand like this—no, one of your hands from the other side. Yeah, like that. And you put your palm against mine, close your hand and move your forearm up and down.

"There! We agree that I won't act like a jackass and get all offended at any little thing you say.

"When you slap somebody's palm, that's a way of saying that person did good—that you liked it. Or maybe that you both did good and you're both happy about it. You put your palm out like this or up in the air when you want a 'high five.'"

She repeated his gestures and nodded her head seriously.

"All right. That's a start. There's one other thing I think we need to get out of the way, and excuse me if I seem forward, because I don't mean to offend, either. But because of what Luca's daughter did, I think we're both a little edgy that either of us might think the uh, male-female thing could be an issue for us."

She turned a darker blue and looked down, and he knew he'd hit the nail on the head. "But let's clear the air about that right now. We are two different species, and I think both of us are smart enough to know that would never work. I'm attracted to human women and I'm sure you go for Blueboys. Uh—Bluemen, I mean."

Letting out a sigh of relief, Sadie nodded her head and looked at him with what he thought might have been another attempt at a smile.

"Thank you for bringing this up. I hadn't thought of that until my father mentioned it. Then I began to worry that my desire to be friends with you might be seen in a different way, and then—"

"That's funny, because before I left, my mom made me promise to marry 'within my species.' I think she was kidding, though. Well, that's a load off, because now I can tell you without worrying about it, that I think your big violet eyes are absolutely gorgeous."

She turned a much darker blue then, but he could tell she was pleased. "Thank you. My mother has violet eyes."

"They're very cool. But back to my earlier apology. So here's why I got ticked off before. It's because at twenty-four, a lot of guys are on some kind of career path, you know, like you're doing with your internship or whatever, on the ship. I'm working, and making my own way, but I'm not sure what I want to do with the rest of my life, and sometimes it makes me feel like I'm not grown up yet, and sort of a loser. I'm kind of embarrassed about it, and that makes me prone to take offense."

He could sense that she was letting her guard down and starting to relax. "Oh, I would never think less of you for that, Colder. On my planet, people may not settle on one path for decades. Before The Rebirth, people were produced to be what was needed at the time. If a new laboratory was being built, people were formed in our repopulating centers with the genetic propensity suited for working in a lab. Their entire childhoods were centered around these future jobs. They were taught laboratory procedures and science as soon as they could speak and learn. There was no choice at all involved in growing up.

"Then The Rebirth came, and everything changed. Now people can choose their mates, their education, their professions, and suddenly, things are much more complicated. Our people live for hundreds of years, so the idea of choosing one path is very intimidating."

"I can see how that would be."

"I tell you this so you'll understand that your hesitation in choosing a path would never make me see you as a 'loser.' Especially since your species has such a short life—oh, excuse me, I should not have said that—"

"No, it's okay. Compared to you, we do."

"Well, especially since your lives are so short, you need to be happy in the years you're allowed. To choose wrongly and be miserable and then die so quickly—that would be tragic."

Colder stared at her, taking in what she'd said, and then a smile slowly spread across his face. "You know, Sadie, you just did a wonderful thing for me. You put into words—you made me see what's been in the back of my mind all this time. I just didn't get it until you spelled it out. Our lives *are* way too short, so we shouldn't force ourselves into a way of life that makes us miserable. That's it. Whoa, I feel so much better!

"And before we go on, I have to ask you something that's been making me crazy. Do Bluepeople smile? I keep thinking you're sort of smiling."

Now she gave a real smile that there was no question about. "Most of us don't—it was never taught to us. But my mother saw your mother smiling at your father on the public viewing system when your parents came to my planet. My mother thought it showed something special between your parents, and when she tried it with my father when they had just met, it made her feel happy. So she started doing it more often, and in public, and many more people have since begun using the smile. I enjoy it, but was afraid that you would mock me for having no skill at it. I know that it comes naturally to your people."

"Are you kidding? You do it beautifully. Really, you brighten up the whole room when you smile. Maybe it wasn't natural to your people for so long because of the way they had to live before The Rebirth. From what I understand, strong emotional ties were discouraged, along with strong emotions period, I presume.

"Smiling comes from emotion. We learn it from our parents when we're babies, although I think it's partly an instinctual response, too. Parents love their children, so when they're handling their babies, they're always smiling, and the babies associate that smile with needs fulfilled, happiness and love. If no parents were there to raise the babies, and no one really loved them, well, geez, what was there to smile about? I think it's cool that your mom was brave enough to try it. You should do it way more often."

She didn't put her head down when she answered him now, but looked him straight in the eye and smiled broadly. "I will. And you have done a good thing for *me*, Colder Sayers. Beginning today, I will enjoy smiling and practice it without shame."

He laughed and held up one hand, and Sadie smiled as she slapped it.

CHAPTER THIRTY-FIVE

That first—night?—they had to tell him when it was time to sleep and how to set a timer on the wrist monitor they'd given him so that he'd know on his own in the future. He didn't feel sleepy and had to will himself to doze, which he did very poorly. His timer recorded his vital signs and calculated the optimum amount of sleep for him. When it woke him in the morning, if it could be called morning, he couldn't say that he agreed with its calculation of his "optimum time."

He went to eat breakfast feeling dopey and halfway sick, but when he sent to Micah and Luigi, who were eating their second breakfasts, they told him that he'd feel better after the next sleep period. He ate simulated oatmeal with some simulated bananas and simulated milk, and then went to soak in the tank where, of course, he promptly fell asleep. He had to be awakened by Luigi, and this time, Colder was properly pruned, with fingers and toes not only shriveled, but numbed up.

Sven and Luca were waiting for the three in the main room when they came in.

"We'll be making our first stop in approximately one hour, and there are things we need to go over with you. Remember that when we arrive on a planet that we haven't explored before, as is our first destination, there may be some danger on disembarking.

"Our sensors will tell us whether life has been found on the surface, and what the atmosphere is like. Unless an atmosphere is caustic to your skin, or the environment is dangerous in some other manner, when we reach a planet, you will place your wrist with its monitor in the metabolic adjuster. This will prompt an inoculation to be formulated specific to your species and condition, which will enable you to tolerate the planet's atmosphere. Never attempt to go out without permission from one of the crew, and without using the adjuster first.

"We will always stay together, unless you're ordered to do otherwise. Follow our lead on *everything*. If there is anything that appears dangerous or odd to you, take no action—allow one of us to handle it. We are here to study, not to change the environment.

"Aside from your monitors and your suits, we have two other pieces of equipment for you. However, since we hadn't planned on having you along, we only have one extra of each piece, so we should discuss which of the three of you will carry which piece.

"The first item is a neutralizer. Aim this end at a sentient being, and not only will it be rendered harmlessly unconscious, but everything that has happened within the last two hours will be wiped from its mind."

The neutralizer looked like a simple silver tube, an inch in diameter, curved like a sickle, with a small raised area on the outermost side of the curve. He laid it on the table in front of the three, and Luigi immediately picked it up, looked into the business end, and fell to the floor unconscious. Micah and Colder, on either side of him, looked down at their fallen comrade and then back up at Sven, who showed no outward reaction.

"It appears your first lesson should be to never point it at yourself. The trigger is on the curved edge, the part that Luigi pressed when he picked it up. The open end is pointed at your subject. Only use this when instructed by one of us. When needed, it could save your life. If you point it in the right direction."

Micah reached down, carefully took the neutralizer out of Luigi's limp hand, and laid it back on the table. He looked peaceful enough, so they left him on the floor where he lay.

"The second piece of equipment is a transporter, which is very, very important. One of these allowed us to save your parents' lives when they were attacked on our planet, Colder. Had we tried to transport them in a vehicle by land or air, it would have been too late for both of them.

"There are different settings: the red transports the subject directly to the medical area, for when a crew member is injured or a subject is in need of urgent medical care. The white setting is to transport back to the ship, either to the controls—the blue button under the white stripe—or to the main room, with the yellow button under the white stripe. If it's necessary to go to the decontamination chamber first, flip the black lever on the end. You simply set it to the desired destination, take off the safety on the outer edge of the disk, and place it face down on the subject's chest or anywhere else on the body. Always aim for the chest, for in an emergency, when one is stressed, the trunk of the body is harder to miss. You can use this on someone else or to transport yourself."

Luigi was starting to move around and attempting to stand up, so Colder and Micah each reached down a hand, while trying to maintain eye contact with Sven and receive his instructions. They pulled Luigi upright, and he looked around the room in confusion. They both sent for him to be quiet and pay attention to Sven, but as soon as he set his eyes on the table, he snatched up the neutralizer, and before either could grab it out of his hand, he repeated his performance and fell to the ground.

Sven looked at the empty space where Luigi had just been standing. "I think we've established who should *not* carry the neutralizer."

Micah carefully picked it up again and this time handed it back to Sven, who put it on his belt. "You'll each be issued a belt like this with holsters to carry your equipment. Micah, since you seem somewhat better controlled than your friend, you will carry the neutralizer, and Colder, you will carry the transporter, as it requires greater dexterity. Do you both understand your instructions?"

They nodded, and when Sven and Luca left them, they took seats in the main room and started sending in excitement to each other about their impending foray. Sadie came into the room and when Colder smiled and motioned to her, she smiled back beautifully and came over to sit with them, carefully stepping around the unconscious Luigi.

"Hey, Sadie, come join us. We're getting pretty excited about going exploring. I guess this is old hat for you, huh?"

"No, not at all. This will be my first time on an unknown surface."

"You're kidding! I thought with you being on a ship so much when you were growing up, you'd have done this dozens of times."

"No. My parents were very protective when my brother and I were children. Anything could happen on an unknown planet, and they didn't think it was right to risk either of us. This will be my first excursion as an adult. I'm just as excited as you."

"So, I see you have a holster belt with a neutralizer *and* a transporting disk."

"Of course. I mean, I do because they were expecting me to participate, so equipment was previously arranged. Not because they thought—"

Colder held up his hand to stop her. "It's okay if they thought we might bungle something. You can send it. It's true. That's the second time in a row that Luigi's put himself out. And since he won't remember the last two times, he'd probably do it again if he could get his hands on a neutralizer."

She slowly put two hands down to secure the covers on the tops of her holsters, trying not to be too conspicuous. "You don't have to be so polite, Sadie. You *need* to cover the holsters. You're a newbie, but we're *newbie* newbies. It's better that Micah and I each have just one thing to concentrate on this first time out." Micah nodded his head emphatically.

"Do you know anything about this planet? Any dangerous, giant animals that might want to eat us?" he asked, laughing.

Confused at his laughter, she replied, "No, those come at our next stop. We've never landed on this planet before. According to our sensors, it has only fungi, bacteria, trees and plants living on it. We've not detected any higher life forms."

"That sounds pretty dull, but maybe dull is better for our first time out."

"I wouldn't rule out danger. Millions of your species die from bacterial and fungal infections every year."

"Oh. Thanks for reminding me. I guess I'd better hold my breath while I'm there, huh?" he asked, with a quick, nervous laugh. "That's just a joke, you know, in case you're wondering."

The Bluemen had evolved socially to the point where they understood humor, but Sadie was having difficulty understanding the point of his. "For this trip, we'll be wearing protective head and face coverings, with a respirator that recirculates air. Oh, and we'll have gloves on, too."

"Not taking any chances are they?"

"That's why this crew is still alive after so many years in space."

"Good point.

"Hey, look who just showed up!"

Luigi came walking up to them, looking around in confusion, and the first thing he noticed was the holster on Sadie. As his hand move slightly in its direction, one beige, one green, and one blue hand reached out and grabbed his arm at the same time, as he received simultaneous sendings and heard Colder shout, "NO!"

He flinched back in surprise, and stared at Colder in annoyance for shouting at him. Colder turned to Micah. "You send it to him. He needs to get the whole picture."

Five minutes later, Luigi sat looking from one to the other. He didn't believe them, and thought this was one big, irritating, practical joke.

"Look, Luigi, probe my brain. I give you permission. Try to get the picture from my memory if you can."

He nodded and placed a hand on Colder's head. Elpies could probe without physical contact, but touching the subject made it easier and the images clearer. Luigi wasn't subtle, like Eli, being much younger, less experienced, and brash on top of that. When Eli did it, it was like the feel of soft material being slid across a surface. With Luigi, it felt to Colder like someone's thumb was poking and pushing around in his brain. Not painful, exactly, but very uncomfortable and profoundly creepy. Abruptly, Luigi jerked his hand back, freed Colder's mind, and lunged backwards trying to distance himself from Sadie's neutralizer.

Micah started laughing, but Colder grabbed Luigi's arm. "Hey, guy, you don't have to be scared of it in her holster. It's only dangerous when it's in *your* hands."

##

Maurice came out with gloves and helmets that had face masks and respirators attached, and holsters were given to Micah and Colder. He explained to the three how to connect the headgear to the protective suits that they already wore, and checked each one carefully after they'd put them on. Then he gave a pat on the top of each helmet and led the group into the decontamination chamber where they would exit and enter while on this planet.

Sven followed them in, reiterating that they should stay with him or Maurice at all times, and only touch their holstered equipment if instructed, or in emergencies. They all sent their understanding, and the portal opened onto the unknown.

#

From the moment they laid eyes on this new world, every one of them was afflicted with a feeling of overwhelming gloom. Everything was gray, darker gray, black and olive green, and it all appeared oppressively dank and slimy. When they stepped down, their feet squelched into soggy ground. The temperature was cool, and there was a light fog that kept them from seeing much in the distance.

Trees, or what they assumed were trees, stood in small, ragged clumps across the landscape, grey and lifeless looking, their trunks and branches covered with fuzzy black or greenish growths, as if they were being consumed by mold and rot. There were no sounds of any animal life, just as they'd expected, and other than the noise of their feet pulling free of the muck and stepping down again, the place was eerily quiet, with only the strange, subtle dripping sounds heard from every direction.

Colder and the Elpies felt it first, while both Sven and Maurice were too busy collecting specimens in small transparent containers to notice. A threat—a sense of danger, as if something had just changed. All three jerked their heads around to look behind them and to the sides, but nothing seemed unusual. Then Luigi looked up, and gave a raspy shriek.

From a tree above them, what looked like a long, black piece of mold was extending downwards from a branch and heading towards the group, moving faster by the moment. When the little band rushed forward to get out of the path of the falling fungi, the form switched its direction to follow them. They moved faster, and so did the black mass of fuzz, until Maurice felt compelled to try his neutralizer on it. The thing stopped immediately when neutralized, and hung limp, a sight much too reminiscent of Luigi after his mishaps.

Colder was shaken by the incident, but didn't dare show it. No one sent to him, so he simply kept following Sven and Maurice. They led the group a little farther, and then stopped. The two began sending to each other, and then Maurice went to the back of the group so that the four new crew members in the rear would now be sandwiched between veterans.

That feeling of threat didn't diminish with the neutralizing of their mold stalker, but steadily increased, and soon all of them felt it.

Thin, olive drab and grey particles that looked like decaying leaves had begun drifting down from the trees to land on their suits. At first, no one paid them any mind, until Sadie attempted to brush a few off of her. When her gloved hand pushed against the first one, it transferred to her glove, and she couldn't pull it free with her other hand. Alarmed, she looked at the other 'leaves,' and saw that they were moving slightly, and reaching out beyond themselves with gelatinous looking feelers that seemed to be trying to anchor onto her suit.

She sent to Sven in alarm, just as he reared back and threw one of his specimen containers a good hundred feet away. When the others saw what Sadie was doing, they started tearing the leaves off of themselves and each other's backs. The ones that Sadie had tried to brush off were stuck on the hardest, perhaps having tightened their grips in reaction to the sweeping motion she first tried. After clearing themselves, Luigi and Colder attacked the ones on her, grabbing and ripping them straight off instead of trying to wipe them away.

Sven turned to them, holding out his box of containers for them to see before he threw the whole box as far away as he could, and sent for Maurice to do the same. Every one of the specimens had begun to move, and most were growing. A few had shattered their containers and were oozing up the side of the box towards Sven, before he hurled them off into the distance.

They'd stopped at an area where the ground was green and black, but more solid feeling than they'd come upon thus far. There were large flowers here, lily-like in shape, and of a different color than anything else they'd seen—a deep, strong green that was actually pleasant to the eye. More than pleasant—they all felt drawn to the color, calmed and reassured by it. All but Micah, who hadn't been looking at the flowers, but at Colder's back, instead, to be sure he hadn't missed any of the leaves. He saw movement in his peripheral vision, and when he turned his head to look, he gasped and signaled an alarm to the others.

Every move the group made was followed by the open faces of the flowers, which stood shoulder high to the Elpies. Not only did their faces move, but the flowers themselves seemed to be getting closer. At first, none of the group responded to Micah's alert, for they had stopped moving forward, and stood staring in contented captivation at the beautiful deep green. Most of them were beginning to reach out for the blossoms.

Seeing what was happening, he broadcast a warning with his whole will, telling them to turn their eyes away from the flowers. One by one, the crew slowly pulled their minds back from the entrapment. Colder and Sadie jerked their wills free first, after Micah covered their facemasks in front of their eyes with his hands so that they couldn't see the flowers. With their minds returned to them, they reached out and did the same for the other crew members. Without the color mesmerizing them, the rest returned to their senses quickly.

None of the explorers could see any actual movement at the base of the plants, and yet there was no denying that they were closer than they had been.

As soon as Sven came back to himself, he sent to everyone to avoid looking at the flowers and to start back to the ship, walking as quickly as possible. As they turned to leave, one of the flowers shot forward and attached to Sven's face mask, its blossom suddenly transformed into a sucker. When he cried out in alarm, this signaled the other flowers to launch themselves at the rest of the group. "*RUN, NOW!*" he sent, and screamed in his own language.

By this point, they needed no encouragement, and took off as fast as the ground would allow, tearing the flowers off of themselves as they ran.

As soon as they'd gotten far enough away from the aggressive blooms for safety, or so he thought, Sven signaled a halt and told everyone who carried transport disks to take the safeties off and be sure the decontamination chamber was selected for their destination.

As Colder looked down at his disk to make the switch, he took a step back to shift his weight. When he put his foot down, his leg plunged into a morass that appeared to be solid, but gave way into a thick, greyish ooze, the consistency of oatmeal. The disk when flying out of his hand as he fell back, but was deftly caught in the air by Maurice. Colder would have landed on his back and been sucked down instantly, had it not been for Sadie grabbing one arm, and Micah whipping his tail around his other. Even with them holding his shoulders up by his arms, he'd sunk up to his chest before they could stop him.

Remain calm, he told himself. Everything was under control. They had him, and he was slowly being pulled out, but it was almost as if the oatmeal ooze was intentionally sucking him down as the others were trying to bring him up. He was completely helpless to aid them, with nothing solid beneath his feet. Sven had rushed over and grabbed the arm that Micah had caught with his tail, and with his added strength, Colder could feel himself being gradually lifted free of the sludge.

They had him out to his waist, when he felt something wrap around his legs, and then the sensation of hundreds of tiny points scraping back and forth, trying to grind through his suit to the flesh beneath. He started screaming then. "GET ME OUT, GET ME OUT, THEY'RE CHEWING MY LEGS! GET ME OUT!"

Instead of pulling anymore, Maurice reached in and slapped his transport disk onto Colder's chest. A moment later, he was in the chamber, alone except for the coverings of dark grey that were wrapped around each leg, like enormous, flattened slugs, moving relentlessly, back and forth, back and forth, scraping, grinding, tearing at the suit, and he could feel the material loosening. He started screaming again and beating at the masses of ooze, but instead of releasing, the ooze stretched out and enveloped his hands, just as he felt something finally penetrate his suit on one leg and then the other, and begin to cut into his flesh.

Suddenly all the others were in the room with him, and Sven and Maurice were using their neutralizers to incapacitate the masses on his legs. Colder was *beyond* fear now, and Sadie and Luigi had to hold him down for Micah to neutralize the masses on his hands. When they fell limp to the floor, Colder, still screaming, saw blood dripping from his hands through gnawed holes in his gloves, and passed out.

#

Heat. Pain. Those were what brought him to. When he opened his eyes, he was naked under a metallic blanket in an isolated medical chamber. There was a tube coming down from the ceiling of the chamber, with a thick looking, golden liquid pumping through it. His eyes followed it down and saw that it lay along his clavicle and inserted beneath the skin into what he assumed was a vein. That was the first thing he saw. Looking around, he became aware of several other tubes hooked up to him, all coming down from the ceiling.

The pain in his hands and legs demanded his attention then, and when he raised his hands, he beheld them bluish-purple and horribly swollen, with puncture wounds that were weeping a clear, pinkish liquid. He gasped in shock and pulled the sheet back to see both of his legs covered with hundreds of the small, oozing holes, and discolored and swollen even worse than his hands.

His head jerked back at the sight of his legs, his mind hardly able to take in the ghastly alteration in his flesh. Holding back a scream, fighting down the panic that threatened to overwhelm him, he wondered if he was going to die or lose his arms and legs. He was burning up and chilled at the same time. His head was throbbing, his chest felt as if a massive weight were sitting on it, and he ached everywhere. Then it dawned on him. Of course—bacteria, fungi. An agonized moaning of, "No, please, no," left his lips as he shook his head in horror.

Enveloped by a covering of protective material, a hand reached through into the chamber, and laid a palm on his face. It was Micah, standing and watching him from outside of the chamber, with Luigi by his side. They sent a joined soothing to him, and it helped to calm him a little, but didn't change what was happening.

Colder looked to the other side, and saw Sadie and Sven staring down at him. Maurice and Mona were at the foot of the chamber, and he could hear Luca talking to the others in the Blueman tongue. He was so disoriented by this time, that he wasn't sure which direction was up or down, didn't know if he was lying on something or floating. When they saw he was awake, Sadie's covered hand snaked in from the other side and closed around his shoulder.

"Am I going to die? Do you know what's happening to me? Please, tell me the truth," he pleaded, in a thin, raspy voice he didn't recognize. He tried to look at Sven's face, but his eyes kept going in and out of focus.

Luca was peering down into the chamber from directly above his face. "No, Colder. You'll be fine. Apparently, a fungus was working in a symbiotic relationship with a bacterial organism. One captures, and the—"

"I *don't care* about the *damn germs* and their relationships! What's going to happen to *me?*" He controlled his voice just short of screaming. On the verge of hysteria, he was horrified by his condition, and shamed by his reaction at the same time.

Before they could answer him, he started shaking all over, and everything began spinning in his vision as his nose started bleeding and his ears began to ring. His throat was burning badly, and felt as if it was closing up. Gasping for air, unable to cry out, he saw Luca moving quickly at the top of the chamber, and then a bright blue liquid started pumping through the tube, and he lost consciousness.

#

He dreamed he was swimming with his brothers, and it was so good to be with them again. Then the rest of his family came down to the water with Genevieve and Enzo, and the happiness that the sight of them brought to his heart filled his eyes with tears. For some reason, he'd thought he would never see them again.

When next he woke, cool, soft material lay against his back, a dark blue sheet lay over him up to his neck, and his head was on a small pillow. When he looked down and saw that he was covered, he was afraid that his legs and arms had been amputated or eaten up. Luigi was sitting on one side of him, and Micah on the other. They both sent soothings to him, with the message that his limbs were fine.

He let out one shuddering breath and got himself under control before pulling his arms out from under the cover. Thank God, they were still there, and whole. The swelling was gone, along with the discoloration and punctures, and there was no pain. He threw the rest of the cover off and stared down at his legs.

Everything looked normal. Tentatively moving each foot and then each leg, wiggling his fingers and toes, he found that all his appendages were complete and in working order. Then he couldn't hold back the tears of relief. He pulled the sheet back up and sobbed quietly, whispering, "Thank you, thank you," while he covered his face with one hand to hide his display of emotion. There was no need to send to the Elpies. They understood.

Alerted to Colder's waking by the monitors, Luca walked in, followed by the rest of the crew. He stood beside him, waiting in silence for his tears to stop and his breathing to come back to normal. When Colder took his hand away from his face and wiped his eyes, he saw Luca standing there.

The calmness in Luca's sending told him more than anything else. "You gave us a scare for a short while, but the serum we used to fight the infection was very effective, and our machines are programmed to regrow damaged tissue without scarring."

"What did that stuff do to me?" He was almost afraid to hear the answer.

"Apparently, there was a fungus and a bacteria in a symbiotic relationship. The sludge is composed of fungus, and it captures, while the bacterial entity attacks and immobilizes. The bacteria sends toxins into the victim to subdue it, and then begins to digest it. What remains after digestion is digested again by the fungus. Which leads us to believe that there were once creatures of a higher nature on the planet, but the proliferation of these more primitive organisms probably wiped them out. Who knows what their normal prey is now? Mutated, ambulatory bacteria? Migrating fungi?"

Colder thought he might vomit at the thought of himself being the digestee, but Luca was really getting into his spiel now, and continued on.

"The toxin was well on its way to killing you, but our ship's instruments were able to analyze it in time for an antidote to be formulated. Serum that we already had available was effective against the bacteria itself. But—it took time for the serum to take hold, and for our equipment to make the antidote. The toxin was faster acting and the bacteria much more aggressive than any we've ever encountered.

"However, our machines are able to regrow damaged tissue without scarring, so we were able to replace—" he dropped eye contact as he finished his statement "—what was destroyed."

The hesitation in his sending made Colder suspicious that he was holding something back. Plus that one terrible word. "Luca—*what* was destroyed?"

Looking back into Colder's eyes, he answered. "Parts of your heart, your arms, and both legs. We had to remove them and grow new ones for you."

Now he did vomit, grabbing a receptacle next to his bed that might have been a waste receptacle. If it hadn't been before he vomited, it certainly was after. When he finally finished, Sadie handed him a glass of liquid to swish around in his mouth, and he rinsed and spat into the beleaguered depository. Falling back onto his pillow afterwards, he ran his hand up his forehead and into his hair. He could feel himself trembling with the impact of what he'd just heard.

"You took off my legs? And my arms? You cut out my heart?"

"You wouldn't have wanted what was left after the bacterial invasion. We kept you unconscious through most of your ordeal, as we felt you'd been through enough already. And of course, you were kept in stasis during the removal and regrowth.

"But don't be distressed. This is your own tissue, regrown, not anything artificial. In fact, these regrown parts will be better than the originals, because we added little safeguards to assure the tissue will be strong, disease-proof, and much less prone to injury. We also manipulated the muscle growth to match the same mass and condition as the original limbs. Your healing abilities were enhanced to speed your return to overall health. Aside from the emotional shock of what you just learned, you're fine now. How do you feel?"

He hadn't even considered the possibility of sitting up until Luca asked him that question. He rose slowly, with an Elpie hand on each side of his back, though now he realized he didn't need the help. "I do feel fine. Wow. I feel fine! How long was I out?"

"Four days, total, since you got back to the ship."

Slinging his legs over the side of the bed, he started to get up, and then remembered he was naked. He wasn't embarrassed at all in front of the Elpies, who spent their lives naked and had always thought clothes an odd affectation, and Luca had been looking at him all this time while he was treating him. But he really didn't want to be naked in front of Sadie, even if she thought nothing of it. Mona came in then, with a sort of smile on her lips, and handed him a new suit, sending him that she thought he might want one.

He thanked her and then looked around the room. "Umm—would you all mind stepping out just a minute for me to get dressed?" Everyone except the Elpies turned without comment and left the room. Luigi and Micah wanted to see how a human got into a suit. "Fine, fine, forget common decency." He started pulling his suit on, mumbling about pervert lizards and their penchant for voyeurism, but the Elpies were unperturbed.

"There, all done. Happy?" Luigi sent that Colder had it way too easy, without a prehensile tail and back mane to deal with. His performance hadn't even been interesting. What a disappointment.

The others came back into the room when he sent to them, and Sven, with Sadie beside him, came and stood in front of him as he sat back down on the bed. Sven threw all three hands up into the air, palms up, and let them drop to his sides with a sigh before he started sending. "What can I say to you, Colder? Yet another Sayers that the Bluemen have almost managed to lose. We have a very poor record for keeping members of your family from harm. I should have thought about that before agreeing to take you on board.

"Your parents assumed that you'd be in safe hands—"

"Hey Sven, I'm an adult. This was my decision to come on board, not theirs."

"Yes, I know. But if something permanent had happened to you, it would have destroyed them. I believed that we had everything under control when we set out, or as much control as is possible in an unexplored world. Our sensors told us there were fungi and bacteria, but they gave no clue as to the evolved and aggressive nature of either. And I should have ordered a return to the ship as soon as those leaf creatures attacked us. I could have gotten us all killed. Even my daughter."

Colder reached out and put a hand on his shoulder. "Sven, you made what preparations you knew to, and in the end, you got us back alive. To my way of thinking, that's what a captain is supposed to do for his crew. If you knew about every little thing on a planet, every little danger, then it wouldn't be exploration, would it? You wouldn't need to even go there. I'm just *really* happy to have my legs and arms back to normal. Oh yeah, and let's not forget my heart. That's a biggie. You did an outstanding job there, Luca, really stellar. 'Thank you' seems a way poor response for what you did for me."

He could feel the pride and satisfaction in the Blueman's mind when he praised his work. Colder slid off the bed then, and turned so that he could face everybody in the room.

"I need to thank all of you for helping me—I know you did so at the risk of your own lives. And I want to apologize for my behavior. You know, all the screaming and hysteria when I was in that mush, and then in the decontamination chamber when we got back. I am an adult human male in every other regard, but I didn't act like much of a man."

Embarrassed to look up at their reaction to his words, he wanted to crawl into a hole when he heard Sven and Maurice start laughing, to be joined by Sadie and the Elpies, which hurt even more. His face turned red, and he was trying to figure out how to leave the room without looking like even more of a wimp, when Sven sent, "I suppose it was difficult for you to hear past your own screams, Colder, or maybe you just didn't recognize what you were hearing, but we were all screaming, too. Every one of us."

His eyes shifted up to look into Sven's. "Even you? The way Jonas tells it, you were totally fearless when you saved him from that big cat on your planet."

"That's because I was dealing with something that I understood, and could even relate to in some way. But the idea of seeing one of my crew being eaten alive by a sentient bacteria or fungus was too much, not to mention the possibility of seeing it happen to my daughter. The disgust, horror, loathing—*the revulsion* I felt for the organisms we encountered there was so—*visceral*, that my reactions and thinking were affected.

"Oh yes, I screamed louder than anyone, I think. And I didn't even know I was screaming until I heard this loud noise while we were neutralizing those things on your legs. When we finished, and they dropped to the floor, still alive, I realized the noise was coming from my mouth and everyone else's in the chamber. If I had been in your position, I think I would have passed out much sooner than you did. We all think you handled yourself remarkably well."

Not only did his embarrassment fizzle away at Sven's words, but he actually felt a touch of pride. "Thanks for that. So I guess I can still make eye contact with everybody after all."

Sven slapped him on the shoulder, and sent, "Let's eat."

CHAPTER THIRTY-SIX

The week on the estate was typical of the Elpie visits. Games, games, and more games. The kids collected ideas for different indoor and outdoor games from the internet, books, and friends; they bought crazy equipment with their own money from the stores where they lived, and stock-piled these up for their visits. They tried everything from horse shoes to Twister, and from Uno to poker. The adults and Elpies spent hours playing with the kids, and for the Elpies, it was always a challenge.

Six inch fingers topped with long claws were not ideal for card playing, so Simon had made them wooden card holders. Certain games were only possible with someone else handling the moveable pieces for them. They had learned early on that Monopoly was probably not the best pastime for Elpies. One long, clawed hand reaching for a top hat or Scottie dog could wipe half the hotels and houses off the board, and when it was one of the Elpies' turn to be the banker, well…

The humans knew that Elpies were intelligent of course, but because they lived simple lives in tents and ran around naked, it was easy to think of them as having less complicated thought processes. Until they played Gin. Or Rummy. Or Poker. At the beginning of the week, they would seem like poor, confused lizards, hopelessly lost in the complexities of new human games. By the end of the week, the Elpies would be cleaning everybody's clock. Elpies loved to have fun, and they *got* games.

There were almost always enough humans, Elpies, and occasionally Bluemen to form volleyball teams, and those games were the highlights of the week. Elpies were allowed to use their tails as well as their hands. The Bluemen didn't often stay more than a day or so, but when they did, three long arms and their height made for interesting games when an equal number of Bluepeople were on each team.

They'd never understood the human obsession about games with balls before, but after a few rounds of volleyball, they began to see the light. They'd had Bess write down the rules for them after playing their first game twelve years ago, and had since formed a league on the Bluemen's planet.

#

Genevieve and Enzo were a part of the activities, but Enzo also spent lengthy sessions sending with Ishmael. In the beginning, they mainly sent about chess. Sitting in front of the computer board for hours, going over different moves and their individual strategies was a pleasure for them that few people, (and *no* other cats), would have understood. The more time they spent together, the more they sent about other things, as well.

Having someone who enjoyed spending that much time with him proved an unexpected gift for Ishmael. He'd never lacked for company when he desired it, and he knew he was a beloved member of the family, but… it was different with Enzo.

He'd never had a best friend. The whole concept seemed absurd for a cat. But though he couldn't bring himself to think of Enzo in those words, that's how he'd begun to feel about him. When was the last time someone had sought out his opinion on something? Enzo did, and not just about chess. Eventually, Ishmael started asking Enzo what it was like to be a fireman, and by the end of the week, he knew almost as much about fighting fires as Enzo knew about chess.

#

Genevieve didn't mind the time Enzo spent away from her, for she was enjoying long periods of heart to hearts with her mom and grandmother. She looked at them differently now than when she was younger. For the first time, she felt an intense desire to know and understand who they were as individuals, beyond their roles as "Mom" and "Grandma." The more she found out, the more she realized how little she'd known about these women who had raised her.

When she wasn't playing games with the children, or exploring with Simon and the other Elpies, Dulcie sent to the human females about what it was like growing up as a triplet Elpie, and her years with her sisters, Eli, and all their children. Since the Elpies could send pictures of memories, the three women felt as if they were living her stories. For Sarah and Genevieve, especially, who'd never been on the Elpie planet, it was an incredible sojourn into another world.

Sarah told stories about when she was a little girl, a teenager, and then a young wife, and those tales brought alive for Genevieve *and* Bess, the visions, sounds and feel of an era they had never seen. Those times became real for them through Sarah's stories, seen through her eyes and told from her perspective. The most astounding realization for Genevieve was the fact that Sarah had been baking for aliens since she was a teenager, and had never told a soul until fifteen years ago. The recounting of her experiences was riveting and occasionally harrowing, and she'd kept them to herself all those years.

Listening to Bess talking about her childhood, meeting her dad, and her time with the Elpies—it was like meeting a stranger who'd been living inside the woman that she called "Mom." After hearing her mother and grandmother talking about themselves so intimately, Genevieve found herself starting to open up more than she ever had. She talked about her feelings for Enzo, her hopes for the future, things in the past that she'd never discussed, and Sarah and

Bess met a young woman that week whose identity they might have never guessed.

The three women each found a treasure in those hours together. It was time well spent, when three generations reached an understanding and learned to appreciate those other people that each of them encompassed—those people who had been there, undiscovered, all along.

#

Walking around the estate held endless pleasures for anyone who appreciated nature, and Simon, Eli, Barnabas, and occasionally Dulcie, spent days exploring. Covering ten thousand acres, the property still contained surprises even for Simon and Bess. Some of the grounds were very hilly, and there were streams, forested areas with thousands of beautiful trees, and lush meadows full of wildflowers and butterflies.

They would pack an enormous lunch, courtesy of Angus and Sarah, take off in the jeep to reach a section they hadn't walked yet, and then spend the day wandering about on foot. There were a few scattered fruit trees, and lots of wild berries for the Elpies to sample. Warm but not uncomfortably so, and still cool in the shade, the weather encouraged days spent outdoors.

The three years he'd spent on their planet in Eli's village before he'd met Bess had made Simon feel a sense of family and a wholeness deeper than he could ever explain. When he fell in love with Bess, she became his family, and he knew that if they wanted children, they needed to return to Earth. But it was like ripping out a part of his soul when he had to leave the Elpies behind. If he'd never met Bess, he might have spent the rest of his life there.

It was the fulfillment of his greatest wish when the Bluemen began making regular visits with the Elpies. He could spend hours with Eli and Barnabas without ever feeling the need to talk or send.

In their hearts and minds, Simon and Eli *were* brothers. The title had come naturally to both of them, and what Eli attested to only in his sendings, Simon often confirmed in spoken words. To an outsider, it might have been laughable, but to those who knew the two, it was merely truth.

ᚁ

During one of their excursions, the three males were sitting on top of a small hill, eating fried chicken, when Eli pointed to an area directly across the road from the estate. The hill was high enough that they were looking over the trees on Simon's property. His woods occluded their view of the road, but he knew which area Eli was indicating by the color of the leaves.

"Oh, that's just another forested area. But it's not on our property, so I'm afraid I won't be able to take you there. I'm not even sure who owns it. Could be, it belongs to the government, or it might be a private owner. I'm just thankful they haven't built anything on it."

They kept eating, but Eli continued staring at the area. The trees were taller there, and had darker foliage. Something about it drew him. He could almost imagine himself walking under those beautiful giants, and feeling the cool, silent air beneath their canopy of deep green. He sent no more about it to Simon, knowing his brother's main concern was to keep his visitors unseen and safe.

It was late afternoon, and time to be heading back. They didn't want to be late and miss supper, he thought happily, even though he'd just finished off a whole chicken. Even if the Elpies had not had friends on this planet, they would have come for the food.

After returning to the main house, the three split up to their separate rooms. Simon wanted to take a shower after walking all day, and Barnabas wanted a nap before supper, which was served later on the days that the three of them hiked. All the young people and the children were back at the lake today, and Bess and Dulcie were hard at work in Bess' studio, as Dulcie learned the basics of painting.

When he was certain that everyone else was occupied, Eli slipped back out the door. They'd been in an area not all that far from the house, and if he loped, he could easily make it before dark. There were always leftovers, in case he was a little late for supper. He set off in the direction of the hill they'd conquered today, knowing that he could find his way from there.

##

He was driving back to Worthington's place after a fruitless day in town. None of the Sayers' had been there. Maybe if he parked a ways down from their gate, he could eventually get some pictures that his boss would like. He was getting desperate. Milt didn't want to "disappear."

He'd thought about getting in the car and just driving—to another province, or maybe to the U.S., but Worthington had long arms, and Milt was sure he'd send people after him. So what was worse—staying here and never knowing if the guy was going to flip out on him for some little mistake and have him done in, or running, and knowing every minute of every day that someone was trying to find and kill him?

So—he'd get some pictures. The problem with trying to stake the place out was that Sayers' people were watching for ploys like that from Worthington. This was a rural area and there weren't normally cars parked along the road. They'd probably spot him right away, and no telling what *they'd* do to him.

On the right side of the road was the Sayers' estate, and to the left, government land. He was stewing on his predicament, when suddenly, up ahead in the distance, he saw a man crawl through the fence on Sayers' side, lumber across the road, and disappear into the woods.

Except it hadn't looked like a man. He was sure it was green and had a tail. There was nothing up here he could think of that fit that description. This could be his salvation if he'd found something new and exotic for one of Worthington's hunts. He sped up and called Francois to come meet him and to bring the van, a net, and a dart gun with extra tranquilizers in case this thing was hard to take down.

He'd marked the spot by a fallen tree on that side of the road, and when he walked over to it, sure enough, in the damp earth he could see where the creature had slid down the embankment. There was one partial footprint and it was unlike anything he'd ever seen before. It was most definitely *not* human.

#

Thirty minutes later, the van pulled up and Francois got out with the net. He grabbed the dart rifle and handed it to Milton. They clipped the wires on the fence and headed in, with Francois looking for signs to track. They searched for an hour, stopping every time they heard a sound, holding their breaths to listen, looking in every direction and trying to see through the gloom. Then, just as they were starting to turn around and head back, temporarily defeated by the increasing darkness, they saw it.

It was a giant lizard, probably six feet tall, walking upright like a man and acting like one, too. It had reached up to pull a branch down from a tree to look at the leaves on it, like some kind of reptilian botanist. When it appeared to be concentrating on what it was looking at and ran a bony finger gently along the leaf's surface, Milton got chills all over and felt the hair stand up on his arms.

He got an elbow in the ribs from Francois, and calmed himself down to make the shot. Suddenly, the thing whirled around and looked directly at him—not just in their direction, but *at him.* It put one hand up in front of itself to make him stop—he knew that's what it meant—as if it understood exactly what was about to happen. He almost couldn't do it, but then he thought about Worthington, and pulled the trigger.

The thing made a weird noise, clutched at its belly where the projectile had hit, and then pulled the dart out and threw it down. It whirled around to try and run, but stumbled, and then stopped itself, as if it was trying to figure out which way to go. It only got a dozen yards or so before it collapsed, but it kept trying to crawl on its belly, like a regular lizard.

They approached warily, not knowing what the thing was capable of. Hell, it might even be poisonous for all they knew. They were almost on top of it when Francois grabbed his arm and jerked him to a stop. "Look at that!"

He pointed to something on the creature's chest. At first, Milt thought it was a branch that had fallen across him, but when he got closer—he could feel the goosebumps coming up all over, as he realized it was a shoulder strap. The thing was wearing a pouch on its hip.

Milt reached out with a foot and nudged the animal, collapsed completely now and seemingly out cold. "Quick, tie its feet and let's get it in the net before it wakes up! Who knows how long it'll stay down."

As they rolled him over and bound his feet and hands, Eli was semi-aware of what was happening, but unable to move or respond. He could still send though, and focused his thoughts on Dulcie, Barnabas, and then Simon. He could only think to call for help, and that he was captured, before he lost consciousness completely.

A few minutes later, rolled up in the net, he was tossed in the back of the van and driven away into the night.

##

Eli hadn't shown up for dinner, and Dulcie said she hadn't seen him since before the three males had left for their wanderings in the morning. It was still light outside, so they all figured he was wandering around the grounds. He was fascinated by the horses, so maybe he'd gone down there to offer a carrot or an apple.

He'd seen a few horses before, the ones that the Bluemen had left on his planet, but he'd been unable to spend much time with them. When he'd first seen one on the estate, he'd spent an hour trying to send with it, and while he'd made some sort of connection, he'd left feeling disappointed. He'd sent that he was going to try a different type of sending with them, after he had time to think about their response to him. Perhaps he was trying again.

By the time they'd finished eating, it was almost dark. Suddenly, Bess started feeling a vague uneasiness that quickly grew into a full-blown, focused anxiety. She motioned to Simon and took him aside as everyone was starting to leave the table.

"You have to find Eli. Something's wrong."

"What do you mean? Do you know something?"

"No, it's just a feeling, but Simon, it's a *very bad* feeling, and very strong. I don't pretend to be psychic by a long shot, but the last couple of times I've felt like this, something bad *was* going down. And right now, all my anxiety is focused on Eli."

"I've been feeling uneasy, myself—I have never known him to miss a meal. *Never.* I'll get Barnabas and Dulcie to start trying to send to him again. They couldn't reach him earlier."

A strangled cry from the next room sent them rushing in, to see Dulcie standing and clutching Barnabas' arm, as they both stared into space, reaching out with their minds. Then Simon gasped and did the same. He tried to find Eli with his mind, but the link had shut down suddenly. When he looked back at Dulcie and Barnabas, he could tell they'd lost it too.

Bess grabbed his arm when she saw his horrified expression. "Oh no, Simon, what is it?"

"Eli's been captured! He called out for help, and then the sending just stopped and we can't reach him. Oh Lord, what will they do to him?"

The children had left already with Hiram and Gisella, all of them exhausted after a day at the lake, but the brothers, Genevieve, and Enzo had stayed to chat with Sarah and Angus. They'd heard Dulcie cry out too, and now everyone was in the dining room again, shaken and at a loss for what to do.

He was looking around the room distractedly, frantic for a clue as to what had happened, when he noticed Elsie sniffing loudly around the back door, her nose to the ground, making a small circle inside and then outside of the entrance

"Elsie, do you have something?" Simon rushed over, desperate for some straw of hope.

"Almost," she sent, and then, "There! I have his freshest scent. He went this way!" When he saw the direction she was pointing to with her nose, it hit him like a punch in the gut. "Wait! I think I know where he went. Eli, load up your jeep and we'll take Elsie in ours. Follow us!"

They bumped and rocked across fields, through weeds and around trees, crisscrossing paths and one road, with Angus holding onto Elsie to keep her from bouncing out. Simon had them stop when they were across from the hill they'd eaten on earlier in the day.

Surely, surely he wouldn't have gone off the estate—he knows better! That thought kept going through Simon's head as they'd raced to this spot, but he remembered the way Eli and been staring at those trees across the road, and he knew.

Simon jumped out and called to Elsie. "Listen. I think Eli went to that forested area across the road from here." He looked at Barnabas. "You know, the one he kept staring at when we were eating."

Barnabas nodded slowly, and then shook his head in frustration. He knew it, too.

"Elsie, he would probably have backtracked to the hill, climbed up to get his bearings, and then headed straight for the fence. He would have had to cross this area. Try and pick up his scent along here."

The dog nodded and put her nose to the ground, running back and forth across the area Simon had indicated. Then she raised her head to sniff the air, and began moving more slowly, until— "GOT IT!"

In less than fifteen minutes they found the spot where Eli had laid several large branches across the lower strand of wire on the fence to allow him to crawl through. Simon reached around to his back, where he'd crammed a wire cutter into his belt when they'd left the house. He had everyone stand back while he cut through all the strands in that section. His phone rang then, and it was Harvey's ring.

When he picked up, Harvey began shouting on the other end. "Simon, what the heck is going on? According to the tracker on your jeeps—yeah, I put them on those, too—you're right at a spot where we picked up motion on the sensors earlier, but figured it was a deer. When I went up to the house later to talk to you, everything was deserted, and now the motion alarms are going off like crazy!"

"Eli's been captured. He wanted to see an area of woods across from the estate, and he went across the road. We're all out here, except for the children and the Guinnesses, and we've found where he went through the fence. Elsie's with us and we're going to track him.

"You know where that big tree fell on the side of the road in the last wind storm? It should be around there somewhere. You'll know because the fence will be cut. Come alone, Harvey, but come quick. Bring night vision goggles. And Harvey—bring Tasers and a gun. Hurry."

He hung up and they all headed across the road, following Elsie. It didn't take her long to hone in on his scent again after they crossed the road, but it wasn't really necessary. The fence had already been cut there by someone else. While Elsie tracked, Barnabas and Dulcie were sending together to try and magnify their call, but there was still no response, no inkling that he was out there.

Loud barking brought them to the spot. "Here! He was here! And there were two men here too, right on top of where he was. I think he was lying on the ground, and they picked him up. He has no tracks leading away from here, but the men do, and they started sweating, like they were working harder. I can smell the sweat, and Eli's scent in the air along with theirs."

"Oh, no." Simon had been sweeping his flashlight back and forth across the area, and now he reached down to pick up the tranquilizer dart. He saw the fresh blood on it and held it out to Elsie, but he knew already. She took a sniff, and sent, "Eli's."

It came as no surprise that the men's tracks led back to the hole in the fence. She tried to track the car, but it had been raining, which normally would have helped the scent, except that more cars had run over the tracks and left mud from other areas. "I just can't be sure from here, Simon. I know they put him in a car or truck, and they went in that direction, but that's all."

He patted her head, trying to keep the panic out of his voice. "You're a great dog, Elsie." Getting his phone out, he dialed Harvey again. "Forget about meeting us on the road. We're heading back to the house, so go straight there. I think we'll be using something else from your arsenal tonight."

##

Per Simon's instructions, Harvey had gone into what he now thought of as the "armory," and found a couple of small tracking devices. He stopped only long enough to call his wife and tell her he might not be home tonight because of a security issue, and then returned to the house. Simon had already called Hiram and explained the situation. He had come over and Gisella had stayed with the children. She'd tell them everything later, when they knew something for sure.

When Harvey walked in, Simon grabbed the devices out of his hand, and after examining them, he smiled and looked back at him. "Harv, I don't know why on Earth you bought these, but God bless you." He grabbed him by the back of the neck and planted one on his forehead. Harvey felt his face heat up—he wasn't used to "Dad kisses" from his employer, but he was pleased at the approval of his purchases. His intuition had paid off.

"Okay, here's what I think, and if anybody thinks differently, or has a better idea, please speak up. This is really a shot in the dark, but it's the only one we've got, as far as I can see."

They all got quiet, with half of them sitting around the long table, and half standing. Dulcie was so distressed that she hadn't been able to stop moving until Barnabas caught her arm and held her captive long enough to send her a soothing. She'd sort of wilted then, and he'd led her over to sit next to Bess, who held one of her hands and rubbed her back.

"I don't know who has Eli, but whoever it is, was prepared, because they used a tranquilizer gun. Just the fact that they had one, means that they're interested in capturing animals. Now they have the grand prize of catches, but if they're true collectors, one catch won't be enough. They'll want to come back and see if there are any others of his kind in the area. We can only pray that they come back soon."

He looked at Barnabas then, and held up the tiny tracking devices. "My friend, with these, we can follow someone's movements from a distance. I hate to ask this of you, but would you be willing to let us insert a couple of these under your skin, and act as bait? If they capture you, we could follow and then go get both of you out. It's dangerous, and there's no guarantee, but it's all I can think of to try."

Before Barnabas could answer, Dulcie reached over and grabbed both trackers out of Simon's hand. She went straight into the kitchen, got a steak knife, came back in and sat down at the table. Laying the trackers down, she made a slit in her upper chest and one on her right side, and then shoved the trackers into their new homes. Bringing paper towels from the kitchen, Sarah pressed them over the wounds to stop the bleeding. Simon left the room and came back with a tube of super glue. Bess took it out of his hand and applied a small dab to each incision, and they were done.

Twenty minutes later, they left Dulcie on the spot where her husband had been felled. She'd brought some blankets from the house, and curled up with them where his scent was the strongest. And waited.

CHAPTER THIRTY-SEVEN

"Our next stop," sent Sven, "will not necessitate leaving the ship."

Colder, Sadie, and the Elpies were sitting on the light blue "chairs" that were normally scattered about the main room. Cube shaped until sat upon, they molded around the body to make insanely comfortable seating. Lightweight enough to be picked up and carried, they were arranged now in front of the monitor in the wall panel at the fore of the ship, per Sven's instructions. He stood before them for the briefing.

Colder held up his hand to stop him from going any further. "Wait. Is this because of me? Because of what happened to me?"

"No. We won't be getting out onto the planet because we've been there before. It's a planet in the midst of an environmental disaster, and we're only going to check on the state of its population."

"It's populated?"

"Not with creatures such as you or the Elpies. There are two dominant species on this planet. One is mammalian and the other, amphibian. The amphibians are predators, living mainly in the water. They spend some time on land, where they are slow and clumsy, much like your crocodiles, and are of a similar size. And like your crocodiles, in the water they are extremely fast and powerful. They're capable of propelling themselves straight up out of the water to catch prey in low hanging branches of trees. Until recently, they primarily preyed on various species of fish and the occasional mammal that was caught when it came down to drink." He turned a screen on to show a clip of one in action.

"Whoa, that thing is hideous! He makes a crocodile look warm and fuzzy."

Several heads turned towards him.

The creature looked like a cross between a crocodile and a giant salamander, with a rounded muzzle and wide mouth like a salamander, but the long pointed teeth of a crocodile. Its face was wet and slimy, but the rest of its body was armored with thick, tough skin. It had a long, wide tail, and Colder could easily imagine the momentum that tail could produce in the water when it chased its prey.

"The highest thought processes of this species are basically: kill, eat, defecate, mate. The planet's primary mammal, on the other hand, is sentient and telepathic. It also is noteworthy for the unique adaptation in its eight limbs. It never uses more than four at a time, and has pouches in its abdomen where the unused limbs lie. It has hooves for running, climbing hills and traversing rocky areas, but when it climbs trees, where it spends much of its life, the hooved limbs are tucked in and replaced with limbs supplied with hands, much like monkeys and apes. And like monkeys, it has a prehensile tail. In appearance, its head very much resembles a rabbit-eared bandicoot, but its size is more that of a deer."

"Come again? It resembles what?"

"A rabbit eared bandicoot. Also known as a bilby."

"Am I supposed to know what that is?"

"We assumed you would. After all, it's a species from your planet. A rat-like marsupial found in Australia and New Guinea."

"Sorry, but that's my mom that watches all the National Geographic shows. I don't think even *she'd* know that one, though."

"We assumed you would, since there's been a good deal of publicity about it in recent years. The bandicoot's population has been decimated in much of Australia, due to the introduction of non-native foxes, rabbits, and feral cats. There's even a campaign to replace the mythical 'Easter Bunny' with an 'Easter Bandicoot' in Australia, and chocolate bandicoots rather than chocolate rabbits are being made by some candy companies for the children's Easter baskets."

"That's all cool, but I still don't know what they look like. And I know what you're thinking—that my ignorance is astounding."

Sven shook his head and ignored the last comment. "No matter. It was just a comparison in head and facial features." He clicked a hand control and a clip of one of them grooming its young came up on the panel.

"Oh, geez, it's really cute. Look how it uses its little hands to comb the baby's hair. That's so sweet."

Heads turned towards him again.

"So what's happening with the environment?"

"There has been unrelenting rain for many seasons now, and the predator-prey balance has been destroyed. As the water has risen, the mammals—"

"The Bandicoots?"

"*All right*, if you want to use that term." The 'Bandicoots' have always escaped from the amphibians by either going to higher ground or climbing trees, and evasion was very simple for them. But sadly, there no longer *is* higher ground. There are patches of unsubmerged land here and there, but these are so small that the amphibians—"

"Can we call them 'the Uglies?' You know, just so they have a name instead of just 'the amphibians.'"

'Fine. The 'Uglies' are able to come up on these small islands and either corner the Bandicoots or force them into the water, where they're easily caught and devoured. The trees, which would normally offer them refuge, have shallow roots, and with the constant flooding, the ground has softened so much that the trees are pushed over easily by the hungry Uglies."

"That's terrible."

"Yes, it *is* very sad. When we visited the planet last, a few months ago, there were only a few small family groups of Bandicoots left. We believe that the Uglies have overpopulated because of the unusual bounty of food in the form of the unfortunate Bandicoots, and this increase in numbers has decimated their normal food source—the fish, whose populations have not increased to match that of their predators. Now they *must* go after the Bandicoots, and when they are no more, the Uglies will begin eating their own young, then preying on the smaller of their number, and eventually slaughter each other into extinction."

"Geez, I'm glad we're not going out. I don't think I could stand to see a poor little Bandicoot get eaten."

Micah and Luigi were sitting and shaking their heads, in complete agreement with Colder's sentiments.

Sven looked at the three and thought, *Geez, I'm glad we're not going out, too.*

##

They were flying very slowly above the water on the surface of the planet. There was no rain at this time, but the clouds looked as if a downpour might start at any time. The water was brown in some areas and green in others, and the only land in sight was in tiny patches, some of which held a few sad, tall, sickly looking trees. The thought of these being the bandicoots' only remaining refuge was appalling. The world appeared—drowned.

Maurice had the hatches open on both sides of the ship, and the crew walked back and forth between the two, trying to spot anything other than Uglies. The ship's company had all taken inoculations so that they could breathe the ship's *and* the planet's atmospheres, and the fresh air was a welcome change for the ship-bound.

"The sensors are picking up something over there in that stand of trees."

Sven turned the ship in the direction his sensors had pointed out, and in a matter of seconds, they were hovering over the trees. An earsplitting screech ripped through the air, and then a horrendous, desperate plea for help hurtled into their minds. The screech came again, followed by what sounded like a human babbling incoherently. A third time, the terrified cry for help was hurled at them, but now with the message that they were "the last, the last." Then, even more horrible, was the sound of two other screams, in a higher pitch.

The intensity of the screams and the force of the sendings had all of them leaning out of the hatch and looking for their source.

"What *is* that?"

Mona sent, "That, Colder, is your Bandicoot. And the higher pitched cries were from the two young clinging to her back."

They curved around a few degrees, and then they all saw them. Two huge, mud colored Uglies were jumping up and snapping at the female Bandicoot cornered in the scraggly clump of trees. She was light grey, with smooth fur, long ears laid straight back on her head in fear, long pointed snout, and round, black eyes that looked up at them and begged for deliverance. Two small bundles of fur, one gold and one brown, clung to the fur of her back and buried their faces there to hide from the terror below.

One of the Uglies stood on its hind legs and leaned its weight against the tree until it slowly began to topple. The Bandicoot leapt to the safety of the closest other tree, over the heads of the other Uglies waiting below. There were only five trees left on this tiny portion of land, and the final disastrous outcome of the female's evasive tactics was inevitable.

She shrieked and babbled again, and the little ones echoed her. Then she let go of the tree with her arms and reached out to the strange creatures staring out at her from the ship, in an unmistakable plea for mercy.

Colder ran over to Sven, who seemed to be calmly watching the scene, with no sign of emotion. He grabbed his arm and stood in front of him. "Please, please, Sven, we can't let the Uglies kill them! They're all alone, the last of their kind, probably. Doesn't that make them worth saving? Couldn't your protocols make an exception for that—to preserve the last of a species? Come on, man, just listen to them!"

The screams came again as another tree slowly tore loose from the ground and began to fall. She jumped again, and almost missed the branch, with the added burdens on her back, and the screams sounded even louder as the leaping Ugly's jaw snapped shut a few scant inches below her.

Sven was shaking his head sadly. He *did* feel for the hapless creatures. He was about to explain protocol to Colder, when he saw that now, not only Colder, but the entire crew stood before him. Mona bowed her head to him, then looked into his eyes and began sending.

"Sven, you are our Leader, and we honor, respect, and obey you always. But take my thoughts to heart, I implore you.

"Those are not mindless insects out there, Sven. She's a sentient being, struggling for the lives of her children, and she looks to us as their only hope. She *calls* to us, Sven! She reaches for our minds, believing that our hearts are there, also. I know what we risk if we save them, but I would rather lose my commission than my soul. I could not live with myself, hearing their cries and her pleas in my mind for the rest of my life, knowing that I turned away—leaving them to be torn to pieces or eaten alive *to satisfy protocols—words,* orders from Bluemen who are worlds away from the reality of this day. We must do as you command, my Leader, but please, command us to act in a way that will not crush our spirits and tear at our hearts forever, I beg of you."

All of them looked at him and sent their agreement, their pleas. Then the Blue crew knelt before Sven, as if he were royalty, and Colder realized they were humbling themselves—acknowledging his right to command them, but begging that he allow his own understanding and compassion to command *him*. Colder looked at Luigi and Micah, and the three of them dropped to their knees as well.

Sven looked downward in defeat. This was the end of everything. Everything he'd worked for, for so many years. He was respected and honored by all the Leaders on his planet. He made a fine living, doing what he had always hoped and dreamed of doing. He was able to bring his wife and children with him to travel the galaxy, even visiting friends on other planets. All that would end when he broke protocol. This time, there was no skirting it. This would be a full, outright breach, and consequences would be severe.

But he knew the others were right. What use was prestige, when inside, he would feel lower than the worst criminal? What use for others to give him honors, if he had no honor within himself? He was a father—how could he turn his back on another parent's plea to save her children?

"All right. When I hover closer, be prepared to transport them."

A cheer went up, part audible and part mental, and Sadie ran forward and threw her arms around him, whispering the name she used for him when they were just father and daughter. He turned away and rushed to the controls. Maurice had an extension line attached to a harness, and his transport disk in his hand, as the ship moved lower over their screaming target.

The Bandicoot was looking up now, screaming louder and sending her soul-wrenching cries for help, but the crew all felt a tinge of resignation beneath the fear. She didn't believe they would help her.

There was a roar as the biggest of the Uglies leaned all his weight against the Bandicoot's present refuge, and this time, the distance between their victims and the next tree was long enough that it was doubtful they'd make it.

Mona adjusted a control on a side panel by the hatch, and a metal rod shot out of the side of the ship, stopping just a few yards from the Bandicoot. Maurice slipped into a harness, clipped it onto the rod, and slid down the bar, using it like a zip line. The tree began to topple, and just as the panicked creature tensed for her suicidal jump to the next one, Maurice reached out and touched her shoulder with the transporter, and she and her babies disappeared.

Seeing their prey vanish, the Uglies leapt upwards, trying to reach this new morsel that had presented itself, but Maurice was back in the ship almost before their back feet cleared the water.

When she appeared in the middle of the main room, the Bandicoot let out another shriek and a babble, sounding exactly the same as when she was crying for help, but with this shriek, came the mental sending of thanks. She slumped to the floor in exhaustion and relief, and lay there unmoving while Luca ran a sensor over the three to scan for viruses or bacteria that the crew might be susceptible to. Sven hurriedly changed the ship's atmosphere to accommodate the Bandicoots. Since the crew could breathe hers, frightening her with an inoculation in order to breathe theirs was unnecessary for now.

When the scan was negative, he ran another light over her and her young to rid them of parasites. Thousands of tiny, red, insectile creatures, slightly bigger than fleas, dropped to the floor, dead. The three had been so heavily infested, that when they were rid of the little monsters, the color of the Bandicoots' fur appeared changed. The adult's grey coat was more a silver now, and appeared sleeker, and the hues of her little ones' fur were richer. Even the shapes of their bodies were more defined.

Luca offered the adult a tablet to kill internal parasites, and after she searched his mind and found no malice, she swallowed it and reached over her shoulder to administer a second and third tablet to the little ones, now sitting up on her back.

After this effort at compliance, she made no further attempt to move, so complete was her surrender to fatigue and stress. Luca brought out another instrument, and after running it over the three, turned to the crew. "They're starving. Even if the Uglies hadn't eaten them, they would have died soon. Most of the plants they normally eat have been submerged and destroyed with the flooding, and the external parasites were draining them of blood. There are so few living hosts left for the parasites, that any Bandicoot still alive would be overwhelmed with them."

Mona left the room hurriedly, and returned with an armful of simulated grass and three different types of vegetables that Colder had never seen before. She laid these before the face of the adult, who lay perfectly still, with her eyes closed, cherishing the first safe haven she'd known since the flooding began. Mona reached out her hand and gently stroked the female's face. Her eyes shot open, and frozen with fear, she stared wide-eyed at the Bluewoman.

Moving very slowly, Luigi went to his knees beside Mona and began sending a soothing and a message of welcome to the female. When he felt her trembling stop, he reached out and began stroking and scratching the little ones behind their long ears and under their pointed muzzles, as he sent the same message to them. After only a few seconds of this, the golden baby leapt off of its mother and into Luigi's arms, hanging onto clumps of his skin through the tight suit, and pressing its little head against his chest. Luigi gasped with the sudden pinching, but then put his arms around the baby to support it. His next five minutes were spent convincing the baby to release his tortured flesh from the vise-like grip of its tiny fingers.

When his soothing and sending had touched her mind, she'd let go of her fear. It was not until she saw how gently he handled the young one, however, despite pain from the pinching, made obvious by Luigi's continuous wincing, that she knew they were truly safe.

As soon as she let herself acknowledge that, her brain changed priorities, and the smell of food had her sitting up in a rush, causing the brown baby to go tumbling off her back. Before it could hit the floor, Micah reached out and caught it, pulling it in to rest against his chest, where it pressed itself and clung to handfuls of suit and flesh, making little purring sounds.

The adult looked around hesitantly before touching the food, but she was already salivating so badly that a little pool had formed on the floor directly below her jaws. Mona nodded and motioned to the mound of vegetation, and suddenly the Bandicoot was shoving it into her mouth as fast as she could. Her pleasure at tasting food again was so exquisite that they all felt it. When Mona put out her hand once to stop her, she froze and the fear returned to her eyes, until Luigi made her understand that she needed to eat slowly and only small amounts at a time, to avoid becoming ill.

When she understood, she sent her thanks again, and handed two vegetables to Micah and Luigi. She put a hand on each baby, sending for the Elpies to please feed her young. When they gingerly offered the food, both babies grabbed the vegetables from their hands. They opened their little mouths wide and began gnawing and sucking on the food, with closed eyes, purring sounds, and looks of such utter contentment that everyone in the room was touched by the sight.

Sadie had been squatting beside Colder to get a closer look at the babies, but now she stood up and approached her father, who was still standing at the controls, face forward, staring out into the distance. It pained her to see the resignation and sorrow on his countenance, but she thought she also recognized a sense of peace there. She walked up beside him and took his hand but let go when he turned to face her.

She called him by that name reserved for family, and looked into his eyes. "My mother chose well and wisely when she picked you to share her life. She must have seen in you that character that would make her children proud to name you 'Father.'

"I know what you may lose because of what you've done today. No one knows better than a Leader's child, what this position means. But understand, Father, no matter what happens because of our actions here, we know that you have held life above matters of state and arbitrary rules, and that is what makes you a true and worthy Leader. A worthy and honorable Leader you will always be, with or without a ship under your command. I will never respect anyone more than I respect you this day. Whatever tomorrow holds, your family will always be proud of today. I love you, Father."

Then she leaned into him and encircled him with her arms. Touched and comforted beyond words, he embraced his daughter, and was glad for his decision.

##

After the three had eaten, they were taken to a small room devoid of anything but a built-in bed. The crew had wondered if she'd be uneasy in a bed, but they needn't have. When they brought her in and Micah sent her a picture of sleeping, she rushed to the bed, climbed in, and held out her hands for the babies, who were already asleep. She lay down, cradled them against her, and was unconscious before the others could even get out the door.

Colder walked into the control room and put his hand on Sven's shoulder. "You did good today, man. Really good. If you need for me to go to your planet and testify, or anything like that, you've got it. This was something that had to be done, and your crew was all behind you. You're the best, Sven. The very best."

The big Blueman turned to look at him. "Thank you, Colder. That means a great deal to me. But I don't want my crew involved in my trial. I am the Leader, and my crew would have done whatever I commanded. They must have no part in any blame. Had I told them to leave the Bandicoots here, they would have complied. The responsibility is mine. The consequences are mine to bear. But I thank you for your offer."

Colder shook his head, and a slight smile began on his lips as he studied Sven. "You know, you're too tall, and the wrong color, the eyes are off, and the nose is definitely different, but geez, you remind me so much of my dad. I can hear him saying those words. He always takes responsibility for what he does, even if he was pushed to it, or it wasn't his choice. I guess integrity and honor are traits that aren't defined by species. I'd bet that Sadie is as proud to be your daughter as I am to be his son." He punched his arm lightly then, and walked out. Sven didn't bother sending to him that punching the leader on a ship was punishable by life imprisonment. After having already destroyed his career today by breaking one protocol, he decided he could let this one slide as well.

#

One by one, each of the crew found their way into the control room that day, voicing and sending similar sentiments. By the time they'd all expressed themselves, he was filled with peace and the determination to continue living the way he had always lived—as the best Leader he could be, on or off a ship.

#

The crew had been worried about elimination and sanitary problems with the Bandicoots on board, but being sentient, telepathic, and exceedingly grateful, the adult followed their directions to the letter. She carried her young into the facilities too, and taught them to do the same.

Meals were something of a challenge, with two infants who had lost all of their shyness and inhibitions with the crew. Because the adult could communicate on a primitive level, they found it easy to forget that she had been a grazer, a vegetarian used to eating off of the ground, or sitting in a tree.

The shape of her snout and muzzle didn't really allow for neatness when sitting at a table, so they encouraged her to eat in a manner that she was comfortable with. Their understanding helped to alleviate the immense pressure to fit in that the poor creature was feeling. She requested a trough on the floor for her and the babies, and with a little ingenuity, Mona and Maurice made a satisfactory vessel from a small metal storage bin.

The biggest adjustment for the crew, by far, was living with the Bandicoots' shrieks. Every interaction with another being, every strong sensation or emotion, and occasionally, even elimination, was announced by a high decibel shriek. The shrieks had a human quality to them that reminded Colder of the way women screamed in those old movies when they saw a monster or found a dead body. Those would have been difficult enough to live with, but the shrieks were always followed by tragic sounding babbling or gibbering noises, again with a human sound to them, as if some completely insane, expresso-fortified tenor was describing the worst day of his life. At one time or another, all of the crew members had experienced that unique sensation of lifting off from the floor when one of the Bandicoots had surprised them with a shriek of welcome or goodbye.

Mona sent that her screams were much harder on the Blue crew members than on the two other species, who had hearing ranges similar to each other. All that Colder, Micah, and Luigi heard were the screeches and babbling. But the Bluepeople heard a much wider range of sounds, and Mona explained that when the Bandicoots screamed, they sent out two different screams, one in a lower range, audible to humans and Elpies, and one in a higher range that only the Bluepeople could hear.

Receiving the two sounds in different ranges at the same time was not only uncomfortable on their ears, but also slightly disorienting. Maurice thought this quality of the screeches was probably a defense mechanism to throw predators off their trails. Unfortunately, it worked very well on non-predators, too. Sven had been forced to put the ship solely on self-drive until he could accustom his brain to the messages it was receiving from his ears.

Having had all of her physical needs met, the adult Bandicoot began communicating more and more with the crew. She did best with the Elpies, whose type of telepathy matched hers more closely. They sent mainly in pictures and emotions, and after each session with her, the Elpies would report to the rest of the crew about what they'd learned.

Colder had dubbed her "Blanche," and the babies "Bunny" and "Bruno," and they had no problem with responding to these monikers. To the surprise of the crew, only Bunny belonged to Blanche. Luigi related their story to the rest of the crew as Blanche had sent it to him.

When Bruno's mother was taken, a large Ugly had sunk its teeth into her heel, surprising her as she was climbing a tree. Before she was pulled down to her death, she'd made a desperate throw, tearing the baby from her back and flinging him by one arm up into the sickly branches, hoping that the few leaves left there would shelter and hide him. By some miracle, he'd managed to grab onto one of the limbs and had clung there pitifully as he tried to shut out the terrible sounds coming from below.

Blanche, hiding in another tree, had witnessed everything. After a few hours, she could no longer ignore the infant's pitiful sendings, and had made the decision to take him into her care.

The Uglies had poor vision on land and an even worse sense of smell, and that had saved him, for they could have downed his tree with ease. Blanche had waited a full day to retrieve him, in order to assure that no Uglies remained in the area. At the time, she'd thought that rescuing the little one was a senseless action. She believed that she and all of the Bandicoots were doomed, with a lack of food, and predators in wait at every turn, but she wanted to at least let the infant die in a mother's arms, rather than wet and alone in a tree. She had seen her mate and all but this one infant taken, and she'd continued living, even without hope, because she saw no other option.

When she'd first begun sending with Micah, she'd picked up right away on his own sense of loss. She'd questioned him relentlessly about what had happened, and in such detail that Luigi finally stopped her because of the pain it was causing his friend. She realized it too—felt it, once she was no longer engrossed in his story, and she expressed her profound remorse for the heartache she'd dredged up. From that time on, she related to him more than any other, because she understood his pain and felt that he understood hers.

#

They would return to Earth in another forty hours. Colder had been spending much of his idle time thinking about all that had happened, and what he wanted to do when he got back home.

One thing that had come as a revelation to him was how much he missed his work. He even dreamed about planting trees, and digging; of planning gardens and landscapes. Even when he was awake, when he thought about working, he could almost feel the cool dirt in his hands and smell the damp earth with the life that it nourished. The more he thought about it, the more he longed for it. He missed the management part, as well—the challenge of making ends meet and planning which flowers and shrubs to have in stock, figuring out how to market the business.

There it was. After all this time, he realized it had been staring him in the face. He wanted to buy into the business and own it someday, or maybe build his own company from scratch—a landscaping company and a nursery open to the public. But first, he wanted to learn everything he could; to pick his boss's brain for all of his knowledge, and to study, really study plants. His own dad was a goldmine of information, and he shared his love of growing things. He knew he'd understand and applaud his decision. He would go back to school and get degrees in horticulture and botany, and then—

He was so excited now, that he could hardly wait to get home and start his new life. He had a goal and dreams, and he was ready to work for them. This was the new Colder. He even had new legs to travel on and new arms to work with.

Twenty-four hours ago, he would never have believed he could joke about that, but it was so much like a bad dream now, that his mind could skirt the trauma. In fact, he found that his brain had a mind of its own when it came to that horrible day. If he started to think about it, his brain would automatically zip away to something else, almost as if it was protecting him, and he was fine with that.

He'd wanted his parents to get sentimental and worried about his leaving, but now he didn't want them to know what had happened. It would be too hard on them to think of one of their kids going through that. He'd tell Sven not to mention it, because he was sure he'd feel compelled to tell them as soon as they returned. Colder didn't need any trauma from the past to mar his future, which he now saw as very, very bright.

CHAPTER THIRTY-EIGHT

"This was a mistake, a terrible mistake." Simon paced the room, pounding a fist into his other palm in time with his steps. "Dulcie's out there, all alone, waiting for *who knows what* to come and take her. They may not even come back. And if they do, will they treat her the same or worse? I'm going to bring her back."

Barnabas grabbed his arm firmly and shook his head, sending that this was the only way, and that Dulcie would not return without her husband. Simon opened his mouth to argue, but no words came that made better sense, so he closed it again and sank into a chair, disconsolate.

The family was in the dining room, sitting around the table. The big picture window at the end of the room looked out into darkness now. There was nothing to say or do other than pray, and that had been done already. The only sounds were the quiet clinks of cups returning to their saucers, an occasional slurp or swallow, and sighs. Sarah had made tea and coffee, and most of them were drinking one or the other. It gave them a task to do, enabling them to accomplish something, even if it was just the draining of their cups.

Harvey was sitting in a car, off the road and hidden in some brush about fifty yards away from the gap in the fence that led to Dulcie. He had the GPS tracker set up on the dash of his car, waiting for something to happen. Praying that it would.

#

Dulcie lay on her blankets, reaching out to her husband. She knew he wasn't dead. She would have felt that. Letting her mind wander back, she thought about their many years together. They had been good years, and she and her sisters had never regretted coming to Eli in marriage. Her family was large and healthy, her days easy and filled with happiness and affection. She would not let go of that. She would find Eli, whatever it took. She would find him.

Slight crunching in the fallen leaves alerted her to stealthy footfalls as someone approached. No—it was *two* beings coming through the brush towards her. She had to fight the compulsion to run and hide. Getting away would be easy, but that would ruin everything. She had to be captured; against every instinct in her body, she had to let them take her.

A noise came from twenty feet to her left. She sat up and stared through the brush, to see two men with goggles on—one pointing a rifle at her. Instead of running, she stood up to give him a better shot.

Jerking backwards with pain when the dart struck her chest, she looked down at it curiously as the world around her became blurry and began to darken. She walked a few feet, but the dizziness sent her staggering into a tree.

Running footsteps. Then the voices—"Perfect shot! It's going down easy. Let's get on it with the net. Great idea, coming back."

As she felt herself falling, in slow motion it seemed, she sent one last sending out into the distance, telling Eli she was coming.

#

Simon's phone rang seconds after he'd begun pacing again, and when he snatched it up and answered, they watched him as he listened and then closed his eyes and mouthed a silent "Thank you." He nodded and said, "We'll be waiting."

Turning to the tense group around the table, he nodded, then nodded again, not trusting himself to speak, until finally he lifted his head and addressed them. "They took her. Harvey's got a strong signal and he's following them now."

A cheer went up, and Bess walked to where Simon was standing, leaning with the back of his hips against the heavy table, his arms folded against his chest. He'd turned away from the others and appeared to be staring out the window into the darkness. When she came around to face him, though, his eyes and lips were clenched tightly in a futile effort to hold back the tears that were threatening. A few had bypassed his struggles and were running down his face. She wiped those away with her thumbs as she took his face in both of her hands, and when he opened his eyes, it was her nodding to him, just nodding. Sometimes words were superfluous.

##

His head felt like it was three times its size, and his tongue was dry and foul tasting. Opening his eyes to see dark grey, horizontal stripes, he lay there for a few minutes, trying to remember what they were. Then he heard voices.

"Hey, it's waking up. Look at that. Pretty bloody amazing!"

Men talking. Voices he didn't recognize. Now he realized he was lying down, and when he slowly pushed himself upright, the stripes became vertical, and they were bars. He was in a cage.

He tried to jump up, but fell back when his wobbly legs gave out on him. There were five men in the room, and he didn't recognize any of them. When he reached out to their minds, it made his blood run cold. There was only one of the five whose thoughts didn't repel him with their violence and malice.

Worthington was squatting by the cage, staring intently at his prize. Everything about the creature amazed him. The size of the thing and the seeming intelligence of its actions, at least according to Milt and Francois, were incredible enough. But the thought that it walked upright and was carrying a pouch full of small balls and leaves of unknown origin was doubly intriguing.

"And you're sure it came from Sayers' place?"

"I'm sure. The fence wires were held down by a bunch of branches so it could crawl through."

"I wonder if Sayers knows these things are on his property."

"Hard to say. I didn't see any more, but I guess if there's one, there might be others. It was probably a good idea to send Francois and Juno back to try and find more."

Worthington gave him a disdainful look. "*Of course* it was a good idea. Get me some water in a glass." Milt ran to get a glass, glad to get out from under his boss' nose. He thought for sure that he'd be sitting pretty after finding this thing, but it seemed like he still couldn't say or do anything right. He grabbed a glass from a cupboard in the breakroom, filled it, ran back in, and handed it to Worthington.

Carefully reaching through the bars of the cage, he set the glass on the floor. He motioned for Pritchard to bring him the chair from behind the desk, then sat in front of the cage to watch.

#

Simon had told him to never go outside of his fence. He'd told them all it wasn't safe. But he'd done it anyway, just because he'd wanted to. And now look at him. He was in a cage, and there were men with frightening minds all around him. Simon had told him that if other Earth people found out what he was, that he'd be taken by those who would want to study him, and who would never let him go.

Maybe he should act like an animal with lower intelligence. If they didn't think he could use his mind, they might be careless in his confinement and make it easier for him to escape. But escape to where?

He saw the water, and suddenly realized how terribly thirsty he was. Instead of reaching for the glass with his hand, he crawled on all fours to the glass and began lapping up the water, never taking his eyes off the man sitting in front of him, staring.

"Look at those eyes! There's intelligence there, I'd swear to it. What stumps me, is why make him wear a shoulder bag? And what are all those balls of smelly offal inside of it?"

"Bugger me if I know. Might be that he found it somewheres and decided to keep it."

"I suppose that could be, but the way he was wearing it, like he's very comfortable with it, makes me think different. I wonder if he's vicious."

Worthington picked up a broom, and slowly pushed the handle in towards Eli's ribs. He ignored the broom until he finished the glass of water, using that time to try and decide the right course of action. If he acted hostile, it stood to reason that they were more likely to harm him. But if he was too friendly, they'd come to realize he had intelligence. On the other hand, he'd seen lizards on TV that were kept as pets, and these seemed acclimated to humans. Maybe he should try something in between.

He slowly slid around on his belly, and taking the handle in his mouth, bit down and snapped it in two. Maybe that would make them keep their hands off of him.

"Bollocks!" At that crunch of wood, the closest man dropped the sandwich he was about to put in his mouth. "Any blighter who'd step to with that minger'd have to be a pillock or off his onion!"

Milt sighed and rolled his eyes, thinking for the hundredth time that he didn't belong here. Most of the men who worked for Worthington had come with him from England, and sometimes he could barely understand a word they said, between their accents and their slang. They were from England—why couldn't they just speak English? Intellectually, he realized that if he was from Canada, and they were from England, then in terms of English, he was the one with the accent. But he wasn't intellectually inclined at the moment, so it just pissed him off.

When he'd gone out for a beer one night with a bunch of the guys, the first and *only* time he'd been invited, he'd felt so alienated by his lack of understanding that afterwards he'd gone to his room in the staff's quarters and googled English swear words. He'd carried a sheet of paper around with him in his pocket, like an idiot, for a week. It was worthless, of course, because he couldn't be whipping out his little cheat sheet every time somebody said something to him.

But the other reason he'd felt alone, was the violence he'd ascertained in the other men. It was always there, just beneath the surface, and even when they smiled and patted him on the back, he had the feeling that they could kill him without batting an eye, and might actually enjoy it. He didn't belong here.

He didn't particularly love animals, but he wasn't cruel by nature, and he felt bad about the hunts. Especially when they used the dogs. They scared him shitless. Nobody and nothing deserved to go like that.

He'd been excited when they caught this lizard, because it was so weird. He'd thought for sure he'd get a bonus or *some* kind of reward. Well, that hadn't happened, and after they started talking about the pouch it was carrying, and that maybe it was really intelligent, he'd started feeling a little guiltier than usual. He didn't belong here.

#

Eli settled down in his cage and watched the men. The one that hadn't seemed as dark inside as the others kept looking at him and looking away, as if he didn't want to meet his eyes. He knew he couldn't speak to the man like he could with the Sayers, but maybe he could just touch his mind, impress on him that hurting him would be a bad thing. He lay on his belly, unmoving, and tried to make eye contact with the man they called "Milt." He sent with all his concentration, but he couldn't tell if he'd reached the man or not. What he did notice, by the smell, was that the man had suddenly started sweating, and there was fear in the sweat. Maybe he'd gotten to him after all.

"Hey, Miltie, I think this manky beast has the hots for you! Look how it's looking at you!"

Milt had felt the eyes on him, and he could swear it was trying to communicate with him. He'd told himself though, that it was all in his mind. But when Benny said that, he turned and looked the thing full in the face. He was right. It was staring straight at his eyes, almost like it was willing him to understand. He'd already broken out in a sweat from the disturbing characteristics of the thing, and when he looked at it now, he got chills.

"I'm stepping out for a smoke."

"Never stepped out for it before, Milt. Why, I believe this blighter's got you freaked, don't he?"

Ignoring the laughter, he walked out and leaned against the wall of the cage room, taking deep breaths. Why did he feel so panicky, so—undone, just because some lizard looked at him? He needed to get out of here. He didn't belong.

##

He lay still on the floor of his cage as the men talked about him, pointing at him, prodding him with metal bars to see if they could make him lunge at them. Once he heard one of the men call the old one "Worthington." What was it about that word? Then he remembered.

What had he done with his foolishness? He'd delivered himself into the hands of the human who'd tried to kill the Sayers. What would they do to him if they knew Simon and his family were his friends?

The old one had grown silent, and sat watching him. He watched his every move, but said nothing. The other men were laughing, and it made Eli afraid. He'd always loved the sound of human laughter, but now it held only threat. He was tired from the drugs and from the constant tension, and despite his situation, had actually dozed off when two other men threw the door open and burst into the room carrying something in a net.

He smelled her before he could see her clearly. *Dulcie!*

They rolled her out of the net roughly, to land on her back in the cage next to him. She was unconscious, and as he watched her breathing, he knew that she was in trouble. She was smaller than him, and had always been the most delicate of the three sisters. If they had drugged her with the same amount they'd used on him, it could put her far enough under to stop her breathing. Even as he watched, her breaths became more shallow and farther apart. He had no choice.

He reached through the bars of his cage, took hold of the bars of hers, and putting his legs up against his bars to brace himself, dragged her cage over until the sides of both were touching. He heard shouts and curses from the men in the room, but he didn't care. He had to help her.

One of the men picked up a long pipe that they regularly used to "discipline," their captives, and he started to go after Eli, but Worthington grabbed his arm and slapped his face. "YOU IDIOT! He's finally showing us what he really is and you're going to beat him senseless? Drop the pipe or I'll have the other men use it on you!"

Worthington was more than capable of making good on his threat, and might do it just for sport. Every man there knew it too, so the clod with the pipe let it fall from his hand and backed away from the cage.

Worthington was almost up against the bars now, enthralled in watching Eli straining against his cage to reach Dulcie. She was too far away to reach with his hand, so he turned around and stuck his tail between the bars. He wrapped it around her arm and then, leaning forwards as he walked in the opposite direction, slowly dragged her over to lie within his reach.

"Look at that! Look at that! Do you know how much those cages weigh? And did you see what he did with that tail? This is incredible!"

Milt had come back inside when he heard the men shout, and now, as his boss was voicing his wonder at what the lizard was doing, he saw the intelligence of its movements, too. Maybe it *had* been reaching out to him. Maybe it knew that he was different from the others. He was a criminal, yeah, but not like these guys. He'd never killed anybody, never even hurt anybody, and never planned to.

Eli whipped around as soon as Dulcie was against the bars, and he reached through and tilted her head back to help her breath. He could hear more air going into her afterwards, but her breathing was still too shallow, and it was becoming irregular. He jumped up to stand on two feet, and reached through the bars to point at his medicine pouch on the table, making a barking sound for emphasis.

"He wants his pouch! Give him the damned pouch!" Worthington screamed at the man closest to the table. The man lunged for the bag and ran at Eli to shove it into his outstretched hand.

Eli grabbed the bag and went down on his knees, pulling the pouch open and rummaging frantically through it until he found what he was looking for. He grabbed two leaves and chewed them, then pulled the mass out of his mouth and shoved it into Dulcie's, raising her head and stroking her throat, while he crooned to her in what sounded like a growl to the humans. When he saw her swallow, he tilted her head back again. It took only a few minutes for her breathing to improve, and the room waited in silence, the men warned to keep their mouths shut by glares and throat slitting gestures from their employer.

Eighteen minutes later, Dulcie began to make odd little sounds and move her head around. Eli held her hand and sent to her, telling her what had happened and where she was, so that she wouldn't panic when she came to. Slowly she opened her eyes, and when she saw Eli, she sighed and reached out to give palm to his face. He leaned his face into her hand, and reciprocated.

"I can't believe it! They act like lovers! This is the most astonishing thing I've ever seen! And what, is he a doctor lizard? Is this incredible or am I crazy?"

A resounding answer to his question, asserting his saneness, and the incredibleness of the moment filled the room, supplied by his oft threatened men.

Since all pretense was useless now, Eli turned to look into the eyes of his captor. Worthington laughed and snapped his fingers at the two men who'd captured Dulcie. "What are you waiting for, you dolts? Go fetch me more lizards!"

##

Almost up against the bars again, Worthington asked Eli, "Do you speak?" He got no response other than a cold stare, and the man answered himself. "No, you don't have the vocal cords for it, do you?"

"Can you understand what I'm saying?" Again there was no response. "Suppose I told you that if you don't respond to me, I'm going to shoot your lizard friend in the head?" Eli jumped up and shook his head, holding one hand out, palm first, and shaking it back and forth in sync with his head movement.

Laughing, Worthington looked at the men around him, and they started laughing, too. When he stopped suddenly, so did they.

"Well, well, what should I do with you then, Green Man? I suppose I could try and breed you, perhaps with your friend there, or I might sell you for a fortune to some collector. *Or*, even more amusing, would be to have a little hunt. I would be the only man on the face of the Earth to ever hunt one of you, I think."

CHAPTER THIRTY-NINE

"Yeah, I realize that, but I tell you, this is really important. I can't talk about it, but can you take the word of one of your American brothers, that this is life or death? You've met me, and we've been emailing. You've talked to the other guys I worked with, and the chief. You know I'm a straight shooter. I know that this is a crazy request, but please, please, Hugo, just this one time, and I'll owe you forever. If I get the job, I swear, I will do your shift anytime you ask me, for the rest of my days, it's that important. All I need is a set of irons and I'll get them back to you in twenty-four hours. I know you have extra, because the other guys were talking about the new ones you just got in. Please man, I'm begging you. Oh, geez, thanks. Listen, I'll go around back. Within half an hour. Thanks again."

Enzo ended the call and turned to Genevieve, who was standing in the hall with him, listening. He turned to her and grabbed her shoulders. "Gen, I gotta go pick something up. I'll be back in about an hour. I think it's something we may need if we go after Eli."

"What? What is it?"

"We call them 'irons,' and if Eli and Dulcie are in cages, like I suspect, we might need these to get them out. You staying or coming with me?"

"I'd better stay and keep up with what's going on. Keep your phone handy and I'll call you if I'm not here when you get back. Thanks for being all in, Enzo."

He gave her a quick kiss, and said, "They're my family now, too, Principessa," and started running for the house to get their car.

Genevieve went back into the dining room to wait with the others. When Simon's phone rang again, he almost dropped it in his frenzy to answer, but caught it and shoved it against his ear. "Yes? Oh no, oh God. I—this can't be happening. No, no, come back here. We need to talk." He put the phone on the table and slumped down into a chair, covering his face with his hands and saying nothing until Bess grabbed his arm.

"Tell us!"

He looked up at her with haunted eyes. "It's Worthington. Arthur's got the Elpies."

Moans and not a few curses spread across the room. Feeling as if she'd been dealt a physical blow, Bess turned away from him to lean against the table. Her thoughts came forth in little more than a horrified whisper, and they tasted evil on her tongue. "He'll never give them back. Never. And once he knows they're your friends, what will he do to them?"

Jonas stood up and walked over to the second Eli. When Eli looked up at him, Jonas raised his eyebrows in a question, and it took only a moment for his brother to understand and nod in answer. Eli got up then, and the two walked over to Simon. Jonas put a hand on his father's shoulder. "Dad, let's go get him."

Simon's head jerked up, and he shook it violently. "No, we can't just charge in there! Arthur must have fifteen—twenty men over there, and knowing him, I'm sure they're all armed."

Genevieve threw up her hands in exasperation. "Well what are we supposed to do then, Dad? We can't call the police, we can't call the army, and we can't leave the Elpies with Arthur. You've got men too, Dad. Harvey hired extra guys. They're all ex-military, and most of them were Seals. They know how to go to war."

"Do you hear what you're saying, Genevieve? You're talking about people shooting each other, and maybe dying. And not just our men. What about Arthur's staff? His maids, his chauffeurs? Will they be in the middle of a blood bath? What about Harvey? Do you want to be the one to tell his wife and children, or the wives and children of *any* of our men, that their husbands, their fathers, are dead? Do you? Could you? And if we go over there, guns blazing, the first thing he'd do would be to kill Eli and Dulcie.

"We are *not* going to war. There has to be another way. If we can wait until the Bluemen come back, they could go in and take them like they took your mother and me, and wipe the minds of everyone over there. It would be simple and bloodless."

"But Dad, they're not due back for another fourteen hours. Who knows what that maniac might do to them before then?"

"I have their communication disk. They're probably too far away to reach yet, but I can try, and maybe they could get here sooner."

They all started when Sarah shoved her chair back loudly and rushed off into the kitchen. Almost as soon as she went through the door, they heard the banging of pans and bowls, and the refrigerator door and cupboards being opened and slammed shut again. Everyone looked at Angus, and he shrugged. "She's gone into a baking frenzy. It's kind of her answer for everything. If she's sad, she bakes. She's mad, she bakes. Happy, she bakes."

"Whatever eases her mind. I'm going to get the disk and see if I can reach the ship. When Harvey gets here, send him to my office, will you?" They all nodded distractedly, each thinking about what Simon had said, and what might be happening to the Elpies while they waited for help to arrive.

#

"Eli, come into the hall, quick! And don't talk to anybody."

The sending hit his brain like a rock, there was so much urgency in it. He recognized Ishmael as the sender, but he'd never received anything from him that forceful before. He walked down to the end of the hall before he saw him. Black cats and shadows were made for each other.

"Hey Ish, what's going on? It's kind of a tense time right now. Can this wait?"

He felt the cat's annoyance before he grasped his sending.

"You think I want to talk chess with you, or tell you about the last bird I caught? Give me a break!"

"Sorry. Have you been listening to everything going on in there?"

"Of course. That's why I called you out. Come with me, quick."

With his dad trying to make a call, and Harvey still on his way back to the house, Eli guessed this was probably as good a time as any to see what Ishmael was up to. Anything that might help the situation was worth listening to, and the cat had come up with good ideas before. You couldn't be stupid and be a chess master.

He followed him out of the house and back up into the property until they came to the stone fence between the Sayers and the Worthington estates. When Ishmael stopped, Eli looked around and saw nothing out of the ordinary. "So, the fence is what you wanted to show me?"

"No. I wanted to tell you that I'm going over to Arthur's property and see what I can scout out around the house. Maybe I can find where the Elpies are being kept, and give you a heads up when you make your raid."

"Hey, that's really gutsy of you, Ish, but who says we're going to make a raid? Besides, it's dangerous in there for a cat. There might be coyotes, or bears, and he has a bunch of dogs. I can hear them barking all the way from my house. You'd better leave this to us."

He jumped up on the fence to be closer to Eli's face, then stood on his hind legs and swatted him several times. Eli jerked back in surprise.

"Weren't expecting that, were you?"

"Uh, no, I wasn't."

"Do you think they'll be expecting a cat to spy on them?"

"Of course not, but—"

"Will you just shut up then, and listen a minute? Geez, you people like to talk!"

"Okay. Mouth shut, brain open."

"All right. Old Arthur over there, being homicidal, crazy, and rich—a very bad combination—probably has a bunch of criminals working for him, and they have guns. Guns kill people. And as much as it galls me to admit it, I'm sort of used to all of you, and I think your getting killed is a bad idea."

"I'd agree with that."

"Shut up and listen."

"Right."

"Yes, it could be dangerous for me, but there's nothing new to read in the library, and I could use a little excitement. Now, you notice what color I am?"

"Black."

"Ooh, you're so sharp. And what time of day is it?"

"Nighttime."

"Right again. Another genius in the family! Okay, watch this." He jumped off the fence and walked a few yards away into the darkness, and then didn't move or send. Finally, Eli got irritated.

"Very funny, Ish. Where are you?"

"Right behind you."

Whirling around, he looked down, and there sat the cat.

"Whoa, I didn't even hear you."

"My point exactly. Black cats disappear at night, and I can sneak up on just about anybody I want to, no problem. It's a cat thing. Yeah, they've got dogs, but they're in kennels, you can tell by the sound. Speaking of which, were you aware that cats have better hearing than dogs?"

Eli shook his head.

"Most people aren't. Just because dogs have that freaky sense of smell, people think that all of their senses are better. People are wrong. I Googled it.

"I need to get in there right now, so I can reconnoiter before any of you get crazy and go over.

"I know your dad is going to go and maybe get himself shot, and I'm pretty sure there'll be some other Sayers there too, sooner or later. Not to mention, if anything happens to your dad, I think Harvey and your mom will lose it and you'll have a full scale war on your hands. Harvey will take that credit card and come back with rocket launchers, grenades, tanks, you name it. And he will use them, I have no doubt. I'm not psychic, in case you were wondering. I was in the room when your dad was on the phone with him.

"Even if they see me on the property with their security cameras, nobody would pay attention to a cat walking through a yard. I can get up close to the house, and send to the rest of you about what's going on. You'll need to know if you're planning on invading. I can't send long distances like the Elpies and your folks can, but within a hundred yards—no sweat. As for wild animals—Arthur and his gun happy little crew have probably already wiped out anything bigger than a squirrel. *Nobody* can kill those little—"

"Okay, okay. I got it. And you know what? You're right. This is a great idea. I appreciate your being willing to do this for us, Ish, I really do."

The cat stood on his hind legs and rubbed his head across Eli's knees. "It's all in the family. I wanted to tell you so that when your dad goes over there, he can send to me, and I'll let him know about anything I've found out that might help. Bye." Jumping down off the fence, he ran into the dark and became invisible.

#

She'd gotten out her pans, but before Sarah started baking, she'd put her macaroon stone on the window sill. Desperate times called for desperate actions, and she felt pretty desperate right now. When her grandchildren started talking about making war, it was time for Grandma to call in the cavalry.

#

Sven had sent that quite a few factors determined how far their disk could transmit. This was not nearly as sophisticated as the one they'd been given when Simon was trying to grow his blood supply back. They'd been given their most expensive equipment then, because it could have meant life or death for one of the Bringers of The Rebirth if he'd had any kind of mishap while he was healing. The disk they had now was strictly a matter of courtesy and a way to make sure that Sarah knew to start baking.

He tried twice, and thought he heard an answer over static. The third time, Mona had Colder answer. Only every other word was getting through, so Simon kept repeating the same thing until he finally felt he'd done all he could, and disconnected.

#

Colder looked worriedly at Micah, and then at Mona and Sven. "All he kept saying was, 'Eli and Dulcie captured. Need help. Hurry!'"

#

As soon as he'd put the disk down, Harvey walked in. "Close the door, would you, Harvey?"

He sat down at his desk, and Harvey sat in front of it. "What do you want us to do, Simon? If I was up front with the guys, I know they'd be willing to take out Arthur and get the Elpies back. But that would mean telling a lot of people about your whole situation here."

Simon covered his face with his hands and then laid them on the desk in front of him, shaking his head. "When you say, 'take him out,' you mean 'kill him,' don't you?"

Harvey looked down at his own hands for a moment, and then back at Simon. "Yeah, I guess I do."

"I can't do that. I can't send you to start a war, knowing you're going over there to kill people and maybe get killed yourselves. I just can't do it."

"Then what? I know you're not thinking of leaving them with him."

"Of course not. I'm going over there alone and talk to him."

"That's crazy, Simon! The guy tried to kill your family *and* you, and you think now you're going to go have a nice chat and he'll just hand over the prize of a lifetime? You're not that stupid and neither am I. What are you really planning?"

He sighed heavily and leaned back in his chair, putting his head back to stare up at the ceiling without speaking. Harvey waited in silence. Finally, he sat back up and looked at the man across the desk from him, this man, he realized, who was ready to risk his life for him. To go to war and leave his family, *for him.* How could he ever repay loyalty like that?

"Harvey, there are two things that Arthur Worthington values: power and money. I can give him both. If I go over there, and beg him, I'll be giving him power over me. He wants to see me grovel. For the Elpies, I can do that. I will also offer him my entire fortune, if that's what it takes. I'm going to talk to my family first, but I know they'll understand.

"If he demands the estate, I will give him everything except the clinic, and the land and homes that I've deeded already to the Allbrights, Eli's family, and the Guinnesses. Those are no longer mine to give. I also have money in trusts for each of my children, the Allbrights, and for you, Harvey. Those, I will not touch."

Harvey was completely dumbfounded. Simon had never mentioned the trust. "I don't know what to say, Simon."

"Don't say anything. It's not necessary, and there's no time. All of my children are grown and can make their own way, and Bess and I have skills that will let us find employment easily. I love this place." Looking around the room, and out the window, his vision blurred a little at the thought of leaving this home where they'd spent their lives together, and raised their children. He shook it off quickly and got back to business. "But in the end, that's what it is—a place. Eli and Dulcie are family. We don't need to be wealthy. We don't need it at all. If I give Arthur everything, in his mind, I'm humbled, and he's rich. And he knows I can't report him, because I can't tell anyone about the Elpies."

"And what if he just decides to kill you, instead?"

"Then call the police, and deliver that letter I gave you. If the police rush in, at least the Elpies have a chance. Arthur still might—no, he'll *probably* kill them if he's attacked, but if the police did manage to get the Elpies out alive, the Bluemen would be able to get them away from the police without a problem.

"What I need for you to do, Harvey, is to stay here and protect my family at all costs. They want to go over there with me, but there's no way I'll see any of them killed. Protect them here. I thought about sending the children and Gisella away, but if Arthur has men watching us, and had them followed—they'd be defenseless anywhere else. At least here they have your army.

"Have all of your men posted here, and *ready* for an invasion. What worries me the most is that he might send men over here to hurt my family, on the chance that they might go to the authorities when I turn up missing. You can't let that happen, Harvey. I wish I had let you buy that tank, now." He gave a short, half-hearted laugh, and stood up.

"Simon, I—" He didn't know what to say. He knew that Simon was going to walk out that door in a few minutes, and he would probably never see him again. He stood and looked at the floor, trying to think of some adequate response to the moment. Then he heard Simon coming over to him, saw his long feet on the floor in front of him.

"Simon, I— I just—"

Simon put a hand on his shoulder and said quietly, "I love you, too, Harvey. You're like one of my sons. And it means everything to me to know that you're watching out for my family. Who better to take care of family, than family."

The two men embraced, Simon kissed the top of his head, and walked out the door.

When he went back into the dining room, they all looked at him expectantly, except for Bess, who was glaring at him in sheer fury.

"We're supposed to be partners, Simon. Why did you shut the door?"

"I just needed to cover a couple of things with Harvey, and I wanted the quiet to think."

"Why couldn't I be in there, then? I wasn't making any noise."

"I'm sorry, I just didn't think about it."

"You are the world's worst liar. I am so mad, right now—"

"I know, and I'm sorry, but we don't have time for this. I need to talk with you all." He laid his plans out for them then, and asked Bess if she was willing to part with everything she owned. He left out the part about him maybe not making it back alive, but they'd all figured that out on their own.

When he finished, Bess was still seething. "You know you don't even need to ask me. I'd give up anything for the Elpies and count it as nothing. But you are *not* going over there alone. I've lost you twice before, and there's no way on Earth that I'll just sit here and wait for the third time. If you're going, I'm going too."

"No. You're not."

She slapped his face hard enough to make her hand go numb. "YOU DON'T TELL ME WHAT I CAN'T DO, DAMN IT!

Everyone in the room was stunned, including Simon and Bess. After she screamed at him, she stood with her fists clenched at her sides, trembling and tearing up silently, glaring at him. Daring him to tell her "no" again.

He looked past her into the room and said quietly, "May we have a moment, please?"

They all stood up and filed out of the room without speaking. He went forward then and took her in his arms, holding her as she cried and argued, and finally went still. Then he sat her down in a chair and sat himself to face her, close enough for their knees to touch, and took both of her hands in his.

"Bess, please, listen to me. If I go alone, he'll be focusing on how much he hates me, and how he'd love to humiliate me. If I give up everything we own to him, he'll feel like he has his revenge. But if you go with me, that will remind him of your rejection, and worse than that, he'll realize that I still have you, and he'll know that you're my real treasure. You always have been. That's something he can never have in his life, and he'll know that when he sees us together. He'll want to kill you in front of me, or degrade you, and you know I'd die before I'd let either of those things happen. So you might be saving my life by staying here. You'd only be putting me more at risk by going. Can't you see that?"

She could. She did. She sat straight up, clenching her lips closed and stopping her tears through pure will. He put one hand behind her head and pulled hers over to meet his. They stayed that way for a minute, forehead to forehead, in silence, and then he called the rest of them in.

"I've spoken with Harvey, and he and his men will be here. Do whatever he says, and he'll be sure everyone stays safe."

Eli stood up. "Dad, we're going with you, Jonas and I. Period."

"No, I forbid it. I'm still head of this house, and I forbid it!"

"Sorry Dad, we're all grown-up, and we won't be in your house when we walk out that door. You can't forbid us, no disrespect intended. And you know, this is partly your fault. You've been killed twice before, but the Bluemen were there to bring you back. All our lives, we've heard you say, 'three's the charm,' and 'everything comes in threes."

"I just say it, I don't believe it. You know I'm not superstitious."

"*You* may not be, but maybe *we* are. So if this is the third time somebody kills you and you *stay* dead—well, we're not going to let that happen. The Bluemen wouldn't be here soon enough to bring you back this time, Dad."

Simon let out a growl and slammed both fists on the table. Everyone but Eli jumped. "WILL YOU LISTEN TO ME?" he shouted. He stopped himself then, and looked down, not sure what to say, now that he had their attention. He stayed silent for a minute, trying to think of the words to persuade them, since bullying obviously wouldn't work.

Shaking his head, he said quietly, "I'm sorry. I love you all, and I admire your loyalty and your courage. But seeing you with me would put him on his guard, and there'd be more of a chance of him killing the Elpies and hiding their bodies. And as I told your mother, if he sees you, he'll be reminded of what he doesn't have and will never have. A family who loves him.

"That would put him in a rage and make him demand more than any of us are willing to give. If he only deals with me, he'll be thinking just of me. You're worried about me getting killed, but if any of you were lost, you'd be killing me anyway, and your mother, too."

Harvey pleaded, "At least take a gun, and wear a vest and a wire, so we can know what's happening."

"Harvey, you know he'll have me searched, after I made threats against his life. And if I wear a vest, he'll think I may be getting ready to launch some kind of attack and he'll kill the Elpies. This is the only way. If you don't hear from me in a couple of hours, go ahead and call the police. I'll make it a point to call you as soon as anything is settled."

"Dad, wait! I forgot. Ishmael went over there already. He's going to try and scout things out for us. He can only send a hundred yards or so, but when you're over there, you can try and send to him, and vice versa. Maybe he can help us. I mean, he can help you."

Simon nodded to his first born as he looked at him approvingly. "That's good. Very good. Thank you.

"Now, I don't want any of you to take this the wrong way, but you know how I am. I always like a hug when somebody walks out the door, and this is no exception. I need a hug from everybody in this room, and make it snappy."

He took each of them in turn into the hall to say how much he loved them and why. He ended with a hug and a kiss on the forehead, as he had a hundred times before. This same goodbye was meted out to everyone, including Angus, Hiram, and Barnabas, and then he went into the kitchen for a moment with Sarah. When he'd spoken to everyone else, he took Bess in the hall and they held each other and whispered and kissed like there was no tomorrow, because they both knew there might not be.

CHAPTER FORTY

He left the house, and Bess and the others went to the front window to watch him drive down the winding road to the front gate. As soon as his car moved out of sight, she turned to look at her family and said, "All right, we need to get our gear together."

The second spontaneous cheer for the evening went up.

"Listen up. As your mother— those of you whose mother I am, that is, I should try to stop you from going. But you're right. You're grown and I can't stop you, so I'm not going to waste time trying. And your father was right about not letting us go with him. We need to go in stealth mode, as the second unit, and sorry if I sound like I'm trying to talk like a commando. I just don't know how else to say it. We'll give him a little time with Arthur to try and do it his way, but if we don't hear from him within thirty or forty minutes, I say we need to move.

"I don't believe that Arthur would just blow him away the minute he walks in the door. He'd want to play with him a little, first. Taunt him. I think your father's offer to give up everything to get the Elpies back will just make him want to keep them more.

"Who all is going?" she asked.

"I am," came from the door of the dining room. Everyone turned to see Enzo standing with his irons in his hands. A firefighter's irons consist of an ax and a Halligan, fit together for carrying. The Halligan is a thirty inch long tool used to break into doors and tear down walls. Both ends are split: one into an elongated version of a hammer's claw, and the other into a rounded pick and a flat lever. With their irons in hand, firefighters can tear through a typical house wall in minutes, and break the locks or pry most doors open in even less time. With his irons in hand, Enzo was ready to work.

Barnabas slammed one hand down on the table as he broadcast his inclusion.

Jonas and Eli said, "We are," at the same time, and Genevieve went over to Enzo and put an arm around him. "I am, of course."

Angus said, "I'll—"

Sarah stopped him before he had a chance to say more. "Angus and I will stay here. I want to be sure the children are safe." Angus looked at her angrily, but when she gave him a pointed stare and raised her eyebrows, he knew that she had something up her sleeve, so he stayed quiet. She rushed back into the kitchen after they declared.

Bess was surprised, but relieved. She'd thought for sure that her dad would demand the right to go with them, and though he was very healthy for his age, he *was* eighty-six. She'd been trying to think of how to dissuade him without hurting his pride. The last thing they needed was for one of her parents to break a hip in the middle of a battle.

What surprised all of them was that Hiram said, "I'm going, too."

Bess looked at him worriedly. "Are you sure, Hiram? What about your Hippocratic Oath?"

"Oh, Bess, if you'd ever read the whole thing, you'd know most doctors never swear by that. In Canada, we go by a code of ethics. Besides, I'm not going as a soldier. I'm going as a medic. I'm also great at knots, and I can tie up or gag anyone you choose to disable. I'm a part of this family too, and I won't stand by while my family is at risk. I'm hoping that I can help keep all of you or even some of the enemy from being killed. I assume you intend to do this with the least possible damage to the other parties."

Five voices gave their assent to that plan. Then Eli took charge, as usual. "Everybody needs to go get whatever you think you can handle as a weapon, and meet back here as soon as you can." Then he looked at his mom, and added, "But after that slap, I don't know if you *need* a weapon. Never thought I'd see the day."

Jonas gave a half smile at his brother. "This isn't the first time she's popped him."

Bess looked from one to the other. "Actually, this was the third time."

Every person in the room had the same thought after she said that, including Bess. *Everything comes in threes.* And they all wondered if this had been Bess' last slap because Simon wouldn't be there to receive any more.

They started to walk out the back door, but Harvey stepped in front of it and held up his hand to halt them. Bess said quietly, "Please, Harvey, stand aside. We're going. You can't stop us."

He put his hands on his hips. "You don't think I know that? Simon swore me to protect his family, and that's what I intend to do. I knew you'd all be going. I just need to give you some supplies before you go, and a little advice. I'll be staying because I think that Worthington will send people here tonight. If he intends to do harm to Simon or the Elpies, he'll be worried that we know about it, and might go after him or tell the police. So I intend to have Gisella and all the kids in your house, Hiram, and have my men ready. Believe me, you don't need to worry about them.

"I have fourteen men, counting myself. Worthington has maybe fifteen, twenty on the outside. And he'll have them split up. I'm sure he won't leave himself defenseless if he sends a party over here. We have another big advantage. His men are thugs, for the most part, and mine are soldiers. There's a world of difference. I'll see you back here in fifteen minutes."

##

Bess frantically searched her studio for something to wield as a weapon. She did know a little karate, but a very little. She painted. So she could…hit someone over the head with a painting? Paint them with ugly colors? Stick a paint brush in someone's eye? She shuddered at that. Could she really just attack another human being? If Simon or the Elpies were at stake, she could. There were several tools she used that were pointed, but she just couldn't see herself stabbing anybody.

Then she saw it. She had the habit of dumping the change out of her pocket book every so often and putting it in a leather drawstring pouch. She used that as a paperweight until it got full, and then she'd take it and empty it into one of those charity boxes that graced the counters at practically every restaurant and pharmacy. She picked it up, and guessed it must weigh five pounds. Perfect. And when she stepped out, she saw something even better by the door. Wasp and hornet spray. It was in a can that could shoot a nest fifteen feet away. Getting a mouthful of that, or maybe an eyeful should stop a man in his tracks. She grabbed it and ran into the tool shed to snatch an extra can.

Jonas strung his bow, a handmade, hickory English longbow with a fifty-five pound draw, and filled his quiver. He'd never shot anything living—even the idea of shooting an animal made him sick. The thought of causing another living creature pain just because he wanted to use his bow was loathsome and repellent to him. But he had no doubt that he could shoot *someone* if he needed to in order to protect his family, and tonight, that was a major possibility. Pulling on his shooting glove and his armguard, he hung the quiver over his back and waited for Eli, Enzo, and Genevieve.

A backpack loaded with baseballs hung around her waist as she stepped into the living room, and Enzo followed with his irons. Eli came in last, with a wooden baseball bat. Of all their weapons, Eli found Enzo's the most unsettling.

"Are you really going to use an ax on somebody?"

"No! Oh, geez, are you kidding? This is to break into doors or go through walls if we need to. We use these all the time, fighting fires. Now, I might use the handle to bop somebody, but the blade? No way. In fact, Eli, since you and I have been talking Jiu Jitsu lately, I thought we might tag team and do a few chokes together. The Mata Leao? We put 'em out, and Hiram can truss 'em up. Whaddaya say?"

"Sounds good to me, Enz. I'd way rather put a guy to sleep than crack his head open. I'll do what I gotta do, but I'm really not into hurting people."

Jonas was listening and nodding his head. "I feel the same."

Genevieve added her, "Yeah, me, too."

Enzo put an arm around her. "Well, at least it's good to know that I'm not marrying into a family of homicidal maniacs. We are a strange looking group, are we not? That SOB is in for a surprise. He'll think your dad's all alone in this, but as my grandma says, '*Non tutte le ciambelle riescono col buco.*'"

Jonas was adjusting the quiver on his back, and without looking up, asked, "Which means?"

"Not all doughnuts come out with a hole." He looked at them and nodded sagely, with a knowing smile. They looked back at him with blank stares.

"Come on, you guys—and lady! It means that things don't always turn out the way you planned."

Eli gave an, "ahh," expression, and said, "Well, here's hoping all *our* doughnuts have got big ones."

Genevieve was staring at the three of them, when she suddenly got teary and looked quickly at the floor in embarrassment. "I'm so afraid that one of us is going to get killed. I mean, what are we doing? This is so crazy!"

Enzo put his irons down, and wrapped his arms around her. "Hey, Principessa. It would make me and your family feel *so* much better if you stayed here. I'm scared to death that something might happen to you."

"Oh yeah, big time, Genny,"Jonas agreed.

"Please, that would be the best thing you could do for all of us," Eli assured her.

"No way! I'm not trying to back out. But I think about how much I love each one of you—and the idea of something happening to any of you…"

Eli came over then, and politely removed Enzo's arms from his sister and replaced them with his own, "Scusa, Enzo. See, I've been listening.

"Genevieve, you're our only sister by blood, and the youngest. Since you were born, something in our genes or instincts, or maybe it's caveman stuff, but whatever—it's like we're programmed to want to protect you. I didn't mention it before because I know you, and Mom too, for that matter, and I know that neither one of you would send your men out to do battle without picking up your swords and shields to join them. But—it's really hard for us to go into something where we might not have a chance to protect you.

"There *is* a chance that something could happen today, but we've all made our choices, and we all know that we couldn't let our Dad and his brother and his wife, which technically, makes them our Uncle and Aunt Elpies—we couldn't let them be harmed and stand by and do nothing. We also know that if anything happens to *us,* Dad will kill us, and that would kill both Mom and Dad, so we've got no choice but to survive this, right? Is that all clear as mud, now? I don't even know why I just said all that, except it gave me an excuse to hold you."

Genevieve had her head down against his chest while he was talking, and now she looked up at him and kissed his cheek. Pulling out of his arms, she went over to Jonas and hugged him, giving him a kiss, too. Then she went back to Enzo and gave him *a kiss.*

"Okay, I'm ready. I guess I just needed to tell my men that I loved them one last time."

"Well, after that kiss, I think maybe I'll go to war every day! That wasn't a last one, Gen. We're going to make it through this. But on that note, guys, I just want to tell you that it's been an honor to get to know this family, and I'm *just giddy* with excitement about being part of it!" He jumped forwards then, and slugged both brothers in the arm, and they affectionately pounded him back.

"Okay, all the mushy stuff out of the way?" Eli opened the door and bowed to Genevieve. "Principessas first."

#

When they got back to the main house, Bess was waiting in the kitchen, wearing a huge tool belt around her waist, with two cans of wasp and hornet spray sticking up out of it, and she had a bag of coins clutched in one hand. When the others walked in, they surveyed each other's weapons, but no jokes were forthcoming, with the enormity of what they were about to do weighing heavily on their minds.

Harvey was standing there beside a table full of equipment, including a mound of plastic cuffs. "Okay, first, I've got bulletproof vests for everybody, and I think I got your sizes right. Put the Kevlar on first, and everything else on top of it. I've got night vision goggles there on the table. I'm not giving you guns, because there's too much of a chance that you'd kill each other or maybe somebody else that you might not want to.

"But—I have Tasers for everybody. The nice thing about this model is, if you miss, then you can use it with direct contact. They've got two darts, and if only one dart hits, the charge won't do much, but if you touch them with the Taser directly, it will set off the charge from the first dart. The direct contact by itself won't knock them down as much as cause severe pain, so use the darts if at all possible.

"The bad thing about these, is that once you use them, they're done. Using more than one cartridge in a pitched battle would be counter-productive. By the time you changed a cartridge and were ready to fire again, you'd already have been targeted and eliminated. So really be sure this is the target you need to hit before you use your one shot. These can hit somebody from fifteen feet away, and you'll see the laser light to help your aim. I have holsters for all of these.

"If you see a large group of men, don't engage them. You have vests on, but they don't protect your heads or extremities from bullets. Use stealth. Get in and get out, and nobody be a hero. Let me give you a little demonstration on the Taser."

He proceeded to give them a quick tutorial, and let them take a few shots with practice cartridges. Of all of them, the most excited and the most accurate, surprisingly, was Barnabas. He put his belt on over his vest, and he was ready to charge out the door. It was killing him to wait, and he stood tapping his foot, long skinny toes flapping like flippers, while the others practiced and got their equipment on. When they were finished, Harvey hugged each one. "I expect to see all of you back here, soon. You got that?"

Sarah and Angus came out of the kitchen then, and she held up her hands to stop them. They were all expecting her to give hugs and kisses, but instead, she said simply, "You need to wait ten more minutes."

Bess shook her head and looked at her mother in annoyance. "For what, Mom? We need to get going and get in position. We don't know what might be going on with Simon or the Elpies. What are we waiting on?"

"Help from above."

Bess sighed and gave her mother a condescending look. "Mom, don't you think we've already been praying about this?"

She was caught by surprise when her mother snapped, "Not *that* above. I mean the above *out there.* I called for reinforcements."

"Reinforcements—as in *aliens?"*

"Yes, and you don't have to say it like that. I put out my macaroon rock and it's getting hot. That means they'll be here in five or ten minutes."

Everyone had been standing, ready to walk out, but now Bess dropped into a chair with a look of angry exasperation.

"Mom, you don't know these creatures! All you know about them is that they like macaroons. I mean, you don't know if they're dangerous, or friendly, or hostile. You don't know what could happen. This is crazy!"

Angus strode up to Bess and got in her face. "Crazier than seeing our daughter and grandchildren go up against a bunch of armed thugs with a few Tasers, a bow and arrow, a baseball bat, a bag of balls, and two cans of wasp spray? You look like exterminators on crack."

Bess raised her chin defiantly. "*And* a bag of coins."

"Well, that's a load of bravado that could get you all killed. You don't understand—none of you ever has—just who your mother is. Aliens all over the galaxy—hell, maybe even from other galaxies, are absolutely addicted to her macaroons. Since she's let me in on her secret, I have seen some of the weirdest, most god-awful creatures you could ever imagine, and they all treat her like royalty. They tolerate me because of her. I'm just trash to them. But they *cherish* her, I kid you not.

"She can't really understand their languages, but they get through what they want with gestures, and sometimes I think they're like the Elpies—they sort of send her pictures. But *they* always seem to understand *her*. And I tell you what, girlie, if your mama tells them to protect you, they won't think twice about doing it. You'd be a bunch of airheads not to let them help you."

Bess looked around at the others, and they shrugged and half-smiled. "Okay, why not? You're right, Dad. I really don't want to see any of my kids get hurt. We wait. If you're sure it won't be long."

Sarah put her arm around her shoulder and gave a quick squeeze. “It should be any minute, sweetie.”

CHAPTER FORTY-ONE

They stood him up against the side of his car at gunpoint, and searched him for wires and weapons. Then they called Worthington.

"Yes, sir, I know you're busy, but you're not going to believe who just drove up demanding to see you. Sayers. Right, already done that, and he's clean. No wires or weapons. All right. Yes, sir, we'll escort him all the way."

Hanging up, he began sucking again, trying to dislodge a piece of the meat he'd had at supper from between two front teeth. Finding this method unsatisfactory, he continued to ignore Simon as he hunted down a toothpick in the drawer of the gatehouse. Finally working out a little wad with his toothpick, he inspected it carefully, then ate it. He hated wasting food.

Turning to Simon then, he said quietly, "You got to be pure nutters to come here again after the last time. We'll take your car up to the house, but I have my doubts you'll be finding it useful anymore. The dead don't drive much. Come on, then."

On that encouraging note, Simon got back into the driver's side, with the other man in the passenger's seat staring at him intently. Neither spoke again. When they reached the house, both got out and went through a door being held open by another one of Worthington's thugs. Considered incapable of handling a possible threat, the butler had been sent to his quarters.

They took him to the office he'd been in the last time he was there, and the two shoved him down into a chair set in front of the desk. Then they backed up to stand against the wall. A few minutes later, Arthur strode in briskly, passing by him without speaking, and sat behind his desk, leaning forwards to put his elbows on the wood. He clasped his hands together, just below his face, steepled his index fingers together against his lips, and looked at Simon curiously.

"Last time you were here, it was to threaten me. I ignored your insults and insinuations as post-traumatic hysteria, added to by your possible concussion, judging from that cut on your head. Which…is…healed already? With no scar? What *is* it with you, Simon—do you have an on call plastic surgeon living in your house? Maybe that would account for you and your wife's unnatural lack of aging. Before you leave here today, you *will* give me his name."

"Arthur, I'm here because I know you have the lizards. I want them back."

He laughed long and hard before answering. "Oh my goodness, so forceful for someone totally helpless in enemy territory. And what lizards would you be talking about?"

"The *big* lizards. Cut the stalling, and let's get to it. They're pets that I've had a long time, and they're very important to me. I'm willing to pay a great deal to get them back. What do you want?"

"What do I want? Nothing that you can give me. All right, I do have the lizards, and I would say they're probably the rarest creatures on Earth. Where did you get them?"

"I found them in the woods when we first moved here. They were hatchlings, and I brought them back to the house. I never saw any others, so maybe a hunter killed the parents. We raised them, and they're like a part of my family. I'm prepared to pay you whatever you ask, but I want them back."

"Who knows you're here?"

"No one. No one else in the family even knows the lizards are missing. They roam the estate at will. I was walking and I saw where they'd pushed the fence down to go through, and followed their tracks. I'd heard that you were in the business of illegally dealing in exotic animals, and put two and two together."

"Mmm, mmm, mmm, Simon, you must be the world's worst liar."

"So I've been told."

"So where did you really find them?"

Simon sighed and leaned back in his chair. "All right, since I can't seem to tell a believable lie, I'll tell you the truth, but you won't believe that, either."

"Try me."

"We call them 'Elpies,' and they're from another planet. I was abducted by aliens thirty-eight years ago, dumped on the Elpies' planet, and I ended up living with them for over three years. Bess was abducted thirty-five years ago, and she lived with them for a while, as well. They were brought here for a visit by the extraterrestrials who abducted us in the first place."

"All right, I take it back about you not being able to lie. If I didn't know better, I'd think you were telling the truth."

"I am. So let's get to business, shall we? How much?"

"You actually believe that I would give them back to you for money? You can't put a price on those things. Plus, I'm positive you have no proof of ownership. What else could you offer me?"

"My estate. Everything except for the land that's already been deeded out to one of my sons, my caretakers, and my adopted daughter. The rest is yours. I'll sign an agreement right now."

Arthur put his hands against the edge of his desk and shoved his chair back, looking at Simon with a huge smile on his face. "Your estate? Good Lord, you must really want them badly. You mean I could have all your land? What about all your cars and the boat, the ATV's, the—"

"They're yours. I just want the Elpies back."

"Ah, Mr. Sayers, dear Simon—I have more money, in more banks all over the world, than you ever dreamed of. I don't need your pathetic little piece of land, and that monstrosity of a house that your dotty old aunt built."

"You want to see me beg? Well, I'm begging you, Arthur. I'm completely humiliated. Just coming here and asking you for *anything* sticks in my craw enough to make me gag. You can take away all that I have. Isn't that enough for you?"

He stood up then, leaning over the desk and raising his voice to almost a scream. "Why, of *course it's not enough!* I'm not taking everything you own if you still have your lizards, am I? Would you like to see them?"

"Yes, please."

"Oh, he said 'please.' Well, since you asked nicely, not only will I let you see them, but I'll let you share their experience with them." He pulled a gun out of his drawer, and shot Simon in the chest before he could even stand. He grabbed his chest, and then saw that instead of a hole, there was a dart sticking out.

He pulled it out and dropped it, turned around and tried to make it to the door, knocking the chair over and stumbling on the legs of it. Arthur's men laughed and turned him around, shoving him back to the center of the room. He attempted to say something, but he couldn't remember how to make words. Trying for the door again, his legs gave out, and he went to his hands and knees. Crawling now, only able to comprehend that the door was where he needed to get to, he was straining to make his arms and legs move in sync. Arthur walked over and put his foot on his back, pushing him slowly to the floor. The two men rolled him over, so that he could see Arthur's laughing face above him, and he heard the words, "I *love* it!" just before passing out.

#

He let Simon wait on the floor while he spoke with his men. "As soon as you deposit him in a cage next to his friends, I want you to take all but ten of the men and hit the Sayers' estate. Kill the men, and bring the bodies of his sons back here for him to see. Take the women and children alive, and bring them back here, too. There's always a good market for those. Before I kill him, I want him to know that I've destroyed everything he holds dear. Do *not* say anything about this to him. I want it to be a surprise."

#

When the old man had left the room, Dulcie sent to Eli, telling him why she was there, and that Simon would be coming soon to free them. Eli was horribly ashamed for being the cause of his wife's pain, rough treatment, and imprisonment. She had risked everything to find him. Reaching through the bars, she slapped him on the head and then put her palm to his face. Yes, he was rash sometimes, and today he'd been a complete idiot, but all would be well. Simon would see to it.

There was a noise at the door, and the Elpies separated and sat back away from the bars to see who was coming. Two men struggled in, carrying something heavy between them, and another man opened the door of the cage next to Eli. They laughed and swung the something back and then threw it into the cage, to land with a thud and a slapping sound as its flesh met the concrete.

The thing fell onto its side then, from the pile it had landed in and—*No, No! Simon!*

If Simon was here, captured, what had they done to his family? They might all be dead. He looked at him, feeling that all hope was lost, and wondering what would happen to them. As he watched Simon dejectedly, he began to realize that his brother was having the same reaction to the drug as Dulcie had. His breathing was shallow and irregular, and his skin had a bluish-gray tinge.

He leapt to his feet and started gesturing wildly to his pouch again. They'd put it back on the table after he'd used it for Dulcie, and he needed to give Simon something *now*.

The old man came in and nodded to the human by the table, so the man picked up the bag and tossed it to him.

He grabbed it out of the air, only to drop it on the cage floor as soon as he had it inside. Then he went down to stretch his arms through the bars and go through the same process that he'd used with Dulcie's, to pull Simon's cage over to his own. When the bases came together, he thrust both arms in and pulled Simon to him. Thankfully, he'd been within reach. Pulling his little Dulcie with his tail was nothing. But dragging a man of Simon's size—

He rolled him onto his back and tilted his head to help him breathe. There was a gasp when he opened his airway—a welcome sound to Eli's ears. Holding his head back with one hand, he rummaged around in his bag with the other, trying to find what he needed by feel alone.

"Look at that! It's like he really does care about him! And he's looking for something to give him. Did he send him to medical school, or what?"

Ignoring everything else around him, he finally found the leaves and chewed a handful as fast as he could. Simon's skin was turning colder. Spitting the chewed leaves into his hand, he rolled the mess into a ball and raised Simon's head forward now, to keep the wad from going down into his lungs. He shoved it into his mouth and sent with all his might to reach Simon's mind, with "SWALLOW, SWALLOW!" He rubbed his throat and kept sending, until at last he saw his throat moving. "AGAIN, AGAIN!" he sent. Though they'd probably received the same amount of drug, Eli needed to get a bigger dose of the counteracting herbs to circulate through a man this size.

Within a few minutes, Simon started moaning and trying to sit up. Eli held him down, not so much for medical reasons, as to be able to send to him without being detected. He started sending everything that had happened, and where he was. After another few minutes, he saw Simon's eyes open and focus on him.

Simon half smiled, and sent, "You're always saving me, aren't you?"

He responded by reminding him that this was the fourth time, and twice he had failed. He needed to stop making it necessary.

Pulling himself into a sitting position, Simon tried not to move, hoping the room would stop spinning if he stayed still. He could see Arthur standing in front of him, gloating.

"I am deeply impressed, Simon, that you could train a creature like this. Did you teach him some of your herbal medicine that you're always dabbling in?"

"He taught me, actually."

Arthur laughed at that, so his men laughed, too.

"Really, I want to know. How did you do it?"

He raised his head and looked him square in the eye. "You're right, Arthur. I am a terrible liar. So look at me now, while I tell you again. He's from another planet. He is a treasure, as is the other one. He's a medicine man, and that's how *I* got into herbal medicine. I was his helper on their planet."

"How do you come up with these stories? And to tell it with such a straight face. I can see I badly underestimated your talent for fabrication. Or are you just insane?"

"You tell *me*, Arthur. Suppose I could train him to walk upright, and do simple tasks. How would I teach him to make independent decisions on which herbs to use to counteract a sedative effect? And how would I teach him language? You can say anything to him, even in a foreign language, and he'll get the gist of it, because he reads the message behind the words in your mind."

"Really? So tell me, Green Man, how many eyes do I have?"

Eli looked at Simon, who nodded and sent to him to answer everything. Eli held up two fingers. Arthur looked surprised, then intrigued.

"Cuantos hombres estan en esta sala?"

Eli let him see him taking a count, including Simon, and then held up four fingers.

"Combien d'amis avez-vous dans cette chamber?"

Eli pointed to Dulcie and Simon as his only two friends and then held up two fingers.

Arthur laughed, as did his men, and then exclaimed, "That is remarkable! Astonishing! I think I'm beginning to believe you, Simon."

Sending to Eli that the Bluemen were on their way back to Earth, Simon stressed that if he and Dulcie could just stay alive until then, they could easily rescue the two of them. Whatever this maniac asked them to do, they should do it.

"Listen to me, Arthur. I know that you hate me, and you're probably planning on killing me. Ordinarily, you'd kill the two Elpies, too, just because they're important to me. But why kill them when they're worth a fortune to you? I'm the one you want dead. You could sell them anywhere in the world. Or keep them for your own private zoo. These creatures can open up a whole new world for you, once you start learning to communicate with them. They live on another planet that you'll never see, but you can through their eyes. Doesn't that tempt you just a little bit?

"Whatever you have planned for me, you'd be crazy to kill them."

One of his men had been studying Dulcie, and the way she was looking at Eli.

"Makes sense, Mr. Worthington. Sir. I mean, look at the way this one looks at t' other. Like they's sweethearts. Most people'd be gobsmacked to see sommat like that. You could charge a good bit for a look at them, no quarrel."

Arthur turned his head slowly to look at the man. "Pritchard, do you recall me asking you for an opinion?"

Pritchard ducked his head and backed away. "No sir, no sir, sorry sir."

"You know, Simon, if you were anyone else, I'd say you were spot on about that. But they're *your* pets, or your *friends*, whichever, and that makes them even more valuable to me for a different reason.

"You have been the object of my fantasies for many years. When I was a very young lad, I used to dream of beating you at every sport you tried. Then I just dreamed of beating *you*. As I grew older, that became boring, so I dreamed of little accidents I could cause you. And then my dreams got bigger, with bigger accidents, and accidents involving your family.

"Do you know, that when I heard about the plane crash that killed your parents and sister so many years ago, I actually cried? I cried because I wasn't responsible for it. I cried because I didn't have enough money or power at the time, to orchestrate the crash myself. I felt robbed."

Simon was standing now, leaning against the bars and listening in silence. He set his jaw, trying to keep his face calm, not wanting to give this creature the satisfaction of seeing his rage.

"I'll have a lovely surprise for you later, but now I have to think about what to do with your friends here. Since there's two of them, I can get rid of one and still have my prize. My men are out now looking for others, but I think I believe you—they won't find any, will they?"

Simon shook his head. "This is it. They're a breeding pair, too, so you could actually raise your own stock. You'll never have another chance like this in your lifetime, Arthur. Don't screw it up."

"Dear Simon, always thinking about my welfare, aren't you? The idea is appealing, I have to confess, but what I have in mind will be more fun. For me. What I'd like to do is to have a hunt. I have a nice corridor cordoned off with electric fencing, full of trees and hiding places, but ultimately a dead end. None of my prey ever escapes.

"I'll leave the female here, I think. I might be able to learn something of what you were talking about, once she gets over the grief of losing her mate." He smiled at her, and she made a small chuffing sound in her throat.

"They really do understand, don't they? A hunt it is, then. Should I go by myself and use a rifle? That way, I can skin him and have the hide as my trophy, or have him stuffed and mounted for my den. *Or,* I can hunt with the dogs. When the dogs catch something, they tear it to pieces. I can bring you the biggest piece they leave. How's that?"

He couldn't do it. He couldn't keep quiet any longer. "YOU SICK BASTARD! What have they ever done to you, other than give you the possibility of being famous, and even wealthier than you are! DON'T DO THIS! If you have one ounce of a soul inside of you, you can't do this! Look at them! They're just as intelligent as you or I! Don't do this, Arthur, I'm begging you." He dropped to his knees in the cage, and repeated, "I'm begging you. I'll do anything you want. Hunt me, instead."

Eli started banging the cage door now, sending to Simon to stop. He saw his fate before him, and he knew nothing would change it, much less having Simon murdered along with him. At least this way, the Bluemen could save Dulcie.

She was huddled in the back of her cage, moaning as she looked at Eli.

"Oh, please, Simon, don't you think you're being a bit melodramatic? You're offering to take his place as if you had a choice about how you're going to die. The choice is mine. And you act as if I wouldn't do this if I realized how human-like these lizards really are. But Simon, I was going to do it to you. Or maybe to one of your sons. Or that spunky little Boston terrier your imbecilic daughter dragged home to marry. I'm only keeping you alive now for a surprise later. But first you'll get to see your friend run a dead end race."

CHAPTER FORTY-TWO

Harvey had arranged for all of his men to stay on the estate for the first two months of their hire, in a guest house on a remote section of the property. He'd wanted them on hand until he was sure that Arthur wasn't going to try anything else. The area was far enough away from the main house that he didn't have to worry about the aliens being seen, and with their ships cloaked, and the Sayers knowing the location of the men, Harvey was reasonably sure that no "close encounters" would occur.

He'd used his time with the men to discuss strategies in case of an attack on the estate, and to go over some possible scenarios, and now he knew his forethought would pay off. He'd sent a group of men to Hiram and Gisella's to prepare her and the kids in case of attack. Both dogs would stay with them. He'd dispersed his other men to Eli's and the front entrance, to stay camouflaged and on alert.

##

A pressure in the air was felt, sudden and extreme, followed by a momentary floating sensation.

Then they heard Sarah's happy exclamations from the kitchen. "Mr. Stench! Blobra! Come in, come in, I want you to meet my family."

An overpowering aroma, like wet dog, concentrated a thousand times, with essence of skunk thrown in, permeated the dining room, even though Mr. Stench was still in the kitchen. They saw Sarah first, pulling someone behind her. Someone who had to bend over and turn sideways to make it through the eight foot high door.

Almost nine feet tall, and massive, he was completely covered with sleek, dark brown hair, including his face. He might have been smiling, but his face was contorted in what looked like a perpetual snarl, showing impressively long, pointed teeth. Rather than just a mouth and nose, he had a muzzle slightly shorter than a Labrador's, but shoved into his face, like a boxer's, making his fangs always visible. It was not a kind face. He had ears on top of his head, tall and pointed like horns, and he was growling.

Sarah was pulling him along as if he were the town minister there for tea. "Mr. Stench, this is my family, and it's very important that you remember their faces."

She looked at all of them then. "Yes, he knows what I call him, and he's proud of it. On his world, disputes are settled through scent gland duels."

Enzo was the closest to him, so he stuck out his hand, and said, "Hey, Stench, I'm Enzo. Nice to meet you." Stench grabbed his outstretched hand and smelled it extensively on both sides, then licked it and handed it back. Not wanting to be rude, Enzo smiled, nodded, and left the room to wash his hands. Thoroughly.

The doggie door banged open then, and Elsie came bounding into the room, broadcasting her sending. "I'll go right back, but the smell—I had to see, had to know."

Then she saw Stench. Genevieve almost screamed, thinking there might be a dog fight and Elsie would be torn to bits. But instead, the dog ran straight up to Stench and around behind, sniffing his derriere in delight, and he seemed completely comfortable with this invasion of privacy. She came around then, wagging her tail, and everyone stopped breathing for a second when he reached down and lifted her up to sniff *her* butt. She held perfectly still in his hands until, finally satisfied, he put her down and made a growling sound. Elsie turned to the room with a blissful expression on her face, for a dog, and sent a broadcast of, "Isn't he wonderful? He's so—masterful, but courteous, too!"

Then she remembered where her job was, but had to run back to Stench for one more delightful sniff before charging out the door.

The group steeled themselves for the next introduction when they saw Sarah rush back to the kitchen door and heard her next words. "Blobra! Come in here, dear." Walking back into the dining room, she looked irritably at the people in the room. "And yes, she understands what I call her, too. I just use descriptions for their names. They understand that, and they're all okay with it. Just in case you were going to ask."

Their new guest oozed more than walked into the room. She was either six or seven feet tall, and four or five feet in wide, depending on her current undulations, and she was simulating legs and arms to put the group at ease. Even with this effort on her part however, no one was sure how to address a cross of gelatin, mercury, and mucous. A sickly greenish-grey in color, which conjured up all kinds of nauseating thoughts, the bulk of her body was constantly moving in waves. Several eye-like structures seemed to peer out from near the top of her slimy mass, but otherwise, she was featureless.

Enzo was back, and he felt he couldn't speak to one alien and not the other, so he introduced himself again, and held out his hand. But before Blobra could reach out with her own, Sarah screamed, "NO!"

All action stopped at the command of the macaroon maker. "Ah, Blobra, dear, remember to shut off your acid before you touch any of mine." Then she pointedly looked at the floor, and following the direction of her gaze, they all saw a path of still smoking corrosion where Blobra had slid into the room.

Enzo turned a little pale, but Blobra looked at Sarah, and then Sarah told him, "It's okay. She'd already shut it off."

Not seeing any way out of it now, he put his hand back out. She met his with her pseudo-appendage, but instead of shaking his hand, hers enveloped it, and he slid up to his elbow inside of her arm. He tried to keep smiling, but he was saying, "Oh, oh, oh," and his eyes looked like they might pop out of his head. Then she made a sort of jerking movement and shot his arm back out of hers. He smiled some more, excused himself, and ran down the hall to the bathroom to wash his arm. Repeatedly.

After the handshake, Blobra turned darker, with a bluish color, and Sarah called out, "Oh Enzo, she liked you! Look, she changed colors!"

Abruptly, Sarah turned serious, as she addressed the two. "Mr. Stench, Blobra, we've known each other for many years, and I have never failed to provide you with macaroons. I have also never asked you for anything in return. But tonight, I need your help. This is my family, and they're about to go and rescue another member of our family, and two Elpies like him," she said, pointing to Barnabas, "that we also consider family, from the clutches of evil humans. Now, the bad people will be using guns, which you know about. If anything were to happen to *anyone* in my family, I would be so distraught that I don't think I could ever bake macaroons again."

Both creatures were visibly affected by this speech, and the group had to believe it was that last sentence that got to them.

"So, will you help us? Help me to carry on?"

The creatures stepped and oozed forward, and put hands and gelatin on her in affirmation.

"All right! We're outta here! Angus, could you drive the truck for Mr. Stench and Blobra? Oh, dear, look at the floor. Well, we'll worry about that later. But Blobra, please hold the acid when you're in the truck. It won't do to have you eating through the floor and falling out before we even get there."

Fortunately, the truck bed was large enough for Stench to lie down and curl up in, out of sight. Blobra sat in the front, with one slimy faux appendage around Angus' shoulder, much to his unspoken dismay. He felt like a giant had used him as a Kleenex. The rest of her mass bulged over and into the back seat.

Carrying his bow, Jonas walked out beside Eli to get into his van. Eli looked him up and down. "Geez, I feel like I'm in Sherwood Forest."

Jonas shook his head and glanced back at him. "*I* feel like I'm in *The Twilight Zone*."

##

As the group sped down the road towards Arthur's estate, they passed a van full of Arthur's men heading in the opposite direction—to the Sayers'.

##

When Ishmael heard Arthur talk about using the dogs, he knew he had to do something, so he started with a sending.

"Simon, it's me, Ishmael. Help is coming, and I'm going to do a little something to screw up the dogs. Don't give up." The crushing despair he'd felt in Simon's mind when he first touched it, gradually changed to hope as his message was received.

With one dog, he might take his chances in a showdown, but with a pack of a dozen, forget it. But—when dogs were on the hunt, they honed in on a scent, and they'd be zeroing in on Eli's. Maybe he could do something about those precious noses.

Running over to the kennels, he stopped when he reached them and backed right up to the first one. The hounds immediately went into a frenzy with their efforts to get to him. *That's right, fellas, open those big mouths.*

As soon as the dogs had their heads down at his level, barking furiously, he sprayed them in their faces. They shook their heads and kept barking as he went from kennel to kennel. There were three dogs per kennel, and they crammed their heads together, jockeying for the spot closest to him. He appreciated this concentration of droolers, since he was quickly running out of urine.

Ammonia in their mouths and noses ought to do something to screw up their sense of smell. He also gave them a good look at him prancing back and forth before the kennels, maddeningly just out of reach. When he heard a man come tearing out of a building, yelling something about the dogs, he split, running for the hunting corridor. He needed a little head start to check out the area before he made his move, if he intended to survive it.

He'd begun to worry that the rest of the family wouldn't make it in time to save Eli. He could stall and confuse the hounds for a little while, but ultimately… The others had better come soon.

CHAPTER FORTY-THREE

Five men, dressed all in black, crept around the perimeter of Eli's house. The lights were on in the living room and one bedroom, and this was made note of. Two of the men went to the back door and two to the front. The fifth stayed out to one side, in case someone tried to escape out a window and into the woods. They knew the sons were big, so they'd decided to hit them first, to get any problems out of the way before they grabbed the women and kids.

Worthington had said he'd overhead the brothers talking at the gallery showing, and all of the brothers and the fiancé were staying in this house. Sweet. They could go in guns blazing, and knock them all out in one swoop.

They had sound suppressors on their weapons, to prevent anyone in the other houses from hearing them and making a run for it. There hadn't been anyone at the gatehouse of the estate to try and stop them, which was odd. Bad time for somebody to get careless, but they would have killed him before he could've sounded an alarm anyway.

All of the guys were really up for this, and they'd been laughing and joking the whole way over. What was the good of having weapons if they never got to use them? It wasn't the same using a rifle on a tiger or antelope as it was on a man. The thrill just wasn't there.

These men had all killed before. That was one of the stipulations for employment with Worthington. All except for Milton. They'd brought him in because he was good at strategic planning on the business side of things. He hadn't realized about the bloody side of Worthington when he'd signed up, and then it was too late for him to change his mind. As for planning, they were planning to off him sometime soon. Boss was worried that he might be having conscience issues.

On signal, the front and back doors were kicked in simultaneously, and the men began to open fire. They murdered multiple sofa pillows, three lamps, a table, some walls, and a three foot tall Mickey Mouse doll, but no previously breathing creature was in the living room or kitchen.

They looked under everything; sprayed every closet and shower with bullets when they first walked into the rooms. They even pumped a few rounds through the mattresses, in case someone was hiding under a bed with a gun, waiting for one of them to look there. Then they took the stairs as a group, expecting to meet some resistance, and treated the second floor rooms the same as they had the ground floor. But nothing alive here, not even a goldfish.

Felix was holding a cigarette in one hand and his gun with the other, while he watched from outside. From the number of rounds he heard fired, there would be no survivors to worry about. He had to chuckle. This bunch of wankers were like little tykes when it came to shooting. They'd been so excited on the way over, he could hardly get a word in. Shaking his head and laughing quietly at how their eyes had lit up when he'd told them to get their guns ready, he put his smoke between his lips.

He was just about to call them on their earpieces for a body count, when the cigarette was knocked out of his mouth, his gun was swept away, a knife put at his throat, and a huge hand clamped over his mouth. The hand pulled him back against an even bigger body. Someone said "Shhhh," directly into his ear and then threw him roughly to the ground, to be trussed up like a hog. Somebody's knee was on his chest, and he couldn't breathe until after they gagged him and the pressure was let up. He was rolled over onto his face, with his knees bent back and his feet tied to a rope around his neck. *Bollocks.*

His men started calling him on his earpiece, and when they got no answer, they came out as a group, guns at the ready, to look for him. Three men went into the woods on the left. "Spread out," Jamie whispered. They hunched down and began creeping from tree to tree to scout the area. As two of the men, walking ten feet apart, passed some clumps of brush nestled between the trees, two specters in black, with blackened faces and brush tied to their heads, rose up at their backs. One of the brush heads grabbed his man from behind, pressing a hand over his mouth, and a gun against his temple. The terrified man threw his hands up and dropped to the ground, as instructed by the pressure on his shoulders and the whispered threats in his ear.

Brush head number two's target started to put up a fight, so he just clobbered him in the head with his gun, and he fell like a rotten branch in a hurricane.

The third man was circling back through the woods to the front of the house, when he thought he heard a noise behind him. He whirled around to search the trees in back of him with his eyes, just as two more brush heads rose up on each side of him, pointing their guns at his head. He tossed his gun down and raised his hands before being taken down, restrained, and gagged.

Neither he nor any of the others tried to say anything in their defense. What was there to say? *We was just strollin' through the woods, got lost, and decided to pepper a house with bullets?* Shite, it weren't hardly worth the effort. Weren't talking their way out of this one.

The fifth man was properly spooked now. Nobody was answering him on his earpiece. Maybe it was this poxy equipment. Worthington always bought the cheapest stuff, but nobody dared say anything about it. Not to that blighter; he was bloody crazy, and vicious on top of that. Better to keep your gob shut around him.

Now he started calling out the other men's names in a loud whisper. Finally, he heard a whispered "Over here."

He let out his breath in a rush of relief, and shouldered his rifle. He pulled his gun out just in case. When he walked past a tree, part of the tree became a person, and knocked his arm hard with a rifle butt, sending his gun flying.

As he bent over in pain, holding his wrist and moaning, he saw boots coming from all around him. One man stuck the muzzle of a rifle under his chin and tapped it upwards to make him raise his face and look at him, and the tap wasn't on the gentle side. A large face, all blackened, with the whites of the eyes almost glowing by comparison, got very close to his, and began to speak. "You can talk to us and tell us what we want to know, or we can slit your throat and gut you, right here. Speaking for myself, I'm hoping you don't talk."

He told them everything they asked and offered much more. There were twelve men here. Two were waiting in the bushes by the gate house to ambush the guards when they returned to the strangely deserted post. They'd already been taken down by Harvey's men. So that left five. They were going to the Guinness' house.

They had figured they could take that house easily, killing the man and then using the woman and her children as hostages to force any people in the main house to show themselves. When his interrogator heard that, he smiled up at the other men and they all had a good laugh. That was a bloody bad sign.

#

Harvey was sitting up in a tree, more excited than he'd ever been, with the exception of his shopping excursion, of course. Thirty feet up, he was ready to fast rope to the ground. He'd *always* wanted to do that. Eight men were stationed around the house, and every one of them was camouflaged so well that even he couldn't spot them.

A crunch of leaves alerted him to a man dressed in black walking under his tree. He braced himself and then went down the rope hand over hand, but before he could get down, the man heard him and turned around, raising his weapon. Harvey had seen him stop and go on alert, so before the man could get his weapon all the way up, he launched all of his two-hundred and eighty pounds off the rope. He hit the man full on, coming from ten feet up. The guy was out before he hit the ground. Harvey had to fight to keep himself from whooping. So maybe he hadn't looked like one of those cool dudes zipping down the lines from helicopters. He'd looked like Tarzan instead, and on retrospect, he thought Tarzan probably had more fun. But he *so* wanted to try this again someday.

One of Worthington's men was in the process of trying to climb in a window, when he was Tasered in his nether region. Two were getting ready to kick in the front door when they noticed red dots on their chests and threw down their weapons.

The last man was at the back door. Harvey had him in his sights, but waited to see what would happen.

#

They'd told him they thought there might be a dog at this house, and that's why he was chosen as one of the ones to go in here—he didn't much care for dogs, and wouldn't mind killing one or two. When he'd approached the door, a frenzied yapping began just behind it, and never stopped. He *hated* little yappy dogs. Hated them. This was going to be a pleasure.

As the man raised his arms to knock off the door knob with his rifle, the hedges on both sides of the porch exploded towards him, and two large non-yapping dogs wearing Kevlar vests launched themselves upwards to grab both of his wrists in their mouths. Elsie had coached Madelyn beforehand to be sure she felt her teeth hit bone when she bit down. A thing worth doing was worth doing well.

He dropped his rifle, screaming at the two dogs hanging from his arms, and the door flew open to reveal a woman and four kids, all in Kevlar vests, night vision goggles, and helmets, and all armed with Tasers. A yappy little dog in Kevlar leapt out and clamped its teeth onto his right thigh.

The woman screamed "Clear!" and one of the kids grabbed the little dog. The big dogs let go and jumped to the sides, just as the whole group fired their Tasers into the man's body. His last coherent thought before he crashed to the ground was "They make those in kid's sizes?" and the last sound he heard was "yap yap yap."

CHAPTER FORTY-FOUR

His parents were captured. What exactly did that mean? Were they hurt, or just confined? Simon had warned them multiple times that if they were ever seen outside of his property, that people would want to catch and study them. Maybe that's all that would happen and they'd be fine, but—it still frightened him badly.

Sven had increased their speed as much as he could, and said they should be there in an hour. Micah couldn't sit still anymore, so he began to pace, and Blanche paced with him on her hoofed legs. She was very upset that his parents seemed to be in some kind of danger, especially knowing that he'd already lost part of his family. She knew what the loss of family meant. As they paced, every so often she would let out a screech, until finally Mona laid a hand on her shoulder and explained to her that it *really* hurt the Bluepeople's ears when she did that.

Horrified that she'd been inflicting pain on the ones who'd saved her and her children, she apologized with her mind, and made her babbling noises for ten minutes to go along with the mental remorse.

Colder watched Micah pacing, and began to wonder what *his* family was doing with the situation. If he knew his parents, they weren't sitting idly by, just waiting for help from the Bluemen.

The more he thought about it, the more worried he got, until he finally got up and started pacing with Micah and Blanche. Pretty soon, Luigi felt like he should show his support, so he began pacing with them. When Sadie started heading in their direction, Sven reached out one arm to stop her. "No, please. Four are already enough to drive me insane."

He was seriously reconsidering his idea of a crew made up of several species. Seriously reconsidering.

CHAPTER FORTY-FIVE

He didn't know what he was supposed to do. Worthington already didn't trust him. But the look that lizard kept giving him was starting to prey on his mind. He *knew* it was asking him for help. If he tried anything, they'd kill him. From some of the hints and little snide remarks he'd been getting from the other men, he was probably up for elimination sometime soon anyway.

He'd heard the other men talking about killing Sayers' family. Unbelievable—how could anybody be that brutal and bloodthirsty? All of Sayers' sons—for what reason did they deserve to be butchered? And after they tortured the guy by showing him the destruction of his family, he was pretty sure they were going to set the dogs on him.

What was he doing here? He wasn't a murderer. He was a strategy guy, good with numbers and planning. Why had he ever let himself get involved with this maniac?

He got his cigarettes out and nodded to one of the men, holding up the pack to show him why he was going out. The other man, Sid, nodded back to him. As soon as Milt was out of the room, Sid addressed Arthur in a soft voice.

"Beg pardon, Mr. Worthington, sir, but I think Milt is having a problem with this whole thing. Maybe he's a risk you don't need."

"I know that. As soon as we're done with Sayers, we'll be adding another body to the pile."

#

The only thing he could think of to do probably wouldn't be any help, but he couldn't live with himself if he didn't try something. Milt wandered past the dogs, who were strangely agitated, rubbing their faces with their paws, and moving their muzzles up and down against the walls of their kennels.

None of them barked, because they were otherwise occupied, and also because they knew him. He reached the office where Darby kept his training equipment and his papers recording the dogs' lineages, and leaned against the wall to light his smoke. He casually took a puff, and when he was sure no eyes were watching, he slipped into the office and closed the door behind him.

He knew that Darby controlled the dogs partly with a whistle. He always carried one with him, but he had several extras in the drawer of his desk. Milt had seen him toss them in there one day when he'd come to deliver some papers to him. Opening the drawer, he grabbed one, and headed back as fast as he could without looking suspicious.

#

"Yes, I think we'll use the dogs. They'll ruin the skin, it's true, but on the whole, it will be so much more entertaining."

"Arthur, you can't do this. Please, whatever you want, it's yours. I'll give you codes to all my accounts, I'll sign over the estate to you, anything, but please don't do this!"

"Simon, this is getting tiresome. You've already begged, humbled yourself, and offered me everything you own, and it's just not enough. But soon I'll show you what 'enough' is for me."

When Arthur turned and walked past him to get a closer look at the Elpies, now holding each other through the bars, Simon shot his hands out and grabbed him by the neck. He pulled him tight against the cage with one forearm across his neck, but one of the men shoved a pipe through the bars, ramming it against the side of his skull. Simon's head was knocked back by the blow, but he managed to hold on until they hit him again. They couldn't shoot him and ruin Worthington's fun—they knew it would be their heads if he was killed before he saw his family destroyed. With the second blow, he lost his grip as lights flashed in his vision and he stumbled, falling onto his back, blood pouring from the wounds on his head.

The blows were painful, and left him stunned for a minute, but he didn't lose consciousness. Since he'd ducked down to keep his head behind Arthur's, the pipe could only be shoved through the bars at an angle, preventing the blows from being as forceful as they might have been.

He fully expected Arthur to kill him for the attack, but he laughed instead.

Rubbing his neck with one hand, he rolled his head around before looking down at Simon with a sneer. "Well, that was a pretty pitiful attempt. I'd have expected better from you, Simon. Darby, go get your dogs." When he looked at Dulcie and Eli, Dulcie turned her head away from him and clung to her husband.

"That's right, you two. You'd best say your goodbyes. You have about five minutes." Then he went outside to watch the dogs being taken out and herded up. Milt acted like he dropped his pack of cigarettes beside Simon's cage, and when he bent down to pick it up, he rolled the whistle under the bars.

Simon saw it, and reached one hand out to help himself into a sitting position, with the hand coming to rest on top of the whistle. Closing his hand, he pushed himself the rest of the way up and then used the bars to pull himself to his feet. He sent to Eli to turn around and embrace him through the bars and to shake his hands with both of his. When he did so, Simon transferred the whistle to his hands, and started sending.

"It's a dog whistle, Eli. I'm not sure how much good it will do you. You blow on the end of it. I don't know what your range of hearing is, but people can't hear these—the sound is too high. Maybe it will confuse the dogs. I think they train them with patterns of whistles, so try blowing different sets of patterns. Worth a try, I guess. Ishmael sent that he's trying to do something to the dogs, but I can't imagine what one cat could do. He said that help is coming, too.

"When you go out, run until he lets the dogs loose, and then go as high up in a tree with foliage as you can. He can still shoot you out of a tree, but maybe you can move around and use the trunk as a shield. If you can't— well— getting shot would be preferable to being torn to pieces."

He reached through the bars, took Eli's head in his hands, and bent his own down to touch foreheads with him while he sent. "Oh, my brother, I am so sorry. If you hadn't valued our friendship, you wouldn't have come here, and this would never have happened. I'm so, so sorry. I'm sure that he's planning on killing me as soon as he's done with you, so perhaps I'll see you soon."

Eli sent that he was to blame for all of this, and probably for Simon's death, too. It was he who was sorry for the terrible results of his foolishness.

"I got through to the Bluemen and told them we needed help, but they probably won't make it in time. I love you, my brother."

He kissed his forehead then, and gave him his palm as he strained to keep himself under control. He didn't want Arthur to see him cry. The more he realized the depth of Simon's love for the Elpies, the more cruelty he'd show to them. He didn't want to get Dulcie killed, too.

He sent to her then, all that had been sent to him, and about the whistle, so that she might have some hope, but he didn't lie to her. She knew Eli's time was almost up as well as he did.

And to think this was all because of a childhood grudge. Murder, because Arthur didn't get his way in school. The absurdity of it only made it worse.

#

A few minutes later, Arthur returned and picked up a high powered rifle with a scope and sound suppress0r on it. Simon stared at him icily.

"You know he'll kill you for this. He'll never let it rest until he finds you."

"Your friend, you mean, whose name you used to intimidate me? I've been thinking about that, Simon. As soon as we clean up all the mess from tonight's festivities, I'll be taking off in a helicopter and then boarding a private jet to whisk me away and out of the country. He won't find me. I have new papers already, with an alias, a new passport, a new life waiting for me. Interpol has been getting a little too nosy about certain interests of mine. And I could always put a hit out on *him*. I'm not worried."

"It won't matter what you do, Arthur. He'll find you. He's famous for it."

"Enough chit chat. Stan, get the lizard out of his cage, and bring him out back."

Dulcie tightened her grip on Eli, making raspy squeaks, but he gently disengaged her hands and gave his palm to her cheek.

Simon was desperately trying to hold back the tears, but it was a losing battle. He sent to him one last time. "Goodbye, my brother. Godspeed."

Stan had a gun in Eli's back as he shoved him out the door, and Simon could hear Arthur talking to him. "Green Man, I always like a good chase, so I will give you ten minutes' head start before I release the dogs. Do you understand, Lizard?"

Eli nodded, and started running.

##

The first of the Sayers' vehicles rolled up and stopped about ten yards down the road from the gatehouse. Jonas got out the scrambler that Harvey had given him.

"Harvey said this might disrupt the signal for the security monitor out here. I'll try it, but he wasn't sure if it would work. It depends on how sophisticated their system is." He fiddled with the knobs a while, and then—"Okay, you guys, you're up."

Eli had wet his hair and slicked it back to make it appear darker, hunched a little when he walked, to downplay his height, and had told Enzo to wear his boots to make him look taller. He wasn't sure how many of these guys would recognize them. Enzo had gargled with Vodka and poured some on his clothes. Making lots of noise as they got out of the car, the two started arguing, with Enzo slurring his speech.

"I'm sorry, but I gotta go, and here's a rest stop."

"It is not a rest stop, turkey. This is a guard house! We've got to go about ten more miles before we get to a rest stop. Get back in the car!"

"No way, Jose. I can't make it another ten miles." He began approaching the guard house, making his gait a little unsteady. "Here, there's somebody in there who can let me in."

"This is the last time you're coming with us, you dipshit. Nothing worse than a stupid drunk who can't control his bladder! Get away from there before the guy calls the cops or shoots you!"

Going up to the window of the guard house, he leaned against the sill. The guard was looking at him condescendingly. When Enzo didn't get the hint, he opened the window. "Shove off, you grotty prat! There's naught for you here, I can promise you. Listen to your friend before I take a club to you."

Eli came running up behind him, looking frightened. "Please, sir, I'm so sorry. He's such a moron when he's drunk, but he doesn't mean any harm. Come on, Hal, let's get out of here." He grabbed Enzo's arm but he jerked it away.

"Did you hear what he called me? He called me a potty brat! I'll show him. You know, the back of his little house is as good a place as any to take a leak." He walked around to the other side of the guard house, and the guard jumped up, gun in hand. He wasn't about to sit here all night smelling some drunk's piss. When he stepped out of the door, he saw Enzo in the process of lining up a shot at the wall, with Eli looking on helplessly.

He walked up behind Enzo with his arm out, gun pointing at him. Eli held up his hands and backed away as if he wanted no part of the situation, but stopped moving when he was in position to the side of the guard. Suddenly, Eli grabbed his wrist, pulling it towards himself, while his other hand came up below the gun, snatching it by the barrel and forcing it upwards, as Enzo went low, whirled around and kicked the guards legs out from under him.

When the guard dropped to his knees, Enzo came up behind, threw his right arm around the front of the guard's neck and grabbed his own left upper arm to lock his right in place. He pulled upwards, and with pressure on both sides of the neck cutting the blood supply to the guard's brain, the man toppled forward, unconscious. The attack had taken less than thirty seconds. They called that move 'Mata Leao'—lion killer, after Hercules' famous battle with his lion. Enzo was no Hercules, but the guy on the ground was no lion, either, so it evened out.

Jumping out of the car, Hiram ran over to apply handcuffs, tie his legs, and put duct tape over his mouth. Eli and Enzo carried him to the van and tossed him in back. When Hiram looked at the screen of the guardhouse monitor there was only static. He pressed the lever to open the gate, and then ran back to the van and got in.

As they drove through the gate, Eli started sending to Ishmael. He got an instant response. "I thought you'd never show! Come around the right side of the house to the back. There's a big added-on building like a barn. Your dad and Dulcie are in cages in there, but they're putting Eli out to be chased down by dogs! The hunting area is straight out behind the building. Hurry! A couple of the guys have shotguns, Arthur and one other guy have rifles, and the others that I've seen all have handguns. I'll try and distract the dogs, but I don't know how much time that will give Eli. They can shoot him out of the trees!"

"Okay, thanks, Ishmael. Oh, and if you see a couple of somethings that looks like an oversized werewolf and a giant slug, they're on our side. Just don't get in their way."

CHAPTER FORTY-SIX

The animal room was the size of a large barn, rectangular in shape, with a tall ceiling and concrete floors that sloped slightly towards the center to allow for the drainage of whatever fluids might be spilled there on any given day. It was attached to the main house by a narrow hallway, and on one side of the hall, a door opened onto the staff kitchen and break room.

Twenty feet down the first wall from where the hallway opened up into the main room, were three cages, large and strong enough to hold a rhino, if required. A small desk and two chairs were situated ten feet in front of the cages, for when a specimen was particularly agitated or overly sedated and needed watching. The room was grotesquely decorated with the mounted heads of the creatures that Arthur had mercilessly slaughtered in his "hunts." While most of the heads were posed to gaze out into space with the marble stares of the dead, a few were sloppily angled, and these seemed to be watching the scene below, as if remembering their own endings. Forever silenced witnesses to each new atrocity.

On the opposite side from the house entrance was a hallway running the length of the room. It was built as an afterthought, so that if a police raid ever occurred, an escapee in the room could be shielded from view long enough to leave by way of one of the back doors at either end of the hall. In this one large room, there were four doors: one from the house, one to the right of the cages, leading out to the kennel area, one along the back wall, opposite the cages, and one in the other far corner of the room, opening onto the back hallway. The door in the back wall was camouflaged by bales of hay, set there not for animal fodder, but to hide this means of escape.

Running along half the outer wall of the hallway was a large sliding door that opened onto the killing field .

Looking like nothing so much as a long golf course, with a downhill, rolling landscape, green and otherwise bare down the center, and tall trees running along each side, the area was deceptively peaceful in appearance. The trees on both sides of the green grew in strips of earth only twenty yards wide each. The whole enclosure was a a dead end, so that the hunts didn't become overly long or tiresome for Arthur. His many years of dissipated living had not left him in the peak of health.

Encompassing this area was electrified fencing, only activated when a new victim was about to be slaughtered. The green could be lit up, with the trees still in shadow, or Arthur might decide to use night vision goggles. Sometimes he hunted in the day, but night was always more provocative for him—"stalking" something at night made him feel more primal and powerful. On days when he was feeling less powerful than usual, or when he followed the dogs, he drove a golf cart to the hunt.

On the night that Eli was to be brought down by the dogs, Arthur ordered the green lit up. Working alongside the dog trainer was a man whose sole purpose was to shine a spotlight on any treed prey, making sure that no advantage be given by shadow to Arthur's intended victim.

##

When they took her husband around the corner and into the hall, Dulcie could no longer see him, but she could understand from the old one's mind what he was telling him as he was led out that door to meet his death. Her legs sank beneath her and she huddled on the floor in horror. One cage away from her was the man she had put her hope in, and now he was to die, as well. She couldn't let her mind come to grips with what was about to happen, so she withdrew into herself to wait. What would become of her afterwards seemed of little importance now.

A sudden scrabbling, whining, bestial noise came from her left, and she was drawn out of herself in time to see through an open door, the animals that were to be set upon her husband. She gasped at the size and power of the creatures, and despaired of all hope when she sensed their drive to kill.

The dogs were enormous and muscular, with ears that flopped forward and hung to their jowls. They were all tricolored, like a foxhound or beagle, but their markings were random on the white, rather than in regular patterns.

Their handler, Darby, had them on leashes, and though they tugged a little against these, they were well-trained enough that he could hold all of them himself until the signal was given for their release. He noticed they were acting a bit strangely, rubbing at their snouts and mouths with their paws, but they were all still eager for the hunt, so he put it out of his mind.

Simon sat against the back of the cage with his head in his hands, in dread and disbelief at what was about to occur. He knew that help was coming, but it would be too late to keep Eli from being ripped apart. When he heard them release the dogs, he leapt to his feet, screaming, "NO! STOP!" Leading with his shoulder, he threw his weight against the door of the cage, again and again, hoping for one loose hinge, one faulty lock, anything to get him out to help Eli. It was probably useless, he knew, but he couldn't just sit and accept Eli's fate as inevitable. He could not.

The two men left in the room thought this outburst incredibly funny, and their reaction brought him back to his senses. He would not give them anything more to amuse themselves with. Stopping his frantic assaults on the door, he slid down the bars to sit on the floor, where he began to pray for Eli's life. Or if Eli was not to be spared, that God would at least grant him a quick death.

Leaning on the desk across from the cages, the two men were still talking about their prisoner's exhibition. In the midst of lighting a cigarette, one of them stopped and held up his hand. "You hear that?"

"What?"

"Sounded like the door opened at the end of the hall."

"Well, Murray, what you waitin' for? Go check it out. I'll guard the prisoners. Can I have a smoke?"

Murray gave an exaggerated sigh. "One. Only one, and this is the last time. I'm sick of your mooching. You get paid, same as me."

Waving a hand at him in dismissal, Pritchard just laughed. "Ah, go on with you!" he retorted, as he took two cigarettes from Murray's pack.

Blasted knob head never takes me serious. But one of these days, he's going to reach for my pack and lose hisself a finger.

Coming from the middle of the room, the door in the corner was occluded from view by the back wall until a person was almost to the opening to the hallway, with the hall on the left and the door on the right. Still stewing about his cigarettes, Murray was making his way over to the door when he felt cool air coming from the corner. Slowing a little, he stretched his neck to try and see if anyone was there before he went closer.

"Well, ain't that brilliant! They went and left the side door open and it's blown wide."

"Don't go on about it, just close it and get back here. This green one's looking mighty dangerous. I may need help." He laughed and smiled a cavity filled grin at Dulcie.

As Murray approached the door, Simon caught the sending of, "Dad, we're here. Hold on!"

He had to stop himself from gasping in surprise and excitement. He sent the message on to Dulcie, who jerked her head up, and then let it drop down despondently when Pritchard caught her sudden movement. Simon stood up slowly, and leaned against the bars of his cage, looking beaten, and avoiding eye contact with the man.

As Murray leaned out the door to catch the knob, a baseball caught him hard on the side of the head, and he dropped like a puppet with its strings cut. Enzo and Genevieve dragged him out and away from sight of the door, and Hiram went to work with the plastic cuffs and duct tape. Eli the second slipped inside and stood behind the corner of the wall.

When Murray didn't return, and there was no sound of the door closing, Pritchard called out. "Hey Murray, what's taking you so long? Murray? Hey, you there, Murray?"

Taking his gun out, he slowly walked towards the back door. He saw something moving on the floor, and stopped to watch it roll towards him. A baseball? Where'd a bloody baseball come from?

Taking one step at a time, and stopping to listen after each one, he finally got close enough to see the back door. There it was, just like he'd said, standing wide open. Aah, Murray had probably gone outside for a smoke. But—he'd left his cigs on the table.

Holding his gun out in front of him with both hands now, he tiptoed closer to the door. He was almost there when Eli stepped out from behind the wall, bringing the bat down hard across his forearms, shattering bones and sending the gun sliding across the floor.

Pritchard dropped to his knees, cursing and crying in pain, and Eli, Genevieve, Bess, and Enzo rushed into the room, followed by Blobra. Pritchard saw her and started screaming when she turned her eyes towards him as she slithered past. Bess hurried back to him and hit him over the head with her bag of coins to stop the noise, but the blow only knocked him over, and not out, and he kept screaming. She shushed him, as if that would work, and then Tasered him, and that did the trick. She gave him a shot of wasp spray too, just for good measure.

Simon saw their gelatinous companion, but he was so relieved to see help coming, that he only glanced at her.

Bess ran to the cage and cried out when she saw the blood dripping from his head and covering the side of his shirt.

"It's nothing, it's nothing. ELI! GET TO ELI! They're setting the dogs on him!! Hurry, out that back door!" Simon was pressed up against the bars, pointing and shouting directions. He knew he sounded hysterical, and maybe he was, a little, but it didn't matter what they thought, as long as they got to Eli in time. Bess put one hand on his shoulder and the other against his neck, saying, "Simon, Simon, it's okay!"

He stopped shouting, and with an expression fierce and desperate, looked down at her face. "Help is already on the way to Eli. And we will be too, as soon as we get Dulcie and you out of these cages." She kissed him and then ran to Dulcie's cage, where she reached through the bars and helped her to her feet.

"He's going to be okay, Dulcie. We're going to get you out of here."

She had to try twice to get to her feet, feeling as if all the strength had gone out of her. When she finally stood on shaking legs, the Elpie reached out and embraced Bess. Hanging onto her for support, she sought to calm and prepare herself to run. For once they had her cage opened, she would be on her way to Eli.

Enzo ran to Simon's cage and separated his ax from the Halligan. "Okay, Simon, stand back in case any metal flies around. This may take a minute with these bars. Hiram, is that one done?" Their assisting physician, just finishing duct taping one more mouth, grabbed his bag full of medical supplies and manacles, and shouted, "On my way!"

He set the claw of the Halligan against the bolt between the lock and the door frame, and then turned to Hiram. "Here, Hiram. Hold this just like that. Don't move. I'm gonna pound this end with the flat of my ax, and if we can bend that bolt at least a little, we can pry the door open with the bar."

Rearing back, Enzo threw all of his weight and muscle into the blow. He felt the jarring in his bones, and the cage shook, but the bolt held. Over and over he pounded, until his hands were almost numb, and his right arm hurt up into the shoulder, but nothing changed. He looked around frantically, and then saw the desk. Seeing his glance, Simon shook his head. "Arthur took the keys."

"There's gotta be a—BLOBRA! That's it! Blobra, come here, sweetheart, we need your very strongest acid here, capisci? Come here, come here. Can you wrap yourself around this metal between these bars, and put your acid to work on it?" He took hold of one of her pseudo appendages and stretched it out to slide between the bars and wrap around the bolt. "Yeah, exactly like that!"

Excited at getting to be in on the action, she quickly saw what he was trying to do, and concentrated her acid as much as possible. To Enzo's happy surprise, she also stretched out a piece of her gelatin to reach the other cage door, allowing her to work on both at the same time. As she strained, her color changed to dark green and then maroon. After just a few moments, smoke and a hissing sound started coming out from the metal beneath her appendages.

He let her work for a good two minutes, before patting her on whatever part of her body that was beside him. "Okay, Blobra, let go a minute and we'll see if we can finish it off. HA! BELLISSIMO!" He turned with the intention of planting a kiss on her, but knowing he'd vomit if his lips sank into that slimy surface, he smiled and nodded instead.

The acid had eaten a deep ridge around the bolt, and he knew they could break in now. He told Blobra to back away and Hiram set the Halligan again.

"Hold it right there, or this lizard won't have no brains!"

They'd all been turned towards Simon's cage, when another of Arthur's men had crept in the side door and put his gun to the back of Dulcie's head. Bess jumped when he spoke up right behind her.

"Now, I seen that you all got Tasers and whatnot, but were you to Tase me right now, my hand would very likely pull this trigger when I started shaking and all. You don't want to chance that, do you?"

He had a cocky smile on his face that faded abruptly when he felt something sharp pressing hard into the back of his neck, just at the base of his skull. "And you have an arrow about to be propelled by a fifty-five pound bow into your brain stem. That could cause you to shake a bit too, but I'm willing to risk it. Are you?"

Dulcie nodded her head vigorously, and everybody else in the room, except for the possible skewee, Norman, added, "Yeah, Sure, Go for it" and "Why not?" Norman threw his gun down and put his hands up. He could feel blood trickling down the back of his neck from where the point was digging in, and he was earnestly hoping that the guy on the other end of the arrow could keep the string pulled back long enough for him to get surrendered with his brain intact.

They'd set Jonas out in the bushes to watch for anyone that might come in while they were freeing the prisoners, and he'd followed Norman in without the man ever seeing him.

"You need to get on the floor, face down, with your knees bent up and your hands behind your back, and you need to do it real fast, because my arms are starting to tremble a little."

Norm moved forward slowly until he didn't feel the arrow digging into his neck anymore, and then threw himself on the floor so fast that he knocked himself out when his face hit the concrete. Eli stuck his foot on Norman's back while Jonas put down his bow, and then the two of them began binding him.

Bess stayed with Dulcie, while Hiram and Enzo had at the lock one more time. One, two, three hits, and they could see the bend in the metal. He threw down his ax, grabbed the Halligan out of Hiram's hands, and repositioned it as a pry bar. "Hiram, on three we pull. One, two, THREE!" The two men strained back, they heard metal snap and the door slid open.

Genevieve was standing near the back, watching the side door where Norman had slipped in. She had her Taser out and ready, aimed towards the door. Eli was just standing up from helping to bind their newest captive, when he saw a man step out from behind the bales of hay, straight behind Genevieve. The man had seen the Kevlar, so he had the shotgun aimed at the back of her head.

If Eli screamed a warning to her, and she took even a second to register what she should do, she would die. If he tried to Taser the man and missed, she would die. All this went through his head in an instant, and then he did the only thing he could think of to protect her.

With one huge running stride, he leapt between his sister and the shotgun, pulling the trigger on his Taser as the trigger on the shotgun was pulled. The man dropped in a quivering heap, and Genevieve was pushed forward to her knees by the weight of Eli's body falling against her. Bess and Simon screamed, "ELI!" in unison when they saw their son go down. Whirling her head around, Genevieve saw her brother lying on his back, right arm a pulpy mess at the shoulder, and blood coming from multiple small tears on the right side of his neck and jaw. His eyes were partially opened, but he was unconscious. She shouted his name, reaching out for his face and shattered arm.

Hiram grabbed his bag and ran over, going to his knees and gently but firmly moving Genevieve's hands away so that he could examine Eli's wounds. He could see him breathing, and when he felt under the Kevlar, he found no puncture. It felt like his clavicle might be cracked, with the swelling that was beginning there. His upper arm at the shoulder had taken the brunt of the damage. There were bone fragments in the macerated tissue, but at least the brachial artery wasn't shredded. The wounds on his neck and jaw were all superficial, so he ignored them while he set to work.

Simon and Bess had both thrown themselves to their knees and were holding Eli's head on each side. Simon was quietly saying, "No, no, no, Eli, no," as if calmly directing him not to die, and Bess was shaking and gritting her teeth to keep from sobbing. Behind them, Jonas stood with his mouth open, feeling he should say something to change all this—to stop his brother from bleeding and lying on the ground like that. Enzo grabbed his arm, and said "Jonas, I need you. There's nothing you can do there, and we still need to get Dulcie out. JONAS!"

When he half shouted his name and shook his arm, Jonas swung around and realized what Enzo was saying. He gave a jerky nod, and went to help him.

Eli was starting to moan and come to, moving his head back and forth with a grimace of pain on his face, and reaching up with his left hand for his right shoulder. Genevieve grabbed his hand, and finally Bess let her tears come, at the sight of her son moving. *He was moving.*

Hiram grabbed a pad out of his bag to put pressure on the wound, and then directed Simon to get out the rest of the dressings and the IV. As he worked, he began talking to his patient. "Eli! Eli! Come on, man! Eli, can you hear me?"

Slowly opening his eyes, he looked up into his mother's face. "Mom, you're dripping on me. Gross."

They all laughed in relief at the sound of his voice, and the knowledge that he was still sound enough to embarrass his mother.

"Gen, Genny! Where—" He tried sitting up, frantically looking around, but Simon and Hiram held him down as Bess moved aside so he could see his sister, who'd been holding his hand.

He let himself fall back then, yelping a little at the pain this jolting cost him.

Genevieve rubbed his hand and smiled, leaning over so it would be easier for him to see her. "I'm fine, Eli. You took a shotgun blast for me. Just my luck. Now I'll *never* get out of debt to you. First you save Enzo, and then me. Will you take a check?"

Trying to keep his eyes focused on her face, he gave her a weak smile and a barely discernible squeeze of her hand.

"Really good to see you, Bean Butt."

A new man appeared in the side door with a rifle trained on the cluster of people around Eli. Jonas saw him before anyone else. How many more were coming? How many in the house, on the grounds, how many? He felt like he was in some twisted arcade game, where the gophers kept popping up out of the holes, to be bopped back down by a fake sledgehammer. Except these gophers had guns.

When he saw where the rifle was pointed, Jonas knew at least one person on the floor around Eli was dead if he didn't do something, so he made a grab for his Taser as he dropped the Halligan. The man saw the movement, and he swung the gun up to fire at him, but before he could, the pipe kept in the room for tormenting the animals was slammed down on his head from behind. The rifle dropped from his hands without discharging as the man crumpled to the floor. Milton stepped into the room and held the upraised pipe over the fallen man's head, screaming, "ENOUGH!"

Jonas ran over and began handcuffing the unconscious man, glancing up now and then at Milton while he worked. Milt was red and shaking, with a look between disbelief and fury on his face. He'd been trying to work himself up to this—to hit somebody on the head with a piece of metal—but seeing the man about to murder someone else had catapulted him into action.

As soon as this newest threat was sufficiently bound, Jonas stood up and held out his hand. "I don't know who you are, but you've got great timing. Thanks."

Milton hesitated for a second, and then shook Jonas' hand. It occurred to him that this was probably the first time in the past three years that he'd shaken hands with someone who wasn't a felon. It felt good.

A bloodcurdling scream from just inside the house entrance caused them all to swerve and look in that direction. The screaming continued until the cry was choked off.

The sending made Jonas smile. Barnabas was broadcasting that he had his jaws around a man's throat in the hallway. He'd already disarmed him, and now he wanted to know what to do with him. He was fine with it if they wanted him to kill him. After the thoughts he'd found as he probed the man's mind, killing him would not disturb him in the least. But Jonas sent for him to bring him into the main room to be bound.

After Jonas' sending, yes, Barnabas was a little disappointed, but being a team player, he let go of the man's throat very slowly, then whipped his head over to stare down into his face. He opened wide his mouth full of very sharp teeth, and hissed. The man shuddered, which reminded Barnabas that he had a Taser he hadn't used yet.

He stood up, tilted his quill-like mane forward after the hiss, just for emphasis, and Tasered the man. He watched the twitching and jerking with interest and more than a little satisfaction, and then grabbed the incapacitated human by one arm and dragged him down the hall and into the animal room. He dumped him behind Jonas, who was still working with Enzo. Once freed of his burden, he sent to Enzo that he was going to find the first Eli, and ran out the back door.

"Uh, Milton, could you do us a favor and get a pair of plastic cuffs out of my back pocket and take care of this guy? There's rope lying on the floor over there, if you could tie him up like the others. Oh yeah, and tape for his mouth is over there by the doctor's bag. We really need to get this lady out."

Milton stared at the departing Barnabas, and then looked at the "lady" that was waiting to be released. She was definitely reptilian, but when she looked into his eyes and nodded her thanks, he understood the title Jonas had given her.

Hiram finished bandaging, and then he traded sides with Genevieve to start an IV on Eli's other arm. He looked up at Simon's stricken face. "He'll be okay. He had the wind knocked out of him when the shot hit his upper chest, and I think his clavicle may be broken. If he weren't eight inches taller than Genny, the blast would have hit him in the face. Thank God for tall genes, eh?"

He looked at Bess, then, with her face set in a mask of grief mixed with fierce determination. He gauged her to be the one best able to handle the rest. "His arm's messed up pretty bad, but he's stable enough that I think you'd be better off waiting for the Bluemen, since we know they'll be here soon. If we take him to a hospital I'm not sure how *aggressively* they might treat this injury, with the bone shattered like it is." He looked at Bess with raised eyebrows, signaling her that "aggressively" had a more ominous meaning than he wanted Eli to know. "The Bluemen can restore his arm completely, and I can watch him for signs of shock in the meantime. Simon—go help the first Eli."

Wiping the tears off his face, he leaned over and kissed Eli on the forehead. "I love you so much, son. Thank you for saving your sister."

Eli gave his father a tight-lipped smile and answered, barely above a whisper, "Go get 'em, Dad."

Simon pushed himself off his knees and began running for the hall. Jonas yelled after him, "Dad, as soon as we get Dulcie out, we'll be there, too!"

Simon raised a hand in acknowledgement, and ran towards the opening to the hall. Just as he reached it, the second man with a shotgun rounded the corner from the hallway. Simon skidded to a stop as the man pointed the gun at his face from a scant twelve inches away. Too close. He saw the man's finger starting to move against the trigger and knew there was no escape. He heard Jonas' scream of "DAD!" as he saw what was happening.

He closed his eyes, and thought, *Three's the charm.*

They say you never hear the shot that kills you, but he did. He heard the deafening roar of the blast, and he dropped to his knees. All sound ceased as he left this world behind. There was no pain, as he'd feared there would be. A direct shot to the brain, he supposed, too fast for his mind to register before it died.

Then he felt a tender touch on his arm, and a gentle voice sounding as if from far away, saying, "Stand up, Simon."

He opened his eyes, hoping to see the face of Jesus, but seeing his mother-in-law instead. When his mouth opened in surprise, his ears popped, and he could hear again. Sarah was talking to him slowly, patiently. "It's all right, Simon, you're okay. Angus took care of it."

Directly in front of him, he saw his father-in-law brandishing the biggest cast iron frying pan in the world over the face of a terrified man with a broken nose and a baseball sized bump on his forehead. With his skillet cocked, Angus leaned forward until his face was directly over his felled victim's, prompting the man to cover his face with his hands and moan. Angus' voice was low and angry, and he spoke slowly, with calculated menace. "She bakes, *but I FRY.*"

Sarah helped Simon get to his feet, and he stood shakily. "Sorry. I, uh, I thought I was dead."

"I know, dear, we all did. But Angus has always had fast hands."

His in-laws had been running in the door at the end of the hall just after the man rounded the corner with his gun raised. He'd had no clue of them before Angus swung his skillet upwards under the gun, causing it to blast a hole in the ceiling, and with a nice follow through, brought the giant fryer sweeping back down onto the gunman's forehead and nose. In his pain and shock, Angus' victim didn't understand the old man's words, but knew he would never eat fried food again.

Jonas and Enzo came charging over to Simon, with Dulcie close behind. Jonas threw his arms around his father, shaking his head. "Dad, will you ever quit scaring us?"

"Simon?" Bess' tortured sounding voice called out. She expected the worst, after hearing Jonas' cry, and the shotgun discharge.

"Hey, it's okay, Mom," Jonas yelled back. "Grandpa creamed the guy with his pan! Dad's fine!"

Leaning into his son's embrace, as much for support as affection, he took a deep breath to make the shaking stop, and put his hand on Angus' back. His father-in-law was having too much fun making his prey cringe to turn around, so Simon bent over and said, "Thanks, Angus. I'm so happy that pan's on our side."

#

When Sarah and Angus finished tying up the shotgun wielder, they dragged him into the middle of the room and laid him beside all the other men that were tied. Sarah was just beginning to think about how pitiful they seemed, all bound up and gagged, looking scared to death, and then she saw Eli lying on the ground.

She screamed and ran over to where he was lying, and grabbed Bess around the shoulders. She looked up into her mother's horrified face, then smiled and nodded her head.

"Eli, darling, it's Grandma. Oh, honey, I'm so sorry you're hurt. But you're going to be just fine." She bent down to lay her hand on his face, and when she did, he looked into her eyes and gave her a wink.

Standing up now, she gripped her weapon tightly. She'd brought the mini-version of Angus' monster skillet.

Hers was only six inches in diameter, but it was still cast iron. She'd never been this angry in her life.

They'd shot her grandson, the sweetest young man in the world. They'd tried to kill her son-in-law, and it was just by the grace of God that Angus had walked in at the right time to prevent it. They were trying to kill a friend. They'd tried to kill her daughter and granddaughter and her fiancé. Damn them! She stormed through the room looking for someone to fight, but the only bad guys she found were already tied up.

So she went down the row of them, popping each one on the head with her frying pan, as she fumed and scolded. "You bastards think you can go around shooting anybody you want?" Bonk. "Think you can shoot my grandson?" Bonk. "His father?" Bonk. "Our friends?" Bonk. "We should just shoot the lot of you!" Bonk. Bonk. "You worthless bunch of hooligans!" Bonk. Bonk. Bonk.

As a neurologist, Hiram viewed concussions as his enemies, although in truth, they did bring him a lot of business. But he was philosophically opposed to *inflicting* them unless absolutely necessary. When he looked up from working with Eli, his attention drawn by the noise of Sarah's tirade, he watched in horror as she knocked two of the bound men out cold.

"SARAH, STOP! What are you doing?" He screamed.

"What does it *look* like I'm doing, Hiram? I'm meting out justice with my little skillet. And these animals are just lucky I can't lift the big one."

She'd already walloped the last one, so he said no more. He was going to appeal to Bess to keep an eye on her to be sure she wasn't going to hit them again, but when he looked at Bess' face as she gazed down at her wounded son, he thought better of it. She might be able to wield the big one.

CHAPTER FORTY-SEVEN

He ran until he heard the dogs moving, and then he climbed up as far as he could into a tree, trying to hide in the branches. Remembering what Simon had told him, he began to blow on the whistle. Little short puffs and long hard blows. He switched patterns on and off, all the while wondering if it was doing him any good. He could have run farther, for he had an easy lope with plenty of stamina, but Elpies were not fast runners. He knew that within a short time they would have caught up with him, and he remembered Simon's other words. If he couldn't dodge a bullet in the tree, perhaps a bullet would be the kinder death, after all.

#

The dogs were acting crazy. When they took the scent, half of them acted confused, as if they couldn't catch the lizard's smell, and the other half kept looking at him for direction. They'd jerk their heads up suddenly and look out into the green as if they were listening to something, and then swing around towards him again. What in bloody hell was wrong with them?

This was Worthington's big moment, and if Darby's dogs screwed up, he was not *in* the doghouse, but most likely *under it.* Six feet under it. Mr. High and Mighty was sitting in his ridiculous little golf cart, waiting to follow the dogs, and he couldn't get them all moving in the same direction. They'd run a ways, and then start circling around, sniffing at the ground and doing that little jerky thing with their heads again.

He looked up when the cart almost ran him down, and Worthington leaned out to scream in his face. "What is WRONG with these blasted animals! We've only gone half the length of the field, and they'd usually be there and back twice by now. Should I just shoot all of them *and you* and start over with a different group of dogs and idiots?"

"No sir, no sir, they've just got the scent of something else, but they'll come round, sir! Just give me a few minutes! That lizard can't go nowheres with the fence on. No chance of losing him, sir."

"I *know* that, but I'm getting bored with this having to stop every ten yards while your mongrels figure out what they're supposed to be doing! *Get on with it!*" He took off then, zipping ahead in his machine, and Darby started laying about with his crop, trying to get the dogs to move. Finally, one of them seemed to catch the scent again and started baying, and the others followed his lead.

#

Ishmael had been watching, and knew how far Eli had gotten. Not nearly far enough. His ammonia loaded urine had put a slight hitch in the dogs' sense of smell, but he doubted it would last for long. He hoped he only needed to stall a little longer to give the family time to get in here. But could *they* handle a dozen dogs bred to rend and destroy? He watched from the base of a tree as the dogs came charging down towards him, and when the pack was close enough for him to see the drool on their jowls, he let out an eerie yowl and sped across the green, directly in front of the pack, and into the trees on the other side.

They saw him and smelled him, and nothing on Earth could have stopped them from going after him at that point. He zipped up the closest tree with yards to spare as the lead dogs lunged up against the trunk, snapping their jaws.

Taunting other animals had always been a pleasure for him, and he truly had a gift for it. If he weren't a cat, he might consider it a character flaw, but since he was, he let himself glory in his skills. He looked down at the slavering, brutish faces, and pondered their inadequacies, until he saw the man with the light rushing over.

They might be able to shoot a six foot Elpie out of a tree, but he was a black cat at night, and he'd give them more of a challenge. He climbed up until he found braches that overlapped into other trees, and began going from tree to tree. It drove the dogs crazy. They were so wild at this point, that some of them were snapping at each other. Ishmael could hear the two dog whistles blowing constantly, which was annoying him, so he could only imagine what it must be doing to the dog brains below, when they were listening to two whistles for directions.

He started going back towards the house as he went from one tree to the next. If he had the dogs going the wrong way entirely, that would give Eli even more time. Where was everybody else?

The guy with the light was having a real problem. Worthington wanted a large, powerful beam, and that meant a light big enough that it had to be held with both hands. He'd sent the man back to find out what was going on when he'd looked back and seen that the dogs had something treed.

Shining the light up into a tree from a distance, at an animal that was treed and frozen with fear was easy. But with Ishmael going in deeper away from the green and moving constantly, the man had to be looking up and walking around trees at the same time that he was trying to navigate through a pack of frenzied dogs without being knocked down or mauled. He'd avoided the mauling thus far, but was working on his fourth knock down.

Finally, the trainer waded in with his crop and whistle, kicking and shoving the dogs until he got them all back on the green. They started moving at a good pace then, and Ishmael knew they'd find Eli soon. He was too exhausted to try anything else, even if he'd had something else to try.

Hang on, Eli.

##

Hovering over the Sayers' Estate, Sven called Colder and Micah to the controls. He pointed to the panel in front of him, specifically to a group of moving dots that had absolutely no meaning to Colder and Micah, and sent, "Look at all this!"

They looked at "this," then looked at each other, and finally, they looked at Sven.

"What is it?"

He sighed in exasperation, having to remind himself that they had no training and so couldn't be expected to know the *simplest, most elementary* readings on the controls. "Look at all this activity," he sent. "There are lots of people moving around on your land. We can't land there. Does your father have a cell phone?"

"Sure."

"Tell me the number. We're close enough that I should be able to go through it."

##

All these years of running, feeling driven to run. Feeling guilty if he missed even a day. And all the strength training—lifting weights, pull-ups, push-ups. Crazy exercise routines for a man his age. Maybe it was all about this day. To get him ready for this day. Simon looked down the long green slope and could just make out the golf cart in the distance.

He set off running, with Enzo and Jonas close behind at the beginning, and Dulcie behind them. In the very rear came Blobra, undulating eerily down the slope, leaving a trail of burned grass in her wake—a grounds keeper's nightmare. Unable to match Simon's speed, the others began to fall behind. The further they ran, the farther behind they fell.

He was telling himself that the dogs hadn't gotten to Eli yet, and he was running to the rhythm of, *Eli is alive, my brother's alive.* A strange vibration on his hip, and suddenly Beethoven's Ninth was signaling a phone call. NOW? Cell phones—they were part of a civilized world that had played no part in their lives tonight.

At the gate, they'd only searched him for weapons and wires—a sloppy job leaving his phone, when some phones could record. But Arthur's staff had far more experience in being searched than in searching. When they'd darted him, they hadn't bothered to look for a phone, knowing that he'd already been searched. He'd forgotten he even had one on him. The whole notion of phones and conversations seemed foreign and useless now.

He kept running, intending to ignore it, and then he realized it could be Bess, telling him that Eli was—their son was— "Hello? Oh, Colder, thank God! Your brother Eli's been hurt. Tell Sven to use the tracking device that they put in your mom when she was young. Have them go to her—she's with your brother. When they get him to Luca, then we need everyone else's help down here. Your sister can lead you to us. Hurry!"

He hung up abruptly and started running again.

#

Hiram was checking the IV when he heard Bess ask Eli, "Honey, why are you shaking?"

He looked down at Eli, and his color had changed in just the past thirty seconds. He'd been pale, of course, but now his lips had lost their color completely, and he'd started sweating. He looked at his pupils and they were dilated—still reacting to light, but very slowly. Blood was starting to soak through the heavy dressing on his shoulder.

"I'm cold. So cold." His teeth had begun to chatter. "Mom?" He looked around in confusion, shaking his head. "What's happening? What is this place?"

Bess stroked his good arm, and leaned over him to be sure he could see her. "Eli, remember, we came to Arthur's to help your dad get the first Eli back. You got hurt, and we're waiting for the Bluemen to come and fix you up. You'll be fine, honey, but you need to relax and lie still."

He nodded to her, but Bess could see he was still confused and close to panic—a complete turnaround from five minutes earlier. His eyes had a glassy look, as if they really weren't seeing his surroundings.

Hiram checked his pulse and looked at Bess, who was staring at him, waiting for an answer. He motioned with his head for her to step aside with him. "Eli, I'll be right back, but Genevieve is here with you. I'll be just a minute." She kissed his forehead, brushed the hair back from his face, and then got up and rushed over to Hiram, who'd moved a few yards away to talk to her.

"Bess, we need to go ahead and call for a chopper to get him to a hospital. He's going into shock and what I can do for him here, I've already done. He hasn't had that big a blood loss *yet*, and I've given him something for the pain, but all his symptoms tell me that we can't wait any longer. I opened the IV up, and I'll get another bag ready—I have a few drugs I can try, but they're all just temporary fixes. I'm a pediatric neurologist, not a trauma surgeon. I'm making the call right now. Nothing would be worth losing him. Nothing."

Bess nodded her assent, and heard Genevieve stifle a sob behind her, as she held tighter to her brother's increasingly cold hand. Hiram had just begun dialing when Bess gasped and grabbed his arm. "Do you feel that?"

He did. A pressure in his ears and all around them. "The Bluemen are here!"

She ran over to tell Eli, but his eyes were closed, and she couldn't make him respond. Dropping to her knees, she stroked his face and called to him, trying to keep her voice from shaking, "ELI! ELI! Come on, Eli, they're here for you! You'll be fine now! Eli, you come back right this minute, do you hear me?"

There was a pounding of feet and Sven rushed through the side door with Maurice, Mona, Colder, and the Elpies right behind. He ran to Bess, and when he saw Eli, he slapped a transport disk onto his chest. When he disappeared, an unintentional shriek sounded from Bess and then she looked at Sven and said, "Please." He nodded and put the disk on her chest as well, sending her to be with her son.

Colder had just caught a quick glimpse of Eli lying motionless on the floor before Sven sent him to the ship. He stood unmoving, in shock at the idea that Eli could—Genevieve called his name loudly and said, "Come on!" and he shook it off to follow her.

Milton dropped his rifle when the Bluepeople and Elpies ran through the door. He didn't scream, because he remembered what Simon had told Worthington. It was true. It was all true.

He watched as they ran out the back door, and then he bent down to pick the rifle back up. He nearly shot himself when he dropped it again as a nerve shattering shriek came from behind him, followed by an insane babbling sound. When he turned to see this new surprise, some grey furry thing that looked like a long-eared rat-deer, came barreling through the room and out the back door after the other aliens.

He *really* didn't belong here.

CHAPTER FORTY-EIGHT

Colders were bigger and had more muscle mass than the village Elpies, but they were still Elpies and hence, slow runners. Without the dogs' confusion, he'd never have caught them, but because of an extra whistle blowing constantly, the cat pee in their mouths and noses, and the offending cat running across their paths and leading them into the trees, their venture into the killing zone had been start and stop. Giving up on the dogs, Worthington had picked his light man back up and gone on ahead in his golf cart.

Barnabas saw Blobra bouncing and slithering towards the group of maddened animals, and was surprised that she seemed to have no fear of the pack. He decided to let her do as she wished, and he'd take care of the trainer. The man was carrying a stick with leather on the end, and using it as a whip to try to keep the dogs on scent, but now they were picking up Blobra's scent in the air.

When the first dog caught her smell, he stiffened his legs and stopped, causing the two dogs behind him to crash into him, bowling him over. Then *they* caught the scent and started milling around in a circle.

The trainer's affection and loyalty for the dogs was not towards them as living creatures with feelings and intrinsic value, but as the culmination of his efforts at breeding. He'd started thinking it would be better for him to shoot them now and profess their worthlessness to the boss on his own. Then he could possibly get permission to try some different breeds. If he stayed loyal to this lot, Worthington was likely to have him shot at the same time his dogs were.

He didn't see what the dogs saw coming their way. He had just raised his rifle to shoot the animal closest to him, when a long, thin, green thing snaked out from behind him and wrapped around the rifle, tearing it out of his hands.

He yelped in surprise and spun around to see his rifle tossed away by a tail belonging to a six foot, four inch lizard with porcupine quills on his head that were all pointing *at him.*

He screamed and started to run, but clawed fingers wrapped around his neck and threw him to the ground. He kept screaming at the thing that came and straddled him, sitting on his chest and staring down at him. Darby looked up at those black eyes studying him and suddenly felt like an entrée.

The problem with capturing these creatures was that then he had to do something with them. Barnabas knew the Sayers didn't want him killing, but how could he keep this one from joining the other evil ones if he had nothing to tie him with? Maybe Simon wouldn't mind just this one. But no, there would probably be bad feelings about it. Looking around, trying to think of something to restrain him with, Barnabas stopped to watch the dogs attacking Blobra, settling onto his human chair for the show.

At first, the dogs whined and backed away as the jellied mass approached them, but finally one took courage and jumped at it. He jumped *at* it, but ended up *inside* of it. Two more dogs joined him, and Barnabas looked on in amazement as the dogs appeared to be swimming inside of the ooze. He thought that surely they would be drowned, but Blobra changed her shape from a rolling mass to an upright one, and popped the dogs out. They stood coughing and sneezing, and trying to wipe their tongues off on the ground. Then Blobra made a little bubbling noise, and when the dogs looked back at her, the first one yelped and began running full blast back to the kennels, with the other two fast on his heels.

As she searched the area with her eyes for any new challenges, she spied Barnabas. Extending a globule of herself in a semblance of a hand, she gave him a wave. He waved back, and then remembered the problem he was sitting on.

Looking down, he saw that his problem had temporarily taken care of itself, for with him sitting on the man's chest, his captive had been unable to breathe and had passed out. Barnabas shoved him around a little to make sure he was still alive, and then tried sending a picture to Blobra of the man being tied.

Being an all-purpose ooze, Blobra left the remaining dogs whining pitifully and pacing back and forth, unsure of what to do. They were still hearing a whistle, only one now, but in a pattern they'd never heard and didn't understand.

When Blobra got to Barnabas, she sent out a thin layer of slime for him to roll the unconscious man into, a human fajita in a slime tortilla, leaving only his head free for breathing purposes. Three turns and the man looked like a booger with a head.

Satisfied with their efforts, Barnabas sent thanks to his mucilaginous friend and started running again towards the end of the green, with Blobra sliming along after.

The dogs were having a very bad day, but the whistle finally convinced those remaining to keep going. Their trainer was on the ground over there, and he wasn't whistling, nor did he smell like himself. There was no love lost between the dogs and Darby, for he'd always treated them as what they were to him: property and a means to a job. If he'd fallen in front of them, they might have considered eating him, but now their only concern was to have direction. They'd lived their whole lives in cages, let out only when they were being trained to run, track, and kill, first with small animals as their prey and then on to larger and larger. They knew nothing else, so they continued the hunt.

##

The Macaroon Maker had expected him to rush out and hunt down her enemies. He understood this, but that was not his way. She and her mate had taken him to the field and tried to persuade him to give chase, which he could have done, but he needed to know the beasts he would call to. It would be much easier this way, much cleaner.

They had finally given up on forcing him onto the green, and the Maker of Macaroons and her mate had rushed inside to tell the others. He'd moved on to the kennels, following the scent. He'd smelled each kennel, from every direction possible, and he knew the beasts now. They were those he could lead, and they would be his. He knew this. He could begin now.

##

Be safe, Father, be safe. Micah was running down the green, hearing the horrible barking and baying, and understanding now that these creatures were hunting his father. Luigi was just behind him, Colder a ways in front, and the Bluepeople, with their long legs, were far ahead. Then a familiar screeching sounded over his shoulder, followed by a crazy babbling, and Blanche passed him as if he were standing still. His eyes followed her, and soon she passed the Bluepeople, too. He admired her bravery, but what could she do against a pack of ravenous beasts?

Loping behind Micah, Luigi's eyes were drawn by movement up ahead, and he saw one of the huge beasts running directly for him. Even if he'd been graceful enough to change course on the spot, there would have been no chance of outrunning the creature. He thought about his father, and then stopped running, steeling himself, and telling himself that *he was fiercer* than the terrifying creature about to kill him. He tried to project that thought, to use it as a weapon, as his father did. At the last minute, when he was sure he was about to be torn to pieces, the dog veered away and kept running towards the kennels.

He'd done it! He'd really done it! Then he saw two more dogs running in his direction, and they ran around him and kept going. So—maybe he hadn't done it. He started running again, rethinking his fierceness defense.

#

Enzo and Jonas were running as fast as they could, but Simon was far ahead of them now. They'd passed the dogs, on one of their many stops, and Jonas hoped they were as confused as they'd looked, and might head back. He could shoot an evil person much easier than he could put an arrow into an animal that was an innocent victim of its training. But if he had to do it to save Eli, he would.

When they heard the newly focused dogs coming behind them, they veered to the side, but not soon enough to hide themselves. The dogs had seen them running, and were so crazed and confused by this point, that anything fleeing in front of them was a welcome target. He knew they couldn't outrun the animals, and he didn't know how many he could take down with his arrows before they caught up with him, but he might be able to save Enzo. He whirled around and stopped to nock an arrow, as he screamed, "ENZO, GET TO THE TREES!"

"No way, Bro," he heard, spoken calmly at his shoulder. Enzo dropped his irons, separated them, and looked at each, deciding which to make a stand with. He chose the Halligan. Holding it up like a baseball bat, he stood beside Jonas and waited, saying a silent prayer. They both still had their Tasers, but there were too many dogs, and they needed to have weapons in their hands that they could use quickly and more than once. And with the dogs moving as fast as they were, the chance of missing was too great to risk.

The dogs had come over a rise and were only twenty yards away and closing fast, when suddenly they all jerked to a stop, looking in all directions, as if they heard something the humans could not.

Jonas and Enzo flinched as an ear-splitting screeching noise followed by a wild babbling sound cut through the air, and a grey streak shot across the path of the dogs and headed back the other way. As soon as they saw Blanche, all thoughts of any other prey were gone from the minds of the pack. This creature, they recognized instinctively as prey, and with the joy of surety in their minds, *for once* tonight, they turned around and followed her, baying furiously.

Blanche was frightened out of her mind, but she had to help the father. Help her friend's father. She'd thought for sure that she would be faster than these animals, but they were gaining on her. She put on a burst of speed, turned sharply to her left, heading for the trees, and just before reaching them, pulled her hooves into her belly and whipped out her hands. Zipping up the tree like a monkey, she climbed just past the point where the dogs could reach her with their frantic jumping. She had to keep their attention long enough for Micah to save his father.

From the top of the hill, where the animal room opened onto the green, came a sound that was heard all the way to the end of the corridor. A huge sound, between a roar and a howl. And along with the sound, the breeze brought a suffocating, stomach-turning, overwhelming odor.

Jonas and Enzo turned to each other and cheered, "STENCH!"

Every dog froze at the sound, and when the scent hit the pack, they went wild, sniffing the air and the ground, and then howling back. They were answering him. At last! On this, the most confusing day of their lives, they had a leader! The Alpha! They were his pack! As one, the dogs began to run back to the animal room, ignoring every human, Elpie, and Blueperson along the way. They were following their leader. At last.

#

As Simon crested a hillock, he finally saw Arthur up ahead, getting out of his cart and looking up into the trees.

Arthur had told the light man to ride with him, so that if he didn't have the idiot dogs, at least he'd still be able to see and shoot the lizard. He didn't want a head shot, preferring to make it slower.

The man had been shining the light into the trees ahead of them as they moved, and had spotted the thing about fifty feet up in a tree. He was trying to hide behind the trunk by shifting from limb to limb, but Worthington had seen this ploy before. He had four double barrel eighty-four caliber muzzleloaders in the cart, in a specially built carrier, fully loaded so that he didn't have to bother between shots. These monsters, most often referred to as "elephant guns," shot a sixteen-hundred gain bullet, and could take down a small tree or a very large branch.

He had to get back at an angle to shoot upwards, and he had a large cushioned pad on his shoulder for the massive kickback when he fired. He carried a smaller rifle, too, but this was his favorite to knock branches down. He'd toy with the lizard with the smaller gun once he had the thing on the ground.

The creature was standing with his feet on two separate but parallel branches, not by the trunk, but trying to blend in with the greenery further out on the limbs. He would have been successful if not for the light. Arthur gave a small laugh when he saw that. This would indeed be a challenge. He lined up his sights and pulled the trigger, lurching back with the blow to his shoulder from the force of the gun.

Arthur and his light man saw the first branch splinter in two and fall, and the lizard man went down after it, grasping at the air and small branches around him. Unable to get a handhold, he bounced against one limb and then another, back and forth, all the way down, until he finally hit the ground and lay still, battered and bloody.

"NOOO!" could be heard from a distance, and Arthur shook his head in disgust when he recognized the voice. Sayers. Not again. Ah well, it might be more fun with him present. Let him watch his pet die slowly, and then give the same treatment to him. He switched to a regular rifle, because if he used the elephant gun, the party would be over too soon.

Simon was only fifteen feet away when he put the rifle to the lizard's chest and shouted, "No further, Sayers!"

Trying to pull up, Simon stumbled and ended up on his hands and knees. Gasping for air, he held one hand out towards Arthur. "Please, Arthur, don't. Just don't." He stopped begging then, and slowly got to his feet, knowing that it was no use. He stood there, watching numbly as his friend, his brother, lay there, helpless to defend himself against this human beast.

"I thought I might shoot off one limb at a time, for a little sport, but you know, it's been a long, trying evening and I'm getting tired, so I think I'll just blow his head off, and follow it up with yours."

He had no time to react to that before Arthur dropped the rifle and began screaming, with an arrow sticking out of both sides of his wrist. Simon raced towards the rifle, but before he could get to it, the light man reached in the cart to grab one of the elephant guns. He never quite made it, being bowled over by a five foot, five inch bundle of muscle and Adrenalin. When Enzo tackled him, the gun flew up in the air and discharged when it hit the ground, narrowly missing Arthur, who was striding back and forth, holding his arm, screaming and cursing.

Once he had his man down, Enzo did a chokehold and put him out. He still had two pair of handcuffs left in his back pocket, so he grabbed one, dragged the man off the green, and cuffed him with his arms around a tree.

Simon was leaning over Eli, looking for wounds and talking frantically to him while he searched. He could see him breathing, but Eli had so many bloodied areas on him from the fall, that he couldn't tell if he'd been shot. "Eli, wake up, brother. Dulcie's okay, she's on her way here. Don't disappoint her. Micah's here, too. Come on—"

A leathery green hand covered his mouth, as Eli sent that humans talked too much. Simon started laughing, and there were tears with the laughter as he helped Eli up and then embraced him, sobbing. A little unsteady on his feet, and bruised and scraped everywhere, the Elpie could still appreciate his brother's relief, and he patted Simon's back like a parent comforting a child.

Simon let go then and turned towards Arthur, who was still wailing and holding his arm. He walked up to the screaming man and began pounding on him, punching his face and stomach, hitting the sides of his head, kneeing him, and when he had him on the ground he kept beating him, not even aware that he was screaming, "NEVER AGAIN! NEVER AGAIN! NOT MY FAMILY, NOT MY FRIENDS, NOBODY, NEVER AGAIN!"

When Arthur stopped trying to fight back, Simon put his hands around his throat and started squeezing. He would end this evil now and forever. Then he felt a thin, strong hand on his shoulder, and the calm sending of Eli, telling him to stop, to let go and stand up.

He was so beyond himself, and wild, that it took a moment for him to understand Eli's sending. He saw his hands around Arthur's throat, and didn't recognize them as his own—bruised, bloody and swollen, and he could hardly tell it was Arthur's face, because of the same condition. He let go abruptly, and jerked his hands off, not wanting to even touch the monster before him anymore.

Eli helped him to his feet, and then to everyone's surprise, since almost everyone had arrived by now, Eli gently pulled Arthur to his feet and steadied him, even though the man was in a stupor. When he seemed able to balance by himself for a moment, Eli backed away, then wound up like a shot putter and slammed his tail into Arthur's chest, sending him flying several yards.

Micah rushed to his father, throwing his arms around him and sending him that he was coming home to stay, because he still had family to love and cherish there.

Walking up to his own father, Luigi simply leaned against him. Barnabas leaned back, threw an arm around him, and sent that it was good to see him again, even if he did look stupid in that suit.

When Micah let go of his father, Eli swayed and the ground seemed to leap up in front of him. Before Micah could grab hold of him, a blue hand caught him across the chest and eased him into a sitting position on the ground. Mona sent that she wanted to send him to the ship for treatment. He nodded and held his arms straight out to the sides, welcoming the idea, so she put the disk on his chest and he disappeared. Then she put the disk on Dulcie as well, so that she could be with him.

Maurice and Dulcie had been the last ones to arrive. He'd seen her struggling to run, still woozy from the tranquilizer and in shock from fear for her husband, so he'd picked her up and carried her the rest of the way. He managed the extra weight easily, but it had delayed his arrival slightly.

Simon had been watching Eli, when Jonas and Enzo walked up on either side of him. Jonas put an arm around his dad's shoulder, and not to be outdone, Enzo put one around his waist, which cracked him up.

To laugh again. How heavenly. He shook his head as he looked at his son. "Jonas, what an amazing shot!"

"Thanks. But I keep thinking I should have gone for his heart."

Simon nodded and then shrugged. Then he looked down at Enzo. "And the way you got those cages open—Dulcie and I would probably still be in there, if not for you. Keeping me from getting shot just now sort of made my day, too. Bless you both for ignoring my orders and coming to the rescue."

Putting an arm around Enzo's neck, he gave it a squeeze. "You know, it's kind of nice having an extra son around."

Another hand closed around his shoulder, and he turned to see Colder standing there, out of breath. The other two let go so that he could turn and embrace his youngest. "Dad, your head! Are you okay? Geez, didn't you just get that fixed?"

They both gave a short laugh, but when Colder had seen the blood after hearing the awful blast from the elephant gun, he'd almost lost it for a second. Then common sense had kicked in and he realized that if his dad was still walking around, he was okay. All he knew now was how good it felt to wrap his arms around him and have his dad hug back way too hard.

"Where's Genevieve?"

"She figured we had enough help now, so she went running to the ship to be with Eli."

"Let's go see about both our Eli's. We just need to tie Arthur up first."

He turned back to find that Arthur was nowhere to be seen. Looking around in a panic, all he saw was Blobra, glopping and oozing her way back up the hill. She was a darker color than usual, and she seemed larger, heavier. Sven looked at her, and when she felt his gaze, she turned back and met it. They locked eyes for a moment, and then he turned away from her to Simon, who'd started running through the trees, screaming Arthur's name, half-crazed with dread as he searched frantically for his fallen nemesis.

Lunging out to catch him as he ran past, Sven put one hand around Simon's arm, and another on his shoulder, to capture and calm him. He was nearly out of his mind with the thought that after all they'd been through, Arthur had escaped, and might still be a threat to his family.

"Simon! Simon, stop!" When he looked into the Blueman's face, Sven sent, "He's finished. Very soon, he will no longer be on the face of this planet. You're done with him. Forever."

And then, in a move that surprised even himself, he put out his three long arms and reeled Simon in to lean against his chest. To let him rest against a friend.

CHAPTER FORTY-NINE

When the first Eli and Dulcie arrived, one after the other in the main room of the ship, Luca stuck his head out of the medical area. One look told him that Eli needed help. The injuries, the drugging, and the stress of nearly being killed had come crashing down on him, and he could barely stand. Luca came out, scooped him up, and carried him into another exam room.

Eli was sending that he could walk, but he didn't protest too hard. Luca's scan showed a concussion, two broken ribs, and he was bruised, bloodied, and battered everywhere. His body was a mass of scratches and gouges after scraping against hundreds of little twigs and branches as he'd tumbled out of the tree, ricocheting downward from limb to limb. Luca intended to keep him for several hours for repairs, so he slid out a built-in bed from a panel in the wall for Dulcie to rest on while she stayed with him. He took a second look at her and saw the stress level there, along with the residual effects of the drug, so he gave her a vial of liquid to clear her system, and another to make her sleep.

##

"Your son is stable now, and we have him deeply sedated for the repair. We need to talk to you about his arm before we start."

Bess groaned and shook her head. "I know, I know, it's horrible. But you can fix it, can't you?"

"That's why we need to talk. The bone was shattered, the surrounding tissue torn to pieces. We do have the ability to piece it back together and mend the bone, but it will never have the function it had before. It would be best to take the arm off and let us grow him a new one. It would only take two days, and the arm would be perfect. It would be his tissue, grown by his body, with our help. Because we like our repairs to be flawless, and to improve the original area if possible, the arm that's grown will be practically disease-proof, and very injury resistant. We feel we need to discuss the options with you only because the idea of amputation is so extreme for humans—even when they find out after the fact."

Colder didn't need to look at Luca to know whose experience he was referring to.

Simon and Bess both looked shaken at first, but then Simon shrugged and tilted his head to the side as he looked at her. "There's only one choice that makes sense." He looked back at Luca with a slight smile. "It's not like we don't know your work. You redid my body twice, and I've never had to go in for repairs. But—"

Bess broke in and nodded to Simon. "But Eli should make that decision himself. We can't speak for him. Can you bring him around and ask him before you start?"

"Yes. I know you want to see him, so why don't you all come in?"

Most of the family, including the Elpies and the animals were there. Only Gisella, Lola, and the children weren't on the ship. Bess and Simon wanted to know how he was doing before they spoke with the kids about their dad.

His parents were by Eli's head when Luca gave a stimulant through a tube in his neck, and he began to stir. Opening his eyes, he looked around the room, and they could see him sizing things up in his mind. He knew they were there, but wouldn't make eye contact until he was sure about what he remembered. Finally, he looked at them.

Bess took his hand and smiled, and Simon laid a hand lightly on his head, afraid to touch his damaged arm or shoulder.

"So, I'm in the fix-me-up place again, eh?"

Everyone laughed, much too heartily, and Eli could feel the tension in the air.

"It's a good thing you and Dad aren't into poker, because he'd have lost the Institute in a week. What's going on?"

Before either Bess or Simon could answer, Luca stepped forward and told him exactly what he'd relayed before to his parents. Eli tried to be cool about it. Took a deep breath and nodded his head, trying to appear like he was thinking instead of going berserk inside. He wasn't fooling anyone.

Simon leaned forward and spoke softly. "Son, this is your choice. But you have the chance to have a perfectly normal arm again, versus an arm that will never function as it once did. Look at your mother and me. Have you ever thought her eye looked artificial? They grew her a new one, and her vision is better in that eye than it was before. Just think about that before you decide."

Trying to keep his tone light and his voice from shaking, Eli nodded at his dad and looked around the room. "Hey, thank you all for everything you did for me—especially you, Hiram. You probably saved my life. But I think I need to be alone for a little while to think, okay? No offense, I just need…"

A tear oozed out of the corner of one eye, and when Bess saw it, she reached for his face, but he held his hand up. "Please, Mom. I'm okay. I just need to think a minute."

They left the room and sat outside, torn by the look on Eli's face. Simon thought this was a no-brainer—that there was no real choice to make. But it wasn't his arm.

Abruptly, Colder stood up and said, "I need to talk to him," and went back into the room before they could stop him.

When he walked back in, Eli had his good hand over his eyes, and a few tears had escaped to wet his face. He wasn't making a sound, other than the jagged intakes of breath on and off. Colder went over to his brother and laid a hand on his shoulder.

Eli started, and turned his face away, rubbing his eyes furiously with his hand, ashamed for anyone to see him crying. Colder reached up and grabbed his hand, pulling it down into his own two.

"Hey, what's the deal, Eli? You said you weren't embarrassed to cry anymore, so why are you hiding it from me? You've got every right to let loose, brother."

He shook his head and tried unsuccessfully to wipe his face on his pillow without using his hand. Finally, he gave Colder an exasperated look. "Dude, I appreciate the support, but I need my hand back."

"Oops, sorry." Colder let go long enough for him to wipe his eyes and face, and then reached over and took his hand back. Eli made himself take a deep breath, blew it out, and sank back into his pillow. He turned to look at Colder. "You don't have to hold my hand, you know. I'm okay."

"I'm not doing it for you. I'm doing it for me." He bit his bottom lip and looked up at the wall above Eli's head, trying to think of a way to say it. He finally sighed and looked back at his brother. "When I was on the ship, all Dad said on the phone was that you were hurt. So for the next ten minutes, I didn't know how bad you might be. Then when we came into that place and I saw you lying on the floor, not moving, with mom holding up an IV, I just— Oh, man, Eli, I love you so much. I can't even imagine you not—" He turned his head away as his eyes filled up.

"Hey, *now* who's hiding? I love you too, Colder. Wow, I don't remember any of us brothers ever saying that in the last ten years without punching each other. Call Guinness."

"He's in the waiting room."

"Not that one."

"The other ones are at his house."

"I'm lying here helpless, and you can't even let me have one little joke."

"I'm sorry, Eli, but you set yourself up."

He sank a little deeper into his pillow, gently pulled his hand back, and covered his eyes again. Without looking at his brother, he said quietly, "I'm just so damned scared."

He took his hand down then, and turned his head towards him. "Colder, why'd you come back in?"

"Because I wanted to tell you that I understand about losing an arm."

"You can't understand unless it's happened to you."

"It happened to me."

"What? Don't kid around with me, Colder. What are you talking about?"

"When I was on the ship, last week, we went exploring and I got attacked by this man-eating fungus partnered up with an even worse bacteria. By the time they finished with me, my hands and both legs were dark purple and swollen and rotten. I would have died, but Luca developed an antitoxin and stuff, except—it was too late for my legs and arms. Oh, and my heart."

Eli stared in shocked silence, trying to take it all in. Then he started getting angry.

"Are you making all this up to try and make me feel better? Because if you are, I still have one good arm to strangle you with."

Colder looked slightly insulted, but not really surprised. "Geez, Eli, how could I make up something that crazy and—sickening? I wouldn't. What you need right now is the truth, and that's what I came back in to tell you."

The anger went out of Eli's expression, to be replaced with dismay. "Oh, man, Colder—I don't know what to say. That's so—*awful.* I didn't know."

"Nobody at home does, and they're not going to. I don't want Mom and Dad to know what I went through. They don't need to know, 'cause I'm okay now. The Bluemen put me to sleep, and I didn't know what they'd done until I woke up, and there were my two legs and arms, all healthy looking and working fine. So then Luca comes in to explain things to me, and…when he told me that…geez, it's still hard for me to say it out loud. When he told me that…that they'd had to take off both my legs and arms, oh, and part of my heart, I just heaved. Barfed right there in the trashcan. It was just this instant, gut reaction. "

"Yeah, we Sayers tend to react with our stomachs, I've noticed."

"Well, I reacted like that *after* I was already whole again. So I understand why you're shook up, and why it's not as easy as it sounds to say, 'Oh yeah, take it off and give me a new one. Good deal!' I just wanted you to know, I get it."

Eli was staring at him and shaking his head. "That's unbelievable. But wow, you'd never know to look at you."

"That's what I wanted you to understand too, Eli. I never would have even known if they hadn't told me, because everything feels, looks, and works normal. Well almost—I did lose a couple of cool tats, but who cares? And something they told me that really made it work for me—they're mine. They're not artificial. The Bluemen made me grow them. It's like I just got to erase the injuries and start over. When I saw my arms and legs all horrible and gross, I knew I was going to lose them. Or die. I remember trying not to scream when I saw them."

"Geez, you must have been terrified. Thanks for telling me, man." He looked at his draped shoulder and didn't say anything more for a while. Colder stood silently, holding his hand again, unwilling to push him.

"It does kinda help to talk about it with somebody who's been there." He rolled his eyes and shook his head. "It sounds stupid, but—it's like I've got some sentimental attachment to it, you know? I mean, we've been through a lot together, me and this arm. How many games have I pitched with it? How many times have I punched you or Jonas, or held Babette's hand, or stroked the hair on my babies' heads?"

"I get it, Eli. I do."

He sighed then, and looked at the covering they'd placed over his shoulder. They'd stopped the bleeding, and then simply covered it so that none of the humans would be shocked by the sight. "Hey Colder, do me a favor."

"Anything, Eli."

"Take the cover off of my shoulder. I need to see why they want to give me a new one."

"Okay, but first, since you *are* a Sayers, we need to get a trashcan handy."

"Oh, right. There's that thing over there. I'm not sure if that's what it is, but—"

"Oh, hey! That's the same thing I threw up in. Cool. Here, let's just tuck it right there, so you can swing around really fast and stick your head in. Want to give it a trial run?"

"Okay. YCCH, I'm gonna spew!" He threw his head over into the sad receptacle, and gave Colder a thumbs up. "Perfect fit. Okay, let's do this."

Colder walked around the bed and then slowly lifted the cover off the wound. They both stared at the mess of chewed up, torn muscle. There were fragments of bone, large and small, sticking up at odd angles, ripped skin dangling in shreds, a few with the underlying fatty tissue still attached, and no sign at all of any muscle or bone that was still intact.

Eli took a long look, and then lay back on his pillow. "That's what I needed to see. No way that could ever be fixed right. Hey, and I didn't even—" Colder grabbed the can and ran to the other side of the room to vomit. It took him a while to finish, and afterwards, he grabbed a glass off of a table in the room, gargled and spit, and then asked Eli, "Was that water? It was water, right?"

Eli shrugged his good shoulder. "Your guess is as good as mine."

"Uughh."

"Colder, I need to see my kids before they put me under. They said it would be a couple of days, and I don't want them to be scared or think something worse is going on that you're not telling them."

"Okay, and I'll call Babette."

"No, I don't want to tell her—it'll scare her to death. I'll tell her when it's over."

"Wouldn't you like to see her?"

The question stunned him. He lay there thinking about it for a minute before answering, and his brother didn't rush him. When he looked at Colder again, he said, "Honestly? More than anything in the world right now. But I don't want her to see me like this."

"You *have* to tell her. The kids are going to need their mom here for the two days they're waiting to get you back."

He slapped his hand over his eyes. "Oh, dammit, I didn't think about that. Then I need to call her first and let her hear my voice so she knows I'm okay. Maybe Dad can hire a car from there to pick her up and bring her straight here."

"He'll hire a car *and* a chopper, if I know Dad. She could be here in a few hours."

"Okay then. Bring my cell phone and my kids, and let's grow some new parts!"

Colder started out the door when Eli called him back.

"Yeah? Think of something else?"

He held out his good arm to Colder, the way their dad always did when he demanded a forehead to kiss. Colder obediently went around to the side of the bed so that Eli could snag him around the neck and bring his head down to kiss the top of it.

"Thanks, Colder. You're a pretty great brother, you know that?"

"Yeah, well, I learned by example."

#

"Hey Babe! Whoa, it's so good to hear your voice! Yeah, well, I didn't call because I was kinda busy. No nothing's wrong. Well, that was a stupid thing to say. A lot of stuff has happened here, mainly bad, but it's too detailed to go over on the phone. Yeah, I'm fine. No, I'm not fine, and—but—I'm about to be fine. The Bluemen are going to fix me in their machine. I sort of—got shot. Oh, Babette, don't— don't cry, I'm fine!"

There was no way to make it less awful for her to hear. He'd just say it as fast as he could and let them both get it over with. "They just need to—take off my arm and grow a new one."

When she shrieked in dismay, he was afraid of what she might do. "Babette, don't hang up! Do *not* get in the car! No, I don't want you driving! And don't tell the other kids. I'll tell them when we get home. No, call your brother to come for them. Tell him—tell him I got appendicitis. My dad's sending a car over there right now, and it will take you to an airstrip where there's a chopper waiting to bring you here.

"I'll be out for a couple of days while they re-grow my arm, and my folks thought that— No. I didn't want to upset you, so I was just going to tell you afterwards, but—-wait, okay? When Colder asked me, 'Don't you want to see Babette?' I realized I wanted to see you so bad I could hardly stand it. Yeah." The last few words only came out in a whisper. Then he couldn't speak at all for a minute, and Babette was going crazy on the other end. He could hear her saying his name, then louder and then shouting it. "I'm here, Babe. Sorry. I just—I just want to see you so bad. You're my rock, you know? I love you. All right. See you soon."

Funny how he'd been fine until Colder had mentioned her. Now he didn't think he could deal with being put under without first seeing her face. It wasn't like he was dying or anything. But two days of his life would be gone, and so would his—no, his arm would be there, in a newer version, that was all. He didn't know why he was so scared.

The door opened and Aluin stuck his head in. When Eli saw him and smiled, he came in, followed by Simone and Gisella. Eli mouthed "thank you," and nodded at Gisella, so she started to back out and give them their privacy. She stopped before she was out of the room, though, and rushed over to the bed, taking his hand.

"I hadn't gotten to see you, Eli, and—I just wanted to say how much I love you, little brother. I'll never forget how excited I was when Bess presented me with a baby brother, all those years ago. And you just keep getting better. I'm so glad they can fix you." She leaned over and kissed his forehead, and he nodded, smiled, and raised her hand to kiss it before she turned and hurried out of the room. This time he was the one to stop her exit.

"Hey Gisella?"

"Yes?"

Rats, his vision was blurry again. This was getting to be a habit. "What can I say to somebody who went to battle with my children, and saw them all through safe and sound? And whose husband undoubtedly saved my life? I don't have the words. Thank you for everything, Sis."

She nodded with a smile, and closed the door.

Simone's big, beautiful blue eyes got even bigger when she saw her dad lying in bed, looking pale and tired, with one arm covered. She didn't speak but came over to his good side, picked up his hand, and held it against her cheek. She was trying not to cry, but her eyes were brimming and her jaw was shaking as she stood and looked at him.

Aluin, on the other hand, came in and climbed up on a stool they'd left there for him, and proudly proclaimed, "We got a bad guy! It was so cool, Dad! This guy with a gun came to the door, and the dogs grabbed his arms and then Gisella and all us kids Tasered him! Wait 'til we tell Mom!"

Oh, wait until they tell Mom… Being unconscious for a couple of days while things got squared away might not be so bad after all.

"Oh, uh, how are you doing, Dad?" he added, as an afterthought.

Simone was so upset with him that she wanted to slap her brother right off his little stool. "How do you *think* he's doing, creep? He's wounded, and all you can talk about is yourself!"

She was third degree peeved, but when she saw the hurt look on her brother's face, she softened a little. Most of the time, he really wasn't bad, for a little brother. She'd seen way worse. So she turned to her dad, by way of apology, and explained, "He doesn't mean to be a jerk, Dad, he just can't help himself sometimes."

Eli smiled at him. "I've had the same experience, myself."

Aluin looked a little ashamed, but mainly just ticked at his sister.

Eli took his hand out of Simone's and stroked the hair on her head gently, and then chucked Aluin under the chin.

"Well, I asked them to bring you two here so we could say goodbye before they put me to sleep."

Suddenly Aluin started crying, and Eli reached out for him. "Hey, big guy, I need to be asleep while they're fixing my arm, so it won't hurt. No biggie."

Looking at him suspiciously, the boy retorted, "When they put Munster to sleep, he never came back from the vet's. Never!"

Eli closed his eyes, amazed by his own incredibly brainless choice of words, but—too late. "Not like that. My arm got shot, and it's too much of a mess to fix, so they're going to grow me a new one. And when I say 'put to sleep,' I mean that they'll give me medicine to make me sleep for a little while so that I won't be in pain while they're working on me."

Aluin was still not convinced. "Then why are we saying goodbye?"

"Because we *always* say goodbye if we're not going to see each other for a couple of days, right? And you know how parents are—any excuse to kiss on their kids. "

Simone was starting to get a little fidgety now, thinking about the implications of what he'd just said. "If they're growing you a new arm, what's going to happen to the old one?"

"Well, honey, you know—they have to cut it off." It still made his stomach drop to say those words.

Simone gasped and teared up.. "Oh Daddy, I'm so sorry! Does it hurt bad?"

He hated to see his kids cry. "Baby, no, no, it doesn't hurt at all—Luca gave me something to stop the pain and it's all numb now. And I'm going to get a new arm, just like the new eye they grew for Grandma Bess."

"So you'll be able to see with your arm? That's pretty weird, but cool, in a way."

Simone glared at her brother. "Will you just listen?"

"What?"

"You know, it hit me sort of hard at first, thinking about it, but I'm getting a brand new, healthy arm. The old one was getting kind of beat up, with pitching and painting, and changing tires. I'm just gonna think of it like getting a new tire. I had a blow-out on my right front, so they'll take that one off and put a new one on, and SHAZAAM! Good as new!"

Simone leaned over the side to kiss her father's cheek, and then stroked his hair back, like he did to them when they were sick.

"So, Dad, are they going to have to balance your wheels afterwards?"

"It's possible."

Giggling, Simone asked, "Will they have to re-align you?"

"My chiropractor can do that." Both kids giggled, and that sweet sound made everything seem better to him.

"Yeah, he'd better, 'cause the last thing you need is a shimmy."

"Good one, Simone."

"Can we see it, Dad?"

"Aluin!" Simone thought she might have to kill him right there on his stool.

"Well, why not? I just want to see what happened to it. Can I take a picture of it with your cell?"

"NO!" Simone and Eli said in unison.

She took his hand again. "Genevieve says you're a hero. She said you got shot saving her life."

"Anybody would have done the same thing. I didn't want to get shot. I just couldn't think of anything else to do."

"I'm so proud of you, Dad." Simone laid her head on his shoulder, and that heartfelt gesture almost made him lose it, but Aluin saved him by killing the mood.

"So can we see it or not?"

"I guess. Simone, don't look if you don't want to. It's pretty gross. Which means your brother will probably think it's cool and want to keep it in a jar or something."

"Whoa, can I?"

"NO!" Simone and Eli answered together.

"Okay, Aluin, very slowly, lift off that cover, get your fill at staring, and then put it back."

The boy jumped off the bed excitedly and walked over to the cover. He very carefully lifted it off, holding it to the side so Simone wouldn't see. His reaction was not what Eli expected. Aluin stared at it for a good twenty seconds, and then with his eyes, he followed the ruined arm and shoulder up Eli's neck to his face and finally his eyes. Then he very carefully replaced the cover and came back to his father's good side. Getting up on his stool, he leaned over and laid his head on Eli's stomach and said quietly, "Oh, Dad, I'm so sorry."

"Hey, don't you get my chassis wet! You cry on my undercarriage, I could lose my brakes!" He ruffled Aluin's hair and rubbed his back, took a deep breath, and quick, changed the subject.

"I did want to tell the both of you how proud I am of the way you handled yourselves the other night. Harvey said you were the bravest kids ever, and you did exactly what he told you to. He said he had his rifle trained on that guy the whole time, but wanted to see how you'd handle it—which I'll be talking to him about again, very soon, if he's still alive after your mother talks to him."

Simone laughed and said, "Maybe we should warn him to put his Kevlar on before Mom gets here."

Aluin added, "Yeah, and to have his Taser with him."

That cracked all of them up, and reminded Eli how much he loved laughing with his children. It also made him realize that he really needed that good arm, so that he wouldn't miss even one time, picking any of them up, or throwing them in the river, tossing them in the air, or hugging them tight against his chest.

All at once, he felt exhausted and horribly drained, and it must have shown on his monitors, because Luca came in suddenly and sent to the children that their dad needed to rest. His kids could see it too, and Aluin, completely serious now, climbed onto the bed to reach his father's face and kiss him, and Simone reached over and did the same.

"We love you, Dad. Be better. And get that wheel fixed!" Simone said, before closing the door.

"Love you more." he whispered, as they walked away.

CHAPTER FIFTY

"This kind of wound stresses the whole body, and he's showing signs of weakening, so we've put him in stasis until Babette comes. It should be safe to wait a few hours to start the procedure."

Bess reached out and took one of Luca's hands in both of hers. "We owe you so much. You have children, so I think you must understand the depth of gratitude we feel for what you're doing."

Simon nodded his agreement with what Bess had expressed, but said nothing, as if the effort to speak was beyond him, and Luca saw him sway a little. The side of his head was cut and bloodied, and had bled enough to cover his neck and that side of his shirt halfway to his waist. His hands were abraded, grossly swollen, and discolored over the knuckles, probably indicative of multiple fractures, and his right arm was bruised and swollen all the way from his shoulder to his hand from throwing himself against the cage. He appeared close to collapsing, and there was much more to go through before this night would be over for all of them.

Luca put a hand on his arm to steady him, and leaned over to look into his face as he sent. "Simon, let me tend to your head wounds and your arm and hands, and give you something to renew your strength. If I don't, I believe you're going to pass out."

He ran his hand through his hair, and saw the blood on his hand afterwards, but more telling, was how much that hand was shaking. Running all that way hadn't done this to him. Having been overdosed and hit on the head twice hadn't helped, he supposed. And maybe the running had added to the strain. He routinely ran much farther, had endured much worse pain, but never under these conditions.

What was telling on him the most was having thought that his brother was being brutally murdered while he sat in a cage, helpless to do anything, as his horrified wife huddled one cage away from him. It was seeing his daughter almost murdered, and his son maimed and nearly killed. It was the look on his son's face when he was told they needed to take his arm off. It was the knowledge that everything that had happened was because of *him*. Because someone hated *him*.

Bess had been so focused on their son and his injury, that she'd barely noticed the shape Simon was in. She looked at him when Luca addressed him and realized that he was on the brink. They'd both been ignoring his injuries and the toll that everything had taken on him. She reached out and took his arm.

"Oh, good grief, Simon—I'm so sorry—since Eli got shot I haven't thought about anything else. Just look at you—Luca's right. You need his help—no excuses. You're about to crash, and it won't help anything if you end up collapsing."

He started to argue, but then realized he could barely speak, he was so physically and emotionally drained. When Colder's new friend, the deer/rabbit thing with the babies hanging on it, had let out one of its shrieks earlier, he'd almost screamed. And he thought if he let himself, he might just keep screaming, he was so tense inside. So he nodded, and went with Luca into another chamber.

Bess sank down into a chair next to her mom, and reclined it as much as she could. Starting to close her eyes, she stopped when Sarah reached over, took her hand, and gave it a squeeze. Such a simple act, but its effect was huge. Tears of relief began leaking out of her eyes, but they were few and short lived enough for her to handle.

Wordlessly, she looked at her mother who was gazing at her with all the sweetness and gentleness she had come to know and expect from her throughout her life. This mother, grandmother, sweet baker of cookies who had just beaten the tar out of a bunch of criminals without a hint of squeamishness.

She squeezed back, and gave her a little smile. Then she raised the back of her chair so that she could look out at her family. She let her eyes drink them in. Each face so precious. Each soul so unique. And not a one lost this night. How had that ever happened? How had it ended like this? Closing her eyes, she thanked God for every life in that room—lives that could have been so easily lost in an instant.

When she opened her eyes and looked out into the room again, she saw that most of her family was involved in the same exercise—searching the room and stopping on different faces to silently celebrate the fact that those faces were still there. Occasionally, when her eyes were pouring over one of them, he or she would look back up and meet her gaze, and the intense connection between them would make her throat tighten with emotion.

In thirty minutes, Luca came back out with Simon, who looked like a different man. His cuts and the bruising from the blows to his head were gone, his hands and arm looked normal, and the shaking, with that appearance of utter exhaustion, had vanished. He looked at them sheepishly.

"Sorry. I guess I let everything get to me, and the injuries just made it too much. I don't know what Luca did to me, but I feel like I've had a five hour nap and a session on a therapist's couch. I'm just so sorry about everything." Several people mumbled that he wasn't to blame, but they knew their words wouldn't change how he felt.

"While Eli's in stasis, we need to go talk to Sven about what to do with the prisoners."

CHAPTER FIFTY-ONE

"Oh God."

They had all gone with Harvey to see Eli's house.

Looking from the outside, with the door kicked in, they could see through into the living room, and the aftermath of the hundreds of bullets that had ripped through the sofa, the walls, everything. The thing that stood out as most horrendous, oddly enough, was the Mickey Mouse doll lying on the floor, torn apart by the fusillade. It seemed eerily symbolic of the carnage that had been intended in this place.

They walked through every room. There were bullet holes in all the beds, in the closet doors, in the showers. In everyone's mind was the thought—what if they had been here? What if they hadn't been prepared?

Jonas, Enzo, and Genevieve saw their mortality more clearly, looking at the ruins of this house where they had all been only hours before, than when they'd been doing battle at Arthur's place. They had gone there armed, with forethought, ready to risk their lives. But this—this would have been a slaughter.

Bess and Simon were shattered at the thought that all of their children except for Colder and Gisella would have been wiped out in a matter of minutes if they'd been here. Angus and Sarah were both thinking the same thing—their grandchildren, almost all gone.

Milton had told them what Arthur had intended—to murder all the men and drag their dead bodies in to show Simon, and to take the women and children for sale at a later time, in a foreign country. When he'd finished, they could hardly fathom a mind so evil. It was such a devastating scenario that none of them could even respond to it at first.

Simon was trembling again, but with rage, now.

When they left the house, he turned to Harvey.

"Where are the prisoners—the ones who did this, and the ones from Arthur's?"

"In Eli's work shed—the one with the dirt floor that he built himself. They're tied up and chained to the walls. I didn't know what you wanted us to do with them."

Simon spoke in a quiet and deliberate voice as he looked at his friend. "Harvey, will you please bring me a gun?"

"What kind?"

"Doesn't matter. As long as you bring enough bullets. Two for each of them."

They all stared at him, shocked, but no one told him not to do it.

He stood before his family and spoke slowly, his voice calm now. "Maurice scanned them all. All of the men at Arthur's, and all of them here. Milton said that every one of them had committed at least one murder before coming to work for Arthur, who had researched each one prior to hiring. Being a soulless killer was a prerequisite. Maurice verified it when he scanned their memories.

"Some have been responsible for multiple deaths, and their mind sets tell him that none feels remorse, and all are prepared to kill again, with no hesitation. If we turned them in to the police, who knows whether or not their pasts would be found out?

"This was obviously attempted murder—we know that, but no one was killed. They could tell the courts that they knew no one was in the house and that they did this as a warning. Even if they were convicted, they might get reduced sentences and be out again, to murder other people, other families, or to come back here and try to finish the job they screwed up this time.

"We can't let them go, knowing what we do. It would be giving them free reign to kill again. We can't do that. We can't allow them to keep murdering people. There are innocent lives in our hands now. We'd be responsible for the deaths of those future victims. And there's no way to prove what we know in court."

He wondered if his family would see *him* as a murderer when he finished what he had to do.

From the shed, they began to hear shouts and curses, thuds and clanging noises, and then Sarah's voice, shrill and strident. They all looked at Angus, and he nodded.

"Sarah walked out of the house and straight to the shed. She'd already asked where they were, and she still has her skillet with her. You may not have to do anything, Simon.

"Why don't you let me do this, son? I will gladly put a couple of bullets in each of their brains, without a moment of regret. Ever. If they have any brains left when Sarah's finished with them, that is."

"No. Thank you, Angus. This is for me to do."

"I'll help you Dad." It was Jonas, still carrying his bow and wearing his quiver. "I can do this, after looking at this house, and after seeing Eli lying on the floor with his shoulder blown apart. And knowing what he intended for the women and kids in the family—yeah, I can do this with no problem."

Simon went to him and pulled his head down to rest his forehead against his own. He spoke to his son in just above a whisper. "I love you, Jonas, and because of that, I don't want this on your hands and in your mind for the rest of your life. But thank you." He kissed his forehead, and then released him.

Sarah was coming out of the shed with her little skillet when Harvey returned with a Glock and handed it to Simon, along with several mags. When he handed them over, he held onto the last one as Simon tried to take it from him. "Let me take care of this for you. I saw what they tried to do. I or any one of my men would be more than happy to finish this. We're soldiers. All of us have been to war, but even we were blown away by how excited and happy to commit murder these animals were. It was like a party for them. None of us wants these guys to ever be out on the streets again."

Simon just shook his head, took the last mag, patted Harvey on the shoulder, and walked down the drive to the shed. He walked in and closed the door behind him. The family stood together in shock and dread, waiting for that first shot to ring out.

A few minutes later, he opened the door and yelled out, "Angus, Jonas, Harvey, I changed my mind. I would like your help. Bring your weapons. Oh, and Barnabas, why don't you come, too. We owe you a little action."

#

Before the other four got to the shed, Simon addressed the men before him. All were tied and chained to the wall, all bearing knots or bloodied scrapes where Sarah had clouted them.

"My name is Simon Sayers. Most of you know that. The house next to the garage, the one that you riddled with bullets—the one that you thought *my children* were in—that's my son's house. I love my children beyond measure, and I understand that you planned to murder my sons and then drag their bodies over to Worthington's to drop in front of me. And then you were going to sell my daughters, wife, and grandchildren."

He leaned into one of the men, so that he was inches from his face, and said quietly, with all the seething anger that he felt, "Do you have *any idea* what that makes me want to *do to you*?"

The man swallowed with difficulty. His mouth was dry and he was sweating. He tried pulling his face away from Simon's, but the chains wouldn't let him.

"You shot one of my sons, my first born. He'll be okay. But *you* won't."

The men had held stock still to listen, but now they started shifting nervously.

Opening the door to the shed, Angus and Jonas were held back by Simon's upraised hand. "One of my sons that you had intended to murder is here with me now. He can shoot a tick off a buffalo in the dark with his bow. But sometimes he misses when he's tired, and he's *very* tired. I'm going to let him have a little target practice. Jonas, come on in."

It wasn't hard for Jonas to figure out what was going on. He walked in and strung his bow very deliberately in front of the men. Then he slowly nocked an arrow and waited for his dad to lead him.

"Jonas, do you think you could hit that knot in the wood, just above the third man's head, there?"

"Geez, I don't know, Dad. It's been a long night, and my hands are a little shaky. I might miss."

"Why don't you try, anyway. If you miss, well…" He leaned forward and spoke directly to the third man. "Nothing lost."

"Okay, if you say so." He made a big production of wavering back and forth, and let a few arrows fly in a haphazard manner, landing them beside his trembling victim and other men at random, terrifyingly close to each. "Wow, I *am* really shaky!" Then he drew back and smoothly sunk an arrow into the wood just above the chosen man's head, skimming his hair. A pitiful whimpering came from the man, who was already trembling badly.

One of the men was sitting on the ground with his legs spread wide, and Simon walked up and stuck the heel of his shoe into the dirt between the man's thighs before he could pull them together. "I'll bet you could hit my heel mark in the dirt there, Jonas. You think?"

When the man tried to pull his legs together, Simon shook his head at him. "Oh, I wouldn't do that if I were you. Then he'd have to shoot right through your legs. He just might be able to do it, but what a mess. You should try and hold very, very still."

"I can only do my best, Dad. I'm a little dizzy, but I can try. Like you said—if I miss, nothing lost."

This time he didn't stall, but pulled an arrow out, nocked it, drew smoothly and fired, all in a matter of seconds, and the arrow sunk into the dirt a few inches below the man's crotch. A quick scream escaped the prisoner. Simon pointed out some additional targets, and had Jonas demonstrate his prowess to a few more terrified men before introducing the Colder.

"This is Barnabas. The lizard that the dogs were going to tear apart? That's his best friend." While Simon was talking, Barnabas walked down the line of men, glaring, sending gory, terrifying scenes of himself eviscerating them, tearing out throats, ripping off limbs. Since they weren't telepaths, they couldn't receive the pictures exactly as he sent them, but the men felt their intent, and his ability to turn intent into reality. He projected ferocity, anger, and even more chilling—*hunger*. He would stop occasionally to open his mouth and hiss in a face, or put his claws around someone's neck.

"He was a little upset at my family for not letting him kill any of you during your captures. But that was before we saw this house. We're going to make it up to him now." Barnabas looked at the men, made his quills stand up and lean forward, and sent his glee at this news into the minds of the killers before him. Then he licked his lips.

"You know that tall, elderly, *very angry* woman that just beat the crap out of you with her little pan? That was my mother-in-law, the grandmother of those people you were trying to murder in that house. She *really loves* her grandchildren. You might have noticed. Now I'd like you to meet her husband, the grandfather. Only one of you—the man with the broken nose and swollen forehead—has met him so far. He's very eager to meet the rest of you. Sarah's good with a frying pan, although she usually bakes. But Angus now, he's a *master* with *his* skillet. Come in, Angus."

When Angus walked in, one handedly twirling his gigantic weapon in the air, one of the men who was already sporting multiple knots, abrasions, and bruises from the six inch version, started crying. Angus was not a small man, and he wielded the monstrous fryer as if it weighed nothing.

Simon pointed out a wooden sawhorse and addressed his father-in-law. "Angus, that thing takes up entirely too much room in here. Think you could minimize it?"

Peering down, Angus walked around it, choosing his target spot. "Shouldn't be a problem." Then he swung the massive piece of iron back and over his head to bring it slamming down to smash through the wood, breaking it in half and sending shards flying through the air, as the two ends collapsed towards their missing center.

He looked up and gave the prisoners an Angus smile. The same smile he used to give Simon in the days before they became friends. The smile that said, "I know who you are, and we're not done." He kicked the wood to the side of the shed, walked up to the first man, raised his skillet high above his head, and asked Simon, "Shall we get started?"

"Not yet. I think it would be kinder if we blindfolded them. I haven't used a Glock in a while, so the first few might be messy. No point in torturing them by making them watch each other go down. Although they don't deserve the mercy."

Gesturing for the other three humans to come help him, Simon took out a utility knife and gave Angus a pair of heavy shears. Harvey retrieved a small knife out of his boot to give Jonas, then pulled a huge one out of a sheath on his leg for himself. They spread out a canvas sail, and the four of them quickly cut twenty-one long strips. Dividing these up, they proceeded to blindfold the men. As they blindfolded, Simon sent to Barnabas, who nodded his head and ran to Eli's house. He was gone for a time, and when he returned, he stood outside of the shed, waiting until the blindfolding was finished to come back into the shed.

More than a few of the men began begging for their lives, giving reasons why they shouldn't die, but no one answered their pleas. Several were crying, a couple shouted, cursing, and the rest sat in numbed silence.

When they'd finished the blindfolding, Simon called the four over and sent what he wanted them to do. Jonas pulled a roll of duct tape off one of the shelves, and tore off twenty-one strips, sticking one on the wall behind each man's head, once they were all blindfolded.

In one hand, Barnabas was carrying a raw leg of lamb that Angus had given Eli to bake and keep for the siblings to snack on between meals. He'd had it thawing in the fridge and now it was nice and soft. In the other hand, he had four coconuts set on top of wet sponges, with each set wrapped tightly in its own pillowcase.

"Harve, are you ready?"

Simon took the safety off his gun, and Harvey pulled out his own and did the same. "Ready and more than willing."

Walking up to the first man, Simon put the muzzle of the gun first in his ear, then against one eye, and the man began crying silently. Next, he pressed it to the top of his head and held it for a moment, before moving to the back of his head and pressing hard against it. Finally, he laid the barrel flat against the side of the man's head and fired a bullet into the wall behind him. Jonas had his piece of tape ready, and as soon as the bullet was fired, he taped the man's mouth shut. He had Barnabas hold his head up while he taped, since the man had fainted when he felt the jolt of the metal against his head and heard the firing just above his ear.

Angus picked the man whose nose he'd broken earlier, and whispered in his ear that they had unfinished business. He laid the enormous pan on his head as if lining up his blow, raised it up high, and the man screamed as he brought it down to lightly graze his head and then connect with a crack and squelch on the wrapped coconut and wet sponge laid beside him. As soon as the pan passed his head, Barnabas hung a strip of raw meat over his ear on that side to dangle wetly against his face. Jonas taped.

Barnabas breathed onto the face of his first victim, and hissed loudly. Then he put his teeth around the man's face and closed his jaws slightly, so that he could feel the pressure building on both sides of his skull. He began screaming as Barnabas sent an image of his face being crushed between his jaws, and then the Colder pulled back and let Jonas slap on the tape. After the man's screams were muffled, Barnabas took a huge mouthful of lamb, ripping it off and chewing noisily, as he waved the meat near the nose of the next man in line, so that he could smell the raw flesh.

Simon chastised him loudly. "Damn it, Barnabas, no eating! There's too many to be sampling them all. I want to get this over with—we've still got to bury them. And they probably all taste the same, anyway." He waited a few moments, gave an exasperated sigh, and then said, "Oh, all right, just the one that you finished off then, but hurry and have your fill and get on with it."

Repeating his own performance with the Glock, Simon had Harvey use the same maneuver on a few of the men. Harvey, however, preferred putting the gun to their stomachs, and then moving it around to their backs and firing into the wall, where they could feel the kick of the gun against their spines. With one last little flourish, he used his water bottle and wet the men's shirts as he fired. The screams his act elicited before his victims' mouths were taped, even more than the gunshots themselves, helped to terrorize the blindfolded men waiting their turns.

Jonas liked that added touch, so he picked up a bottle of water that had been left on the workbench, warm after sitting there for days. Every time one of the guns went off, or Angus slammed his skillet down, Jonas would simultaneously flick a handful of water onto the face of the man next in line. Blood *is* thicker than water, but under the circumstances, none of the blindfolded could tell the difference.

They started at one end and worked their way slowly to the other. Each man waiting his turn heard the shot or the blow aimed at the man bedside him, or listened to the rending of flesh and felt the warm, wet droplets splattered onto his face. Each was aware of the increasing silence from that side of the room. A silence heading his way.

By the time all twenty-one men had been dealt with, no lives had been lost, but five had fainted and a good number had soiled themselves. Two had emptied their stomachs on their neighbors. When the avenging five left the shed, most of the men were sitting or lying blindfolded, wondering, "Am I the only one left? How bad is my wound?" They were already in so much pain from Sarah's ministrations that most couldn't distinguish one injury from another, on heads that were hurting all over. None made a sound, for fear that their punishers would come back to finish them off if they realized any of the captives were still alive.

As a parting blow, Simon spoke loudly with Angus on his way out the door. "Angus, we can use that steam shovel I rented for the pool excavation. The hole's already dug, and there's a ton of dirt and rock just sitting there waiting to be pushed back in. We can drag the bodies into a pile, pick them up in the shovel, dump them in and have the hole filled within an hour or two. We can always rent a mixer and add cement later. What do you say?" Now the men had to choose between telling their captors that they were alive and being subsequently executed, or trying to appear dead and being buried alive. Food for thought.

The five made their way up the drive from the shed to the rest of the family, who had settled onto the grass to wait. When they reached them, Simon shook his head in resignation. "They're all still alive. We just gave them a taste of the terror that some of their victims must have felt. I couldn't do what I intended. I couldn't shoot them when they were tied up, and already bloodied by Sarah. I'm sorry. I should have, but I just couldn't do it."

He looked at them in shame, but everyone was smiling. There were audible sighs of relief, and Bess put her head down, with one hand to her chest and one covering her mouth. Then she stood straight, rushed over to Simon, and wrapped her arms around him. She raised her face and whispered in his ear. "I'm so glad."

Simon shook his head again and held up his hands in a gesture of helplessness. "I don't—I don't know where to go from here."

Sven let them have their moment, and then asked, "Can we go back to the main house? I'd like to sit down with everyone and discuss something. I have an idea that may satisfy all of you."

CHAPTER FIFTY-TWO

When they got back to the house, Sarah calmly washed the blood off her skillet and then went into hostess mode, making coffee for everyone, and putting out macaroon laden plates on the counter.

Stench and Blobra had gone back to their ships to wait for word from Sarah. Harvey had all his men secluded and relaxing in a guest house until they received further orders from him. Sarah had already sent milk and macaroons to them earlier.

Sven stood while he sent, looking at each of them in turn, because all needed to agree. "First let me say, Simon, that I am greatly relieved at what you see as your lack of determination. I see it as your lack of cold-bloodedness. I could not agree with wholesale execution, but it was not my family they tried to murder, so I didn't interfere.

"What I propose to do is to notify Interpol. When we scanned their minds, we found that most of these men had committed the majority of their murders in the U.K. or Europe. Before I do this, however, we are going to make some adjustments to their minds. First, we are going to wipe any memories of this family, the Elpies, ourselves, and Sarah's friends. Then we're going to implant the idea that Arthur had ordered them beaten, bound, and blindfolded before he left the country. He had cruelly let them know that he was having people come with a truck to take them to some remote spot and dispose of them, since he wanted no witnesses left to his crimes. Particularly, the murders of two of his wives, and the slaughtering of endangered species in his despicable hunts.

"This should come as no surprise to Interpol, since Arthur has actually rid himself of most of his employees like this twice before, in order to save money when he moved from one country to another. Murder is significantly cheaper than air fare.

"We will leave them with the belief that the only way they can save themselves is to tell everything they know about Arthur, so that the police can capture him and protect them. We will also leave them with an overwhelming compulsion to confess to every crime they've ever committed. We're going to transport them all back to Worthington's house, still bound, and make an anonymous call to the local police, as well as to Interpol.

"At first, their confessing will seem too bizarre, and the police will think they're under some kind of influence, which they are, of course. *But*, they'll be duty bound to fingerprint them and check out their stories, particularly when Interpol calls them. All should be extradited in short order, I would imagine.

"When we were scanning their minds, what struck us as most tragic was the fact that so many of the murders they committed were never found out, and the bodies never discovered. Think how many families have never known what happened to their missing relatives. By doing this, we can at least give closure to their grieving survivors, and the satisfaction of knowing that these murderers have been brought to justice at last.

"The only part of this plan we regret is that Interpol will be wasting manpower looking for Arthur."

He remained standing when he finished, and looked at each face to gauge the reaction to his plan.

Hiram spoke first. "Sven, you and your crew are absolute geniuses, you have wonderful machines, and you are probably the best friends this family ever had. That's—that's just an amazing solution to this quagmire. We can never thank you enough."

Everyone began voicing and sending the same sentiments, and the relief at a final solution was evident on the faces in the room. That question of "Now what?" had been looming heavily over all of them.

When Simon asked, "What about Arthur? Where is he?" the room suddenly went still.

"What you need to know first," Mona sent, "is that Blobra's species are the Magpies of the universe. They have no real culture of their own. Everything they know, all their machines and ships—they have all been copied from other planets and their civilizations. You saw the way she copied your general shapes. She can also make an exact copy of any machine, if she oozes into and covers it, which she can easily do. Her slime has a memory that can recall in fine detail anything it has touched. She can go back to her planet, and from her memories of her visit here, her people can make facsimiles of anything she's come in contact with. Even you, Enzo"

He shuddered to think there might be a globular Enzo oozing about the galaxies someday.

"When I say they are Magpies, it's because they're collectors. They entertain themselves by accumulating things that catch their eyes, the way Magpies do."

Sven picked up the story.

"Blobra sent to me that she's always wanted to take a human for her collection of creatures she keeps on her planet, but has never done so for fear of incurring the wrath of the Maker of Macaroons."

Sarah sat a little straighter at this, and Angus looked around the room with raised eyebrows, leaving "I told you so," unsaid but understood.

"I saw her moments after Arthur disappeared, and recognized her increase in bulk for what it was. She knew I'd caught her, and was ready to disgorge him if I had protested. When I didn't, she took him back to her ship."

"She *ate him?"* Colder gasped.

Maurice shook his head. "No. She enveloped him. She can cocoon another being for a short time, and keep it breathing in the small amount of atmosphere she absorbs for the cocoon. It's really quite a remarkable system."

Sven continued. "She's waiting for me to clear it with Sarah before she takes off. Oh, and of course, she was hoping to take some macaroons."

Simon was staring into his coffee, concentrating intently on every word of the sendings. Finally, he spoke up. "So there's no possibility that Arthur will ever return to Earth? That she might feel sorry for him, and decide to bring him home some day?"

Sadie looked at her father for permission to send, and he nodded his approval.

"We studied her species in school, and from what I understand, many of her kind enjoy keeping collections of living creatures, but they're not usually successful in keeping them alive for long. They have to simulate their nourishment, and while the simulations look perfect, they don't have the nutrients or flavor that the original food would have. After a while, these simulations become intolerable to the creatures they keep, and their helpless menageries soon perish. We've tried to convince them to quit collecting living specimens because of this, but we haven't been persuasive enough yet. They're not a cruel species, but they have short attention spans, and limited understanding of the suffering of others, much like very young children."

Sarah had started gathering the empty dishes, and looked up as she took Sven's plate. "Sven dear, would you tell the lovely Blobra that she can have Arthur with my blessings, and that I'll even give her extra macaroons for getting him out of here. With the condition, of course, that he never gets off her planet, as unlikely as that sounds."

"I'd be delighted to."

Jonas asked a question that had been bothering several of them, Elsie and Madelyn in particular. "What happened to the dogs?" The two canines in the room looked at Sven expectantly.

"Oh, they will have wonderful lives. Stench is of a species that relates to all Canids on any planet. With his size and overwhelming odor, he is the Ultra-Alpha." The two dogs looked at each other and nodded, and Elsie sighed as she remembered sniffing him. She'd made Sarah promise to let Madelyn meet him before he left. No one should miss that.

"Canids flock to him, and want desperately to be part of his pack. They are driven to be near him—his vocalizations and smell seem to have an almost hypnotic effect. On his planet, many of his species keep alien Canids as pets, and he was particularly taken with the look of this pack, since they were different from any he'd seen. They're going back home with him, which means they'll be in an almost euphoric state for the rest of their lives."

Everyone seemed pleased with this development. Ishmael had not been particularly impressed with Stench, but that came as no surprise to anyone. He was just glad to get that slobbering horde out of the neighborhood. No one noticed when Elsie and Madelyn quietly left the room.

Simon looked at Harvey and cleared his throat. "That only leaves one problem. Your men. We can't have all of them remembering what happened here."

Harvey sat straight up, looking at Simon with sudden distrust. "What are you proposing I do with them?"

"Oh, come on Harvey, you know I'd never do anything to harm them! They saved my family! But Sven, I was wondering if you could—"

"Wipe their memories of last night? Maurice already took care of it. They think they were just fending off a mock raid to prepare them in case something ever actually happened. And Harvey, what they do remember is that the practice went very well, and that you were an excellent leader."

He still looked a little uneasy, but after a minute or two, he seemed to relax and shrugged his shoulders. "Well, I guess that's all right. You didn't take away any other memories, did you?"

"No, of course not. We only wiped the parts of memories that we needed to."

"And Harvey," Simon added, "you can tell them for me that I was overjoyed at their efficiency in protecting my mock family, and that I'll be doubling whatever pay you promised them for that 'staged' battle. That includes your regular salary, too. Permanently. I could never pay you enough for what you did."

He looked at his family before him and had to stop for a moment, thinking of what could have been. Then he turned back to Harvey and continued. "What I thought of as your extravagance in obtaining equipment saved our family. Your planning and the execution of your ideas worked remarkably well. You are an outstanding soldier and commander, a wonderful friend, and you've been an extraordinary blessing to this family. Thank you."

Simon had walked over to him when they'd started talking, and Harvey had stood in alarm at the mention of his men being a problem. Which was perfect for Simon, as he grabbed him in a quick bear hug. He stepped back after adding a Dad kiss on the top of his head, and this time, Harvey was okay with it.

They all had a say about his work, and Harvey smiled broadly, slightly embarrassed, but mightily pleased at all of the praise, for he knew full well it was justified. Without the supplies he'd provided, and the planning, tactics, and positioning of his men, they knew there would have been deaths in the family.

##

The Bluemen were like guardian angels that night and the next day. They left the Sayers and Elpies in the living room with little vials of liquid for everyone to take so that they could sleep, for they all desperately needed the rest and let down from the Adrenalin charged evening. Then they left to insinuate their suggestions into the minds of the prisoners. After making sure that all fingerprints and DNA on the duct tape, bindings, and surroundings at Arthur's had been eliminated, they transported the mentally modified prisoners back to the animal room.

When Simon thought of his family trying to clean up and bring this whole matter to a conclusion by themselves, it almost made him sick with fatigue and anxiety. It would have been impossible. Instead, they were left to decompress a little longer together over cookies, plus roast beef sandwiches that Angus had somehow produced in a matter of minutes, while their blessed Bluemen took care of everything.

CHAPTER FIFTY-THREE

Colder excused himself to go upstairs and change out of his silver suit when he realized people had started checking it out. What had seemed great looking to him on the ship, now just made him feel ridiculous. All of the clothes he'd brought with him were most likely shredded by the bullets shot into the closets at Eli's, but his old room here still had some clothes left in the drawers for when he might need some spares. He took his time changing, since like everyone else, he was experiencing the physical and mental exhaustion from the tension of the night. He felt like he was underwater—his movements slow and difficult.

When he came back down into the living room, his parents had been weeping. Both of them. Sarah looked horrified, and when he walked through the door, she gasped and covered her mouth, shaking her head and staring at him through tear-filled eyes. Jonas was sitting with his head in his hands, and Genevieve was leaning against Enzo with her face turned to his shoulder. Even Blanche and her babies looked upset. Ishmael looked the same as always.

He rushed over to his parents, grabbing his mom's shoulder.

"What is it? What's happened? Is it Eli?"

She looked up at him, and then stood up to throw her arms around him. His dad followed suit, and they both began to tell him how sorry they were, and that they loved him. Then his grandparents were there, too, making it an extremely uncomfortable crowd.

He accepted the loving politely, but then gently pulled himself away from the embraces. He started to demand again to know what was going on, and then he noticed Luigi, standing by the fireplace, pretending to look at the fire, which wasn't lit, and avoiding eye contact with him.

Micah shook his head and pointed at Luigi when Colder sent to him.

Oh, no. "Dad, does this have anything to do with—"

"Luigi sent us his memories of what happened to you on that God forsaken planet, and showed us your wounds, that horrible infection, and then he sent us—sent us about what they had to do to you. Son, can you ever forgive us for encouraging you to go on that trip—laughing at the idea of it being dangerous?"

He glared at Luigi, who looked back at him now and shrugged his shoulders—the universal Elpie response when confronted by humans about anything obnoxious they'd done. Then he sent that Colder's parents were wondering why he'd had to go in and talk to Eli, and what he'd done to help him make up his mind about the amputation. He'd just satisfied their questions by explaining why Colder could empathize with him.

Seeing his parents, or actually, his whole family so distraught made him feel terrible. He couldn't believe that he'd *wanted* someone to cry over him before he'd left the planet. Geez, hadn't they gone through enough in the last few hours without this? He could strangle that little reptile.

His dad put a hand on his shoulder and he turned to face him. "Son, we need for you to drop your drawers."

"What?"

"We need for you to take off your pants so we can see your legs. We just need to see for ourselves that you're okay now."

"Dad! I'm a grown man! You can't just tell me to drop trou in front of the whole family!"

Genevieve tsked. "Oh, come on, Colder! Except for me, the rest of the family, including Jonas, used to change your diapers, and I've seen you in your shorts plenty of times, growing up. We just want to see your new legs."

"Well they haven't changed my diapers in the *past couple of years*! I've matured just a little since I needed their help. Hopefully, they wouldn't even recognize me."

Enzo laughed at that, but stopped and wiped his grin off at a look from Bess and a squeeze from Genevieve that didn't feel at all affectionate.

"You've all seen me already, at the lake!"

Simon shook his head. "But those weren't your new legs. And we hadn't seen those horrible pictures from Luigi's memories. To see your limbs so—destroyed, and then to see you when they—"

Colder whirled around to stare at Luigi in shock. "You showed them that, too? What they did?"

Luigi shrugged again and sent that he'd just shown them what he'd seen.

His mom looked at Colder with tear-filled eyes. "Please, honey. It would help us so much to see with our own eyes that you're healed. Luigi's memories—it was like watching a movie, and I can't get that picture out of my mind—the way your legs and arms looked before they—and then—oh, please, I need to see your healthy legs and replace that horrible vision in my mind."

Enzo was holding Genevieve's hand now, but leaning forward towards him.

"Hey, Colder, you know there's really not a big difference between a pair of boxers and swim trunks. If it makes them feel better? They've been through hell, and—"

"Okay, okay, I'll go upstairs and get a pair of Dad's swim trunks to put on. But *only* because I don't want to see Mom cry anymore." Then he looked at Simon. "*Not* because you ordered me to, Dad. I'm not a little kid anymore, and you can't order me to do something like that."

"Okay, sorry. Sorry. You're right. I—we just want to see. My swim trunks are in the left bottom drawer in the bureau."

Five minutes later, he was back in the living room dressed in a swim suit. He thought they'd all just look from a distance, but oh, no, they had to gather around him like he was a specimen in a museum. His dad reached out, pulled the leg of the trunks up on one side and squeezed his thigh muscle.

Colder jumped back, almost shouting at his dad, "Hey! What are you doing?"

"Oh, good grief, Colder, I was feeling the muscle tone. That's truly miraculous."

"Geez, Dad, you can't go around squeezing people's thighs!"

Simon sighed and rolled his eyes. "It's not like I was squeezing anything higher."

"Well, I hope not, because even if you are my dad, I'd have to hurt you."

"And well you should. Well you should."

Finally satisfied, his dad, gramps, and Jonas slapped his back, his mom and grandma hugged him, Genevieve kissed his cheek, and Luigi slipped out the back door.

##

Madelyn and Elsie trotted with their noses in the air, tracking the scent until they found Stench's ship near the woods. He had a camouflaging mechanism on the outside, and even when they were next to it, they could barely see it. But their noses told them where it was. With Stench's aroma, they didn't need to see.

"Well, we're here. So now what?" Madelyn sent.

"There's no doorbell. Should I bark?"

"Maybe we should scratch at the door?"

"Which would be less intrusive?"

The next moment, their questions were irrelevant as a large panel slid to the side, and Stench stepped out. He saw them standing there, and knew that they needed to see him.

For his species, he was actually a pretty friendly guy. He knew the power that he had over Canids, and he had never abused it or denied any creature access to his presence if he felt it was needed.

He didn't understand why these two were different, but he could receive their sendings, and not just as dogs. They sent in pictures, like the lizards, and in words, like the humans. Very intriguing.

When he stepped towards them, his incredibly powerful stench proved he'd been rightly named, and Madelyn began trembling all over. He turned his back to them in introduction, and they sniffed to their hearts' content. Then they turned their backs to him and he picked each one up and sniffed their rears in polite reciprocation.

Elsie had been determined to see him and smell him once more, but now she didn't know what to send. So they stood and stared at each other until he finally asked them if they'd like to come and live with him. He asked it in pictures, the way the Elpies did, and his meaning was very clear.

Looking at each other, the two dogs were fighting between an almost irresistible yearning to follow him, and the need to stay with their family. Madelyn reminded Elsie that there were children to guard, and Elsie reminded her that after all their people had been through, they would likely need her company when they went to sleep at night.

They both sighed and hung their heads, and then sent that they would love nothing better, but that their duty was here, with their family. He bowed in respect for their faithfulness, and then turned to go back into the ship. He stopped himself though, and instead of entering, as a courtesy and for a remembrance, he went out and peed on a tree. Then he bowed to them again and returned to his vessel.

Running over to the tree, they both sniffed for a good twenty minutes before getting their fill. Madelyn was overwhelmed by his gesture.

"He left this just for us—and he barely knows us."

One more sniff, and the two turned and began walking slowly back to their family, who would never know what the dogs' loyalty had cost them. Looking at the ship a last time, Madelyn bumped shoulders with Elsie companionably and sent, "I think he concentrated the scent in it to make it last."

"So much kindness in one being. Unbelievable."

They strolled on through the night, yearning still, but content with their decision. They'd always have their memories. And their tree.

CHAPTER FIFTY-FOUR

A few hours later, they heard a chopper landing on the site marked out in the field. Colder and Jonas ran out to meet Babette, and each gave her a hand down from the door when it was opened. They waved to the pilot and ran back towards the house.

In spite of how long he'd known her, whenever they'd been separated for a while and Jonas saw her again, he was as stunned by her beauty as he'd been when he first laid eyes on her, and he thought that Colder probably felt the same. Babette was only five feet, three inches, with a perfect little figure, and an air of sweetness mixed with self-confidence and femininity that was hard to resist.

It wasn't that they'd never seen a woman with black hair and blue eyes before. But Babette's face was sharp and soft at the same time. Baby blue eyes with long black lashes, and thick, soft black eyebrows, high cheekbones, skin that always looked just kissed by the sun, sharp straight nose, and a full, sensuous mouth, melded together inside of an oval face set off by an abundance of lustrous black hair—that was Eli's Babette.

Besides her generally sweet nature, one of the most attractive things about Babette was her complete lack of vanity. She never thought of herself as beautiful, though she'd been told all of her life that she was. In her mind, she was simply herself, and what showed on the outside was none of her doing. It had been given to her through genes, so she felt it was nothing to flatter herself about. In this, she and Eli were a perfect pair. Disdainful of their own looks, both thought the other beautiful in body and soul.

She didn't bother greeting her brothers-in-law, other than to thank them for helping her from the chopper. As soon as they were far enough away to hear each other, she asked only, "Where is he?"

They took her straight to the ship, and when they entered, Luca changed the controls on Eli's inducer to wake him for his wife's visit. The rest of the family was waiting there for her, and she nodded to them, but didn't speak. She would do nothing else until she saw Eli.

Luca opened the door to the chamber for her and stepped aside. When she walked in and saw him lying there, propped up slightly, looking so pale and strained, it broke her heart. What hurt the most was that he looked frightened. In all their years together, she had only seen him afraid for *her,* during childbirth, and for the children, when they were hurt or ill. Never had she seen him frightened for himself. He never allowed himself to be.

He tried to smile at her reassuringly, but was having difficulty making it work. Before she spoke to him, she went to the cover over his shoulder and lifted it to look beneath. She gasped and moaned once, and then she stood and stared at it. After a moment, she gently covered it back up and went around the bed to step onto the stool they'd brought in for Aluin. She kept it together until she looked into Eli's face, and then she began to cry.

He reached out his arm to her, and she laid her head against his shoulder, kissing his neck, and raising her head to find his cheek and then his lips. "Oh, *mon coeur,* what they did to you!"

He let a few tears mingle with hers, and he almost felt whole again, just having her next to him, as he buried his face in her hair. Then he fought back the panic and realized he could be strong now. He could be strong for her.

"I'll be fine, Babette. Two days to a new arm—not bad. I'm okay now. I just needed to see you."

"You *will* be fine, Eli. And I'll be waiting right here for you when you wake with your new arm."

She climbed up on the bed then and stretched out next to him. They whispered to each other in French for a while, for she had taught him to speak the important words in that language. He loved telling her how he felt in French.

Somehow the words seemed to hold a deeper meaning that way, because he had learned it, and used it, only for her.

Finally, Luca sent to Eli, "Are you ready to begin? The sooner we start, the sooner you can be back with your family."

He said he was ready and told Babette that she needed to leave him so they could put him to sleep and begin. Suddenly, she was terrified for him—at the idea that they would take away his consciousness and then take away his arm. She sat up but couldn't force herself to let go, with one hand on his arm and the other holding tightly to his hand. Simon came in, enfolded her in his arms, so like his son, gently pulled her free, and helped her down from the bed. She stood on the stool and leaned over to give him one last kiss, and say, "*Je t'aime. Toujours,*" and then let Simon lead her away.

After escorting Babette to the door, he came back and bent over his son to kiss his forehead. "I love you, Eli. Thank you for what you did. Even as big as you are, I'll never know how your body makes room for a heart that huge. I'll see you in a few days and we'll have us a ball game."

Eli smiled and gave him a thumbs up, took a deep breath and corked up the tears. When everyone had left the room, Luca told him he was going to sleep, and he did.

##

On the third morning, he heard Babette calling his name softly and felt her hand on his face. He smiled without opening his eyes, and rolled over to put his arm around her. Her happy laughter brought him awake, and when he opened his eyes he saw tears on her face. She was laughing and holding his right hand to her cheek. His right hand, that he'd moved from the other side of the bed with his normal right arm connected to his normal right shoulder.

His face split in a huge grin and he began laughing. He sat up, started to slide out of bed, and then noticed he was naked. He was about to ask for clothes, but after he'd looked under the sheet, his mom, with a smile so big he thought her face might break, handed him spares she'd thought to bring from his old room. He smiled back at her and nodded his thanks, then addressed the room. "Could everybody turn and face the wall a minute, please?"

They all complied, with the exception of Babette, who couldn't stop looking at him. He slid out of bed, expecting to be dizzy but feeling fine, and had his clothes on in seconds. Then he laughed and picked up his wife to swing her around with his two good arms. He kissed her thoroughly with his two good lips, and then saw what was waiting for him over her shoulder.

His entire family, Harvey, and the Elpies were standing there, smiling, laughing, misting up, and holding their baseball gloves and bats.

"YES!" he yelled, and then whooped, and it was Eli as usual. They hadn't had a good family baseball war in six months, and it was high time for him to whup somebody.

As they were heading out the door, Eli the second, with one arm around Babette, stopped when he saw Luca standing back and watching them. Eli asked his wife to wait for him by the door, and hurried back to Luca.

Having already been the recipient of Eli's thanks once before, Luca was expecting many boisterous acclamations, handshakes and back slappings, but instead, Eli stood in front of him silently as he looked into his eyes. Then he spoke quietly. "Thank you, Luca. Please—look into my mind to understand the meaning behind those words. There's so much more intended."

#

The game was a blow-out. They were used to Eli hitting home runs, but when he hit them that day, those balls were gone for good. They stopped the game just to let him keep hitting, and to watch him celebrate feeling strong and whole once more.

Babette and his parents could have watched him forever, but his grandparents had left earlier to finish the feast they'd been preparing, so the group finally called a halt. They headed back to the house for the meal, despite the fact that they all felt very full already.

CHAPTER FIFTY-FIVE

Two days after their battle with Arthur's men, an incredible story was making its way around the world. Television networks in North America, the UK, and most of Europe and Asia carried the tale, its weird and violent content too intriguing to pass up. Local papers were particularly enthralled, with scandal, mystery, and murder in their own back yard.

Interpol, in conjunction with local authorities, has released a statement to the press concerning a man named Arthur Worthington, recently a resident of this community. Due to an anonymous tip-off to local police, Worthington's home was raided yesterday. Twenty-one bound and blindfolded men were found in a room that had been used to keep animals prior to their release for hunting. All the captives had been beaten, several had cracked bones in their forearms and hands, one had suffered a broken nose, and almost all had sustained concussions, which varied in degrees of severity. A bizarre and frightening story unfolded when the rescued men began telling their tales to police.

At the same time the first call was being placed to local police, another anonymous call was received by Interpol, who contacted the local authorities before the men from Worthington's had even been discovered. The caller had informed Interpol that Worthington had fled the country, but that his men, who had all committed one or more murders in the UK or Europe, were about to be brought in and would give details on their own crimes as well as Worthington's.

Although both agencies were suspicious of a hoax, in the interest of public safety they agreed to pursue the investigation. The rescued men reported that when Worthington was preparing to leave the estate, he'd had all of them corralled at gunpoint by parties unknown to them, beaten, and bound. They were then bluntly informed by Worthington that they had become a liability to him and privy to too much to be allowed to live, so they would be picked up and delivered to their graves by truck.

Worthington has long been suspected by Interpol of smuggling, dealing in the illegal transport and slaughter of exotic and endangered species, money laundering, and multiple murders—in particular, the suspicious deaths of two of his wives. He had also been suspected twice before of the large-scale executions of men who were believed to have worked for him. There has never been enough hard evidence to indict, however, much to the frustration of various law enforcement agencies and the families of his supposed victims.

The almost hysterical confessions given by every one of the men again raised doubts as to the veracity of their stories. But police have reported that when the said individuals began supplying names, dates, locations, and specifics on numerous unsolved murders, DNA testing and fingerprinting were ordered for comparison with existing evidence. The men have expressed to police that they felt their lives would more likely be spared by the government than by Worthington, if he were to lay hands on them again, especially since they could give details on his wives' murders.

At the time of this report, all of the incarcerated men have declared their willingness to testify against him in court. With this curious case of multiple murder confessions, Interpol has expressed the hope that many unsolved murders and disappearances may finally be brought to light, and that justice might be served.

CHAPTER FIFTY-SIX

The water rippled gently in response to the slight breeze, and as the sunlight glittered across the surface, the scene exerted a spellbinding effect on the human and Blueman who sat staring out at the lake. Blanche, Bunny, and Bruno had tagged along when Simon had asked Sven to take a walk with him, and the three Bandicoots were ecstatic to be around water that contained no Uglies. The little ones were even splashing in the shallows, something impossible on their own planet. It would have been an idyllic scene, if not for the piercing shrieks and crazed babbling of the happy threesome.

Sven and Simon had barely sent or spoken as they walked, both simply enjoying the beauty of their surroundings and the company of a friend, and both lost in their own thoughts. Now Simon leaned back against a tree, and continuing to gaze out at the lake, began to talk quietly.

"Sven, my old friend, as usual, we have so much to thank you for. I know that you were able to help us without breaking protocol because the Elpies, your charges, were involved in this nightmare. But you've always gone so far above and beyond to make sure that our lives are left intact whenever you've helped us. Everything you did for us—well, you know how we feel.

"I believe that if this thing with the Elpies hadn't occurred, that sooner or later, Arthur's hatred for me would have driven him to the same horrendous actions that he tried to take against my family this time, only then, we might not have been prepared when it happened. Seeing that house torn apart by bullets, and knowing that my *children* could have been, as well—" Overwhelmed by the vision those words brought to mind, he could say no more. But he didn't need to. Sven was a parent, too.

"Well, anyway, I believe this was a Godsend to spare our family. You know my heart. You can look into our minds and know the gratitude that we feel but can't express in any way that suffices."

Having found his own tree to lean against, Sven reached out without moving the rest of his body, and laid a hand on Simon's shoulder.

"We know. We've heard your words and your sendings, and we do see how you struggle to express more. There's no need. We understand.

"Simon—our relationship with your family and with the Elpies over the years, has been—now *I* don't know how to send it. It's been—one of the driving forces in *my* life, at least. Without you and Gisella, we might not have had The Rebirth, or at least, not as soon. Without Bess' care and understanding, her insight as a female and a partner in your lives, I would never have met Cleo, never have been a father—or at least not to the wonderful two offspring that we've had together.

"Seeing how you and Bess relate to each other and to your children has taught me a great deal. And I have had the privilege of knowing and caring for exceptional human beings. We've met many humans, you know, but we've never truly been friends with any of them. And certainly not good friends—until you and Bess and Gisella came along. Our lives are so much richer for having known you."

Then he laughed. "And our visits have never been dull or uneventful! I think we've used our regrowth machines and other medical equipment more on your family than we ever have on ourselves in all our years of travel together. For a good man, you're very adept at making homicidal enemies."

Simon shook his head, and gave a short laugh. "Don't I know it."

Suddenly, Sven tightened his grip on Simon's shoulder. "Oh, Simon, forgive me. I didn't mean to make light of all you've been through. You and your family have suffered so much pain, and I didn't—"

"No, no, Sven, don't apologize. I understand. It *is* crazy. Bess told me once that she almost feels like it's my destiny to be murdered. I don't. Although when I was looking down the barrel of a shotgun the other night, I found myself agreeing with her. And yes, I'd have to concur that our time together has never been dull."

Sven gave a huge sigh and turned to face Simon. "I was glad when you invited me on this walk. I needed this time with you to say goodbye, Simon. I don't believe I'll ever be able to return. This will be my last trip."

Sven's hand had dropped to his side, and he'd turned back to the lake as he sent those last words. Simon could feel his despondence as he put his hand on Sven's shoulder. "Sven, look at me, please."

Sven turned his head, and his huge eyes focused questioningly on Simon's.

"Colder told me about what happened on the ship—about saving Blanche and the babies. I've sent with Sadie and the rest of your crew since then. They told me that you stand to lose everything because of that one choice you made, and that you made it partly so that *they* wouldn't be haunted by having to leave those innocents to a horrible death. They also told me that you have forbidden them to speak to The Seated to plead your case."

"It was my decision, ultimately. A Leader has to be responsible for the choices he makes. I would not ruin their careers because they have compassion. I would not see their good hearts punished to fight a losing battle. I have skirted protocol and compromised it many times, as I think most Leaders have. But this time, there's no denying it. I willingly, knowingly, made an absolute breach of protocol. The Seated have no choice. They must take my commission away."

He put his head down onto his tall, bent knees. There were no tears. Simon didn't think that Bluemen *could* cry the same way that humans did. But that one posture, so uncharacteristic of this proud creature, spoke clearly of the abject misery he felt at the prospect of his loss.

Without lifting his head, he sent, "But I would not change my decision if I could. I will live many more years, Simon, long after you and Bess are gone. I can live those years without being a Leader, though in truth, the pain will always remain with me. But I could not live those years without a soul, and that is what a different choice would have cost me."

He lifted his head then, and turned to face Simon once more. "My daughter and my crew, including your son, have all expressed their pride at what I did, and that will be enough to sustain me. It will have to be. Sadie assures me that Cleo will feel the same, but of this, I'm not sure. She will still have her commission, but everywhere she goes, she will bear the shame of being married to one who's been removed from his position. Simon, if she leaves me—"

Now Simon saw something else he'd never seen on Sven's face—fear. Fear that the female who had filled his life and his heart for these past fifteen years would reject him. When he felt the emotion behind that sending, he didn't believe that Sven could survive that blow.

"Sven, that's one of the reasons I wanted to talk with you. I want you to let Mona make a disk of me to present to The Seated. That way, your crew won't be penalized. They'll just be delivering a message from me, one of the Bringers. And from Sarah, the Macaroon Maker. I'd go in person, but I'm just too leery after the last couple of times I left Earth. I guess you could call me a coward for that—"

"Never."

"Well, I want—we all want to do this. Please. This is not your doing, or your crew's. This is something that I need to do for myself. For all of us. You are too good a Blueman, too good a Leader, too good a *friend,* to be lost this way. Please. Let us do this."

Turning his head, Sven looked back out at the water, and then at the Bandicoots, shrieking and babbling, *living* and enjoying their lives. "Very well. I don't believe it will change anything, but I thank you for the effort, my friend. I will always be proud to call you that, Simon. I have seen you dead twice, and nearly killed a third time, and yet it hasn't changed who you are. I wish that your race were not so short-lived, though you and Bess will undoubtedly live longer than most. I will miss you greatly."

Simon laughed at that. "Whoa there, I'm still alive, and I intend for you to be making lots more visits here, so don't go missing me just yet. And Sven—you will always have a place in my heart."

The two sat in silence for a few more minutes before rising to head back, comforted by and clinging to the camaraderie that they knew might be at an end. When they finally started walking, Simon spoke again. "Besides, you have to come for the wedding. Genevieve said if you and the Elpies can't come for the ceremony, a big wedding without all of you would make her too sad, so they'll just elope. Bess wants to give her only daughter a huge wedding, and she'd kill me if I didn't make it right for you so that you can come. You don't want to be responsible for my getting killed a third time, do you?"

"Certainly not."

"It's settled then. We'll see you in six months."

##

"Hey Sven." Colder, Luigi, and Micah stepped into the ship after taking their own walk. Sven nodded to them, and then continued in his preparations for take-off. "Uh, could we talk with you for a minute?"

Sven stopped what he was doing, stood up and came to sit on one of the main room 'sofas.' This seemed to be his day for talks.

"Well, you probably already know what we need to say. In fact, I would imagine that *you'd* be starting this conversation if we weren't." The Blueman's expression was noncommittal, as usual, and no sendings were flying into his brain, so Colder continued.

"The thing is, none of the three of us feels like—I mean, the Elpies and myself—"

"Why is this so difficult for you to tell me, Colder? You want to say that you don't think traveling in space is the life for you. You're right. It isn't. Are you afraid that I'll be angry, or disappointed with you?"

Both Elpies were sending an affirmative. Colder had a little different mindset. "Well, yeah, because we'd hate to do either—disappoint or anger you. But I have this feeling that just maybe you'll be relieved at our decision, so that you won't have to throw us off the ship."

Sven began to laugh in a way that they didn't think Bluemen could. They'd seen chuckles, and little polite laughs, but this was a belly laugh. Coming away from her pre-departure duties at the sound, even Sadie was shocked. Then Colder realized it was one of those laughs that hit, not because something was so funny, but because it served as a release of tension. The kind of laugh that was hard to stop, and occasionally turned into tears. His mom had this weird laugh that only came out when she was super tired or stressed, and it creeped out everybody in the family. This reminded him of that.

Sven laughed for a full ten seconds—a very long laugh for a Blueman. Sadie sat down beside him, putting a hand on his arm. "Father, are you all right?"

He settled himself, looking at her sweet eyes, so full of concern, and laid his hand on her face, the way the Elpies did. He'd learned much from them. Then he smiled at her, the way Cleo had taught him after watching the humans. He'd learned much from them, as well.

But he was so relieved that these three would not be 'crewmen,' anymore. They were not suited for this life. And with his record for putting one or more Sayers in mortal jeopardy whenever they left Earth, he couldn't risk having one of them on his ship again. It was a moot point, though. This would no longer be his ship once the journey ended.

"Colder, you're a very astute young human. I would never have *thrown you off,* but I did feel that we needed to discuss the possibility that this was not the place for you. I'm greatly relieved that you've come to that conclusion yourselves. I'd been dreading causing offense to any of you.

"None of you were meant to spend long hours confined in a ship. I was made in a laboratory that picked the attributes necessary for prolonged space travel and put those into my make-up. The same genetic manipulation was used in the making of the rest of my crew, except for Sadie, and she's been traveling in space with her mother and me for her whole life. It's a natural choice for her to make. It's only right that you should choose more natural lives for yourselves."

Colder was overcome with relief. And he realized now, that part of the dread he'd been harboring about telling him was because of the way he felt—no, the way *they all felt*—about Sven.

"Uh, speaking of natural, I know that this isn't a natural thing for Bluemen, but I also know you understand it. I saw the way you hugged my dad when he was about to lose his mind at the thought that Arthur had escaped the other night. That was exactly what he needed right then—somebody bigger and stronger to just stop him and take over for a few minutes. I want to thank you for that, Sven, and for everything else you've done. I think you're a great Blueperson, and I can't imagine anyone being a better Leader. And after saying all that, what I'd really like right now is to give *you* a hug, if that's okay with you."

Sven was flattered and moved by Colder's speech *and* by the request, but could think of no appropriate response, so he simply stood up and opened his arms.

Colder walked up and plastered himself against his friend, hugging him tightly, thinking that this might be the last time he had a chance to. Before he could break it off, Luigi and Micah had piled on, too, with their bony arms poking his back and ribs here and there, but nothing potentially fatal. Then Sadie added her three arms, and the rest of the crew, who'd been watching, came out and threw their bulk into it.

Now it was more like being buried in an avalanche of flesh than a group hug, and Colder thought he might actually die in there. Maybe Sven was right about it being lethal for the Sayers on his ship. He started pushing back, saying, "Hey guys, guys, a little air here!"

The Elpies caught his panic and need for oxygen, so they began to push back too, and the hug was ended with no casualties. Goodbyes were said, spacesuits returned, and Colder felt another huge weight come crashing off his shoulders.

##

Two days later, the ship left Earth. It was a more prolonged and sad goodbye than usual, for Sven was sure he would never see any of these humans again, and that thought hurt him beyond what he ever would have imagined. Genevieve informed him that she would take no excuses for him missing her wedding, and refused to consider the possibility that he might not return. Bess' face was so red and puffed up by the time they'd finished seeing Sven off, that even her own mother thought she looked—only at this particular moment, of course—fairly hideous.

Simon and Sarah, with the crew's help, had done their best with the disk, and could only pray that The Seated would be lenient. It was unthinkable that someone like Sven could be destroyed for an act of kindness.

Blanche and the little ones were going home with the Elpies. Micah was planning to take them under his wing and introduce them to the Elpie way of life. He knew that his village would accept the three, and give Blanche that sense of family and tribe that she felt the loss of so keenly. If he could just stop her shrieking.

Eli the first and Dulcie were overjoyed at the thought of their son coming home to stay, and Eli believed that helping Blanche to deal with her grief would help him to live with his own.

CHAPTER FIFTY-SEVEN

After the ship left, Colder had a talk with both of his parents, and asked if he could stay in his old room for about a month. He was going to take a leave of absence from his job and work some things out in his head.

He hated lying, but he had to tell his boss something, so he made up some lame story about a car accident, and his nerves being frazzled since the wreck. Surprisingly, the man was very understanding, which made him feel even more like a low-life for lying, but also made him even more sure that he'd like to go into business with him.

Nightmares had begun plaguing him more and more lately, and they were so frightening and ghastly that he'd started going to great lengths to avoid closing his eyes. He would read, draw, write, drink coffee, take long walks in the dark by himself, but eventually his body would rebel and he would once again be plunged into the horror of the past. Trying to get by on as little sleep as possible was wearing him down physically *and* mentally, so that when sleep would finally take him against his will, his dreams were even more terrifying than before.

He'd be back on that planet, falling into the pool of sludge again, but in his dreams, he would be sucked down over his head and gasping for air as he saw those gray masses of slime coming towards his face from all directions. Or he would find himself in a room, all alone except for the masses that were on his arms, chest and face, chewing, slowly chewing through his skin to get to the blood and meat beneath. Several times, he'd awakened the next day with deep scratches where he'd tried to claw the things off.

His dad had woken him once, his mom twice, when his thrashing about or his screams had brought them rushing to his room in the middle of the night. He was so terrified after one dream, that he actually held his arms out to his mother and let her hold him as if her were a child, until his shaking stopped.

She sat there on the edge of his bed as he leaned into her arms, and she stroked his hair with one hand while she held him close with her other, rocking gently. His dad sat on the bed, leaning against the headboard and rubbing his back, quietly reassuring him with his voice and his touch, that he was safe.

When Colder calmed down enough to feel embarrassed and told his parents to go back to bed, Bess left him and went to the phone to call Gisella and Hiram. They agreed to send Madelyn over straight away.

After his mom had left the room, his dad told him that he wanted to stay for a while, and Colder didn't argue when he made himself comfortable in a chair, with his long legs stretched out on the bed. He pretended that his big feet just happened to be planted up against his son's. Had Colder still been a child, he would have climbed into bed with him and held his hand while he slept, but at his age, the foot approach had the same effect without insulting his manhood.

Even as shaken as he was, Colder was so exhausted from his chronic lack of sleep that he slipped off again within a few minutes. Instantly, he was back in that room, with the slime stretching out to cover his face, but this time it was different. Just before it touched him, he saw a hand reach in front of his face to intercept the hideous mass, grasp it roughly, and throw it to the ground. And there was his dad, stomping mercilessly on the creature to crush it under his boots. Picking up the remains of it then, he held it up so that Colder could see it, and shot fire out of his hand to set the thing ablaze. He held it up, oblivious to the flames, until the offending mass had turned to ash. Then he leaned over, kissed Colder's forehead and left the room.

He thought he was safe then, but when he looked around him, he saw that now he was underwater and the thing was swimming towards him like a shark. He was trying to scream and swim away, but couldn't move or cry out. Suddenly, a hand shot down through the water, and this time he knew it was his dad's.

He grabbed his arm, pulled him up out of the water and set him on his feet on dry land. Then he reached back in the water, taking hold of the huge, slug-like mass, and with a furious roar, pulled it out of its refuge. He held it up in front of him and snarled, then folded, wadded, and rolled it up to the size of a gumball, and popped it in his mouth. He chewed it for a few minutes, and Colder could hear the horrible screeches of the creature as it was being pulverized. When his dad finished chewing, he spit it onto the ground, where it dissolved into foam and water. Then he brushed his hands off loudly, in a gesture of finality, gave a curt nod to the spot where only wet ground remained, winked at his son, and walked out, and Colder was no longer afraid.

He slept then, for seven hours straight, the longest period of undisturbed sleep he'd had since the dreams had started. When he woke up, his dad was still in his chair, feet still firmly pressed against his own. He was awake, watching him as he sipped on a cup of coffee.

"Were you awake all night?"

"Pretty much."

Sliding out of bed, Colder went to his dad's chair and stood beside it. "I need for you to put down your coffee and stand up, Dad."

Simon raised his eyebrows, but did as requested.

Colder looked closely at his father's eyes as he spoke. "You followed me into my dreams, didn't you?"

His dad gave a slight smile and shrugged his shoulders.

"You chewed up the damn boogie man for me."

He reached out and pulled his father into his arms, hugging him tightly, and when their heads were side by side, he spoke, his voice cracking just a little. "I don't know how you did it, Dad, but thank you so much. You don't know what that sleep did for me. It's like my whole body was starving for it."

When Colder let go, his dad put his hands behind his head and tilted it forward to meet his own. They stayed that way for a few seconds, touching foreheads in silence. Then he released him and sat back in his chair. Colder sat on the bed and leaned back on his pillows to listen as his dad began to talk quietly.

"When I was living with the Elpies, in those years before I met your mother, I was Eli's assistant—you know that. Sometimes when patients had a high fever, or had been injured, fever dreams or recurring nightmares would keep them from getting the sleep they needed to heal, so Eli taught me how to go into someone's dreams to help."

Bess walked in to listen, newspaper in hand, and stood leaning against the door sill behind Simon, who heard but didn't acknowledge her.

"It was the most difficult skill I ever had to master, next to living with your mother—" He winced as the rubber band she'd just taken off the paper popped him in the back of the head. He half smiled, but kept talking. "—and not even all Elpies are capable of it. The same as when you're tasting someone's pain, if you're not careful, or don't know what you're doing, you can get lost and that pain or terror becomes your reality. But Eli was an excellent teacher. That was so many years ago, I'd forgotten about it until I saw you last night. Then I wasn't sure I could still do it.

"No matter how old you get, Colder, I'll never stop wanting to protect you. It kills me to think of what you went through on that planet, and now to know that you're still being hurt—to see how it's draining you—" He shook his head, his expression full of anger and frustration. "When I saw you last night, all I wanted was to go in there and destroy that thing that's been tormenting you—to smash it to dust or rip it apart with my teeth—whatever I had to do. And suddenly I realized that maybe I could, for a while. At least long enough for you to get some solid sleep. I'm just sorry I didn't think of it sooner."

Madelyn had been waiting for him to wake up, and when she walked into the room, Simon stood up, bestowed a dad kiss on his son's head, picked up his cup and turned to leave so that the two of them could be alone to send in private. Colder watched him walking away, blithely sipping his coffee, and he wondered if his father had just risked his sanity to slay his son's dragon.

He jumped off the bed and grabbed his dad's free hand. When he turned to look at him, he tried to send as he spoke, so that he would really understand.

"Thanks again, Dad. For this and—everything else."

He knew his dad had caught his sending, because his expression changed and his eyes were suddenly shiny. He nodded and gave a warm smile.

"Just doing my job, son." He closed the door but then stuck his head back in and winked. "And I really love my job."

Madelyn and Colder sent for a long time that night, and she sent that she intended to sleep in his room with him for as long as he chose to stay at the house. She began spending her time with him during the day as well, for she understood that her gift for healing was the real reason that Colder had remained. Pride had kept him from asking for her—asking for her to leave the children to come and stay with him, a grown man. Madelyn loved her family, but sometimes they could be so addlepated.

##

Genevieve and Enzo were packed and ready for their drive to the airport, when they asked to sit down with Simon and Bess.

"Mom, Dad, we wanted to talk about *after* the wedding."

"Okay."

"Well, we'd like to take you up on your offer of building a house for us on the estate. We'd like to live here."

Bess screamed and clapped her hands and Simon pumped the air and hollered, "YES!"

Enzo was grinning from ear to ear. "You know, when Gen first told me about you wanting to give us a house, I really wasn't for it at all. I always pictured providing for my family, and this seemed like too much of a handout. My pride was dinged. And the idea of living close to her parents didn't particularly appeal to me, either. But that was before I got to know you.

"This has been the craziest, wildest, most exciting, dangerous, gut-wrenching two weeks of my life. I could never go back to just being around normal people all day. I want to be able to have my talks with Ishmael about Chess, and get Elsie's take on Gen's dog. And I want to know that when we have kids, Elsie and Madelyn will assign themselves guard duty, like they do with Hiram and Gisella's kids. I want to visit with the Elpies and Bluemen when they come to call, and I *really* want to be able to *talk* about the Bluemen and Elpies and everything else without worrying that I'm gonna be locked up.

"There's this other thing, too. When I was growing up, I always wished I had brothers. That's one of the things I love about being a fireman—I have a bunch of brothers at the station. But when I came here—well, geez, within a couple of days, I felt like I had myself three new brothers, and I'd like to be able to see everybody more than just once or twice a year."

Then the two proceeded to tell them about the tentative job offers that both had looked into already. Neither had any doubt that they'd be employed as soon as they were free of their present commitments.

"You have no idea how happy you've just made your father and me."

Enzo smiled at Genevieve, and then turned to them. "We're pretty happy about it ourselves."

"Now all I have to do is break it to my parents. I'm sure my mom will see this as a complete betrayal. She probably figured we'd move back to Boston eventually. So if there are four empty chairs on the groom's side at the wedding, you'll know why."

"You don't really believe that, do you?" Bess asked.

He thought about it for a minute before he answered. "No. I know they'll come to the wedding. Well, at least my dad and sisters. Mom will come too, but she may never forgive me. She might not speak to me at the wedding."

"I have an idea about that, but let's deal with it later. We have to get you to the airport on time. I'll call our architect tomorrow, and get some plans in the works. I'll be sending you his ideas, to get your approval and input. Umm--how many kids are you planning on?"

"Dad, don't even go there right now. It might be a bunch, or maybe just two. Or three. We don't know yet. Let us be married for a while before you start demanding offspring, okay?"

"Well don't get all defensive. I wasn't giving you a deadline. I just wondered how many bedrooms we should have built."

"Let's help them get their luggage loaded. We can talk about family planning later."

#

When they'd gotten into their car, Simon, after saying goodbye to both of them, went over to Enzo's side and made him roll down the window.

"One more thing, Enzo. I just wanted you to know that I'm very proud of my daughter and—"

"Yes sir, you should be."

"I'm very proud of the choices she's made—"

"Yes sir, you should be."

Simon sighed and looked around Enzo to his daughter. "Can you make him be quiet long enough for me to finish?"

She laughed and Enzo zipped his fingers across his tightly sealed lips.

"Anyway, I just wanted to tell you that I think you're the best choice she ever made."

He sat there, shocked and delighted at the same time, and then got out of the car, reached up, snagged Simon's neck, pulled him down, and planted a Dad kiss *on him.*

CHAPTER FIFTY-EIGHT

When they landed, Sven had to wind things up on the ship before he could leave. Sadie left while he was still working, to give the crew time to say their goodbyes. She knew these would be difficult for everyone.

Sven was so thankful for The Rebirth on this day. It would have been impossible before, and it still felt awkward, but Sven was able to look all of his crew in the eye and tell them how much they meant to him. He thought them the finest crew he had ever served, and he loved each of them for being loyal voyagers, and his true and faithful friends. To be able to tell them that meant the world to him.

The crew told him much the same, but also spoke of their respect for his skill and wisdom as a Leader, and thanked him for the honor of serving under him.

#

When he'd finally finished checking the instruments and sealing the ship, he turned to leave, only to find Cleo standing just beyond the landing pad, waiting for him. Her face was a picture of grief and anger, and he knew then that Sadie had told her, and that his marriage was over.

He walked over to stand before her, as he must, not knowing what to say, or if he could even speak. He found himself unwilling to meet her eyes; unwilling to see the look of betrayal and reproach that would lie there. The look she would pierce him with before leaving him. He stood desolate, awaiting her castigation.

"Sven, why won't you look at me?"

"I don't—I don't think I *can* look—I don't want to see you walk away."

Her three arms slid around him, and then he did look at her.

"I came here to say how privileged I feel to be married to a Leader such as you. When our daughter told us what you did, and how proud she was of you, I couldn't stay and wait for you at home. I needed to tell you here, so that your heart would be at ease when you walked away from this ship. The only anger I feel is at the thought of you being hurt because you made the right decision, in spite of what it might cost you.

"If the Council is foolish enough to censure you for this, then it is *their* loss, not yours. You have always been and will always be the finest Leader I have ever known, and the finest Blueman. So never, *never* let me see you with your head bowed in shame. You will face the council with dignity and pride in the knowledge that you have served with decency and honor, no matter the cost to yourself. For that is what a true Leader does."

In that moment, he wished fervently that he could shed tears like the humans did, for the relief, joy, and love that her message unleashed in him were beyond the skill of words. So he simply folded his arms around her as he let his heart soar.

##

The Seated stared at the log screen on the table and then looked at Sven standing before them. They had not had him bound, as they thought his sense of duty would prevent him from fleeing.

"We have read the charges against you, and your plea of guilty to all of them. This is most unusual for a Leader to bring forth evidence against himself. We have also viewed the disk made by the Bringer, Simon Sayers, and the Maker of Macaroons, Sara McPhinney.

"Furthermore, your entire crew reported to this assembly two days ago."

"What? But I ordered—"

"Yes. You ordered them not to appear. You took the responsibility of breaking protocol on yourself, as you should have, since you made the final choice. Your crew disobeyed you by coming here. They broke protocol by disobeying your order. How should we punish them?"

"Please, do not censure them. They did this out of loyalty to me. And perhaps—perhaps it's not a true break, since they were no longer aboard ship, and they knew that I would be stripped of my Leadership."

"Have you watched the disk?"

"No. I thought that would be—inappropriate."

"Be seated, Leader. We want for you and your family to know its contents."

In the air above The Seated, Simon stood, nervously looking at a handful of notes, unaware that he was already being recorded. Suddenly he jerked his head up, almost dropping his papers, and looked into the recorder. The translation of his words was written in the Bluemen's language at the bottom of the picture.

"Most Honorable Council Members, my name is Simon Sayers. I have made this disk in order to speak on behalf of my friend and your Leader, whom we refer to as 'Sven,' being unable to pronounce his true name.

"My family and I have known Sven for many years now. He has saved my life twice, and on your planet, risked his own life to save two other members of my family. On his most recent trip, his crew was responsible for keeping two of my sons alive when their situations had become desperate.

"The longer I have known Sven, the more I've come to respect him. He is a Blueman of the utmost honor and integrity. He leads his crew, but will always put their welfare before his own. His crew members have informed me that, against his wishes, they intend to speak with you and show you recordings of the beings that they saved from certain death.

"My son was aboard that ship, and he spoke to me of how this Leader led a party of his crew into an environment that was hostile far beyond what the ship's instruments had indicated. Every member of that party returned to the ship alive, on a large part, because of the courage and wisdom of this Leader's actions.

"I have spent time with the beings that he broke protocol to save. These are not soulless creatures merely going through the cycle of life and death, but individuals with hearts and minds, who suffer and long for the family and friends that have been lost to them. The adult female, whom we call 'Blanche,' sent to me in great detail about the life and death of her mate and her family. She sent to me about the fine qualities that her mate possessed, and how she still dreams of him lying next to her and her children at night. She sent to me of the loss of her other children to the animals that Sven's crew saved her from, and it was the agony of a bereft mother that I felt in her sendings.

"Blanche risked her life to save an orphaned infant on her planet. This was a courageous act to preserve the life of one unrelated to her. Even though she was already taxed almost beyond endurance by the effort to keep herself and her one remaining child alive, her mother's spirit would not allow her to leave an infant to die alone.

"When a madman on my planet captured our Elpie friend, Eli, he was going to use him for *sport*—to be torn apart by huge Canids. My family launched an attempt to free him and his wife, who was also a prisoner. At one point during this attempt, my son Jonas and my daughter's fiancé were about to be attacked by these beasts, and both men would have been mauled and likely killed, had there been no intervention. But Blanche ran across the path of those Canids to distract and lead them away—an incredible act of bravery to save the lives of two humans—members of a species she had only a slight knowledge of.

"These are the acts of a being worth saving. Of a species worth saving. The purpose of the ship that Sven leads is exploration—to gain a knowledge of all living things in the universe. The fact that this female and the two little ones might very well be the last of their kind, should by itself be reason enough for Sven to have broken protocol to save them.

"As I understand it, these protocols were written before The Rebirth, when you were all told who you were and what you were to become almost from the time you were created. Protocols took the place of judgement. There was no room for independent decision making or compassion in the old world. Nor in the protocols. When you established The Rebirth, you gave your people the gift of free thought, emotions, and relationships.

"I am told that after I was killed and given back my life here, that a sort of shrine was made in remembrance of my actions, and those of my family. We are deeply honored by this. The actions we took were to protect each other. I sacrificed my life to save my family, as any father would.

"What Sven did is far more remarkable. He sacrificed his life as a Leader, for beings that he had never even met. They reached out to him as their only chance for survival. Their pitiful cries of desperation tortured his crew, and all of them, my son included, begged him to save these helpless ones. When he agreed to do so, it was also to save the hearts of his crew, who knew they would never be at peace if they turned away and let these creatures die a terrible death.

"Sven has always been an exemplary leader, but on that day, he personified everything that The Rebirth stands for. He let his love for his crew and his compassion for other living souls make his choice for him, knowing that he would be ending his career. A career that he was *created* for. A career that has been his life.

"What is the purpose of protocols that disallow everything you've worked so hard to regain with The Rebirth? If compassion and kindness are crimes, then Sven is more than guilty. But I say that if the protocols make crimes of these, then it is the protocols that need to be changed, and not this Blueman.

"I believe that Sven is a credit to his station and a gift to his society. I beg you to see him for what he is—more than worthy of his title; a true Leader who brings honor to the world that he serves.

"Thank you for hearing my words."

Simon bowed and stepped out of sight.

Then Sarah came into view, and she was holding a macaroon. She took a slow, lingering bite, and sighed in pleasure as she chewed. After she swallowed, she stared directly into the recorder and licked the crumbs off her lips. The Bluepeople in the room were close to drooling.

"You know who I am. I am Sarah, the Maker of Macaroons. Sven is my friend, and I can't imagine there being a better Blueman on our world or yours. I know a lot of extraterrestrials, as we call them, but Sven is different. He's kind, honest, wise, and he has this great dignity. It would be hard not to respect someone like him.

"Now, I don't know *beans* about your protocols, except that if they cause him to lose his job, then they stink to high Heaven. I know that he wouldn't want me saying this, because he's too proud, and too much of a —a soldier, I guess you'd say. But if you hurt my friend, I would be so upset that I would likely lose my desire to ever make macaroons again. I might just wither away and die of grief.

"I've given the recipe to you people, but you swear that no one can make them as good as I can. So if you really love your macaroons, then you'd better *damn* well take care of me and *not hurt my friend*! Do I make myself clear? That's all I have to say. Except that I'm sorry if I sounded rude, and I really shouldn't have cursed. That was bad manners on my part. Sorry. I'm just so mad. Please excuse me."

The picture went black, and the court addressed Sven again.

"Leader, stand before the Council of The Seated to receive your sentence."

Sven came forward and stood with his back straight and head up.

"Leader, this council has listened to the disk of the Bringer and the Maker of Macaroons. We have discussed the Bringer's words at length, and we believe them to be true and wise. You have always served well, Leader, with dignity and loyalty befitting your position. This council finds your actions honorable and your courage in taking these actions, commendable.

"However, we must find you guilty of knowingly and willfully breaking protocol, and therefore retribution is required of us, if our laws are to have any meaning. It is the judgement of this Council, therefore, that you will be sequestered with the members of your crew for five hours each day, for however long it takes to write new protocols.

"Understand that we do not hand down such a despicable punishment lightly. We know full well the fear that lengthy committee meetings strike in the hearts of all civilized beings. It is the hope of this Council that you may survive your sentence to serve our world as a Leader once again. This Tribunal of the Council of The Seated is dismissed."

CHAPTER FIFTY-NINE

Four hundred guests were assembled in a meadow across from the lake. An archway had been built over a raised platform where the couple was to say their vows, and it stood at the end of the meadow, almost touching the trees of the forested area behind it. Within the trees, painted in colors to match the woods and blend in as much as possible, was a two story chalet whose second floor was done all the way across in heavily tinted glass.

The giant float, swing, canoe and all the normal water toys the family used had been removed, so that a pristine picture of a crystal clear lake lay to the right of the guests. Actually, to the left of fifteen of the guests—the guests in the chalet in the woods. They faced the wedding arch from the opposite side, and they would see the bride and groom from the front as they said their vows.

These fifteen guests had come from a different direction than the rest, and had arrived a day early, in the dead of night, to get safely situated beyond the view of the rest of the guests. The chalet was long, to prevent the quarters from feeling cramped, but narrow in the front, so as not to be too visible a distraction behind the platform.

The archway, bare wooden latticework yesterday, was now completely covered with roses. The roses at each end of the arch were deep red, but as it rose from the ground, the colors changed to reds in increasingly lighter shades that gave way to pink, light pink, and eventually to white above where the couple was to stand.

The chalet had been lavishly stocked with every kind of goodie imaginable to keep Elpies and Bluepeople amused while they waited for the ceremony to begin.

At the opposite end of the meadow, two tents had been set up: one for the groom and his party, and one for the bride and hers, and within each tent were partitions allowing for a dressing room and a waiting area.

#

He was pacing and going from sitting to standing, to pacing again. "Aah, geez, I'm nauseated now. Is it hard to breathe in here, or is it just me? It's—there's just no air in here. I feel like I might pass out. I *never* shook like this before, even when I walked into my first fire. What's to be nervous about, right? I know I want to marry Gen. But oh, geez, I'd rather be in a burning building right now."

Enzo's best man, his cousin Umberto Uccello, who'd also been his best friend almost since birth, was starting to worry a little. "Enzo, chill. You're looking a little pale, my man. Oh boy, you're not going to keel over in the middle of your vows, are you? And please, please tell me you're not going to hurl on her dress."

"Do you *have* to put ideas like that in my head?"

His groomsmen consisted of Vincenzo, another cousin, Ernesto, a fellow firefighter, and the three Sayers brothers. They were all milling around in the little dressing room area, waiting to be called out, until Eli opened the flap to the waiting room. "Hey guys, could you all please step out and let me talk to Enzo for a sec?"

It was getting pretty claustrophobic in there, and none of the others had ever dealt with a semi-hysterical groom before, so he was happily obliged.

Taking Enzo by the arm, Eli physically sat him down in one of the folding chairs. He'd brought in a cold glass of water and a dry cotton towel from the caterers, and as he sat down across from Enzo, he offered these up to him.

"Oh, thank you, thank you." He guzzled the water and blotted his face. Eli thought he really might faint, he looked so panicked. He took the glass and the towel back, set them down, and leaned forward to get Enzo's attention.

"Hey, buddy, look at me. That's right. Breathe with me now. Good. Slow, even breaths. Yeah, that's better. You got it now, smooth and easy. No, no, keep looking at me. Good. Enzo—you're sure you want this, right?"

"Oh, yeah, yeah, yeah. I can't even imagine a future without Genevieve in it. I don't want to. I think it's the crowd and the fact that everything changes after today. I don't know why I feel so wired. It's like inside I'm just one big coiled spring."

"Let me tell you a secret. You know how much Babette and I mean to each other, right? From the first time I saw her, I wanted to marry her. As corny as that sounds, it's the truth. But I was just like you at my wedding."

"For real?"

"Oh yeah, maybe worse. My dad thought he might have to knock me out and carry me down the aisle. My legs were shaking like crazy and felt like they were going to give out on me, but I finally made it to the front of the church. So I was standing there, wondering if I was going to faint at the last minute, and then—I saw her.

"I saw the most beautiful woman in the world coming down that aisle, and it hit me that she was coming *for me*. She was giving her life *to me*. She looked at me and smiled, and her eyes—oh, geez, I can't even describe what her eyes said to me. And at that moment, all the nervousness left. It was like— it was just Babette and me, and this was where I'd been heading my whole life. Seeing her coming to me made everybody else disappear, and all I could feel was happiness and love. And gratitude that God had somehow worked this out."

"Oh, that's beautiful, Eli. You think it'll be that way for me?"

"I know it will. If we can just get you to that arch without you losing it, you've got it made. When you see Genevieve in that gorgeous dress, your beautiful bride coming *for you*—to join her life to yours, everything else is going to just melt away around you."

His shaking had almost stopped while he listened to Eli's story, and suddenly he felt calm. He was here *for her*. She was here *for him*. And nothing would keep him from being there under that arch to take her hand when she offered it.

Eli stood up, leaned over and did a dad kiss on the top of Enzo's head.

"Or, if that doesn't work, we can always set the arch on fire and you'd *have* to run up there."

They laughed and punched each other, and then Enzo said, "You know something Eli?"

"What?"

"I'm so freakin' happy that you're gonna be my brother."

Eli smiled and punched his arm again, but very lightly this time. "I already am, Enzo. I already am."

##

Bess couldn't get over it. Genevieve was the coolest, calmest bride she'd ever seen. She laughed and chatted with her bridesmaids as if she was having lunch with them at the mall. Gisella was her matron of honor, and her childhood friends, Abigail, Justine, and Bethany, and her nieces, Viola Marie and Simone rounded out the bridesmaids. Little Noele, Eli's youngest, was the flower girl.

Duncan and Aluin were going to carry the rings on the pillow together, and they were both in the groom's tent, waiting with their dads. Simon was pacing around outside like a caged animal, because he didn't want to see Genevieve in her dress until he got ready to walk her down the aisle. He thought it was a good thing that the Bluemen had replaced his heart, because as anxious as he was, he might have blown an old one all to pieces.

Straightening Genevieve's veil and train, and then coming around to look at her face, Bess sighed and steeled herself one more time. She'd been working on self-hypnosis with tapes and books for the last two months, to be sure she would *not* cry at the wedding. For once in her life, she was not going to have her face blow up like a puffer fish and turn red and blotchy. She was NOT going to have her eyes swell up, because she wanted to see the *whole* wedding and everybody in it. She'd made it, so far. She would let herself cry *after* everything was over. But today, she wanted her daughter to be proud of the way she looked, and not feel like she had to make excuses for her mother's grotesque appearance.

She was dressed in a full length, shimmery, silver sheath, with a slightly darker jacket in the same type of material flowing past her hips, with silver cuffs and silver borders down each side of the jacket, and she felt beautiful and elegant. But nothing like her daughter. Genevieve made the *gown* look gorgeous.

"Honey, aren't you even a little bit nervous?"

She smiled at her mother and shook her head. "No, Mom. In fact, I've never felt so---serene. I am so sure of Enzo--- I know we were meant for each other. And as for the wedding and the reception, I was nervous about all that before today. But now, everything that needed doing has been done, and if something goes wrong, big deal. At the end of the day, we'll still be married. The time for worry is over, Mom. Let's just enjoy. This day feels completely, absolutely---right. I am so ready to marry him."

Bess hugged her gently, careful to avoid putting anything askew. "You are the most beautiful thing I've ever seen. I love you so much, and I can't say that anymore because I am NOT going to cry and be a freak show at your wedding."

"All right, Mom! You can do it!" Genevieve cheered. The whole family was rooting for Bess.

#

The bridesmaids were up at the platform with the groom and his groomsmen. The relatives had been seated, and Simon stood outside of the tent, waiting to see his daughter. When the tent flap was pulled back, and she emerged, he cried out, "Oh my!" and his eyes filled up. Everyone turned to see what Simon had shouted about, but then they saw her, and they knew.

She took his arm, and whispered, "Sshh, Daaad." He tried to say something to her but he couldn't without losing control. She looked up at his "Dad eyes" and trembling jaw, and whispered, "I love you, Daddy." He caught those words and wrapped his heart tightly around them. Then he took a deep breath, stood tall, and started down the aisle with this vision that was his daughter

They had laid a temporary floor between the chairs to make the pathway to their destination straight and smooth. The bride and her father walked down that pathway to Handel's Water Music, and she looked like royalty. When Enzo saw her, he knew Eli had been right. Everything else disappeared. No hesitancy, no nerves, no more. He had never seen a more beautiful woman than this serene, statuesque, flame-haired principessa in white, coming *to him*. For *him*.

##

When the party in the chalet saw Genevieve, Blanche let out a deafening shriek and a babble, and Dulcie frantically grabbed her muzzle, clamping it shut. Everyone in the room sent a mental "Sshhhhh!" and she did her best to restrain herself after that.

The earsplitting cry was heard by the whole congregation. They'd stood to face the bride, but half of them whirled back towards the sound. Bess leaned towards them, and said in her loudest stage whisper, "Peacocks. Crazy, crazy birds!"

#

When they'd said their vows, and had that first kiss as husband and wife, before they turned to face the congregation, they both looked towards the window of the chalet and blew kisses.

When Sven saw that, he thought if he hadn't been a Leader anymore, he would have stowed away with Cleo to be here today. He looked at his crew and knew they felt the same. And he knew, like him, they were probably remembering the start of all this.

Simon lying dead from poison in an Elpie tent. Bess, crazed with fear, anger, and grief, attacking Sven when he stepped out of the ship, demanding that they help this man. They could tell by the state she was in, that she must love him. They had restored him, and when they had opened the ship's door, not only Bess and Gisella, but the whole Elpie village had been waiting there, hoping and praying for his survival.

Sven and his crew had watched from the ship as the three humans had flown into each other's arms, and then the whole village had descended on Simon. Sven had felt the mass of sendings expressing love for these humans and joy at Simon's return to life.

That was the start of it. A family had begun that day, not just of humans and Elpies, but of Bluepeople as well. They'd become a part of each other's lives, and formed surprising bonds that had grown stronger over the years. They seemed to have come full circle today. Simon and Bess, giving their youngest in marriage. And instead of turning away and going into the waiting arms of all their human friends, these two who had just become a family, had turned to the *rest* of their family in *this* house, to express their love. His own daughter and son, Eli's son, and

Barnabas' son stood here to receive that love along with their parents. The next generation of family.

Cleo squeezed one of his hands, Sadie held another, and his third hand rested on the shoulder of his son, and once more, he wished that Bluemen could cry.

##

At the reception, Simon and Bess sat across from Enzo's parents. Enzo's mom had been a bit cool at first, until he and Genevieve had driven them to the house the Sayers had built for them, and they saw that twenty yards away was a little cottage, with a sign over the door that said "Giuseppe and Angelina's Place." Having a guest house already prepared for them made them understand that their visits were welcomed by everyone, and that helped to take the sting out of the new couple's moving away.

Genevieve had let her men choose the music for their two dances. When Simon had his dance with Genevieve, to the song, "I Loved Her First," by Heartland, he couldn't dance it all the way through. He heard the words, and they rang so true that finally, all he could do was just hold her and sway to the music with his eyes closed. He wanted to memorize the feel of her in his arms one last time—his baby, his little girl, his young woman—before she went into another man's arms to stay.

When the song ended, he took both of her hands in his and kissed them, and then walked her over to Enzo and placed her hands in his.

Bess thought she might be having a stroke. Trying to hold back the tears was giving her the worst headache she'd ever had, and she was trembling with the effort. The visualization trick she was using was to see herself crying inwardly, to satisfy the emotions, but to imagine all the tears going in the opposite direction. What a *stupid* vision. Maybe they were backing up into her brain and her head would just explode all over the room. Which would be worse to have at a wedding: a mother with a red and swollen face or a mother with an exploding head? Who wanted brains in the punch?

When she'd watched Simon dancing with their daughter, she'd almost lost it, but had held on, a fighter to the end. *He'd* practically been bawling, and all he got was a wet face. It was so unfair.

Then came the moment they'd all been waiting for. Enzo had chosen "When I Said I Do," by Clint Black. The question that had been on so many minds was about to be answered.

Enzo took Genevieve's hands from her father, and kissed them himself. Then he put one arm around her waist. She put one hand on his shoulder and their other hands entwined to lead them. The music started, and they began to dance—beautifully. Just beautifully.

EPILOGUE

When the wedding reception was finally over and the happy newlyweds seen to their car, showered with birdseed by friends and family; when all the guests were bidden farewell, and the alien contingent settled into their lodgings for the night, Bess went upstairs and cried her eyes out. Thinking about every beautiful moment that had tugged at her tear ducts earlier, she let the dam break. They'd all known this was coming. She could only keep her emotions in for so long.

Simon changed out of his tux and then climbed onto the bed with a box of Kleenex, pulled a trashcan next to the bed, and held his bride while she wept.

After half an hour, her sobs settled down to sniffles, and she leaned back against the headboard, completely spent and barely able to see. Loving her, and being true to his inner gentleman, Simon tried not to look at her face, lest she read the horror in his eyes.

There was a soft knock on the bedroom door, and when they both called out, "Come in," Colder stuck his head around the edge. One look at his mother, and he tactfully said, "Whoa, Mom! That face of yours is—pretty revolting."

A laugh exploded out of Simon before he could stop it, but he immediately resumed being comforting and supportive, shaking his head with a stern look at his son. Bess threw a pillow at Colder and would've glared at him, had she been able to focus her eyes.

"Seriously, Mom, I just wanted you to know that the whole family is really proud of you for holding it in all that time. I mean, we were *all* crying a little. None of us thought you could actually do it, even though you've been in training. Your face looked gorgeous all night. Well, at least until you got home."

He leaned over and kissed her cheek, and then from behind his back, he brought a glass of ice water with a straw and umbrella in it, and left the room with a smile. She looked at Simon and they laughed together, and then she cried some more because she just loved that kid so much.

He stuck his head back in a little later, and said, "Hey Mom, I was just wondering. Do Blanche and her babies remind you of anything?"

She looked puzzled at the question, and then thought about it for a minute. "Well, now that you mention it, they do look a lot like rabbit-eared bandicoots. Or maybe you've just heard of them as bilbies. Why?"

"Never mind."

##

Arthur lived in Blobra's menagerie for a month or so before he passed. Blobra was determined to take care of this creature so that he would last longer than her others usually did, and thus had raided his kitchen before the police came, taking every food item from there onto her ship. She'd also taken the glasses and all the booze from his various liquor cabinets.

Arthur never could quite grasp the reality of his situation. One minute, he was being beaten by Sayers, after coming so close to breaking him, and the next—he was in this place, with this *thing*. Maybe Simon had beaten him to death, and this was Hell.

Even though Blobra tried to be a responsible keeper, by offering Arthur the huge slabs of raw meat she'd taken from his freezer, along with various other enticing items she'd found there, he spurned the offered sustenance. He decided instead, to get drunk and stay that way.

When he finished all his brandy, he started on the fifty or so other bottles in the stash that she'd set up for him in his little room/prison. At first, every drink was toasted by a cursing of Simon's name. But after a few bottles, Arthur couldn't remember Simon's name, and after a few more, he couldn't remember his own.

He set about his mission with a single minded dedication, and succeeded in drinking himself to death in a fairly short time.

The Sayers learned about this from Sven, who sent that Blobra had come inquiring of him about whether he thought she might be able to get another human to replace the one that had gone bad on her. His reply, of course, had been a resounding *"NO."*

As terrible as it seemed, the news of Arthur's demise left Simon and Bess feeling immensely relieved.

##

Because Milton had a hand in saving Eli from the dogs with his stolen whistle, and had probably saved Jonas' life when he'd used the pipe on his cohort that night, and most importantly, because when the Bluemen scanned his mind, they found no past murders or any leaning towards violence, they simply wiped his mind of his experience with the Sayers. Then they implanted in his mind the compulsion to stay as far away as possible from anything even mildly illegal, and dumped him just outside of town.

He never understood how he got there, but he made his way into town, thrilled to be out from under Worthington's thumb. He eventually moved to the States and became a CPA.

##

Every one of Worthington's thugs was extradited by Interpol, who sent them to several different countries to stand trial. Convictions were speedy, since all of the men insisted on confessing to each charge in minute detail, and most will be incarcerated for the rest of their days.

##

Worthington's estate was confiscated and sold by the government to a delightfully eccentric old couple who use the animal room to sleep their fifty parrots at night, when they aren't flying about the estate or wandering through the house destroying furniture.

##

Because of the second Eli's injury, Eli the first had waited to inform the family of the role that Ishmael had played that night at Arthur's. Ishmael had led the family to where they needed to be upon arriving there, and this had saved precious minutes. He'd confused the dogs with his noxious spraying, and risked his life to lead the dogs astray in order to give the family more time to save the first Eli. The family learned of it later, and praised him as a hero cat once again. Ishmael decided that being a hero must be in his blood, so why fight it?

Eli the first had watched his actions on the green from his tree, and he knew that the ending of that evening might have been far different, had it not been for Ishmael's performance. As soon as he was restored by the Bluemen, he had sought the cat out and praised him for his bravery and intelligence, and thanked him for helping to save his life. He gave his palm to Ishmael's face—a first for cat *and* Elpie, and Ishmael reciprocated by rubbing his face against Eli's. Which is when the first Eli discovered he was allergic to cats.

##

Jonas took his father aside two days after the Bluemen and Elpies had departed.

"Dad, you know how we talked about that 'Three's the Charm' thing with you, and how we were afraid that the third time you got murdered, that was going to be it?"

Simon shook his head in denial. "Jonas, I told you, that's just a saying. I never really believed that." *And I tell my children not to lie.* "I've never been superstitious."

Jonas nodded his head but the look on his face told Simon he wasn't buying it.

"Well, Dad, you can say what you want about that. But I wanted to tell you that I don't think you have to worry about getting murdered a third time anymore."

"That's smashing news, but how did you come to that conclusion?"

"I saw that shotgun a foot from your face, and the guy was pulling the trigger when Grandpa clobbered him. That was your third murder. But three *is* the charm. This time it went the way it was supposed to all along. The third time, you didn't die. You were never supposed to die that way, Dad. That's why you got brought back twice.

"Have you never thought it just too weird and unbelievable that both times before, the Bluemen arrived at *exactly* the right time to be able to bring you back? I have, lots of times. I mean, once would have been crazy enough, but twice? And now it all makes sense. You got do-overs, Dad. The third time, things went the way they were supposed to, and you didn't die. Three's the charm."

His words hit Simon with an almost physical jolt, and suddenly he felt the cloud that had been hanging over his subconscious for all these years, just separate and drift away with the breeze. He didn't say anything. Couldn't really, so he just took Jonas' head in his hands and planted one on his forehead.

"And Dad?"

"Uh-huh?"

"If Mom's face is red and swollen when you see her, it's because I told her, too. She's not superstitious either."

#

The Bluemen continued to monitor Blanche's home planet, and eventually the waters did recede. By this time, most of the Uglies had eaten each other, and with a greatly decimated number of Uglies, the fish population began to increase, and a normal natural order began to emerge. But what was most exciting was that the Bluemen had found a small enclave of surviving Bandicoots.

Blanche loved the Elpies, and appreciated everything they'd done for her, but when she heard that there were more of her kind on her planet, she and her young were on the ship and ready to boogie before the Bluemen could even get back on board.

For the Elpies' part, they loved Blanche and her babies, but they don't miss their vocals.

##

Colder went back to school and earned a degree with a double major in horticulture and botany. He used his trust fund first to buy into the landscaping business he worked at, and then to eventually buy his partner out when the older gentleman was ready to retire. The man had no children, and so was thrilled to know that his business was going to someone who loved it as much as he did.

Next door to his new business, Colder opened a tree nursery as well as an adjoining nursery specializing in ornamentals and plants used for cooking and herbal medicine, thanks in part to his father's influence. His interest in all things growing often leads him to spend long afternoons working the earth with his dad in his garden, or talking plants with him, and Simon has found in him a kindred spirit as well as a much loved son.

After having Madelyn move into his apartment on a temporary basis, and allowing her to go to work with him, Colder's nightmares gradually went away. He never allows mildew to form anywhere in his house, and if he finds mold on any vegetable or fruit, he takes the offending piece out and burns it. He realizes this is unnecessary, but finds the practice very satisfying.

He met his wife, Vivienne, when she came into the nursery looking for herbal remedies for her dog's sick stomach. As they were discussing natural medicine, they found they had much more in common than just plants. Eight months later they were married, and now live in their own home on the estate. Since Vivienne loves to bake, Sarah has taught her how to make her double fudge caramel macaroons, so that when she passes, Babette will have help in providing for their sugar-starved alien friends, and preserving intergalactic peace.

##

When Eli and Babette first saw what had been done to their house on the estate, they were both so horrified at what might have been, that Babette wanted the house leveled. She also wanted Simon to change their deed and grant them their acreage someplace else, as far removed from this memory as possible.

Eli had loved this house, but he knew Babette wanted no part of it ever again. Simon understood her feelings and had no problem with a change in deeds and building them a new house with completely different specs. Eli went along with the new house, but put his foot down at moving to another location.

He explained to Babette that he'd grown up on the estate, and this had always been a favorite spot for him. That was why he'd asked his dad to deed it to them. He didn't want to give Arthur the power to take that away from him. He didn't want to know that there was a lonely, deserted piece of land here where once there had been a family. His family had survived. *He* had survived. The house was ruined, yes, but the land was still intact. He wanted to make this acreage a home again, in defiance of everything Arthur had tried to do.

When she saw how important this was to Eli, Babette relented and put all of her staggering energy behind making this place radiate the spirit of her family—to make it a testimony to their lives. It would be spitting in the eye of the monster if they laughed and loved on this spot that he had meant to be an abattoir, and she very much wanted to spit in his eye. She would rather have put an ice pick in it, but she would settle for saliva.

Arthur's men would never know how lucky they'd been that sweet Babette had not been present when their fate was decided. If Babette had been polled about these men who had tried to murder her husband and his brothers and attempted to steal her children, the only question she would have had was where they should bury the bodies.

Simon and Bess had a bigger house built, with a bedroom for each of the children, and Babette made all the choices of materials, designs and colors. She loved the finished product so much that a few years later, when her mother passed, the family moved to the estate on a permanent basis and kept their home in Quebec for when they went to visit friends.

##

Eli the second was profoundly affected by his amputation and the story of what his brother had experienced. He clearly understood that he had no idea of what a person must go through when an amputation takes place in the real world, where injuries cannot be completely overcome in a few days. Having been shaken almost beyond reason by the mere threat of amputation, even knowing that a new arm would be grown, he felt drawn to those who had to live with the results of the loss of one or more limbs.

He had always been an artist, but few people knew that he also had an affinity for machines and their design. He began to do research on prosthetics, and eventually convinced Simon to invest in building a company dedicated to developing new and better prosthetics for amputees.

Painting will always be a passion for Eli, but he has found that working with the men and women who need his products, and trying to improve their lives, has become, after his family, the main focus of his own.

##

Jonas was sitting and sending with Madelyn one day, when something just clicked. He'd been thinking about how much this one dog had done for his mom, himself, and eventually Colder, after their traumatic experiences, and how much she meant to Gisella's patients. There would never be another dog like her, since she possessed much of his dad's memories, and therefore had his view of life mixed with her own canine perception. But Jonas began thinking about everything he'd read on therapy and service dogs, and knew that this was something he could put his heart into.

He began searching the internet until he found people who could train *him* to train dogs. He wanted his dogs to be able to help people with problems ranging from PTSD to Diabetes and seizures. And after Gisella's experience with Madelyn, he wanted to investigate the possibility of training alert dogs for high risk pregnancies. Traveling across the U.S. and Canada, he reached out to people who knew what he needed to know.

He also trained for and received his pilot's license. When he felt he had finally learned enough to begin his own company, he began taking Madelyn with him to pounds in the southern U.S. to help him chose suitable dogs for training. He always brings many more dogs back with him than he can use, to be adopted out in Canada.

He'd found his passion in life. Or so he thought, until he met Babette's younger sister, Jolie. So it must be said that he'd found *one* of his passions, for his greater passion is his family, Jolie and their four children, who all speak French just as well as their mother. Jonas and his family eventually moved to a house of their own on the Sayers estate, where he has also built a gym sized structure to use as a training facility.

#

Bess began teaching free art classes two nights a week, first using Gisella's clinic, and eventually moving the classes to Jonas' training area. She started her classes to help victims of PTSD, to make them see that they could take control and master a facet of their lives. Since people who suffer through amputations are often PTSD sufferers as well, her classes soon began including Eli's *and* Jonas' clientele. Learning to manipulate the brushes and other tools used in her classes was excellent training to hone the fine motor skills of a new prosthetic user, so joining her classes became an automatic recommendation for many of Eli's clients.

The brothers often work together with their dad to help Eli's clientele, who always end up becoming his friends. Eli makes the new limbs, Jonas' dogs provide a new outlook and support, and Colder and Simon have become involved in concocting herbal remedies for the sore muscles and stressed, cracked, blistered, and battered flesh that unfortunately often goes hand in hand with the use of prosthetics.

Though she can't send to Jonas' dogs the way she can with Elsie, Madelyn nevertheless guides them and shows them by example as they train.

Genevieve provides free veterinary care at her clinic for all of Jonas' dogs in training, and all that are now owned by his and Eli's clients.

On his days off, if Genevieve is working and the kids are in school, Enzo often goes to Eli's, Jonas,' or Colder's place and helps in any way he can, partly because he admires their work, but mainly because he loves being with his brothers, and the feeling is mutual.

#

As a wedding present for Genevieve and Enzo, Eli did a painting of a forested bluff looking out over a tumultuous, stormy sea. It occupies a prominent space over the fireplace in their home, and while both of them love it, Enzo can stare at it for hours. When he's tired or stressed, he can go to that bluff, smell the storm and the wet leaves, feel the wind on his face, and find his energy renewed and his mind freed of clutter.

Eli is teaching Enzo to paint.

##

Genevieve and Enzo have three children: one short, one tall, one medium. And they are all just right.

##

Lola has enjoyed every moment of her life with the family, and she divides her time between playing with the children, cuddling in Genevieve's lap, shadowing Elsie and Madelyn, and inhaling amazing treats when Angus and Sarah are visiting. When the Bluemen and Elpies arrive every six months, the moment the door slides open, Lola bounces up into the ship, tongue at the ready for slobbering greetings. Since there is no stopping her, short of locking her up and making her crazy in the process, she has now become the official Sayers Estate Alien Welcoming Committee.

##

Colder, Jonas, and Enzo manned up enough to be in with their wives when they gave birth, and to their happy surprise, found that Eli was right. Again.

##

After the Bluemen had restored Bess and Simon's bodies at the end of their horrendous trip to the Bluemen's planet, the couple had been concerned about one thing: their life spans. They were aging, but slower and better than anyone else around them. Neither of them had any desire to outlive their children, or to eventually look younger than them. Since their re-grown organs were fairly disease proof, stronger, and healthier that the average human's, the Bluemen had no concrete idea as to how many years the lives of the two might be prolonged.

To ease their minds, they supplied their human friends with a fail-safe. When the time comes, if their children have reached old age and the two of them have not, or should the two of them become old enough to warrant scientific investigation, or perhaps when they have just grown tired and realize that it is enough, they will be able to simply let go.

Neither would ever consider this suicide, for their lives have been, out of kindness, unnaturally prolonged. At some point in the future, Bess and Simon will discuss this with their children so that they will understand if and when their parents decide to take action.

They also have it on record with their attorney, and have made a separate, notarized document for themselves, explaining that they had studied an ancient eastern discipline that would enable them to leave this life at will. They needed to assure themselves that there would never be even a slight suspicion of foul play involving their passing. Fortunately, the western world will generally accept any wild story that has the words "ancient eastern discipline" tacked on.

Because Bess had already lost Simon twice, she was determined not to lose him again, even if for only five minutes, so she made Simon swear that when they are ready to go home and they lie in each other's arms on their bed, he will hold her while she lets go first. Not until he is sure that she is gone from this world, will he allow himself to follow. She has made him promise, and he always keeps his promises.

When they told the animals about this plan, Elsie sent that if she is still living, she would like to go with them, and they made arrangements for this with the Bluemen.

Madelyn wants to keep helping Jonas and Gisella for as long as she is able. Ishmael sent that if he could still play chess or read, he was good, thanks.

But this action, should they need to take it, is far in the future. Their lives are very full and satisfying, and neither has any wish to pack it in just yet.

##

The arch in the meadow has become a tradition with the Sayers and their friends. Colder and Jonas had their weddings there, as well as Sadie and her brother, Tristan. Micah joined with his second wife under the arch, and Harvey Washington's children eventually married there. Over the years, many more humans, Bluepeople, and Elpies close to the Sayers chose the lovely spot for their weddings, with the Sayers' blessings and generosity

Each new generation of Sayers grows up knowing each new generation of Elpies and Bluepeople, and because of this, the friendship that has become such an integral part of their lives is still growing. Sven and his crew, Simon and Bess, Eli and his wives, and Barnabas and his family assume that it will continue to grow long after they are gone.

Three species, so dissimilar, yet they have learned to reach out with their hearts and souls to find a place of understanding in one another, turning what was once only a medley into *family*. The metamorphosis of their friendship into something greater—something truer, would be thought undesirable by some, and improbable by most. And yet in this life, the three have danced, and will continue to dance—beautifully. Just beautifully.

ABOUT THE AUTHOR

L. M. Nisgow was born in San Antonio, Texas, where she still resides with her husband and their dog---the gold one at the bottom of the picture. The one in her lap is just a publicity hound.

Made in the USA
Middletown, DE
25 August 2021